EAGLE VISION
Return of the Hoop

D0573349

Ed McGaa, Eagle Man

Illustrated by
Daryl No Heart, Hunkpapa Sioux

Contributing Artist
Harrisson Lone Hill (Grandson of Chief Fools Crow)

Four Directions Publishing

Four Directions Publishing

P.O. Box 24671, Minneapolis, MN 55424
Phone: 612-922-9322, Fax: 612-922-7163
E-mail: eagleman4@aol.com
Website: http://members.aol.com:/eagleman4

First Edition

Cover and art illustrations by Daryl No Heart
Cover: A Sioux Sun Dance and the Power of the Hoop. Late 60's.
Contributing Artist, Harrisson Lone Hill (Grandson of Chief Fools Crow)
Art Direction: Kimberlea A. Weeks

Copyright applied for, U.S. Library of Congress

98, 99, 00, 01, 02 <<>> 10 9 8 78 6 5 4 3 2 1

EAGLE VISION
Return of the Hoop

Note: The subjects: Lakota, Dakota, and Sioux will be used interchangeably throughout this text. At this time, my tribe is still officially addressed as the Oglala Sioux, as is the adjoining tribe, the Rosebud Sioux. That is how the tribal councils have been referring to themselves for quite awhile. The terms Native American, American Indian and Indian will also be used. Most older Native Americans have been called Indian all their lives and have become quite used to that term, therefore interchange is preferred by the author who is much more concerned about historical content, than linguistic semantics.

* * * *

The Lakota language has been spelled phonetically in some words to help the reader pronounce words which are being mis-pronounced due to an archaic, language system that has severely confused native languages. Example-The "proper" way to spell white man is wasicu and most readers erroneously say wah see coo or wa see cuu. Washichu (wah shee chew) and similar phonetics will be used throughout this writing in an attempt to establish practical pronunciation rather than "correct" or "proper" linguistic spelling.

FOREWORD

I began this book long ago, yes, long ago when the characters and adventures were still very fresh in my memory. So long ago that one of the holy men read a portion of the original manuscript before he passed on. His accurate prediction followed: "It will be some time before the white man can accept that Indians have their own religion, let alone can write their own books." I tried to explain to him that I would write it in fiction. He shrugged his still powerful shoulders. "Just do it Nephew. In time it will all come about. Don't give up."

This novel was written for the present generation and the generations unborn so that they too can experience that rich cultural time; a difficult and often sad time, when there were but a few that actually stood for the return of the Old Way. Many readers of my earlier books have constantly asked about the characters herein. I hope that you now may enjoy them as much as I was privileged.

For close to a century, my tribe was forbidden to think in terms relating back to their spiritual past. Religious missionaries, supported by a federal government, blocked all two-legged thought toward that realm. Two staunch and determined Sioux holy men fought back and challenged the absolutist dictates of established religion along with its supporting, dominant sea of the white man's world. Why shouldn't they? The North American native people had a track record of Humanitarianism, Truthfulness, and Generosity. They kept their own portion of Mother Earth viable as long as they were here - for thousands of years - maybe hundreds of thousands of years.

They were beautiful people - those old timers. To control, establish a hierarchy, or to impart fear of Creator, or fear of a possible after life - never entered their thoughts. They had a simple mission and a simple message. Life was a Mystery. Benevolent Creator was to be respected yet not feared. And, all were related and meant to become like Created Nature, which certainly reflects an ongoing harmony. Mitakuye Oyasin. Ahh ho Wakan Tanka! Pilamiya (Thank You).

Note: Protestant missionaries also shared in the overwhelming zealotry imposed on a captured people. My personal experience was with the Jesuit Order. I wish to thank the Benedictine Order, however, who were very fair and generous at St. John's University (MN) and the Sisters of all Orders. It is a world-wide loss that the good Sisters of the Roman Catholic faith cannot have an equal policy making voice. Maybe this book would not have had to be written had the church been balanced, as is Creator's created Nature.

ACKNOWLEDGEMENT, APPRECIATION & DEDICATION

Acknowledgement: Poem-Chapter: 13 – Beth Heffinger, an Eastern Airlines Flight Attendant.

In Appreciation: To Editors, Robert M. Patterson, Bowie, MD and Sharon Bahringer/Red Eagle Woman, Cornell University, for your generous interest and perseverance. To my Publisher: Joe Thunder Owl Brewer, a courageous warrior who has also fought the Blue Man.

Dedication: To my older sisters, LaVerne Heiter and Chick Cutschall who were both raised in the boarding schools. One must always appreciate being blessed with a pleasant, fulfilling mate, and daughters and sons that make you proud. But to be granted sisters as well... two, who know your very soul down through all your time, your journeys, your missions, your mistakes, your foolish errors, your triumphs, romances, laughter, tears, harrowing escapes and all those other far away ports and places a few fortunate men are cast by a mysterious, magical fate. Indeed, that warrior is truly blessed! But most important are their memories of characters and places, happenings and rich history. Of, course, to the brave holy men, the old time sun dancers and the grandmothers. To Buddie Red Bow and Sonny Larive, the first of the young sundancers to bring back the Way.

MISSIONARY
BOARDING SCHOOL

CHAPTER ONE

There are many stories and many story tellers.
Most will tell you what you want to hear but only a few will tell you
what the Blue Man forces don't want you to know.
— Thunder Owl
Mdewakanton Sioux

High aloft, a pair of eagles scanned a prairie dog town. It was an unusual winter day. Warm wind and sunshine had enticed the stubby tailed creatures and now evening was drawing jack rabbits from their dens. To the south, the eagles could view the missionary boarding school. Northward, the desolate Badlands stretched for almost a hundred miles. In that vastness of silence, high walls crested with cedar and isolated wind carved buttes touched down to alkali flats, gullies, creeks and a lone river knowing no street or village. Only a post office/store and a few cattle ranches upon fenceless range bore witness to two-legged (human). The rest belonged to the eagles, owls, rattlesnakes, bullsnakes, kangaroo rats, prairie dogs, rabbits, deer, antelope, badgers, bobcats and coyotes. In those days, maybe a few mountain sheep and possibly a pair of prairie wolves still lingered - such was its remoteness and solitude.

The Indian boarding school was a sprawling establishment. The Church had acquired hundreds of acres; choice bottom land once covered with buffalo grass, now sprouted hay pasture, grain fields and garden plots. So far, it was a mild winter, the first Sunday of December and pond ice had formed only once. A statue, proclaimed by the Jesuits as the 'Mother of God', beamed down on open water melted by a warm Chinook which had been blowing on and off for about a week. Upstream from the pond, red brick buildings, classrooms and dormitories clustered around a spired church. Several battered cars, mostly thirties' vintage, were parked in a graveled lot. A sporty team of matched dappled grays pulled a buggy up to the church. Another team, plow horses hooked to a wagon, stood in sharp contrast next to a shiny black sedan. The fenders and grill of the new 1941 Ford gleamed from a fresh wash and polishing by boarding school students. The West River Bishop's Mass was about to conclude a weekend retreat. Most of the brothers, priests and sisters had been sequestered in silence and subsequently, all mission school activities had been curtailed. Even radios had been banned for the weekend; such was the devotion to solitude, isolation and contemplation. Barns, hog houses, chicken coops and machinery sheds spread out downstream. Range cattle stood inside a fenced enclosure, isolated from a herd of milk cows waiting to be stanchioned for the evening's milking. Hogs grunted in the hog yard while a pair of roosters tried to outdo each other for the last crow.

Oglala Sioux youth scurried around the milk cows like trained sheep dogs, obedient to the barking commands of well muscled Jesuit brothers. A bell tolled from the church, and the brothers fell silent for a few moments. At the opening of a cattle gate behind a hesitant milk cow, one youth looked perplexed. He didn't know whether to follow the last command of the Jesuit or the dictate of the bell. He wisely dropped one knee to the ground in an act of prayer, while the milk cow ambled back to a tuft of hay she had pulled from a feeding stall. On a hillside rising beyond the church steeple, a cemetery waited beneath leafless cottonwood and elm trees. Tombstones and wooden crosses arranged in rows, poked out of brown winter grass and clusters of tumbleweeds. In the center of the fenced graveyard, a European featured human God was nailed grotesquely to a cross and another life-sized statue of the grieving 'Mother of God' also bore distinctly European features.

Three boys hidden by stacks of prairie hay behind the hog house ignored the bell while it tolled. Two half-breeds listened closely to a full-blood boy pronouncing Sioux words. "*Pilamiya,*" Cross Dog spoke, then went on to enunciate each syllable. "Pee lahm eey yah. Pee lahm eey yah." He paused to explain in English. "*Pilamiya.* That means, thank you." He repeated, "*Pilamiya,*" then added a new word, speaking yet in syllables. "Pee lahm eey yah wee choh nee." In heavily accented, guttural English he said, "Now say it."

"*Pilamiya wichoni.*" Lawrence Charging Shield, the older of the two half-breeds, answered comfortably with almost as much Siouan accent as the full-blood, Cross Dog. Lawrence was the oldest of the trio, almost too old looking for high school. He was strong in build like Cross Dog but lighter complexioned. The youngest of the three, Kyle Charging Shield, was still in his early years of grade school. He was thinner than Lawrence and close to his brother in degree of complexion. All had the pronounced hawkish Siouan nose and rangy bearing. The two older boys, still growing, were close to six feet.

"Real good, brother." Cross Dog responded while he gathered up loose hay to make a comfortable mound. The full-blood could have displayed a more fierce look but the hunger and loneliness in his eyes erased it. "*Pilamiya wichoni.* That means, I am thankful for my life. That is a powerful prayer or something good to say to the Big Spirit- *Wakan Tanka.*" Cross Dog was not a blood relative but used the customary term of relationship reserved for a close friend.

"*Wakan Tanka,*" Lawrence replied. "I know that is the Great Spirit, Great Mystery, but what else does your father and your grandfather say about that word.

They were all holy men, weren't they?" The half-breed spoke with a calm self-confidence.

Cross Dog looked around cautiously and nodded affirmatively. "They must have been. I get beaten at this school more than anyone else... and I don't look for trouble."

"Why don't you just throw in with these Catholics? That's what I told my little brother. Lay low and keep your mouth shut. What they say ain't any mystery. Hell, he's even made his first communion."

"*Wakan Tanka*, means Big Holy... Big Everything," Cross Dog responded in halting English, ignoring the advice. The *washichus* (white men) have a word. You just said it." A glimmer of deep pride still flared within the full-blood.

"You mean Great Mystery or Great Holy." Lawrence offered.

"Yes that's the word. This 'Great Mystery', it is too powerful to be killed and hung up to die like the *washichu* claims. I am too old now to believe that. For your little brother, I can understand but I would be lying if I say that I believe the way the *washichu* wants me to."

Lawrence chewed on a stem of hay. "That's why the Brothers of the Cross are beating the shit out of you and not giving you as much to eat. But as long as I'm around, you'll eat." With that statement the husky youth pulled a half loaf of bakery bread out from a gunny sack. He broke two small pieces off handing one to his brother and then passed the major portion to the full-blood. He reached down into the grain sack and served up four boiled potatoes. He offered two to Cross Dog, one to Kyle and took the smallest for himself. Kyle handed his larger potato back to Lawrence, then swiped the smallest potato out of his brother's hand despite a bite already taken. Lawrence laughed in admiration. "*Heyyyy, heyyy*, look at this little guy. Already he's learning to be an Indian." He pointed his potato at Kyle. "Cross Dog, my brother, you look after this little guy next year. Keep the bullies away from him." He noted a sparrow looking down from the roof of the hog house. He broke a pebble-sized crumb and threw it up to the bird. "That little bird is our witness. Beat the shit out of them the first week of school. That's the way I've always done it. I taught you enough about boxing. You can do it."

Cross Dog ate his potato and smiled confidently. "You still plan on joining the Army?" he asked after he swallowed the first potato and reached for the bread.

"A Sioux should never join the Army. goddamn cavalry," Lawrence spat the words. "Going to try the Marines. Don't know if they will take an Indian. They don't allow Negroes in the Marines. Navy doesn't either. That's what I heard. Don't know what they'll say to an Indian."

"I think I heard about the Marines but never saw any. Are they the ones with that real pretty uniform, all red, white and blue?"

"That's them. But guess they don't wear it much. Just for show and parades. I guess they are some real tough sons-a-bitches."

Cross Dog admired the way Lawrence could swear and sound like a white man. He wanted to swear like Lawrence and promised himself he would practice swearing once he could get away and be by himself. Lawrence had learned to swear from working summers in the West River lumber mills next to white men. He was a baseball player too, for the lumber mill team; even though he was Indian, he was that good. He liked Lawrence Charging Shield. Not many full-bloods had the opportunity to hang around with half-breeds. The school seemed to reward the half-breeds more and was harder on the full-bloods. But Lawrence, he was different. He didn't care whether you were full-blood, half-breed or even quarter-breed. He could out box any one in the school, even the brothers... and they knew it. Took three to hold him down for a beating. Cross Dog's chest rose. Took three of them, last time he was beat and he had gotten a couple of good licks on that one smart aleck brother, the one that really hated Indians, especially the full-bloods. He looked at Lawrence. "My father saw real live soldiers, right here on the reservation."

Lawrence threw his hay straw to the wind and offered another piece of bread to the sparrow. "So did mine. That's the reason none of us should join the Army. They worked hand in hand with these goddamned missionaries. I heard they left not too long ago. They still got a fort north of West River. Don't know whether they use it or not."

Cross Dog liked the way Lawrence was so unafraid of the missionaries. So many of the breeds and even the full-bloods thought that the priests and nuns had some sort of hidden power but not Lawrence. The way Lawrence could fight, he didn't have to take anything from anybody. No priest or brother could take him alone. At the age of six, Lawrence had been severely weaned when he entered boarding school. Those were the lonely years. The isolation from his parents and grandmother left a growing hardness that developed into a bold disdain for the missionaries. Cross Dog looked at the lengthening shadows and knew it was time to resume his language teaching. "Your parents speak good Indian, Kyle. You had better learn from them when you go back home this summer."

"Our mom, the priests have got a hold on her. She won't let us learn. Dad, he sneaks, like you have to. He teaches me some times," Lawrence spoke as he looked at Kyle. "Dad's afraid of the priests. He believes the same way as you do but he says the priests are powerful with the way they can be boss, and you best stay out of their way." He paused and studied his younger brother. "It can all cause this little guy a hard time. Me, I'm getting the hell out of here. Wish to hell I could take Kyle with me." He found a cockle burr in a tuft of hay and threw it at the hog house with a perplexed, worried look.

"What about your brother Hobart?"

Lawrence scowled. He reached into the sack and pulled out an empty pint jar. "Kyle, go down to the creek and get us a drink of water," he commanded. Kyle

4

responded with a quick hop to his feet, eager to please. "And get the water upstream from where the cows drink." Lawrence called after him.

Once the boy was out of earshot, Lawrence growled with sarcasm, "My dear brother Hobart. That son... of... a... bitch. That son... of... a... bitch." Lawrence noted the quizzical look on Cross Dog's face. He stammered, adding hurriedly, "I don't mean my mother is a bitch. I like my mom and she would probably kill me if she ever heard me call one of my brothers or sisters that. But, it is about the only way I can say how I feel about Hobart." The breed's voice carried a warning note. "Stay away from that guy and my sister Leona. Both of them are out for themselves."

"They don't even bother to look in my direction or any of the rest of the full-bloods." Cross Dog replied. "Your sister Mildred. She talks to me and has even snuck me some bread, once or twice. Gave me some apples last Christmas."

"She's okay," Lawrence added. "Long as she stays away from those other two."

As Kyle ambled down to the streambed, a bearded Jesuit brother pitched wads of manure out of the cattle barn into a manure spreader. Milking chores exempted some brothers from the final retreat hours. Raised on a harsh Kansas wheat farm, Brother Herman had known nothing but work. He was solid muscle and could out last anyone at the Mission when it came to cutting wood, fencing, milking and a host of unending tasks to care for the fields, animals and gardens. Recreation, sports, social festivities and girls were never an experience to the Jesuit. Most German farm families steeped in Catholic tradition, selected at least one or even two of their own to serve the church; and he had been chosen - no questions asked. Raised in sheer discipline and religious fervor, he had never expressed remorse or questioned authority regarding personal ambition or worldly desires. Out of curiosity, he watched the boy with the jar shuffling along. He returned to the milking area and gathered up more manure with his shovel. After the manure loader was nearly full he noted the boy returning with his water jar back toward the hog house. He tossed his shovel into the manure load and proceeded to sneak in a low, clumsy crouch toward the front of the hog house.

By the time they had finished their bread, both boys were thirsty and appreciated the cold spring water brought by their companion. Cross Dog took a long drink before handing the pint jar to Lawrence. He smacked his broad lips as he spoke, "Well, let's find out how your little brother is doing at learning Indian. Now say my name in Lakota, Kyle."

Kyle was proud that the older boy included him in his lessons. "*Hinya za, hin yan za shaunnka.*" he pronounced his answer, trying to copy his brother's Siouan accent.

Cross Dog rolled back from his perch of gathered hay in laughter. He poked his head up again with tears in his eyes. "Again," he commanded.

"*Hinya za, hin yan za shaunnka.*"

Cross Dog disappeared behind the hay mound again, moaning in laughter. He poked his head up. "Remember how I told you to say horse? Now say that."

"Tah Shaunnk ah Wah kahn."

Cross Dog fell back from behind the hay mound, this time landing with a thud on a bare patch of ground. Lawrence caught on to the joke and rolled away from his brother in laughter. He held his sides and stared up at the sky. "What does that mean, Kyle?"

"It means Big Dog Holy. That's what Cross Dog told me," he answered with a proud smile. "Is that what you guys are laughing at? When Indians first saw a horse, they said it was a big dog and since a man was riding it, they said it had to be holy." Kyle beamed. "*Tah* means big, *shaunnka* is dog and *wakan* is holy. Big Dog Holy."

Cross Dog leaned closer, his mouth agape with a huge grin. "Little guy, I don't mean to make fun of you but it is really funny how you say 'dog.' 'Dog' is supposed to be said like this, Shuuuunn-kah. Shuuuunn-kah." He overly pronounced the sylla- bles. "Oooohhn-kah, oooohhn-kah -not shahhnn-kah," he tried to sound the way *washichu*s pronounced Sioux words. "You are saying Shaunnnnnk -ah. There is a big difference between Shuuuunn-kah, and Shahunnnnnk-ah." He couldn't finish his explanation and started laughing so hard he had to quit looking at the younger Sioux. Every time he looked at Kyle his laughter would get the best of him. Lawrence remained on the ground laughing up at the clouds turning red from the sunset.

So used to being raised in an environment where children were seldom ridiculed, Kyle couldn't help but to laugh along with the two older boys, happy to be respon- sible for such a degree of amusement at the restrictive, rule bound school. Finally, Lawrence joined in on the mirthful explanation. "What he wants to say, little brother, is that when you are saying "*shaunka*" the way you say it, you mean a "woman's thing," you know, that thing she pees through between her legs. You are calling Cross Dog an angry woman's thing. *Shuunka* is the way you are supposed to say "dog." A "horse" you are calling "a great big woman's thing that is holy." In Indian, that really sounds funny. *Tah* means "big." *Tah shaunka* means "a great big woman's thing." You know, *shaunka* is the same thing that babies come out of." He dropped down quickly and howled at the sky. "White people, *washichus*, they call it a pussy. We call it *shaunka*."

All three sprawled in helpless laughter. Kyle Charging Shield howled along with the two bigger boys, knowing that he would never forget this lesson.

At the corner of the hog house, Brother Herman wanted to rush in and end such hooliganism but he knew he couldn't handle Lawrence. The Sioux was a shade taller and too quick with his fists. He would tell Father Prefect. The Father would punish them. Punish them all. They'd get the belts for this, even that young one. They'd get it harder than those two girls got it last time. He had been thinking about the last beating as the boys were talking and laughing. As he relished the thought of holding down the girl for Father Prefect, it began to happen again and it wouldn't go away. It wouldn't go away from his dreams either.

Brother Herman began to look worried. Beads of sweat rolled down his brow. He would have to go to confession. How could this be happening? He had a rock hard erection and it wouldn't go away. While Lawrence was explaining what was down between a woman's legs he even had a slight ejaculation when he heard the word, 'Pussy'. And then thinking about that Sioux girl moaning when she had caught each blow of the belt; her pain, and those damned unforgettable moans, even her smell was haunting. And then when her dress got pulled up and he saw her legs... the damn sight and the sounds wouldn't go away. And just now he had even delighted in such a foul evil word. How could he tell this in confession? He would agonize but he would never be able to tell. This was evil. Yes, it had to be some form of evil. These boys and their laughter, it had to be evil. They had caused him to sin. Yes, he was guilty. Guilty of some sin but God only knew. Maybe it was a merciful God or maybe the fires of everlasting hell awaited him, but he would never tell it in confession because no one would understand and the confession wouldn't make it go away anyhow. He did not understand. He was perplexed. He wished he never had snuck up on the evil boys behind the hog house.

Mulling over the report in his sparse, solitary office, Father Prefect sat tensely rigid. Upon the rolls of the Jesuit Order, Reverend Paul Buchwald, S.J., was his name. Since he had been assigned as Mission Disciplinarian he preferred to be addressed as Father Prefect. The waning moon made a silhouette out of the church spire through his window. His thoughts focused on discipline and order. 'Many a lash had fallen upon recalcitrant Indian youth for the breaking of rules. Rules were designed by learned men to keep order, perfection and obedience to a holy, controlled society. Even some of the girls had to be lashed. Mostly full-bloods. The breeds could be punished with less severe punishment, it seemed. But the full-bloods! God knows they were but a generation or two away from arch paganism. None of their ancestors knew the risen Christ. It was God's redemption, God's resurrection, and God's perfection that often had to be beaten into them lest they lose their wretched souls!'

Paul Buchwald heard approaching footsteps in the hallway. He imagined he could smell manure from Brother Herman even though he had given him strict orders not to bring the boys until he had fully bathed. He could smell manure! It wasn't imagination! It had to be Brother Herman. God help him if he had not bathed! He would make him stay up all night saying rosaries for his disobedience.

"Is that you, Brother Herman?" he barked, convinced the smell was not mere imagination. "Bring in the boys," he commanded not waiting for an answer.

Brother Herman stumbled in with a rim of hog manure covering the seam stitched to bind the sole and toe of his boots. Buchwald's top lip drew back and upwards as if to hold back the smell. Long in the manure shed and hog yard, Brother Herman was oblivious to odors even after he had showered and soaped and lathered and put on clean clothes. His erection had risen again as he lathered but he wouldn't tell that in confession. The boys... the laughing, evil boys, they were responsible for this reoccurrence of sin. They should be beaten. Beaten for their laughter and the sin that was descending upon him.

Buchwald looked at his watch. He had an important meeting scheduled with Father Superior. New donations from wealthy eastern patrons; more letters to write by the students and the retreat had kept him from his business duties. Money was more important than beating these ignorant pagans. A new form letter would be drafted for them to copy. The breed kids, especially the quarter-breeds, were best at writing the soliciting letters. They made the least mistakes. He would be late if he did not act promptly. There would be no time for a lengthy speech and it wouldn't work on the older two anyway. He planned to expel Lawrence in the spring as soon as horse breaking was over. Lawrence was as good as his father at breaking horses. Finally, they would be rid of the belligerent breed. The younger one would shape up in due time. And Cross Dog. The Devil would get Cross Dog. The sons of the holy men; they were too brain washed in the old traditions. They had to be isolated and even starved down to keep from spreading their evil influence. They either ran away for good or committed suicide. There wasn't much hope for them. Besides, they could poison the minds of the rest. It was a worthy sacrifice. All could not be saved. Even the Bible said something like that. He noted the black missal standing upright on his desktop; his book of prayers and devotions sandwiched between a heavy pair of polished agate bookends. Every word was actually written by the hand and voice of God - the Savior.

Two priests and two brothers brought in the older boys. Father Buchwald looked nervous. Both seemed to have grown in stature. Lawrence was big enough but yet it seemed he had suddenly become larger and even stronger looking. Lawrence looked down at the floor twitching nervously. Buchwald looked over at Cross Dog and found him shaking with fear. 'Damn,' he thought, 'these boys should have been tied. But they're scared and there's six of us,' he tried to reassure himself. Brother Herman went back into the hallway and with a firm hold on Kyle's ear, pulled him into the crowded office.

"Lawrence Charging Shield and Cross Dog. You are charged with speaking Indian within this institution. This act is forbidden at U. S. Government Boarding Schools and this rule includes Mission Schools upon Federal Reservations. We of the Jesuit Order, pride ourselves in being lenient as God is caring but we must follow government dictates that foster discipline and good order. You are also charged with using foul, obscene words as witnessed by Brother Herman in your sojourn behind the hog house." Buchwald frowned. He wanted to sound formal and military for the sake of the newest priest holding on to Lawrence. He noted that the priest, somewhat effeminate, appeared fearful by the look in his eyes. 'Hog house, hog house', damn that took away from the formality of the charge, his mind wandered uneasily as he looked at the young priest. "Kyle Charging Shield, you are so equally charged." he added with a loss of forcefulness.

Brother Herman thrust the youngest of the accused forward to within an arm's length of the Prefect. Buchwald reached behind the side of his desk to draw out a thick leather strap. He folded it once and held it under Kyle's nose. The priest felt a surge of power as Kyle's eyes widened. The boy had felt the sting of the strap before. Kyle smelled the leather over the hog manure on Brother Herman's shoes and began to be afraid but he was more afraid for Cross Dog and his brother.

"Bring the accused forward." Buchwald commanded with warden-like authority. Cross Dog held back as if afraid while Lawrence stepped forward. Buchwald made a polite gesture. "The first shall get the least of the lashes while the last shall receive the most." He wanted to pit both of the older Indians against each other. Neither of the two older boys indicated an acknowledgment. Lawrence took another small step forward but hung his head low as if to convey a conciliatory gesture. "As an indication of my leniency, I shall not punish the youngest within this room as harshly but nevertheless, he shall receive his due." With that statement he was pleased to see Lawrence nodding in acknowledgment. A stool was pulled out from a closet. Lawrence moved forward and bent over, his backside to the disciplinarian priest. The youngest priest was over anxious to let go of the accused and stood with a girl-like pose; his mouth open with a chagrined gape and knees knocking while a brother, smaller than Lawrence, still clung rather awkwardly and loosely to an arm. "Brother Herman, switch with your companion holding Lawrence." Buchwald barked. The smaller brother moved to stand beside Kyle.

At the touch of Lawrence, Brother Herman was brought back to the last beating. The pair of full-blood girls that had run away; both of them had got the strap and he, Brother Herman, had to hold them. He had an uncontrolled erection while they were being beaten and had ejaculated when the girl's dress came up. It was a good thing that he had worn his long flowing habit. Now he was beginning to come erect thinking back to the girls, their moans and grunts. They were full-bloods and refused to scream out like most of the breed girls did. It was the closest he had ever been to a girl... 'Yes... he could revel in it! Those moans... he could still hear her moaning!'

Buchwald reared back in the crowded room, letting the strap loose to its full extension and accidentally bumping one of the agate slabs on his desk. His balance shifted slightly and as he brought the strap down hard, his aim was amiss and he partially missed the backside of Lawrence. Brother Herman let out a howl from the end of the strap stinging him solidly upon his erection. The brother began dancing a jig, howling in pain.

It happened. Not according to plan but close to it. Lawrence came up strong with an elbow to Buchwald's temple sending him down and out cold. Cross Dog spun free from his two handlers. A brother went down gasping from a vicious jab to his throat. One of the stone desk slabs smashed down across the ankle of the brother

next to Kyle, sending him limping and howling out of the office. Kyle took the remaining bookstand and crashed it on Brother Herman's foot, fracturing his instep. The two remaining priests were no match. One priest sailed out the window, receiving cuts from jagged glass. The effeminate priest cried out in fear and began sobbing as he was stuffed into the closet, brandished by the stool across his backside.

Under the clouded moon, the boys hustled down the gravel road leading away from the reservation, bearing a gunny sack and bound for the railroad tracks connecting to West River. Whenever a car would come from the direction of the

Mission, they would hide off to the side of the road until it passed. Few cars passed from either direction as the night drew on. Back at the Mission, the infirmary was too busy tending to the injured to bother looking for runaways. Lawrence had always planned to run away and kept a sack of stores put away for the occasion. They would be long gone before the Mission could track them. They would catch a freight train at the bottom of the first steep grade and by morning they would be in West River. Enough Indians, including an uncle working at the lumber mill, were camped along Rapid Creek. They felt confident they could hide for awhile.

When they came to the grade, they hid beneath a tall stand of choke cherry bushes. The Chinook wind blowing out of the Badlands kept them warm. Cross Dog told them that the Chinook was a good omen and the waning moon hiding behind the clouds was a sign that the spirits were with them. Kyle didn't know about spirits but he liked Cross Dog. He figured that spirits must be like guardian angels. His legs ached, making him appreciate the rest. "What exactly is a spirit?" he asked Cross Dog.

"Being Indian, I have to say truthfully I don't know for sure," the full-blood replied. "I suspect it is simply a person that was here before and has gone on."

"You mean a ghost?" Kyle's voice wavered.

Cross Dog laughed. "Ghosts," he spat the word. "That's what those missionaries preach to keep you scared so you won't run away." He held up his hand. "A spirit isn't like a scary ghost. It is a helper. It can watch over you and help you out, especially if you do something important like going off to war. A spirit helper is a good thing to have on your side."

"How do you know this?" Kyle pressed.

"I have seen many *Yuwipi* (You wee pee) ceremonies and these spirit helpers came in. I would be lying if I said that I didn't hear them and even see them - in a way." There was no hesitancy or stammering in Cross Dog's response.

"Kyle," Lawrence spoke. "You are too young to hear this and it probably scares you. But I went to a *Yuwipi* once. It was powerful and these spirit helpers came in and made some helluva big predictions. They always make good predictions, I mean they are in line with what the people are asking. I wouldn't call them ghosts. They ain't spooky like it sounds. I want you to believe me." He looked at his brother closely. "Have I ever lied to you?"

The younger boy was starting to droop. "No," he answered quietly before laying his head in his brother's lap. "You mean they ain't nothin' like a devil?" he mumbled.

Cross Dog spat an answer, "Our *Wakan Tanka* is too powerful to have to make what the washichus believe in. We never had a devil before they brought it here!"

"Fucking missionaries and their goddamned made up devils and Satans." Lawrence growled as he defiantly looked back toward the Mission. "Yeah, the sons a bitches, they brought the devil here. Our people never had a devil before the white man brought it." After a pause he added, "I learned that from my Grandmother."

Lawrence broke out some bread and each boy ate a mouthful, washing it down with water from a quart-sized jar. Before long they were rehashing their episode. "You did a good job shaking," Lawrence complimented Cross Dog. "I figured if we didn't get tied up, then we could get the jump on them."

Cross Dog laughed and looked at Kyle who was now fast asleep. "Your little brother, there. He did his job well. I always had a good feeling toward those fancy rocks that Buchwald kept on his desk. All along they had some good medicine inside of them. Kyle really bombed them two brothers with those rocks. Maybe he'll grow up and fly an airplane. He'll be bombing the Germans if we get into a war with them."

"The white man will never let an Indian fly an airplane but we might go to war with more than the Germans. They say the Japanese are making trouble. That one cook that lets me sneak you food. He's always telling me what's going on from a newspaper the mailman brings." A coyote's doleful howl made the breed's head nod. "I'm starting to get sleepy but one of us has to stay awake to hear the train."

Cross Dog looked back down the track and rose. "I'm going to put my head on the rail and listen for the train. They say that you can hear it coming from a long ways off." He turned with a strange smile. "You get some sleep and I'll wake you up when I get tired... if the train hasn't come by."

Lawrence called after him, "Cross Dog, Brother, I have one last question before I sleep. Why do you think the disciplinarian put you on half rations? Was it because you are a full-blood or your father and grandfather were holy men?"

Cross Dog laughed and walked off speaking back over his shoulder. "It was because I would never take a name."

"A name? What do you mean?"

"You are 'Lawrence' and Kyle is 'Kyle'... Mildred, Leona and Hobart... Paul and Herman." His voice rose. Deep pride could be sensed. All hunger and the loneliness vanished. Even Cross Dog's face took on a fierce warrior's expression. "Me, I am just 'Cross Dog' and only 'Cross Dog'... like Crazy Horse, Chips and Red Cloud. The priest... Father Prefect told me I could have double rations for a month if I would just set an example, make holy communion and take a holy name... even one like his." His voice lowered, "I am a traditional Indian. I couldn't do it." Sternly he spoke, "It would be a lie to myself." An owl hooted loud and clear. "It would be a lie to myself," Cross Dog repeated softly. "Thanks to you Brother, you kept me from starving. I'll make it up to you some day. I'll look out for you and that is a firm promise." There was a resolute echo to Cross Dog's words, as if somehow, he would carry out his promise.

Several tears for Cross Dog flowed from Lawrence as he drifted into sleep. The full-blood's pronouncement ushered in a lonely feeling. Cross Dog was so alone at the Mission. He wished that none of them would ever have to return to the boarding school. He could hear the soft hum of "*heyyy, heyyy, heyyy*" as the full-blood walked away. He looked up to see Cross Dog hunkering down on the railroad bed, placing his ear on the track. A muffled "*heyyy, heyyy, heyyy*" could still be heard. The coyotes howled while a pair of owls echoed their chorus. Both breeds slept and for the moment, Cross Dog was free.

"Son of a bitch. Son of a bitch," Cross Dog began to practice in earnest as he listened on the rail.

Lawrence dreamed of his grandmother and his father. Some how he would have to get his younger brother back to his father and mother who still had their small ranch at the northern edge of the reservation. The actual worries of life and duty permeated his dream. After leaving his brother with an uncle in West River, he saw himself marching off to war in a red and blue Marine uniform. He saw his little brother wearing the same uniform and fighting also but he was in a strange looking airplane and was dropping rocks. The rocks turned to bombs just like Cross Dog had said. He had to laugh at his little brother flying an airplane, and it was a big one too. He would have to get him out of that flying machine and return him to his parents.

A loud rising rumble, like roaring wind filled his dream. Cross Dog flashed so vividly before him. "Thanks to you Brother, you kept me from starving." The full-blood spoke in a soft, reassuring voice. "I'll make it up to you some day. I'll look out for you and that is a firm promise." Cross Dog was elevated and reached out to touch him.

The ground shook as the freight train raced full steam into the steep grade. Lawrence bolted from his resting place, forgetting about his dream. He yelled at Kyle who was already awake from the clamoring noise of the slowing train. Lawrence grabbed up the gunny sack with one hand and his brother in the other. "Cross Dog!" he yelled as the pair stumbled toward the track. Red-orange daylight was just beginning to crack out from the rim of Badlands to the east. "Cross Dog! C'mon, let's catch this son of a bitch!" At the spot where he had last seen Cross Dog, he could make out a severed arm and a leg; the rest had been swept on up the grade. Cross Dog had fallen asleep.

Several hours later on a Monday dawn, the bleary-eyed boys hailed a rancher on a gravel road. Before they could speak, the rancher rolled down his car window and yelled out. "Looks like you boys heard the news. Japs bombed Pearl Harbor! We're goin' to war!" He looked at Lawrence with wide-eyed respect. "Hop aboard, Son. Bet your headin' into West River to sign up. All the young guys are enlistin' and gettin' their papers started."

Life changed abruptly. The War Department declared the northern area of the reservation as a war emergency aerial gunnery and bombing range. Kyle's parents had to vacate their ranch and moved to West River. Lawrence joined the Marines. The runaways never had to return to the boarding school.

Eagle Feather's Vision

CHAPTER TWO

Lawrence saw heavy combat in the South Pacific,
fighting in bloody landings from Tarawa to Okinawa.
He won more than his share of medals and was one of the few Marines
in his original unit who came back with no more wounds than a few pieces
of Japanese knee mortar shrapnel across his backside.
After the invasion of Okinawa he learned how to operate heavy equipment.
The trade fit well on the reservation where he built stock dams
for a government contractor. Lawrence kept an aloof distance from
organized religion but believed adamantly that the spirit of Cross Dog
had helped him return almost unscathed from the long war
with the Japanese. Rarely outspoken but emboldened by several bottles
of illegally possessed-on-the-reservation beer, he stated his personal belief
at the honoring ceremony held by the tribe for the returning veterans.
He swaggered to the announcer's booth at the dance grounds
when his name was called for an Eagle Feather Award.

Using the loudspeaker he told the crowd, "It was the spirit of Cross Dog that protected me. He was my *wanagi*. " He projected a bold sweep of his audience. Jutting out his chin and adding volume to his voice, he scanned the audience with a defiant attitude, "He watched over me all through the war. Twice he came to me in my dreams; before Tarawa and again before we went ashore at Okinawa." The sternness of his expression and tone of voice warned against anyone contradicting him. Despite the fact that most of the Oglalas had been converted to the white man's belief system, a respectful hush followed his comments until, finally, a tall holy man in a trailered warbonnet rose to speak. Frank Fools Crow said, *"Oh-hunnh. Hetch etu aloh. Waste aloh* (I believe you. It is so. Real good)."

Kyle Charging Shield followed his brother's footsteps into the Marines. Both remained close through occasional letters and Kyle's annual leaves. Lawrence jokingly claimed that Cross Dog's spirit had to be helping his younger brother because Kyle had unexpectedly risen to officer's rank, a battlefield commission in Korea and unbelievably, was flying airplanes.

Time had gone by but old memories would never leave either of the two brothers. Neither cared much for churches, which still preached the white man's beliefs to the Indians. Changes had begun to stir, however. Maybe the return of the many World

War II veterans and now, Korean veterans, had something to do with it. Both were long wars and these men had seen much of the outside world. The military had its' discipline but living with white men for such a long period of time had brought on many changes, new attitudes and ways of thinking. Many of the Sioux warriors had gone beyond the call of duty in the military and had won respect, especially in combat theaters. Most had joined or sought out front line units where they were readily accepted. After the war, the suppression of Indian religion on the reservation slowly subsided. Not that the many denominations of missionaries had eased up on their blind zealotry, but the returning veterans were no longer obsequious sheep. On the Oglala Reservation, two holy men stubbornly brought the Sun Dance out into the open. Lawrence, like most of the Sioux, was unaffected by the return of the old ways. He spent his weekends with veteran friends in West River bars crowded with breeds, full-bloods, cowboys and tourists; even during this particular weekend, the Sun Dance weekend. Kyle Charging Shield was drawn the other direction. Maybe, somehow, the spirit of Cross Dog still lived.

An August dawn pierced the Atlantic seaboard, reaching inland to probe somber, smoky steel towns. The advancing rays of morning found no encampments of Iroquois, Assiniboine, Huron or Algonquin. They had all vanished, like the vast hardwood forest that had once stretched almost unbroken past the Great Lakes and on, beyond, to a once blue Mississippi. Instead, black asphalt, concrete highways and talking wires laced the land while patches of putrid haze hung high - a gloomy pallor to mark settlements and cities of the new inhabitants.

In the continent's heartland a meager stream emptied Badlands alkali water where it met the Missouri. Upstream, westward and then southwest, the Sheyela (Cheyenne) River... a moving oasis in that parched and lonely land... reached back for over a hundred and fifty miles to the Oglala reservation.

Campfires began to wink in the receding darkness as early risers began to stir on the Oglala reservation. Long endemic to the continent with thousands of generations preceding the newcomers, who labeled them 'Sioux,' the Lakota/Dakota Nation was, once again, gathering for the annual Sun Dance ceremony. Most of the participants were Oglalas, along with many neighbors from the Sichangu Tribe, commonly called the Rosebuds. But there were also present a number of Hunkpapas, Minicoujous, Yanktons, Yanktonais, Santees and members of other Lakota/Dakota bands, now stirring in their tipis, tents and portable lodges.

It was Saturday morning and, inside an army surplus tent, a Sichangu Lakota holy man turned restlessly before rising. He didn't like having to pierce on this, the third day of what should have been a four-day ceremony. "Why doesn't the priest say his Mass in his church like he does all the rest of the Sundays?" Eagle Feather had protested to no avail. He grimaced in annoyance at the memory of losing an argument before the tribal council.

The Oglala tribal council had ordered this year's ceremony to be ended a day early, on a Saturday. Everyone knew it was the Jesuit missionary who was behind the disruption so that he could hold Sunday Mass in the Sun Dance arena. Bill Eagle Feather moved to the edge of his buffalo robe mattress to unroll the bundle of clothes that had served as his pillow. He dressed quickly in khaki pants and a flannel shirt, then flipped open the door flap, raising his face to greet the chill air of a new day.

The morning star sparkled its' greeting as the big man, well over six feet tall, walked down the road away from the campsite. Despite the fasting and scant water ration, his bladder demanded relief. Ignoring the outhouses, he walked well beyond the tents and sagging barbed-wire fences of the camp area. He turned his nose when he passed by the outhouses. They always had an unhealthy smell, especially those in crowded campgrounds. The Bureau of Indian Affairs and the Public Health Service had provided an ample supply of limed and serviced facilities, but Bill Eagle Feather preferred the privacy and clean air of the spacious prairie.

The holy man from the Rosebud reservation lumbered along like a bull buffalo into the sage-dotted grass range. His rummage-sale clothes and plodding gait belied a keen mind, the awareness of which extended far beyond life on the reservations. His was a commanding presence, whether he was conducting a Yuwipi ceremony or leading beseechment in a sweat lodge. Even his face was over-sized, his bulbous nose and heavy lips calling to mind the head of *tatanka*, the buffalo. Eagle Feather shivered in the morning chill, knowing that in a few hours he would be bare-chested under the hot sun. His broad chest bore more scars than that of anyone else because he had danced in every Sun Dance since its revival more than a decade ago.

In the still dim light Eagle Feather located a flat-topped boulder on which he rested his heavy frame. After he found a comfortable sitting position he pulled from his pocket his *wotai*, an agate with a rainbow-hued rim. The stone was his amulet, his talisman, and had come to him after his first piercing in the Sun Dance. Four times it had flashed from a Black Hills stream where he had gone to wash off the dust of four days of dancing, fasting and prayer. It was a dynamic stone, his personal *wotai* stone and, from that day on, Eagle Feather's power of foretelling had grown stronger.

Eagle Feather sat in the growing light regarding the images within the stone. A broad band of crystal centered the rainbow rim of the agate. A buffalo, a warbonneted man and a woman... a woman of strong character... resided in the stone. He didn't worship the stone. Only *Wakan Tanka*, the Creator, was acknowledged as the highest of all powers. But it was obvious who made the stone, and it was equally obvious that Eagle Feather was meant to have it. *Wakan Tanka* still spoke to the Oglalas, the Sichangus, and the few who remained of the old tradition-practicing tribes. Through ceremonies and *wotai* stones that came to them in special ways,

Eagle feather

through the daybreak star, the four legged and winged ones... all created things, they recognized and acknowledged the Great Spirit.

The holy man held the stone up to the fading morning star. He had felt no breeze and seen no clouds, both good signs for a Sun Dance. The first breeze should stir at the ceremony's beginning, a sure sign for a meaningful Sun Dance. He was troubled in spite of the favorable conditions. "What good can come from a three day Sun Dance? Can the white man ever allow the Red People to have their own visions?" He spoke out to the spirit world.

As he spoke these words, a covey of four prairie chickens burst from a clump of sage and flew toward the Sun Dance grounds. One bird broke formation and plummeted directly at the base of the cottonwood tree, while another bird circled just above the tree. Soon, the lower bird joined the circling bird and flew away.

'Four,' he noted. 'Such a strong sign.' He peered at the stone, holding it so the crystal caught the rays from the rising sun. The rays moved a degree up the boulder while Eagle Feather stared at the *wotai*, mesmerized by it. Deep within the stone he saw a warrior... a tribesman dressed in a uniform... walking toward a warplane. Eagle Feather looked eastward. Somewhere out there, where the sun first touched the continent, he knew a pilot of tribal blood was about to take to the skies from a military flight line. Eagle Feather returned the stone to his pocket as he bowed his head to thank the Incomprehensible Mystery who made all and allowed all. When he raised his head again he wished he had his peace pipe.

*   *   *   *

On a runway in North Carolina, a Marine fighter-bomber began its takeoff roll. Roaring afterburners, providing 34,000 pounds of thrust, launched the McDonnell F4B Phantom jet. Once airborne, the pilot turned the plane westward. Passing through 500 knots, the throttles came back from the afterburner setting, lest a sonic boom cause a barrage of complaints from coastal residents savoring their Saturday morning's sleep.

The Marine pilot's face was covered by a sun visor and oxygen mask attached to a helmet that bore an unusual design... a feathered warbonnet made from bright reflective tape. The tape was designed to aid searchlights spotting pilots bobbing at sea after a nighttime ditching. Soon, however, this particular pilot would have his helmet stripped of the reflective tape, replaced by dull, non-reflective camouflage paint, in case he had to eject over the enemy held jungles of Vietnam.

The pilot wore a jungle-mottled flight suit. Around one of his biceps, sewed to an elastic garter he wore a beaded armband bearing Teton Sioux design. Embossed gold Marine aviator's wings centered a black leather nametag above the left, zippered breast pocket, with his name and Captain's rank stamped below the wings; Capt. Kyle Charging Shield.

Following the broad valley westward, the pilot retraced unknowingly, the route his ancestors had taken centuries before. Possibly, around the time of the Columbus voyages, the Dakota had elected to avoid the rising numbers of fierce Iroquois. Migrating southward from their Adirondack territory, they settled as corn planters, tilling the comfortable piedmont slopes that would later be called Carolina. Several centuries passed before the tribe began its western migration. It was the *Yuwipi*, the foretelling power that told the Dakota to move. The *Yuwipi* directed the vision-

seekers, and from their visions, the spirit helpers foretold the *washichu*; the white men, would come and make it difficult for the Dakota.

A wall of thunderstorms waited at the confluence of the Missouri and Mississippi. Not that the Phantom would be hindered by the most massive weather front, for it could easily fly above and beyond any thunderstorm. A refueling stop had been planned for Olathe Naval Air Station, but heavy rains and dangerous turbulence circled the field. The Phantom turned northwest to intercept the Mississippi and from that point flew northward. Refueling would take place at the Naval Air Station in Twin Cities and, then continue westward to an Air Force base not far from the pilot's home reservation. When the plane turned upstream at the Mississippi, the migration route of the Dakota was followed.

Near the headwaters of the river, they would name the area *Minneahtah*, land of much waters. Later, immigrants would call it Minnesota. These immigrants and the Ojibway called the Dakota... Sioux. Towns would bear evidence to the passing of the Sioux - Waconia, Winona, Chaska, Shakopee, Wayzata, Mahtomedi, Minnetonka and Waseca. But it would be the Ojibway, with the help of French guns, who would push most of the Sioux out of *Minneahtah*, out onto the Great Plains.

On the Great Plains teeming with *Tatanka*, the buffalo, the Sioux would flourish. The new mobility allowed by *Tashuunka wakan,* holy dog or horse, and the rich provisions from *Tatanka*, the all- providing one, would allow expansion into Canadian and Colorado territory, from the Red River to the Big Horns. From band to tribe to nation, their numbers would increase. The Hunkpapa, Oglala and Sichangu bands would become the larger tribes. These western most bands would develop an 'L' dialect and would refer to themselves as Lakota. Together with the Yankton, Santee, Sans Arc and Minnecoujou tribes and lesser-known bands, the descendants of the peaceful Carolina corn planters would make up the Lakota/Dakota nation.

Annually, the people would gather, tribe camping alongside tribe, forming a huge circle of buffalo-hide lodges surrounding an inner circle with a lone cottonwood tree at its center. The *Yuwipi* continued to predict and foretell, while most of the other red nations were fading into oblivion.

The *Yuwipi* ceremony protected. The *Yuwipi* was instrumental in predicting where and when enemy ambushes would take place, but credit must be given to the warriors and their chiefs who simply out-horsed and out-fought an army ill-suited to the vast expanses of the plains, its torrid heat and arctic-like winter storms. Kept inside forts, Cavalry horses were seldom exercised. Sioux warriors rode tauntingly before the forts, prompting the soldiers to give mounted chase. After the Cavalry became strung out on winded horses the Sioux, riding on fresh mounts, would emerge from concealing draws and gullies to defeat their adversary. Such tactics added weapons, ammunition and horses to Sioux arsenals.

EAGLE VISION

In 1868, long before Custer's campaign, Chief Red Cloud brought the blue-coated military to its knees, the Cavalry losing eight soldiers for each Sioux lost, forcing the signing of a Treaty at Fort Laramie. After solemnizing this treaty, Fort Laramie and other intrusions into Sioux territories along the Bozeman Trail were, by mutual action of Cavalry and Sioux warriors, reduced by burning. The area specified by the treaty encompassed all territory west of the Missouri, to and including *Paha Sapa*, the sacred Black Hills, and north of the Nebraska Sandhills to the Cannonball River. The treaty said the land would be the Indians' for "as long as the grass shall grow, as long as the waters shall flow, as long as your dead lie buried, this land shall remain the Sioux Nation's".

Despite their success, the tide of immigrants behind the U.S. Army could not be held back forever. Eventually the tribes were herded to reservations. At least to the Sioux, it was a reservation won in honorable combat, and the area was adequate as long as the *washichu* honored his part of the agreement.

But then gold was discovered in the Black Hills. Gold was the yellow metal that drove the *washichu* crazy. Lands were excluded from the treaty where immigrants could settle and grow corn and wheat. Disregarding the binding agreement, made honorable by the sacred pipe and the feathers of the eagle, tribes were issued boundaries and separated by the untruthful Blue Man of greed and corruption. Back into the desolate reaches the Sioux were pushed, under the watchful eye of the Cavalry.

*   *   *   *

A drum boomed, breaking the morning stillness. The first breeze stirred. A melodic chanting began, accompanied by a chorus of throbbing drums and the high, piercing notes of eagle bone whistles. The rhythmic movements of a dozen sun dancers waiting outside the Sun Dance arena graced the ancient music. Six male dancers wore shawl skirts; an equal number of women wore plain cotton dresses. All wore wrist and ankle gauntlets of braided sage and a rolled sage crown. Other than a few bearing a solitary sunflower necklace made of painted rawhide, the male dancers were bare-chested and all carried peace pipes. A tall holy man wearing a warbonnet led the procession into the arena, his proud posture masking an arthritic limp; his only concession to age.

The participants gathered at the base of the cottonwood tree, shuffling a slow dance step to face each of the four directions, beginning with the East. Offertory songs played as the dancers held out their peace pipes, the portable altars of the plains tribes.

Now, fingers of light reached westward for the continental divide. Yellow sun, paled to white heat as the arduous ceremony progressed. After honoring the four directions, the dancers turned from the North to return to the base of the cottonwood. Pipes touched Mother Earth, raised to Father Sky, then lifted higher to *Wakan Tanka*, the Great Spirit.

Several holy men addressed the gathering of several thousand, holding the crowd's attention by their quiet dignity. The speeches allowed the dancers, weakened from days of fasting, time to rest under the bower of pine boughs surrounding the dance area.

When the holy men finished speaking, a woman escorted by men on either side waited at the west quadrant of the dance arena. Behind them lay a buffalo skull. The

FOOLS CROW

dancers, each in turn, presented their peace pipes to the assembled trio. The woman accepted each pipe, leaning it against the horns of the buffalo skull. Afterward, the pipes were presented to the drumming singers sitting at the four compass points in the shade of the bower. Each group of drummers sang out their high-pitched, staccato songs on rawhide-bound, barrel-sized drums. Each of the four groups had in front of them a flag; red, yellow, black, or white.

As the sun reached its zenith, Fools Crow, the powerful Oglala holy man and Sun Dance Chief, strode toward the cottonwood. From a shirt pocket he brought forth a small whetstone to sharpen the thin blade of his pocketknife. Bill Eagle Feather, slightly taller and heavier than Fools Crow, was waiting in the shade under the pine-covered bower, having changed out of his rummage sale shirt and khakis. He was now wearing a breechcloth and pair of leggings as he shuffled out of the bower to don a buffalo-horned headdress. He moved slowly toward the center of the dance arena with a graceful and measured step. Fools Crow put his knife under his wide belt as he watched the approaching Sun Dance pledger who had been pierced more than anyone in his time.

The pair of holy men mirrored scenes common a century before. Fools Crow, the Sun Dance Chief, wore a long warbonnet, its trailing eagle feathers covering the back of his fringed, buckskin war shirt and leggings, down to the top of his moccasins. The sun dancer wore only the buffalo headdress, a plain deerskin breechcloth and a pair of blue leggings. His broad chest and expansive belly were bare. The eagle bone whistle in his mouth uttered a deep, moaning bellow each time he dropped his horned head. At this moment, he was a bull buffalo about to confront an adversary on some mystical plain.

Fools Crow's age was unknown. His proud carriage and keenly perceptive mind denied creeping age. He was from that era of Oglalas who had ignored the white man's directive to record their beginning, so that now the Teton beaded, geometric tipi patterns on his war shirt were as mysterious as the man himself. He had the classic sharp features of the Oglalas, a hawkish nose with flaring nostrils, wide-set eyes that missed nothing, high cheekbones, and a tight jaw that guarded against casual speech. His regal manner carried with it a sense of sadness, suggesting that the knowledge acquired throughout his many years and his foretelling ability left him unable to reveal all that he knew.

Eagle Feather was younger than Fools Crow and had been his pupil, but the many piercings he had experienced and his dedication to bringing back this annual ceremony had brought him close in stature to his mentor. He too, was far advanced in foretelling and healing power. He reclined on a bed of sage at the base of the cottonwood tree while an assistant tested the rope's strength. Looking up at the striking picture of the tree against wide sky, he wondered if this might be a sign that one of the mystical forces would come to this center of the tribal nation, the focal center of their prayers. He believed that on piercing day a revelation would be delivered at the

Sun Dance ceremony. He trusted the combined power of the sacred tree, the praying people and the Sun Dance itself to bring a vision. Pierced sun dancers often received strong visions.

A dozen men and women stood close to the tree while onlooking members of the Sioux Nation: Sichangus, Oglalas, Hunkpapas, Yanktons, and Minicoujous, rose in hushed silence from their seats at the edge of the dance arena to watch with electrifying intensity, the two holy men. Even the drums fell silent in the magnetic atmosphere. Fools Crow kneeled to insert a narrow blade cross wise into and out of the skin of the sun dancer. The knife blade flashed and the wooden skewer was thrust through the incisions in Eagle Feather's chest. Fools Crow bound the buckskin rope to the skewer with a leather thong and then grasped his pupil's shoulder with a sympathetic grimace.

Once again, Bill Eagle Feather, the Sichangu holy man, was pierced. He held the weight of his rope while rising gingerly from the bed of sage to don the buffalo-horned headdress. The flaming pain in his chest caused his hulking frame to waiver for a few moments. Fools Crow steadied the heavier man. Both men were tall, but Eagle Feather was at least an inch taller. The buffalo headdress was befitting for the Sichangu. Eagle Feather was built like a bull buffalo but, whereas Fools Crow was well-muscled, the Oglala's physique and stature called to mind a regal hawk or a mysterious and powerful eagle. Mysterious! This was the only way to define or express the seemingly remote, yet dominating aura of Fools Crow the holy man.

Eagle Feather tested his eagle bone whistle while taking a westerly position away from the tree, close to the end of the long braided rope. Just below the pruned branches of the tree, his rope was attached. A leather thong tied the other end to the wooden peg Fools Crow had tunneled through the pair of slits in the skin of his chest. He waited and watched while Fools Crow pierced five more sun dancers who had pledged to endure the *Wiwanyag Wachipi*.

In time, six women took positions beside the six male sun dancers who were spaced around and equidistant from the tree. The women wore plain, egg-shell colored cotton dresses, which were significantly cooler than buckskin dresses. The men wore shawl skirts, somewhat resembling a Scottish kilt, and were bare-chested. All of the dancers were barefooted and, with the exception of the buffalo-horned Eagle Feather, all wore a sage crown headdress bearing a pair of spiked eagle wing feathers inserted into the sage crown and standing upright above each ear. The pointed feather spikes evoked the idea of spiritual antennae used to communicate with the world of the beyond.

The women did not have to pierce. They suffered far more pain and even risked death when they gave birth to children… "so that the people may live". Sioux religion was perceptive and balanced and, unlike most male-dominated religions, the woman was specially acknowledged. It was a powerful spirit woman, Buffalo Calf Woman, who appeared to the Sioux, bringing them the sacred red pipe. Her first act was to kill a man, a man who was selfish and thought only of his own desire. She lived among them, long enough to teach the use of the pipe in seven sacred ceremonies. For this reason, a woman sat in the place of honor, holding the sacred pipe in some of the ceremonies. It was a woman who opened the sweat lodge. For the most sacred ceremony... the annual Sun Dance Thanksgiving... a woman took the first cuts during the felling of the cottonwood tree. After the tree was implanted at the center of the nation, a woman would open the Sun Dance ceremonies by circling the tree clockwise, before any other person entered the dance arena.

The twelve dancers held their positions equidistant around the tree before the respectful, silent crowd. It was Saturday, the third day of the four-day ceremony. Sioux way did most spiritual things in fours. Always, the fourth day would be the piercing, the culmination of the *Wiwanyag Wachipi*, the Sun Dance Thanksgiving. But this year, the local missionaries... one missionary in particular, the Jesuit priest, Father Buchwald... made a concerted effort and successfully manipulated the tribal council into disrupting the ancient custom. The following day, the fourth day, the priest would drive his pickup truck into the Sun Dance arena, set up his portable altar, and say Mass at the very base of the tree. For this priest, Sunday was the Lord's Day, and that excluded *Wakan Tanka*, the Creator of All.

Several drums boomed the breaking song. Eagle Feather had been disturbed that entire morning, having to pierce on this, the third day, but it was now the time for a vision. A sun dancer could have a powerful vision while connected through the wooden peg inserted in his chest and tied by rope to the Tree of Life implanted at the center of the Lakota/Dakota nation. The sun dancer was connected physically and spiritually to Mother Earth. Eagle Feather was intensively aware of how powerful this time was, having sun danced more than anyone in modern times. Eagle Feather had revived the ceremony more than a decade earlier and his mentor, Fools Crow, the aging Oglala, had pierced him every year since then. Despite the interference of the missionaries and of the many turncoat tribal members who had adopted their religion, Fools Crow and Eagle Feather had stood up to numerous detractors. The turncoats were the most affluent on the reservation and the most powerful politically. They were rewarded by the Bureau of Indian Affairs with paid positions and whatever other economic advantages were available. They also controlled the majority of votes on the tribal council.

For the moment, Eagle Feather set aside these disappointments. The weaseling of priests and politicians was less important than Sun Dance ceremonies and visions. Vision was direct communication with the universe, the spirit world. *Wakan Tanka* had made it so. The Six Forces and their mysterious helpers directly beneath the omnipotent *Wakan Tanka* could now provide powerful contact, powerful vision.

The dancers moved in rhythmic unison toward the tree, the drums stirring primal instincts imbedded within the flesh and cells of every Sioux. The collective strength of the praying crowd seemed to lighten the steps of the sun dancers, lifting them like eagles soaring on a spiritual wind. Rawhide cutouts of *tatanka* the buffalo and one of a man, placed high in the tree by the Sun Dance Chief, began to twirl. Lower on the tree, twelve chokecherry branches, symbolizing the twelve moons, vibrated in rhythm with the drums and dancers.

The dancers touched the tree, then backed off to the end of their ropes, lightly tugging backward, experiencing the first of four breaking pains. The drummers at the periphery of the arena increased the tempo of the drumbeat. The pledgers, blowing their bone whistles, danced forward again, touching the tree and then backing to the end of their tethers. As they touched the tree for the fourth time, the tree itself emitted a shrill whistle, as though in response to the eagle bone whistles being blown with increased intensity by each dancer.

Now, as Eagle Feather leaned back for the fourth time, the pain intensified. His chest felt as if it was on fire. He begged the Great Spirit for a vision. His pain was his offering for a deep vision. He focused on the outer edge of the sun. The holy man had fasted for three days, drinking little water. The pain, the fasting and the sun at high noon transformed the tree into a giant sunflower. The four colored cloth banners decorating the tree became the four quarters of Mother Earth. *Wiwanyag Wachipi Topa*! Sun Dance Four! The four quarters revolved slowly, becoming a multicolored base for the sunflower. The sunflower bent forward, pulling Eagle Feather into its interior. The sunflower sucked him upward, spiraling him clockwise like a swirl of smoke in a still room.

Two spirit men appeared. Eagle Feather began his spirit journey in much the same way as Black Elk, a Sioux visionary, had done a century before. One spirit man held a peace pipe, the other a flowering stick. Eagle Feather ascended with them to ride on a cloud floating above the encampment. The spirit man threw the pipe down to the Sun Dance tree. The tree budded, bursting forth with vibrant green leaves. A yellow hoop spread outward from the tree to the perimeter of the Sun Dance arena.

Eagle Feather understood. The Sun Dance would be a strong force to bring back the spirit of the Lakota/Dakota people. The cloud drifted west over the Badlands toward the highest peak cresting the dark mountains.

"Heyyy, heyyy, heyyy, heyyy," he heard a cry as he drew close to Thunder Being Peak. There on the mountaintop, a forlorn Black Elk, the aged seer, raised up his peace pipe while lamenting and crying out, piteously. Eagle Feather looked back at the Sun Dance grounds, but the encampment was now in another time, occupied by Cavalry troops. The tree was withered, without any trace of decoration. Eagle Feather was staring into the past, watching the Cavalry that had been defeated by the Sioux. A treaty had been signed, followed by the smoking of a sacred pipe. The Cavalry pitched their tents in a meadow, then began shooting a herd of buffalo crossing a clear rushing stream. A flaming Blue Man scurried back and forth, passing out ammunition. While the buffalo were being exterminated, missionaries built large, square structures, which Eagle Feather recognized as boarding schools.

A bugle sounded. The Cavalry mounted to intercept a pitiful band of ragged Indians walking wearily, returning peacefully to the reservation. Chief Big Foot, the headman walked forward waving a white flag of truce. He was told to camp for the night. The next morning the Cavalry opened fire, mowing down men, women and children. Afterwards, medicine bundles and peace pipes were gathered and brought back to the encampment. There, the rest of the Sioux stood like captives while missionaries poured oil on the pile of sacred objects. The Blue Man appeared with a torch, and with it, set the pile aflame. Missionaries held high their revered crosses, requiring the Indians to kneel in subjugation while the Cavalry looked on. The solemn treaty made by the *washichu* with the Sioux was forgotten. "Heyyy, heyyy, heyyy, heyyy." The mournful voice of Black Elk made Eagle Feather understand why the old prophet of Thunder Being Peak had lost hope despite his once-powerful vision.

A snarling and growling commotion to the north caused Eagle Feather to turn to the Black Hills. At the top of Spirit Mountain, a blue aura surrounded an ugly figure with fiendish fangs threatening a two-legged approaching from below. The Blue Man of Black Elk's vision challenged a warrior climbing the mountain while the warrior's eagle mate circled high above. The warrior was a Lakota Sioux, like Eagle Feather, but a generation younger. A *wotai* stone glimmered on the warrior's chest. The Sichangu holy man sensed that he would play a part in the life of the warrior who possessed this stone. A compelling test and a vivid journey awaited the warrior, Eagle Feather surmised, as he watched the fight between the ugly creature and the warrior draw to a standstill. The eagle continued to circle while the warrior descended from the mountain.

After the warrior had left the mountain, the eagle landed, taking on the form of a woman. Once again time changed, but Eagle Feather sensed he was now looking into the future. It was a new era on the mountain and, while the ugly creature taunted the advancing woman, she designed a set of colored stairs: red, yellow, black and white. The woman also wore a glowing *wotai* stone. As Eagle Feather moved into closer view he recognized the stone as being his own.

Thunder shook the horizon. To the east, a bright rainbow flashed. Flames descended from the rainbow and, where they landed, flowers bloomed. The flowers turned into two-leggeds representing many clans and bands. Most of them were *washichus*, yet they stood straight and tall... conveying an aura of decisive spirit... close to the natural appearance of tribal peoples. Among these people, Eagle Feather saw that the men were strong, yet gentle, and that the women were equal to all and also leaders. This image struck Eagle Feather with awe. He knew that this was a powerful part of his Sun Dance vision.

The cloud carrying Eagle Feather and the two spirit men now drifted south, back toward the Sun Dance grounds. Beneath the cloud he saw an airplane, a military fighter jet. It was embedded in the barren clay and shale of a badlands ravine; its war colors bleached clean like fossil bones. The warrior he had seen at Spirit Mountain climbed from the wreckage to pick sage with which to make a sun dancer's wreath. The warrior left the airplane to stand beneath a drooping, withering Sun Dance tree.

"Heyyy, heyyy, heyyy, heyyy," the old man from Thunder Being Mountain called out, his spirit swooping down to the warrior. While Black Elk led the warrior around the Sun Dance tree, priests and those who took orders from the black robed missionaries gathered at the encampment. They tried to attack the warrior, but he beat them back using the power of his *wotai* stone. The tree straightened, changing to a bright red stick with sprouting leaves. The yellow hoop spread outward to the horizon. Other Sun Dances spread to other reservations, even to other tribes. "Heyyy, heyyy," Black Elk called out, this time in a happy, joyous tone.

Eagle Feather leaned back, pulling taut the braided rope. The vision had ended. The peg tugged at a hand-width of chest skin as the heavy dancer tilted backward to tear the peg free. The vision had been so overpowering, that it created a shield against pain as he strained to bring the dance to its proper conclusion. As the drums intensified, all prayed for the ordeal to be ended. One by one the Sun Dance pledgers broke free.

Later that afternoon, after the long line filed past to shake the hand of each sun dancer, Eagle Feather and Fools Crow were starting to leave the arena. Suddenly, a stone struck the cottonwood tree with a resounding crack and fell at their feet. A puff of dust lingered where the stone landed. Eagle Feather bent his hulking frame to pick up and examine the smooth stone. Fools Crow stepped forward, cupping his hand to shade the oval shape in Eagle Feather's palm. When he made out the image of a defiant eagle deep within the grain, the Oglala holy man nodded slowly without changing the solemn expression that rarely left his face. The stone was the color of a golden eagle. "*He wotai, lelah wakan,*" he exclaimed. "It is one of those holy stones." He turned the stone over to look closely at its other surface. There, embodied against the golden background, was a misshapen man with claws, like the figure on Spirit Mountain. The figure's color was slate blue.

Eagle Feather also saw the images. "*Toe wichasha lelah shee cha. Wanbli hey Wahste aloh.* This blue man is bad but the eagle is good," he added in English. "They are on opposite sides of the stone."

Both men let their eyes drift to the east and when they looked back at the stone; a woman appeared upon the eagle's side of it. Eagle Feather flipped the stone over. The blue man's image was gone. Both men knew that the bearer of this *wotai* stone would be associated with eagle power, and that he would meet a powerful woman.

High above, the resonant roar of jet engines broke the quiet as a thin contrail traced a soft white line across the clear blue sky. Both men looked upward at the plane. *"Okini he wotai, wanbli ouye,"* (Maybe that is the stone's eagle power) Fools Crow declared, as they watched the plane disappear far across the Badlands.

Eagle Feather smiled. It had been a warplane, exactly like the one he had seen that morning, in the vision within his *wotai* stone. The warrior pilot had arrived. He held the *wotai* stone up to the rays of the afternoon sun. *"Hetch etu aloh,"* he exclaimed in Lakota. "It is so, indeed."

GRAND MOTHER

CHAPTER THREE

The jet sped above the rugged Badlands terrain. The pilot surveyed the boundless expanse broken by jagged spires projecting from the floor of an ancient inland sea. Where dinosaurs once roamed, the Sheyela River coursed like a pale ribbon to mark the edge of the barren reservation, the final destination of the wandering Oglalas. A tiny portion of the sprawling reservation nestled beside a badland wall captivated the airman for a long moment, but the diorama of landscape, unfolding inescapably like life itself, stole him away from its enchanting spell.

The aviator looked longingly over his shoulder. He reached to silence the radar transponder, hesitated momentarily, then abruptly slammed the control stick to full aileron. The plane rolled upside down, descending swiftly, steeply, turning back to a lonely trio of badland buttes rising sharply beyond a shallow stream. The altimeter unwound, losing miles of altitude before the huge warplane leveled smoothly into a wide arc over an isolated abandoned cabin.

The pilot placed the circling Phantom on autopilot and saw himself as a boy sitting beside his grandmother, listening to the rustling leaves of the tall cottonwood that sheltered the old woman's dirt-roofed dwelling.

*　　*　　*　　*

A peace pipe rested in the old one's lap as she rocked slowly on the hard alkaline soil facing the trio of badland buttes.

"How did the pipe come to us?" the boy asked.

The old one studied his city clothes before she replied, "Your mother will not like what I tell you." Her pessimistic eyes fixed on the pipe. "No, she will not let you stay with me if I tell you about our way. You live in the world of the *washichu* (white

CHARGING SHIELD

man), my grandson. Everywhere there are *washichus*. There are only a few of us. Our ways will die, *Takgozha* (Grandson)."

"A wolf can travel in a herd of buffalo," the boy rebutted. "Besides, Grandpa wasn't an Indian."

While a breeze stirred the leaves of the cottonwood, the old woman glanced at the early evening moon. A smile smoothed the wrinkles from around her mouth as she remembered an event from long ago.

Watching his grandmother's face, *Takgozha* persisted quietly, "All I've heard is the white man's ways. Why can't I hear about our Indian ways? If you don't tell me, who will when you're dead and I can't learn any more from you?"

Although a worried expression chased the quiet smile from her face, she nodded slowly. Encouraged, he persisted, "No one stopped Grandpa from learning. How come you won't tell me?"

The woman relented and told him about the Old Way, cautioning him not to tell her daughter, the boy's mother.

"She won't care. She's getting better about those things," the boy said.

"Maybe," the old woman cautioned, "but what I tell you, she might not like." A trace of bitterness crossed her face. "The boarding school, they taught my children that the Old Way was bad." A look of relief crossed her face as she stared intently at the boy admiring the peace pipe. "You were lucky, Grandson. You didn't spend much time in the boarding school." Her lips formed a brief smile. "Maybe this pipe will lead you away from the road of the white man."

She told him how the foretelling powers led his people from their cornfields near the eastern shores, when the Dakota Nation had been peaceful corn planters on a piedmont rise close to the eastern ocean of the continent. Beans, squash, pumpkins, and potatoes supplemented their wholesome diet along with a plentiful supply of fish, venison and wild turkey. Their abundance made them a straight and tall people who used tobacco in clay pipes for ceremony; ceremony to beseech the Great Mystery, *Wakan Tanka*. The smoke from their pipes was regarded as their visible breath and symbolized that their words and actions had to be straight and true. This virtue alone preserved their portion of the planet for all the generations that they could remember. These two-legged had lived in harmony; leaving clean waters, endless forests, no endangered species and did not poison the land when crops were planted. This two-legged did not experience the famines that ravaged those across the waters and despite the absence of the *washichu's* diseases, this two-legged did not over-populate. The nature respecting two-legged had acquired an earth harmony and had been upon this continent much longer than the destructive ones who would come later.

The people's ceremony and lifestyle brought forth their deliverance. A great danger was approaching. The *washichu* was foretold and would not only destroy the more powerful tribes to the north but also many of the winged and the four-legged would disappear. Even the waters and the land itself could be destroyed by the *washichu* whose myths and values told him he did not have to respect Mother Earth and all of the related things upon her. "I have dominion over the Earth and all creatures," he declared from his myths. Later, in his history books, he would also assert that this new land had unlimited resources.

The ceremonies, the communication of the spirit calling, warned the Dakota. They were to leave their abundant land and migrate westward; down the Ohio River valley. The Catawbas and the Wakama, the people from the stars, chose to remain. In scattered clans and bands, the rest of the nation slowly followed the retreating buffalo down the plains of the Ohio. Even the eagles left with the tribe, for they knew also, the *washichu* would bring their winged numbers to the edge of extinction. Where two mighty rivers merged, the Mississippi and the Missouri, bands went upstream. Omahas and Mandans went northwest. Biloxis and Arkansa went downstream. The Kansa band crossed over. The main body of Dakota traveled north to the source of the greatest river in the land. In the "land of much waters" the Dakota camped while their scouts and ranging bands followed the buffalo into the rich grazing plains to the west. When advance scouts returned with the horse, the Dakota followed into an enchanting destiny. Another tribe, the Ojibway, who named them Sioux, drove most of the remaining Dakota out onto the plains. Their loss was a blessing, however. The *washichu* swallowed up the Ojibway while the Sioux enjoyed several more centuries of freedom.

Upon the Great Plains, they came upon more of *Ta shuunka Wakan*, the horse and the vast buffalo herds. Many of the Sioux who were now speaking in the L dialect broke away from the main body of the Dakota and called themselves Lakota. Lakota or Dakota, meant allies or friends. These western Sioux, were the first to advance onto the plains. The tribes flourished and grew in numbers large enough to call themselves the Lakota/Dakota (Allies) Nation. The larger bands became tribes: the Oglala Tribe, the Hunkpapa Tribe, the Sichangu Tribe; all under the banner of the Allied Nation. Their leadership was unselfish, truthful and therefore, quite formidable. When they were attacked upon their own portion of Mother Earth, the Allies retaliated by killing eight blue-coated soldiers for every warrior lost and won their treaties in combat from the ones who did not understand or care to respect the land.

The Lakota/Dakota beseeched the Great Mystery through the Six Powers and held annual Sun Dances to thank *Wakan Tanka*, the Great Provider. Hundreds of buffalo hide tipis would form around a Sun Dance tree at the center of the nation, when the meat had been cured and dried from the summer buffalo hunts. The Sun Dance ceremony would express their appreciation and respect as a nation, for all that had been received and for their extended time of freedom upon their *Ina Maka* - Mother Earth.

Upon entering the Great Plains, the people would be blessed by the Buffalo Calf Woman and her gift of the sacred pipe. "The Buffalo Calf Woman was sent to us by the Great Spirit. She came to us carrying a bundle wrapped in a buffalo robe. Inside was a sacred red pipe. This pipe, and ones made like it by the people, are to be used in the ceremonies."

Her eyes held a ray of hope. "I've heard that the white man's weapons are big, maybe so big he'll be afraid to have any more wars. You'll see a war though maybe several *Takgozha*. You will have to cut your braids. I know an old man named Black Elk. He has made some predictions but no one believes much in what he says. He said he saw all the winds of the world were fighting and it was like rapid gun-fire and whirling smoke. One of his predictions is about a flowering tree. The tree will flower some day and around it all nations will gather, but we haven't seen that yet. Two spirits gave him the herb of understanding. Black Elk threw it down onto Mother Earth and it flowered, spreading peace over the whole world. Maybe that will really happen. Maybe there will be no more wars. All of Black Elk's visions are coming true, so far. Maybe white men, as powerful as they are, maybe they will reach out to the herb of understanding. But, before you go to war, you be sure to see Fools Crow." She saw the question of disbelief in his eyes as he nodded his head.

"Grandson, long ago there were those among us who could come back, but first they had to be a warrior. Those that stood by the holy people and fought for the Way. They were called Mystic Warriors. The Mystic Warriors would aid the holy peoples' visions... important foretelling visions for the good of the tribe. They would acquire a power of their own, as long as they were truthful. They could have powerful things happen to them and as long as they remained truthful, nothing could bother them. Not until their task... what was set before them... was finished."

"A Mystic Warrior?"

"Yes, something like that. You will have to do what the holy men say. You may have to help the foretelling power and fight for our way. If you show you aren't afraid, you might get your chance to come back."

"Come back? From a war?"

"No, more than that. When you get older you still may not understand, but it will be in your heart. It will be what you really want after you have been a part of the white man's world."

"Is that the way of the Mystic Warrior?"

"Yes, Grandson... in a way. In the old days, before the white man, they lived for the way so that they might be allowed to come back." An owl hooted closer, seeming to draw a curtain against the night. "Even if I am no longer here, you do what I say. Fools Crow... Fools Crow and Eagle Feather, they will help you."

Closer now, the owl called again. "Ouh heay, ouh heay," she acknowledged, turning her head to listen. As the night-hunter spoke again, *Takgozha* remembered that some Indians said the owl was a bird of warning.

She held up a cautionary hand as the owl hooted once more. "Listen to that. The spirit people, our ancestors, sometimes speak through the winged ones. They are

warning that there is truth in what I say." The owl hooted a steady staccato of tones once more, as if it were carrying a conversation. The old woman held her fingers to her lips to still any interfering questions from her grandson. When the great night winged one was silent, a smile erased her intense composure. "You are going to dance, Grandson. Soon you will become a dancer and you will braid your hair. But soon afterwards, you will go off to war and they will cut your hair." She paused as if she were seeing a vision. After a long pause, she exclaimed with a proud smile, "Oh huhhn! You will be a warrior, Grandson. *Lelah ahtaah wichasta* (You'll be a great warrior). You will fight like a braided warrior of long ago!" She enjoyed a sense of reverie brought back from the mystery of the past. "Le le le le lah. Le le le le lah," she sang out to the night loud and shrill. The call, a tremolo honoring a warrior echoed among the distant buttes. "Later, you will meet a powerful woman, and in times to come. But it is all a mystery." Her smile became one of allegiance to her own gender. "You will be a warrior but this woman will have the power where the warrior way cannot." She sensed that her last words would be difficult for even the holy men to grasp. She waved her hand. 'In time though, maybe in another time, this mystery would come to pass.'

At that time in the boy's life he could not understand, and did not suppress a frown brought on by the thought of association with a woman other than a relative. He could love *only* his grandmother <u>forever</u>, he had once innocently vowed.

She understood his devoted attachment, yet leaned forward to look sternly into his face. She saw something there that gave her a surge of strength. The old woman told her grandson of the Sun Dance and Black Elk's prediction that it would return. When he grew into manhood he sat with her as a young Marine among a pitifully small crowd, to watch Eagle Feather and Fools Crow bring the Sun Dance ceremony back to life.

The Korean War raged before he graduated from high school. Not long after he had tasted combat in that war, the old traditionalist joined the spirit world. Before her departure, she made a last prediction, "Grandson, you're going to see another war. You will still be a warrior."

"No," he disagreed, "The war is over." A frown formed. "No more wars Grandma," he muttered. His childish dream to be a Marine and fight in a war like Lawrence had been fulfilled.

"There will be others," she corrected. "If they can make a business out of their religion, war can be a collection plate too. This time, you be sure and see Fool's Crow before you go off to war."

She smiled and sighed. Turning his eyes to the moon that was touching the tips of the buttes, he saw her head nod. He watched the moon paint the night with silver as he pondered his Grandmother's words.

"I guess we'd better go to bed, Grandma," he called, thinking she might have fallen asleep.

The screen door slammed. He turned to see a clump of sage where the rocking chair had been. The cabin in the background had suddenly grown old and abandoned.

"Marine Jet," West River Radar called. "Marine Jet, squawk Code 44. Over."

CHARGING SHIELD

CHAPTER FOUR

The throttles pushed forward, igniting the afterburners. The Phantom jet surged like an airborne racehorse leaping skyward, climbing for several minutes before the power was set for cruise; only then did the pilot activate the radar transponder, transmitting his position. During the ascent, he guided the plane toward a tree-lined creek joining the Sheyela further downstream. The creeks meandering course pointed back at a town, West River, taking form at the edge of a mountain range rising darkly on the western horizon. Before the town, a pair of airports offered their runways. He radioed a request to the municipal airport as the plane drew closer.

Charging Shield was all the people he had been. Deep within his sub-conscious, his warrior pasts were always there but far enough down where they could not surface, at least not yet. Since the death of his grandmother, new voices, suggestive voices, ancient and mentoring, tantalized a life made up of several lives, separated by separate times. Vainly, he wished to recall those lives, perhaps because he so missed the entwined comradeship of fellow warriors and of course, there was the woman. Yes, *that* woman.

He craved to revisit those pasts, but the darkness was always uncompromising except for those occasional slivers of revelation, a trace here and then there from deep within. He knew, and this could only come from his Indianness. He knew his tribe would point him to his destiny and he believed that to try to change destiny would be akin to throwing rocks at the moon.

Although he favored his native side, Charging Shield had another distinct stream to his makeup, his European Celtic side, one he tended to downplay, yet it was an equally important factor, more so because of the reality of the dominating sea of the white man's world. Within those traces of past revelation there was a cautioning command to appreciate and seek the abundant adventure offered by the new inhabitants and to covenant an accord with his other blood, for he was the sum of those other lives as well.

Charging Shield wasn't afraid to respond to his ghostly subconscious mentors. Bloodied in the Korean War as a sergeant, he had won a battlefield commission. After the war he was rewarded with flight school and went on to fly helicopters and then finally his ultimate goal - jets. He had volunteered for a combat tour even though he was eligible to leave the military, having served more than the six-year requirement for pilots. So many were leaving, even combat-trained pilots. The war in Vietnam was becoming unpopular and costly, but for him, he had to taste combat in this time and he was patriotic to his country as much as he was to his tribe. He had no trouble obediently following the demanding discipline of the Marine Corps. He preferred it to any other service. They were warriors, no question about that.

Charging Shield was an Oglala - his features attested to that. The warrior look still remained as it did on so many Oglalas, even to death. His look was not fierce, however, for he was tempered by a quarter English from one grand parent and a quarter Scotch-Irish from another. Strangely, he could have ridden easily with the Lakota Teton Dog Soldiers or the Kit Fox warrior society, or sat in a far-off, ancient, forested glade, listening spellbound beside the campfire of Merlin, the overseeing magician, or jousted and rode with the Knights of the Round Table, if ever that warrior society existed.

In wintertime, like many of the Sioux breeds, he was light complexioned for an Indian, but the Carolina sun had tanned him quickly and deeply. His thick black hair was military cut and unlike Fools Crow, he had to shave what would become a light moustache, a trait inherited from his European side, a trait he wouldn't have minded doing without. His cheekbones were somewhat pronounced and his eyes wide-spaced and observant.

He had many of Fools Crow's Oglala characteristics: the erect stature, a sweeping hawkish gaze and a quietness when not among friends indicating an almost reclusive nature. His eyes, however, would never carry the penetrating sweep of a holy man and Charging Shield was thankful for that. He would fight for a holy man to protect the Way but he could never be one. He wanted to see the world through a warrior's eyes - to be a hunter, a nomad, an adventurer - and, so far, the Marine Corps was a perfect vehicle for his time.

"Roger, Marine jet, cleared for low pass. No reported traffic," West River tower replied.

The Phantom passed low across the edge of the north-south runway, aiming at a high hangar. A plump figure below waved excitedly at the aircraft rolling smoothly over the asphalt and prairie. The pilot delayed the roll, holding the fighter inverted. His left hand pushed the pair of throttles outboard and forward, igniting both after-burners with a deafening roar. The plane rolled upright to rocket into vast sky. Several seconds into the climb, the booming afterburners silenced. Radio frequencies switched to call a military field several miles further north. Within a few minutes, the Phantom settled on an Air Force runway to taxi to the visitor's line.

The pilot climbed down the side to stretch his lean six-foot frame. He had wide shoulders and the slender legs of a horseman. His face was etched with an unmistakable hardness from being raised in a reservation border town. Yet, when he reached for a Marine garrison cap bearing captain's bars and closed his flight plan in the operations terminal, his manner bore an accomplished confidence, not unusual for a man who had left his small town past behind to become a fighter pilot.

After retrieving a folded garment bag from beneath the Phantom's ejection seat, he boarded a blue shuttle bus for the municipal airport.

"Kyle Charging Shield!" His name was called by a boisterous, overweight, yet gentle-appearing man lumbering, with a limp, toward the Air Force bus. The man's hands displayed two massive Black Hills gold rings. An equally impressive gold bracelet exhibited more of the specially designed jewelry, the unique etching and coloring process invented by the burly man. Ernie Hale, the wealthy owner of the local flying service, a business he dabbled in as a hobby, clasped a bear's hug around the pilot after he stepped onto the curb, then berated him good-naturedly for not landing to offer a ride.

"Can't, Ernie. White man's regulations." The Marine threw his head back and laughed, exposing straight white teeth.

"Geesus, I was flying before you was born, and I ain't never been in a jet," the businessman moaned. "I mean a real one like that Phantom, that can get upside down and all." His ponderous figure seemed to swell. Hale pleaded again as they walked toward a graveled ramp, "How much you want? Just to let me sit in the back seat of that big baby?"

The pilot appraised a row of airplanes before his eyes searching for the hazy buttes far away on the prairie horizon. His thoughts traveled to the reservation. In the background, his hometown, West River, spread itself to tourists flocking to the Black Hills.

He glanced back at Hale. His answer matched his detached stare. "Ernie, I would, but I have to get to the Sun Dance."

Hale's eyes flashed under his bushy brows. "Every time you come home, you're going to some war dance." His growl was amiable. "You're missing a rodeo this weekend."

"Sorry, Ernie. I'm an Indian, not a cowboy." Charging Shield's eyes glinted with amusement. He enjoyed teasing the man whose slouchy appearance belied the power he could wield in the town sprawled beneath the mountain backdrop. Charging Shield was well aware that Ernie's coarse speech could be brutally vindictive. He took liberty with the fact that he was one of the few friends Ernie Hale allowed to be close. The Marine turned toward the airplanes. "You got a bird for rent?"

"Take that Cessna," the brawny man pointed. His voice carried a tone of rejection. A red biplane was parked across from the Cessna. The radial engine of the red plane sitting back on its tail wheel held the pilot's attention. "How long that Sun Dance last?" Hale queried.

"Four days. It'll be over tomorrow. Sunday's the last day," Charging Shield replied over his shoulder as he started for the red plane, ignoring the Cessna. "Every morning they dance, but the main part's tomorrow. Tomorrow's the piercing. I want to be there for the piercing." His words carried an added note of enthusiasm.

"That Sun Dance - that thing's against the law, you know," Hale grumbled, as he trailed slowly behind.

Hale's remark cut into him, forcing a tired retaliation, "You want to abide by the law, Ernie? The treaty says Indians own the whole goddamned half of this state. You're breaking the law just standing there."

"Geesus Christ, kid," Hale returned defensively. "Don't get so hot under the collar. I got nothing against your people's doings. You know that."

Charging Shield apologized. He stopped in front of the biplane. "Holy smokes, what's the story on this beauty?" He looked at the rear of the plane and down at the tail wheel. "You still got that old Piper Cub?"

"Yeah," the older man replied with a relieved voice. "Gonna trade it on this bird you're looking at right now and when I do, I want you to come back and solo it." Ernie Hale enjoyed the big grin spreading across the pilot's face.

"You do that Ernie, and the next time I come back I'll figure out a way to get you through that Air Force flight line. For damn sure, I'll taxi you around in a Phantom." He patted the red plane as though it was alive. His eyes glowed. "Damn, Ernie. I feel like I'm in love. There's something about this big baby that just draws me to it. I'd hug this big bastard if I could get my arms around it."

Hale shot out his hand excitedly. "It's a deal, Kid. C'mon let's shake on it. Ol' Ernie will get it for sure. I got a crop sprayer that's goin' broke. Course I'm squeezing him hard, right now." Ernie winked as he pumped the pilot's hand. "You wait and see what I'll have the boys in the shop do to that cockpit. We'll make a two seater, side by side, out of it. Pop a bigger radial engine on it, an' you an' me, we'll go spinnin' around an' do all that fighter pilot stuff."

After the handshake, Hale watched while Charging Shield took a dipstick from the Cessna's engine to check the oil. Satisfied, the Marine inspected the rest of the airplane, which seemed dwarfed by the burly red plane across from it. "That was lots of fun, eh, kid? The old days - you and me. That tail wheeler Cub, bouncing around on them cow pastures?"

Charging Shield answered with an eerie, detached, reminiscent nod. His mind was on the tribal happenings south, back across the Badlands where he had just flown despite Ernie's enthusiasm. The Sun Dance circle below, as he passed over in the jet, was etched like a moving film in his mind.

Hale's nostalgic mood continued. "I think about you, kid, whenever I see one of those jets go by. And now you're flying that Phantom. You're not planning on staying in, are you?"

"Don't know, Ernie. Might get out and finish college. Expect I'll do a combat tour first, though. Got to get my degree, can't get anyplace without it - not even in the Marines."

"I always told you to get that degree, kid," Hale encouraged. "That war's starting to heat up. Secretary of Defense is talking about building an electronic fence between South and North Vietnam." Hale unconsciously looked over his shoulder at the end of the runway and lowered his voice. "Them computers are gonna win this war," he revealed. "But guess you can't talk about that stuff to a civilian, can ya?"

While he moved the rudder, Charging Shield's eyebrows shot up in disbelief; amazed at Ernie's blind faith or sheer gullibility - he wasn't sure which.

Ernie was startled by the fighter pilot's calm reply, in which he equated the Secretary to an idiot, along with most politicians, adding that the war was being lost by the way they were forced to fight.

Ernie Hale swished his foot at a grasshopper sitting on a cloverleaf. "I heard over the news they're going to send more troops. They get that fence built and the war'll be over," he mused weakly. He wondered if the pilot studying the ailerons had heard his remark. His voice took on a plaintive note while he looked wistfully in the direction of the military field. "Why don't you go sundancin' tomorrow? This evening we could get some folks over and show you off. Tell 'em how you rolled that jet." He looked above the passenger terminal. "Sure was a pretty sight, upside down and all. Folks around here, it would do 'em good to meet a Phantom pilot. Lot of 'em... can't believe..." His words trailed off. "I mean..."

"Can't believe an Indian can fly the big one?" Charging Shield's voice was cold.

Hale grimaced clumsily, "Oh, I didn't mean for it to come out that way. You know what I mean." He pushed his hands into his pockets as he watched the Marine check the gas tanks. The mounting silence forced Hale to continue, "I ain't denying there ain't no prejudice in these parts, Kyle. You know I know that."

Ernie's twisted left foot projected forward, turning over a stone. A clumsy cow beetle ambled out from its hiding place. Ernest Ivan Halevitch Hale, the only son of Russian Jewish immigrants had been struck with polio not long after his parents opened a tiny jewelry and watch repair shop in the railroad hotel. Nicknamed "Gimpy" by his grade school peers, the name had clung to him through high school. Ernie had been the first Jew to graduate from West River High, where, like his flying companion, he had no dates and little social life.

The August sun beat down while both men watched the awkward insect crawl precariously close to a red ant mound.

Ernie continued, "Kyle, all I want to do is show them, if you'd stay over. You coming off that reservation, making a name for yourself." His smile was paternal, yet sincere. His voice rose, "It's a tribute to free enterprise. Anybody can still make it in this country. I'm damned proud of you, boy."

The Marine Captain's face tightened. Ernie's words touched a nerve. Second class citizenship in a white school flooded back. The alternative was boarding school. Prejudice was so thick that most West River Indian youth chose the latter. He jerked the door open. At that moment, a vintage plane descended slowly across the skyline behind Hale's head. The old plane in the background glided down to touch its tail wheel on the runway. Memories revived: Hale at his side in the J-3 Cub, darting in and out of the Sheyela River breaks... and the day the man had turned him loose, a teenaged youth, for his first solo. Charging Shield's gaze softened, shifting to Hale's puzzled grin. If it wouldn't have been for Ernie's boundless generosity; all of the flying hours, he never would have had the opportunity for military flight school. He relaxed his grip on the cabin door, offering Ernie a warm glance before he spoke in a conciliatory tone, "Sounds like a good idea, Ernie, but I have to get to that dance."

Hale shrugged reluctantly, then ambled over to grasp the pilot's shoulder with a fatherly squeeze. "You get out and go to college, you'll always have a job with me - summers and semester breaks."

"I volunteered for a combat tour, Ernie," Charging Shield confessed. "It gets me out in time for college next year."

"Volunteered for combat?" Ernie jumped back with a pained gasp, which was almost a shriek as if he had just discovered a coiled rattlesnake.

Charging Shield's expression clouded. "Combat!" he answered with a hissing dark pride, his eyes growing suddenly bland, masking all emotion. He turned cold rattlesnake like eyes to his friend, his face indifferent, and added in a voice almost foreign, "I'm looking forward to combat."

Ernie Hale felt a tingling sensation as if he were talking to some ghost from a distant past. When the unfamiliar voice spoke of combat it was like some seamy veteran, devoid of sensitivity or fear. In Korea, he had killed with the instinct to survive and would not lack that fatal hesitancy, which cost men their lives. Lawrence had told him. Surrounding the bomb crater full of wounded Marines, dozens of Chinese lay strewn, many in pieces from the barrage of grenades hurled out by Kyle. Ernie blinked, wanting to blame his foolish apparition on the hot sun, or maybe, aging. Nevertheless, he felt a clammy assurance that he would see his friend return from another war.

Kyle climbed into the hot cockpit and buckled his seat belt. After locking the door and nodding to his flying mentor, he fixed a steady gaze on the instrument panel. When he looked up again Ernie had stepped back to avoid the blast of propeller wash.

After the engine came to life, Hale stood in deep thought watching the little craft taxi across the parking ramp. The businessman never had a son who reached maturity. In the old days, Kyle had been like a son, which made it difficult for him to adjust to Kyle's overwhelming interest lately - Kyle seemed to be drawn like a moth back into the cultural flame of his people's past. Ernie wanted to ignore the gap which was widening between them. It was only temporary, he told himself. After all, Kyle was no longer a shy, fledgling Indian boy.

To ease his depression, Ernie's thoughts shifted back to the flaming afterburners and the rocketing Phantom after its roll over the runway. Kyle had evolved into Ernie's alter ego, flying a machine Ernie's money couldn't buy. Looking at the limp windsock hanging near the runway, Ernie forced a grin to dispel his hopeless fantasy of being a fighter pilot.

He frowned as he turned to locate the Cessna. It was parked on the taxiway, cautiously distant from a Western 737 about to take the runway. The limp windsock indicated that dangerous turbulence could be hanging over the takeoff point. He nervously lit a cigar so he could study the cloud of smoke ascending lazily, barely drifting east toward the north-south runway. He hoped Kyle would respect the airliner's turbulent wake and delay his takeoff.

Waiting to see what Kyle would do, Ernie found himself comparing Kyle with Hobart Charging Shield. As different as night and day, he mused. He could never be as close to Hobart as he was to Kyle, but the older brother had won his respect. Hobart was an exception to the rule - now there was an Indian with business sense. He was doing well in his carpet business. Hobart never turned down an invitation to Ernie Hale's house, he belonged to all the right organizations: Jaycees, Optimists, Lions - he couldn't be a Mason, but he was a Knights of Columbus and that was just as good in this town. Hobart was a veteran too. Got in at the end of the war and didn't see combat like Lawrence, but you couldn't call him a draft dodger.

Hobart was doing a good job running for city Alderman. Soon, Hobart Charging Shield would become Mayor of West River. Ernie Hale had enough money and political IOUs for it to happen.

He fixed his gaze on the run up pad. The engine's revolutions rose for run up and magneto checks. A faint ember of hope glowed within Ernie Hale... 'Maybe the war would be good for him after all, especially if he came back with some more medals. He didn't do too badly in Korea. Got him a commission for savin' those Marines and getting them out and then goin' on into flight school. His brother Lawrence got the medals but he couldn't stay out of the bars. Not an out and out drunk, though and was one helluva ball player. Always a dependable bulldozer operator and got a good personality but bars and politics never mix. Lawrence and Kyle are pretty close, probably the Marine thing. Don't think either one is what you could call a Christian.' The big man's thoughts gave him optimism. Ernie wouldn't discount a career in politics for Kyle... 'once he got his degree and learned to court the right people... not on a reservation. No future on a reservation. Kyle will learn that in time.'

Ernie turned a scathing look on the town huddled beneath the mountains. "goddamn town," he spat out viciously, a snarl curling his lips. West River held lasting scars for its most successful businessman.

'Gimpy' had a long memory. It had been a terrifying ritual - being chased, caught, and beaten after school.

"They're going to get Gimpy. Gimp's going to get it." He always overheard the conspiracy of whispers that would pass around in the schoolroom after a recess.

And poor Gimpy would dread the clock reaching half past three. The pathetic figure would limp toward his doom, standing forlornly within the waning protection of the school boundaries, watching the fading sun approach the mountains. But he had to go home. The dirt path toward his simple frame house was only a quarter of a mile away, but he knew he'd never make it in peace. So, with a fearful moan, he'd begin his hobbling run toward his house.

Sure enough, the sixth graders would emerge from behind the trees and bushes that offered hiding places along the way. "Gimpy! Gimpy!" they would scream. He was always surrounded just where the path dipped before winding up a slight rise, and the fifth or sixth grade bully would boldly confront him. Gimpy would kneel and plead and beg and cry, but he would still pay tribute: a bloody nose, a cut lip, bruises on his legs and arms when he tried to protect himself.

The beatings abated in high school, but the cruel exclusion was no less subtle. He was still Gimpy, and Gimpy had no dates, no companions. Puberty had stimulated attraction for the opposite sex, but they had shunned the limping Jewish boy. Social life was relegated to the jewelry store which, by now, had moved to Main Street. Starting out with janitorial chores, he had become progressively adept at repairing watches and broken jewelry. Eventually, he developed the primal beginnings of a talent for design which ultimately led to his fortune, but, as a youth, his tinkering with the various amalgams and metals had begun only as a distraction to carry him through the long, lonely winters. With no friends and no social life, it was damned lonely.

Summers brought a contrasting respite, most of it spent at the swimming holes on Rapid Creek. No playground bullies bothered him there for it was the undisputed domain of the Indians. Up from the reservation boarding schools, the Indian youths would frolic and play in the swift flowing stream, their parents finding seasonal employment at the packing plant or the sawmill. The war years found many employed as laborers building the new military airfield. The polio epidemics had placed an official off-limits on the stream, but the edict had been ignored by the Native Americans since they had been swimming in streams for thousands of years. Besides, the dreaded disease seemed to prefer non-Indians anyway.

The Indians never minded the heavy-set Jewish boy who was generous with his stacks of comic books and an occasional brimming sack of unusual, doughnut-looking treats the boy called "bagels". Most important, the crippled boy would loan out his bicycle in exchange for rides on an old plug mare.

By the end of the summer, Ernie would be almost as dark as his transient companions and the old mare would be spoiled and fattened from choice patches of clover along the creek banks. One summer, a few years before the war broke out, the same bully along with his retinue, came down to the creek and pulled him off the mare. It was some years after grade school days but the same scene was about to repeat itself all over again. Utter, stark, paralyzing fear set into Ernie as he sat in frozen panic, watching the mob of fomented, jeering high school boys circling like wolves about to disembowel a deer. Lawrence was staying with an uncle who worked at the sawmill that summer and swam often at the creek. 'He came out of the water like lightning. He took that bully apart.' Lawrence cursed down at the crying bully and forever threatened his wrath upon anyone who would ever attempt to hurt the crippled boy. The rest of the Indian youths came out of the water and chased all of the intruders away. Ernie never forgot his rescue, the worst of his child-hood nightmares, finally, was forever abated. 'Now, Lawrence could build all the dams he wants. That government contractor won't ever have any trouble gettin' his equipment loans and some good business advice from Ernie Hale - and... on... who he should hire running the bulldozer.'

Autumn would bring the somber departure of his boarding school playmates. Fall gold brought bereavement in later life, for in successive autumns, his beloved parents passed away and so did his only son, a newborn infant.

It was another gold, however, that brought Ernie out of the cruel isolation of his youthful years. A gifted student in science and math, the shy Jewish boy would spend hours on national science projects which, in turn, would lead to amalgam experiments on Black Hills gold. Ernie would have finished college with honors in metallurgy were it not for his invention of a zinc and copper toning application for locally mined gold. Rings, pendants and earrings soon bore Ernie Hale's unique and tasteful mark.

The full throttle whine brought Ernie out of his memories. Kyle Charging Shield had noted the slight drift of airliner jet exhaust. Keeping the plane on the west side of the runway, gathering ample speed before he rose, he turned southwest from a shallow climb and then toward the Badlands and the reservation.

In less than an hour, the Cessna passed over the Jesuit boarding school. Within a few miles he crossed a community of several hundred dwellings. New housing clustered on naked flats surrounded by paved streets while gravel and dirt roads trailed down to weathered log cabins, sheltered by tall trees in the protected gullies. On a hilltop, a government hospital overlooked the town of Oglala. A dry creek coursed down near the main crossroads, one corner occupied by a Bureau of Indian Affairs headquarters, its glassed entryway and modern construction contrasting sharply with the adjacent, tribal council building. The vintage brick and wood framed windows of the council hall peeked through old, sweeping elms, separating the two structures. Across, on the opposite corner, a cafe squatted beside a general store and gas station. A community hall, its architecture and age matching the federal building, occupied a third corner, while on the remaining corner, a row of white framed churches were in line, each displaying a prominent cross and related signs promising salvation and redemption. Few cars were parked around the residential dwellings except for wrecks and junk heaps squatting on summer-burned lawns since most of the community was at the Sun Dance grounds near the edge of the town.

Over the hundreds of tipis, tents and campers surrounding the tall cottonwood tree, the Cessna stood on its wing tip to hold a tight circle. Kyle's adrenaline flowed, for he was home; home with his tribe, his relatives, and tomorrow he would watch the Sun Dance. The pilot flew low over a silver camper trailer before landing at a dirt airstrip several miles further east.

A pickup approached. As he taxied the Cessna off the runway, bouncing on gumbo ruts, Charging Shield's sister, Mildred, and his brother-in-law, Ralph, waved to him. After he stepped from the plane, Kyle embraced his chubby sister who was short in comparison to the rest of his family. His sister also had a round face and looked almost Navajo in appearance. He apologized for not arriving a day earlier, explaining that weather had delayed his departure. He shrugged good-naturedly, saying he couldn't complain since he would see the main ceremony, the piercing, the following day.

His older sister's dark eyes fixed on him, revealing her disappointment. "They pierced today, brother. There won't be a Sun Dance tomorrow. Father Buchwald's going to say Mass. They say he's going to stop Indian religion if he has his way."

"Buchwald?"

Mildred nodded with a bitter grimace.

"Missionaries." Charging Shield's anger welled up. "Missionaries!" he echoed, staring helplessly at the gray gumbo soil, shaking his head in disgust.

Mildred glared across the sage and sunflower covered prairie. "They've taken away everything… *everything*… and now our Sun Dance." Her voice trembled and she started to cry.

The Sun Dance had grown since Kyle had sat as a boy with his grandmother among a curious gathering. The ceremony had taken root despite its humble rebirth. For almost a century, the Sioux had been forced to take the white man's ways, but now many were choosing to return to their old beliefs. From Standing Rock Reservation, Wakpala, Red Scaffold and Turtle Mountain they would come, carrying tents and tipis on top of battered pickups and vintage cars. Most would have little gas money and balding tires, yet the annual coming together would draw them. The long journeys from Los Angeles, Minneapolis and Chicago would bring more scattered members of the tribe; hungry to believe their way was a good way. They returned every year in increasing numbers, drawn by the belief that a Supreme Power above had appeared to all tribes in various ways… not just one.

MISSIONARIES

CHAPTER FIVE

United States Constitution:
Congress shall make no law respecting an establishment of religion,
or prohibiting the free exercise thereof; or abridging the freedom of speech,
or of the press; or the right of the people peaceably to assemble,
and to petition the Government for a redress of grievances.

Time had gone by. Children had grown to adulthood and now, startling social changes were reaching out across the land. Some of these early awakenings were beginning to agitate Reverend Paul Buchwald.

But for a few sabbaticals, the Jesuit had spent his priesthood on the Dakota reservations. Except for decaying, yellow-brown teeth and a graying crew cut, his spare wiry body gave him the appearance of a man much younger than his early fifties. The thick lenses of his steel-framed glasses magnified his dark eyes, pinched closely together behind a pointed nose bristling with protruding hairs, a nose that seemed to sniff the horizon with quick darting movements. His forehead sloped sharply toward tiny flattened ears, underscoring his Indian nickname, earned since his prefect days, *Tunkasa*, the Ferret.

Within the sandstone walls of Sacred Rosary mission, clad in a slate-black Roman-collared shirt, black trousers, and high-topped shoes, Paul Buchwald, S.J. peered in the direction of the Sun Dance grounds. He had heard the airplane pass low overhead, drawing him to his window. Nonplussed, he had watched it buzz and circle. He was sure who was behind the controls. He focused his keen memory. 'Out of hundreds of names and faces, there wasn't one he couldn't remember. Hard to believe a runaway could go on and become a pilot circling around over his tribe, showing off.'

'There was something unusual about Kyle Charging Shield. Why did he keep coming back to this forsaken place?' Buchwald's brow furrowed into a worried, perplexed expression. 'Those who left, the few who made any decent military rank, never came back. And why should they?' His features hardened. 'The year before, Charging Shield had brought that jet down right over the Sun Dance grounds - had gotten all of his tribe whooping and hollering. They'd even put him in the parade.' The first trace of Buchwald's envy had been spawned the day when Charging Shield rode by in the makeshift parade, dressed in a lieutenant's uniform, sitting on a hay bale in the back of a pickup. The applause the Marine pilot had drawn had made

Buchwald twinge. 'None of the Jesuits had ever been honored in the parade that lately had become a part of the Sun Dance celebration. The Jesuits had been here a lot longer than Kyle Charging Shield. Why, Charging Shield wasn't even Indian any more, not a real reservation Indian anyhow. He hadn't grown up on a reservation, and yet his people took to him like he had never left - just because of an officer's uniform and a big fighter plane looping and rolling over their heathen ritual!'

Buchwald's view overlooked the highway that ran by east and west. His silver jubilee, twenty-five years, had been recently celebrated. He had spent most of that time on the Oglala Reservation, save for summer sabbaticals, a few on the Rosebud, and a recent stay at the West River Mission, an assignment he had relished.

West River had creature comforts, a white man's environment, sorely appreciated by one who had been so long away. Buchwald was loath to admit he would never get used to reservation life. It was as foreign as another country. The Indians had converted to placate the white man, accepting his jobs, his rules, even his religion - albeit because the Cavalry was there in the beginning. Now they were returning to their old ways. Not that the steady regression to what Reverend Buchwald termed, 'the unholy heathenism' had been any secret.

'Thank God for the sacrament of Penance. The wrath of the Lord could be wielded in that confessional box. It was a sin if they even knew about those devil *yuwipi* ceremonies - or any other voodoo rites for which hell could claim their souls, especially so if they didn't tell a priest!'

He tired at times, running back and forth across the sprawling reservation, loading and unloading the old portable altar from the back of his pickup truck to say Mass in community halls, dingy cabins, and deteriorating framed churches steadily succumbing to harsh winds and crushing snows. Yet every time he set up the altar, his energy would rejuvenate and the zeal of times past would lash out at the native paganism. 'If it took his last breath,' he vowed, 'he would end the evil ceremonies.' Lately, however, his mind would lapse whenever he thought of the city comforts of West River. 'He'd stop this sun dancing once and for all - then he'd retire, retire off this infernal reservation.'

His appointment as pastor of the Oglala Parish a few miles east, where he baptized, married, buried, and administered the sacraments, afforded ample opportunity to sermonize to four generations of boarding school indoctrinated Sioux. At Sacred Rosary Mission Boarding School, he was now the business manager, keeping track of the lucrative solicitation program made up mostly of wealthy addresses in the east. His mission position allowed a selective role in the hiring of teacher aides, janitors, cooks, drivers, and related menial employment where jobs were dear. His hiring procedures rewarded and reflected faithful attendance at Sunday Mass.

Buchwald's duties were demanding, more than most men would undertake. In the past, the priest's intense fervor had made light of any workload. He never smoked, ate sparingly, and for quite some time even diluted his altar wine, a habit starkly in contrast to the rest of the priests who had been exposed to the remote reservation for any length of time. They had taken the vows of chastity, obedience, and poverty; wine in quantity seemed a justifiable vice. Lately, over the past few years, however, he had imbibed in altar wine from time to time and with increasing frequency.

Fresh from seminary, he had been assigned disciplinarian duties. Though he was slight of build, he was strong and sinewy. During the seminary years, he worked in the dairy much the same as he had when he was a youth developing hard muscles on a Missouri farm not far from the Jesuit monastery that founded most of the midwestern reservation missions. As an ordained priest, Paul Buchwald left many a deep welt on rule-breaking Indian youth who openly resisted during the nine months of the school year.

He remembered across the years to a time not long after his ordination. He relished the memory of the time when Kyle and Lawrence Charging Shield had first run away. He enjoyed his successful breaking of most runaways. 'The Charging Shields were still living on the reservation then.' He knew the Charging Shield family well, quite well, considering that hundreds of families had been associated with his parishes and the boarding school. 'Bill and Julie Charging Shield had done better than most who had left the reservation to settle in West River. It had been early fall when the two boys had run away. Catching runaways was easy. They either trailed down the lone railroad track toward home or traveled one of the few roads that linked the tiny communities sprinkled throughout the sprawling reservation. For his age, Kyle had taken a decent beating. Lawrence was like hitting a mule, never allowing an expression either way. Each boy had to look on while the other received his discipline.' Buchwald's black belt had cracked across backs, buttocks, and thighs until the boys yelled out in pain. 'Didn't take that little one long to yell out.' There was little pity from the Jesuit, his own father had beaten him just as severely… and Buchwald's zeal provided the alibi. 'It was the heathen blood, the paganism, that cried out; the savageness was only a generation or two behind them.'

Buchwald's face contorted while he instinctively rubbed his temple. 'That damned Lawrence almost killed me the last time and Brother Herman still walks with a limp. No one could come up with who did it to him - what with all the commotion.' The two priests had to be sent off not long afterwards. 'Turned into homosexuals. Probably the violence those boys brought on triggered such an evil. Course, Brother Herman has had his problems but no one knows and no one is going to find out. Who ever broke his foot, they're responsible. Responsible for the homosexuality, too. Siouxs, they were all hostiles at one time. That Kyle, I imagine he is just as hostile as Lawrence. He'd better stay in the Marines.'

'World War II had just begun when those two had run away with the full-blood. Got run over by the train, that one. Stubborn, just like Lawrence. Part of the reservation became a bombing range for the military air base outside of West River. Ironically, Bill Charging Shield had gone to work on a construction crew that made the runways for the bombers. They couldn't be brought back to the boarding school unless they volunteered. Lawrence quit school to join the service and Kyle enrolled in West River where he could receive a white man's education but miss out on a sound foundation in the one true religion.' A perplexed look crossed the priest's face. 'Both boys needed Jesuit discipline, and God knows they'd been hell bent on losing their faith. They missed what could only be offered by Sacred Rosary; Mass every morning and religion, as much a part of their curriculum as was academics. Life at Sacred Rosary was laced with a good dose of servile Christian work, too; in the barns, hog houses, fields, gardens - even a chance to work among the brothers learning a trade if they minded the rules and set an example. There was carpentry, welding, electrical, plumbing, and other basic skills to be acquired if they obeyed and, of course, showed a zeal for morning Mass. Boarding schools had little focus for college academics. That would be a waste. Indians weren't ready for white academics. Every one knew Indians were good with their hands. Why, Lawrence proved that. Might be a drunk now but he can handle heavy equipment.' The priest had always wondered how Kyle Charging Shield could fly a fighter plane until he found out - 'it was that rich Jew in West River that taught him how to fly.' It was still difficult for him to swallow. 'Flying was a motor skill,' he concluded, 'and those big jets, they were so fancy and costly, surely the government made them mostly to fly themselves. They had to if they turned an Indian loose in one.' Still, it was hard to believe, 'an Indian could fly one.'

A mirthless smile formed. 'Now, take the oldest of the Charging Shield lot, Hobart and Leona. Why couldn't more of this infernal reservation be like those two and of course, Julie, their dear mother, Julie. Now there was a churchgoer, a leader among the Indians up in West River. No woman could clean and scrub an altar like that woman and see to it that the priests had their laundry and quarters at that West River Mission just as spotless. She was a leader, that Julie. She got the work out of those parish Indians: the bazaars, the rummage sales, the clothing drives.'

Buchwald's elation turned sour. 'Now Julie's husband, old Bill Charging Shield, that was another story. He was a good worker, had to say that much for him. He provided a decent living for his family, better than most who left the reservation and settled down for good in West River. Bill couldn't let go of that pagan streak, however, but the church allowed him a Christian burial, thanks to his wife. He never would have amounted to anything if it weren't for her. He never went to Mass but he never interfered. Had to give him credit for that. Of course, Julie cracked the whip there. She made Kyle go to Mass every Sunday, and confession, too - as long as she could handle them.'

Buchwald shook his head painfully. 'And Mildred, at the boarding school she was always somewhere between Lawrence and Hobart, depending on who had been the last to influence her. Now she's got herself married to that big white man. He's a stubborn devil if ever there was one: a divorced man, ran off and left a wife and some kids for Mildred, and she up and got divorced to marry him. Now she's eating her heart out, whining because she can't receive the sacraments.'

A nervous twitch pulsed Buchwald's eyelid. He didn't want to think about Mildred's husband, Ralph. Ralph had actually grabbed him once, threatening the priest and claiming he'd inflict bodily harm if Buchwald didn't leave his wife alone. 'To receive the sacraments she only had to live as brother and sister with Ralph. He wasn't trying to divorce them. She only had to give up, relinquish her conjugal relationship. Why, she never had any kids; she had to be sterile anyhow. The essence of marriage is reproduction, what else?' Buchwald didn't want to remember that huge fist, cocked, ready to break him apart. The priest had been so petrified that he slimed his pants. 'Indians, at least reservation Indians, rarely ever threatened a priest. They knew better. They knew whom the men of God were, the chosen who had been given special orders. Something bad would happen if you ever hurt a priest or a nun or a brother or any part of the true church. They learned that in boarding school.' Buchwald never told anyone about Ralph's threat. He wanted to tell Mildred or Julie Charging Shield, but he was afraid to do so. 'If only Ralph had been an Indian, the sheriff would have come and hauled him away.'

A car pulling a trailer stacked with spruce poles and partially covered with white tipi canvas passed down the highway, followed by a dented pickup, its box crammed with camping equipment. Another stream of cars passed by. Buchwald shook his head; he had heard the reports. This was the biggest crowd ever, with more coming in every day. He didn't like the looks of it. 'That damn pagan rite. No one at the mission listened to his warnings, but now they finally were beginning to see.'

An eagle high above the Sun Dance grounds set his heart pumping and brought a bead of sweat to his brow.

"Damn!" A foreboding fear swept through him. He knew the Indians and their superstitions. 'They would interpret the bird as some kind of sign. The holy men, the old fools would jump on that one. 'Damnedable' idiot of an eagle!' Oh, how he wished for a long-range rifle. 'Why would a stupid eagle wander over that 'damnedable' pagan rite on this of all days?' The bird's presence electrified him - 'it was a positive omen for the Sun Dance! Too positive. No, he had to get hold of himself. He was starting to believe in stupid Indian signs. That eagle was coincidence, sheer coincidence,' he tried to convince himself, but his brow sprouted new beads of sweat.

His features grew taut as his eyes were drawn to the huge bird hanging like a kite, sailing lazily over the Sun Dance grounds. He had learned too well the pagan beliefs gleaned from years of instilling God-given fear in the confessional box. He knew 'these pagans believed their false god controlled the animals and when this *Wakan Takan* wanted to send a sign, it simply sent forth some animal to act in a hocus-pocus manner. This idiot of an eagle or some air current it had decided to sit on, would be interpreted by those below as some kind of blessing from their savior-less God.'

He fingered an old copy of the Indian Sentinel: 'Ahh yes, the Indians could only be saved through God's revealed true nature in the one and only Judeo-Christian tradition and of course its rituals and prayers necessary for human salvation. These nature based heathen systems such as the Sioux practiced, were manifold with illusions and barbarities obviously susceptible to Satan's power. Devil-dominated heathenism was totally unacceptable to church missions. A Lakota ceremony could never coincide with the true sacraments and was antithetical to the Jesuit strategy of replacement, civilization and assimilationist missiology. The most formidable opponent to mission work was the Satan influenced medicine men. Frightening illusions and tricks that only Satan could empower in their ceremonies... and now this Charging Shield was under their spell.'

He was disgusted with his peers for being so lackadaisical regarding the resurgence of the Sun Dance. He felt a malevolent suspicion for the man in the airplane. He suspected that Kyle served as some kind of cultic omen to the Sun Dance crowd. The pagan religion was rising from its ashes in defiance of the historically effective methods the Jesuits employed: usually subterfuge and religious fear. A sixth sense warned Buchwald that he would need to be wary of Kyle Charging Shield.

PIPES & CRUCIFIX

The thought brought back memories of Kyle's grandmother. Buchwald's eyes tightened. 'Kyle had always been hanging around his old heathen grandmother's skirts. More than once the boy had caught a ride to her home from West River missionaries traveling to the reservation. The old woman had been a Badlands witch, resisting the Lord, clinging to her pagan ways. She was like the rest of them, denying the existence of the devil, preaching some drivel that their Great Spirit made only that which was good.' "No such thing as a bad waterfall, or a bad thunderstorm that brought the life giving rains. The bear and the buffalo were all good." He had squeezed out her statements from those in the confessional. 'No doubt the old witch claimed the rattlesnakes and the grasshoppers, the droughts, storms and blizzards were some kind of good. Or the maggots, wood ticks and spiders that crawled for blood and bones. She even claimed the devil was an invention of the white man and that none of the Indians had ever seen one and never would because such a thing had never been created by their infidel *Wakan Takan*. Oh yes, he knew well her smart alecky words. The old witch had no education and he had always been quick to point that fact out to destroy her credibility. And she lived out alone in that cabin, all the more reason to stay away from what she had to say, for that is where the devil lurks. Out in forsaken places. Witches lived out alone where they conjured up a communication with the devil world. No doubt she had been responsible for poisoning Kyle's mind,' Buchwald had warned Kyle's mother, a dedicated convert.

'Why hadn't he thought of it? No wonder Kyle keeps coming back and never takes the sacraments. The old dead witch is still in him!' A gleaming stare projected at the eagle as the fanatically intense revelation descended to squat on his meager optimism. Buchwald's knuckles pressed white against the windowsill.

"We'd have burned that one at the stake!" he muttered aloud, satisfying an inner urge.

He dwelt on the Jesuit Order's role in the Great Inquisition, 'ridding the world of heretics, witches, and similar sinners whose souls had gone over to the devil.' If he had his way... 'But that was a thought he dared not confide, not even to the Father Superior. These evil times had reached deeply into the Church. Now good men had to bend to public opinion. Father Superior had become so political lately, always testing his decisions, usually to appease the liberals coming out of the seminary. That was all that came out of the seminary lately. Liberals, peace marching liberals.' A worried look, coupled with envy, the same look that thoughts of Kyle Charging Shield had generated, clouded over him as he thought of the latest priest, Father Weitz, who had joined the mission staff. 'Fresh from the missionary, a pup priest, and already he was influencing the Father Superior! That smart aleck had the gall to question his plan to say Mass at the Sun Dance grounds.'

Weitz had eyed Buchwald squarely. "Let them have their traditions. They're no doubt praying to the same God we are. Constitutionally, gentlemen, they are within

their rights. And we, regardless of a belief that we have the true faith, are on constitutionally shaky grounds if we interfere."

The rest of the mission might not be aware of it, but it was clear as day to
Buchwald. He had to feel sorry for the mission head. Even though the man was
losing his zeal, he wouldn't complain. The Father Superior seldom interfered with
Paul Buchwald. 'Oh, a little admonishment here and there to placate the liberals.'
Buchwald had come down hard from the pulpit on those who attended the devil's
Yuwipis. 'And the children of the traditionals - they needed to be singled out and
lectured in the boarding schools. They were backward full bloods, pretending they
didn't know any better.' Buchwald longed for the old days, the days when they
wouldn't have dared to build a sweat lodge or have a *Yuwipi*.

'The reservation needed a good purging. The witchcraft would be sent packing
by an old-fashioned inquisition. Maybe there was something after all to what these
pagans called the circle. Maybe the saints who had cleansed the true church were
now circling back from time - the unsung saints back in those times when evil had
run rampant throughout Europe. Maybe they were rallying Buchwald to tear down
that Sun Dance tree?'

Suddenly, he was positive that his instinct was right. 'He was being called by the
saints, by the Lord, to stop this heathenism. His altar was already waiting in his
pickup. He'd go out to that Sun Dance arena and say Mass for the Lord. The Lord
would come forth beneath the devil's tree and Satan would be sent fleeing when he,
Paul Buchwald, said Mass tomorrow morning under the Sun Dance tree. And
Buchwald would be the Indians' savior, the Lord would be speaking through him as
their savior!' The power of that feeling was overwhelming.

He imaged himself - 'standing beneath that Satan tree. He would hold forth his
arms. His hands would anoint all that looked on. Anoint, bless, save, redeem these
pagans who were so fortunate to have the white man come upon them to purify and
forgive their godless souls for the gates of heaven. The Savior would come forth
through him to save all of these ignorant, nature-worshipping, savage heathens who
denied even the existence of the devil. The power of the true and only salvation for
mankind would flow from Paul Buchwald. Without such a blessing, they would
never see the manly face of God.' His elation was cut short by a knock on the door,
notifying him of a meeting concerning the Sun Dance.

A handsome young priest, light haired, of medium build and newly ordained,
made an impassioned plea to the balding Father Superior sitting at the center of a
group consisting of three tribal councilmen, Buchwald, and several Jesuits from the
mission staff. One councilman, Rousseau, the only Indian to hold a white-collar
position at the mission, was a finance clerk under Buchwald's direction. The other
two councilmen, one a boarding school bus driver, were Rousseau's relatives. They
were a squat, heavy-set family, half French and half Sioux.

EAGLE VISION

The Reverend James Weitz, S.J., was calm, undaunted, and certain, even though he knew that what he said wouldn't make a difference. In contrast to the other missionaries, Weitz was attired in jeans, worn cowboy boots, and a black, western short-sleeved shirt.

In the seminary, Weitz had risked being expelled. Nearly half of his class had been placed on probation for taking part in the freedom rides for integration of southern blacks. It was not that Father Weitz was in the habit of frustrating the desires of his seniors, he was simply not the kind to be content with speaking out from the pulpit. He was an activist, motivated by a disdain for the age-old practices of prejudice and injustice. In the South, he had marched with thousands for civil rights, and now a growing protest against the war in Vietnam was beginning to sweep the nation.

When Weitz boldly questioned Buchwald's plan to say Mass at the Sun Dance grounds, it brought the senior pastor to his feet, sputtering adamantly. Weitz made the Jesuits uneasy. "Aside from the constitutional freedom of religion protection, gentlemen, what is wrong with tribal citizens of this country expressing their love for God? Granted, their methods may seem strange to us. No doubt our customs appeared abnormal to them."

His statement brought the stone-faced audience to the edge of their seats. Buchwald and Father Superior exchanged despondent glances. Both had the same thought. Neither wanted that statement made before the Indians. 'Rousseau and the bus driver could be trusted - possibly - but the other Indian wasn't employed by the mission. Civil rights, protests, bussing, freedom of speech, freedom of assembly - these were fast becoming household words, and there had been incidents throughout the nation testing constitutional guarantees.'

Buchwald cringed. 'Freedom of religion!' He tried to judge the reaction of the mission's superior. He didn't like the worried stare that Weitz had managed to evoke from the aging priest.

The old superior was indeed troubled. 'Sooner or later,' he thought, 'this liberal mood could spread.' He pulled his hand from beneath the fold of his old-fashioned cassock to pat his huge girth. He sought solace through the window facing the late afternoon sun, setting behind a classroom annex, which housed the solicitation mailing room with its addressograph machine and long list of donor's names and addresses embossed on metal printing cards.

The old priest looked like Friar Tuck without his walking staff, his fat hidden under the black pullover robe. His shining, balding pate crowned a hallowed ring of hair. He stroked his broad belly again, which was just beginning to growl. It was a half-hour past his customary stroll through the mission galley, sampling the first courses of the evening meal. Only a couple of years were left until his retirement. 'The donations to the missions were important,' he thought, 'damned important for the retirements.'

Equally important were the landholdings, and those were immense - a quarter section here, a half section, at times even several sections, willed and deeded to the Church. 'A small price to pay for last rites and the soul's salvation.' His hand began to tremble at the thought of how all those land-holdings could be misconstrued. 'The government officials, the Bureau superintendents, made their trades perfectly legal,' he rationalized. 'The mission traded the scattered parcels of land willed over by the aged and the dying for the tribal land that surrounded the mission. It was true that the verdant valley running below the mission was appraised at a higher price than the traded Badlands parcels but,' he consoled himself, 'the services donated by the Jesuits had their value.' It made him shudder to consider how embarrassing it would be if the mission was portrayed as the largest landowner on the reservation. 'The whole issue was far too important to risk not keeping Buchwald and Weitz in check. Both of them were too independent, too separate from the mission in their ways.'

'Funny thing,' he thought. 'Paul had never been that way until after he had taken over the accounting section. Now, as the mission comptroller, he was more head-strong than ever in his handling of the mission's budget and the confidential financial statements known only to Paul, himself, and the mission's superiors. Paul was trustworthy, but he exacted the privilege of independence as his payment.'

Father Superior's eyes fixed on the black pickup parked beside the annex. A high-backed altar projected from the truck box. 'That altar,' he mused, 'brought by wagon train across the prairie, was the first real altar at the mission. But why on earth did my predecessor ever award it to Paul? He'd already been zealous enough. If you listened to Paul, that old antique was milled from the Holy Cross and sheltered the Blessed Virgin herself.'

Buchwald's meddling with the Indians had caused the Father Superior more than one sleepless night. 'Paul was devoted, too damned devoted. In the old days, Paul had been the ideal missionary,' the Father Superior reminisced. 'No one questioned authority then. The boarding schools had done their jobs well, exceptionally well. The entire mission staff: priests, brothers, sisters - all had been one in spirit, wielding the one true faith from the one true Church on the catechized, indoctrinated faithful. In those days, the reservation was akin to an expansive cloister.'

'He'd been like his peers - resolved, righteous, and unquestioning. Oh, he'd admit that he'd never been the burning proselyte that Buchwald was, but he had paid close attention to detail. He was an effective administrator, and he was a Superior which was more than Paul would become.' Father Superior often reminded himself of his selection whenever the conscience of his strict up-bringing coerced his thoughts to envy the adamant zeal and controlling drive behind men like Buchwald. The conscience of his past had been propagated by fervent, well-to-do parents dedi-cated toward their only son's priesthood. In the seminary and during those first years following ordination, that conscience pricked at him, but it had long since withered, receding to the part of the brain used to store memories. In truth, he had succumbed through time to the hardened acceptance of reality that neutered him toward his faith and toward life in general. The bleak remoteness, the stark contrast for too many long years, had finally eroded his spiritual and apostolic resolve.

He wasn't bitter about it. 'His life was comfortable, better than most, better by far than anyone else's on the reservation,' and that, for the time being, was his immediate world. He was like a gelding in a herd of mares; there wasn't much over which to be frustrated. He had few diversions. He relished his wine, but limited it to being consumed with meals and Mass. Food was his gratification. He dearly loved his fare at the mission and was dedicated to the daily menu, particularly the evening meal. He seldom exercised his authority over the rest of the mission staff.

Otherwise, he had become more complacent with each succeeding year, allowing the complement of priests, brothers and nuns, numbering almost thirty, a fairly liberal atmosphere by Jesuit standards. He was a loner, like most Jesuits, but certainly not a hermit. 'Only a hermit or a zealous lunatic would want to remain on a reservation, especially this reservation.' He could ache for the day when he would be allowed to retire to St. Louis, but he was pragmatic. He would simply accept his assignment and be patient and guard the retirement fund.

The Father Superior turned away from the window briefly to study Weitz. Weitz reminded him of the changing times. 'Negroes were calling themselves Blacks, there were sit-ins, demonstrations and marches concerning Vietnam, and maybe the Indians would be next. Maybe Weitz would be the right man to have around for these times. He was intelligent and personable, and he came from an eastern family that was influential - highly influential. They were lavish donors to the diocese in West River.'

Father Superior had always appreciated class. He firmly respected lineage and discriminate upbringing. 'For that alone, he could be closer, in time, to the younger priest than he could be to Paul. Paul had zeal, determination, and a mind that was almost photographic, but what was that compared to lineage and connections? The Bishop had been well pleased with Father Weitz, the new arrival to the reservation.'

A smug look held Father Superior for a moment. The old priest was proud that the Jesuits were fiercely independent of any diocesan bishop. 'Jesuits answered only to the Order and maybe to the Pope, but not some Cadillac-driving diocesan.' There was unspoken, mutual cooperation and, technically, they were within the bishop's territorial Diocese. Historically, the Diocese and the Order had worked well together for nearly a century in the Dakotas. The proud look lingered on Father Superior's face as he reminisced over four decades, his thoughts dimming the debate flaring between Buchwald and Weitz. 'No diocesans could have accomplished what his order had undertaken. They could not have forged it all into a landmark of stone, landholdings, and fiscal success.'

'Fiscal success' - the words rang. 'Retirement in just a few years.' He made up his mind then and there. He turned back to the debate, his hand raised, ending the discussion. He fooled Buchwald with a benevolent smile.

'He'd allow Paul his rein for now, but in time, Paul could get them into trouble. The vow of obedience,' he thought. 'It was the essential vow for a superior or an abbot. He'd assign Weitz to be Buchwald's parish assistant. They would have to work together amicably, because it would be the Father Superior's desire. They would watch each other like hawks, at least until it was clear which way the wind would blow.'

He allowed the meeting to last only a short while longer, for his stomach was beginning to rumble audibly.

Sunday, Buchwald drove his pickup truck onto the ceremonial grounds. Several Indians, who were employed at the mission boarding school, helped to unload the high-backed altar, placing it against the cottonwood. The missionaries had convinced enough tribal council politicians that the Sun Dance should last for three

days, not four. Sunday was the Lord's day, and that did not include the Great Spirit who was supposed to be the creator of all two-leggeds and all things.

Buchwald raised his chalice with a triumphant flourish, vainly positioned at the heart of the annual gathering. Not even the Sun Dance Chief would allow himself to stand so long near the center of the power of the hoop - the eye of the Great Spirit, the very spot around which those of the traditional nation had gathered.

Buffalo Calf Maiden had instructed the people. "You shall gather together for four days and offer thanksgiving during the Moon of the Ripe Cherries. As long as you do this, your nation will live." Buchwald, the missionary, believed otherwise.

A Marine captain dressed in a short-sleeved summer uniform decorated with Korean War ribbons, stood apart from those who watched the ritual Buchwald performed. His people were used to the domination of the missionaries, but the young Marine felt the level of his frustration rising. He had traveled a long way to observe the Sun Dance, and instead he could see only this intruder who understood nothing of the Power of the Hoop, the Natural Powers of the Universe under *Wakan Tanka*.

As Charging Shield stood beneath the hot Dakota sun, he was unaware that he was the subject of a discussion taking place within the tall tipi adjacent to the dance arena.

The holy men had gathered quietly in the ceremonial lodge to hear Eagle Feather's vision and to relate to the happenings of the previous day. The crucial discussion of this event outweighed any missionary's ill-mannered interference. No resentment showed among the mystics. The prophecy of the return of the Indian Spirit was unfolding, and only pity could be exhibited for the oppressors of its return - only pity for those who played with the intentions of *Wakan Tanka*.

After Chief Eagle Feather had elaborated on his Sun Dance vision, Fools Crow remarked, " I had a vision in the sweat lodge. It ties in with what you have said." Fools Crows' hand made a sweeping motion toward the tipi's entryway. "The warrior in your vision is here now. The eagle on the stone - it has the power to protect him for this new war, this Vietnam into which the white man has got himself."

All within the lodge knew the *yuwipi's* dire predictions for the nation. The Sioux, the mystic warriors of the plains, still retained their mysterious ceremonies that sought the predictions of their ancestors; their ancient spiritual gift fortified and honed through lonely vision quest vigils on isolated buttes and mountaintops by the holy men.

"Topa wiwanyang wachipi! Sun Dance Four!" Fools Crow exclaimed in Sioux to Eagle Feather. "Your vision saw the tree on the four quarters of the circle." His elaborated expression brought forth a clamoring of *haus* and *oh huhs* from the audience.

The group sat quietly lost in thought, digesting predictions of two powerful men. The wind rippling the tent covering muffled the priest's sermonizing and the chime of communion bells coming from the center of the arena. Fools Crow's tone remained calmly complacent. "The stone has struck the tree. That is why we are gathered. As for this warrior, if he fights against the one who would destroy our way, the stone will aid him." A questing tone crept into his voice. "This one here today - he is not a full-blooded Lakota. Would he be willing to sacrifice himself so that others may live?" The Oglala shrugged. "Nothing is guaranteed. It is possible he will not come back, and another will have to take his place. We shall see." The wind rattled the tent flap before the holy men filed out of the lodge.

FOOLS CROW'S PROPHECY

CHAPTER SIX

Hokahey! Hokahey! Hauuuuh!
Come with me into battle brothers.
For today is a good day to die!
— Sioux Chief's war cry

The gray Marine fighter-bomber hung motionless in the clear Vietnamese sky. The high tail of the Phantom was decorated with a silver eagle above a red, white and blue ribbon. In the forward cockpit, the pilot's helmet was stenciled with an image of a warbonnet sporting camouflaged feathers. As the craft flew north, the pilot keyed a radio switch on the throttle handle. "Ground Shark. Yankee Echo Eight approaching target."

"Yankee Echo Eight. Hold ten miles. Report feet wet at angel's twenty," Da Nang control instructed.

The Phantom turned toward the South China Sea. When the coastline passed below, he banked the aircraft before engaging the automatic pilot. The plane dipped slightly, correcting its altitude as it circled off the coast. "Yankee Echo Eight. Feet wet. Holding at angel's twenty," he reported, circling at 20,000 feet. He checked his gauges and, through the intercom, told the radar intercept officer (RIO) in the rear seat to record a fuel estimate.

Alone with his thoughts for the moment, he rested his head against the ejection seat. He had flown over fifty missions, and all that had been foretold in the ceremony held at Fools Crow's cabin had come true. Spirit people had entered, predicting that he would see the enemy many times. 'Bullets would bounce from his airplane,' they said.

He pictured Fools Crow waiting at the horse gate when they arrived for the *Yuwipi*. His grandmother's last request was that he attend a *Yuwipi* ceremony before he left for war. In the centuries old calling, Fools Crow would beseech the spirit people for protection. His mother had been with them that clear summer night as they drove from West River to the holy man's reservation home. His grandmother's prediction that he wouldn't come back if he failed to attend a *Yuwipi* was enough to dispel the black magic aura drummed into his mother by the missionaries. He wished his father and grandmother were alive to attend with them.

The tall, trim man held them for a few moments with that mysterious look, the penetrating stare of a hawk or an eagle. Fools Crow was like a Badlands hawk or an eagle - regal, keen, and observant - alone and aloof within his own vast spaciousness, oblivious to the encroaching *Washichu* world.

The straight postured man spoke from the gate as they got out of the car, "What took you so long? You should have been here earlier."

We're sorry, Grandpa," Charging Shield's older sister Mildred answered. "We stopped to get groceries." Grandpa was a common and respectful form of address for Sioux holy men.

'Fools Crow had no telephone, so how did he know they were coming to see him?' Charging Shield wondered, as the holy man led them into his mud-chinked cabin. Kate Fools Crow stood by the wood-burning stove and welcomed them with her warm smile. Speaking in the rich Sioux language, they visited and laughed together as the blue enameled coffee pot was filled, meat was cut and put into boiling water, dried *woshapi* (berry cakes), were set in a pan of water and frybread preparations were made. The laughter flowed. Charging Shield's sister, Mildred, his mother, Sonny Larvee's grandparents, and Fools Crow's son-in-law, Amos Lone Hill, exchanged conversation in Lakota Sioux. Blacktop, a bashful eight-year-old, sat fiddling with the damper on the pot-bellied stove near the west wall.

When Fools Crow went to the closet for his medicine bundle, it was a signal for the women to push back the furniture and draw the curtains. Sonny helped prepare for the tying ritual that preceded the *Yuwipi*, while Mildred unrolled a long string of tiny cloth tobacco offerings. The four directions were represented by red, yellow, black and white flags, which were placed in earth-filled bowls to form a square before an earthen altar in the middle of the cabin. Mildred wrapped a string of tobacco offerings around the bowls, marking the limits of the spirit area. Sage was passed to all participants, who placed some in their hair and over one ear.

The holy man entered the square to place two leather rattles on the floor before raising his peace pipe to offer an opening prayer. Afterwards, he stood ready to be bound. Sonny tied his arms and hands behind his back with bailing twine before

YUWIPI

draping a blanket over the Oglala's head. An eagle feather hung from the top of the blanket that covered the holy man down to his moccasin tops.

Next, Sonny wrapped Fools Crow with a rawhide rope, beginning with a noose around his neck and then seven times around his body, down to his ankles. Each wrap represented the seven sacred ceremonies. While the holy man was lowered, face down to the floor, Mildred sat at the place of honor with the peace pipe, behind the dirt altar with her back against the stove. The kerosene lamp was extinguished.

EAGLE VISION

Amos tapped a drum and sang a centuries-old call to the ancestors of the Sioux, the spirit beings. They came quickly from the west, rattling the stovepipe and swishing the rattles through the room, as if they had been close by, waiting for the call. Charging Shield prayed. Would he return from the war? Would he be a prisoner? He knew the spirits would tell and if he prayed humbly and promised to live for his people, they would try to protect him. Tiny blue lights entered through the stove door behind Mildred while he prayed. They flickered and danced with the heartbeat of the drum, raised to the ceiling, circled the participants and, then, as the song ended, disappeared back through the stove door behind the pipe holder. The buckskin rattles that had accompanied Amos Lone Hill's song now fell to the floor, silent.

Fools Crow's muffled voice spoke out in the darkness, telling them how a stone had fallen to strike the sacred tree at the summer Sun Dance, while an airplane flew overhead. The stone bore the image of an eagle. Later he had a vision. "I saw the airplane land in a far-off place, and a warrior walked away from it without looking back. He walked toward the sacred tree and stood there with a boy. The stone was brought to the Sun Dance lodge. I took the stone from Eagle Feather and put it in my medicine bundle. It remained in the bundle only a short while and then it was gone." The group waited while the holy man took several breaths.

"The stone has returned and is now among us here. Charging Shield, you must pray hard so it will remain."

Charging Shield answered quickly, "Grandfather, ask the stone to stay with us. Tell the spirit people I offer myself for the Sun Dance. I will live for the people and the power of the hoop." A shrill tremolo pierced the darkness, followed by a chorus of "Hau". The cry came from the women to honor a warrior who would go off to battle. It would be repeated when the warrior returned, or at his grave.

Then Fools Crow spoke with uncharacteristic volume and excitement. "The eagle on the stone is for a warrior who will fly with the winged. Charging Shield, you shall wear this stone as your *wotai*. When you are across the ocean, you shall carry it. As long as you wear it faithfully, the bullets shall bounce from your airplane. You shall see the enemy many times. You shall not fear battle and shall laugh at danger."

After a long pause, he spoke more cautiously. "There is no guarantee, however, that you shall return and become a new warrior to stand beneath the Sun Dance tree with Blacktop."

Fools Crow paused with a cough, weighing what he would reveal. The rattles buzzed. No, he wouldn't tell Charging Shield about the vision quest. He had enough to worry about. Vietnam could destroy him. He could make a mistake with the stone. And before the vision quest, he must dance and defend the Sun Dance.

The holy man coughed again, stilling the rattles, then shuddered as he saw the Sun Dance tree standing in the four-quartered circle, as the circle began to turn. "*Ohuze wichasta, wayuecetu*," he said, although he knew those in the room wouldn't

understand. That sign, he knew, came only when a powerful message must be delivered and the warrior had been selected to fulfill a mission. Charging Shield's circle had begun. In the old days it would have cost the sacrifice of one or several, warriors who would pledge to live for the way, as this one had just done. The trials would be difficult, but the reward would be whatever the warrior wished, if he succeeded.

The rattles clashed, each shaking a different rhythm, their discord breaking the stillness. The force on the mountain, he thought, it will try to threaten him away. It will try to keep this one from bringing back a message for the future.

Maybe... maybe the forces will scare him off, or worse. The force on the mountain could be too much for him. Fools Crow breathed great breaths and pondered. Eagle Feather's task will be to get Charging Shield ready; to steer him to one who can direct his thoughts toward a powerful vision.

"*Hehaka Sapa, Hehaka Sapa* (Black Elk, Black Elk)," the spirit spoke. Fools Crow was confused. The old prophet had been his mentor and had passed on into the spirit world. But the image of a cabin in the Black Hills beside a trout stream solved the puzzle. Black Elk's son, Ben Black Elk, lived in the Black Hills.

Charging Shield would be led to him and become a warrior of the four-colored circle, a mystic warrior.

The rattles stirred again in unison. The exhilaration caused by the turning circle made him draw his breath beneath the yuwipi blanket in deep gasps. That woman, she would be good to look at; she will test him. Then ... in time, she will lead him back... back to the only way good enough for a true warrior, at least in this time. A warrior of the eagle hoop, a warrior of the four-colored circle... a Mystic Warrior! His tired smile showed a rare trace of envy. The woman will direct him, get his thoughts ready. The rattles stirred again. *"Hehaka Sapa, Hehaka Sapa.* Black Elk, Black Elk," he cried out in Lakota to his old mentor. The Tree of Life, the red stick bearing green leaves, stood out vividly before him. The red stick became a flowering tree, sweeping eastward in a flash. He saw a horizon with a rainbow beyond. It was like Eagle Feather had described. A pair of eagles flew toward the rainbow. They are this warrior and the woman. Fools Crow glimpsed beyond Eagle Feather's vision. When the eagles reach the rainbow she is a meadowlark. She has power! The woman will come into her own.

The rainbow became a symmetrical cottonwood growing from the edge of a lake. The cottonwood flowered. Fools Crow was startled. The rawhide cutout of the buffalo appeared in the top branches, then transformed into a bird that looked like a mourningdove. The rawhide cutout of the man appeared. It transformed itself into a woman, a powerful woman. The flowers on the tree were rainbow-colored.

He spoke again from beneath the blanket, "If you make it to the Sun Dance, you will fulfill part of your mission. You will fight the one who would destroy our way. Remember to respect this gift or you will lose its protection. *Ho hetch etu aloh.*"

A concluding song, the untying song was sung. When the lamp was lit, Fools Crow was sitting up untied. His blanket was neatly draped over the stove. The tying rope was wrapped in a tight ball. No one, including Fools Crow had moved during the untying song.

*   *   *   *

The voice on the radio receivers in his helmet startled the pilot back to the present. "Yankee Echo Eight. Yankee Echo Eight, you are cleared to your target. Heavy anti-aircraft fire reported. Over."

"Roger, Ground Shark," he responded. "Keep your eyes open," he called to his radar man in the rear seat as he pushed both throttles forward and disengaged the autopilot. He used a cluster of lakes called Finger Lakes as a reference to seek the four artillery positions that he had studied earlier from the photos in the briefing room. He reached for the ordnance selection switch. "We'll make four passes, three bombs on each pass. Talk to me if you spot any flak."

"Chief, most guys don't make too many passes up here. It's a hot area."

The pilot laughed, sensing fear in the radar man's voice. 'Most radar operators don't have a *wotai* either,' he thought. He squeezed the small stone in the buckskin pouch hanging from his neck. 'Fifty missions,' he almost spoke aloud. 'Fools Crow was right and, so far, not a scratch on his plane despite the heavy anti-aircraft fire he had flown through. I will honor Grandpa by doing a victory roll over the enemy. Fools Crow would appreciate that,' he thought with fearless amusement.

He swept the target area in a long arc, seeking a gun position identified by the reconnaissance photo he had studied that morning during briefing. He rolled the jet on its back, preferring the inverted position at the beginning of the bombing run to have a clear view free of the black radar snout protruding in front of the cockpit. Then he slowly rolled the aircraft to an upright position, letting the nose fall into a steep dive. To the crewmember in the back seat, it seemed as if they were heading straight down into the earth.

The pilot squinted through the electronic gunsight. A dim circle with a center light projected as though it was outside the cockpit. He maneuvered the Phantom to hold the target in the sighting circle by coordinating the rudders and his control stick.

As he broke through a cluster of cumuli, a tempo of exploding flak puffs rushed up. The black and orange blossoms looked like harmless mushrooms on red stems as he danced the fighter down through their deadly bursts. He concentrated on a defoliated area that looked like a gun emplacement. A smile formed beneath the oxygen mask. It was time for confidence. In a bombing run, he had learned, tension and fear only increased the danger.

He was now the buffalo warrior living again in a new time, weaving and dancing down through the exploding sky, riding a great *tashuunka wakan* (horse) and galloping through the thundering herds. At times like this, when he rapped brazenly at death's door, he was allowed revelations so intense that he didn't need to pursue their meaning to reap their strength.

The flak was above the plane now. This was a part of the long war that he actually enjoyed. Courting death high in the sky, raging down, down through the curtain of fire, and then escaping to wait, high out of reach, like an eagle that would attack again.

At these times, a feeling would flare, like St. Elmo's fire, that he was part of an ancient heritage of societies: Kit Fox, Dog Soldier, Owls Cap, Strong Hearts, back into time, Mystic Warriors, and, yes, even higher: wolf, eagle, owl. Stalking, preying, being preyed on. Part of a great mystery, a great circle, seeing, teaching, learning, sometimes a two-legged, sometimes a winged. The man-brain questioned. The pure things never questioned, didn't need to, they would probably laugh at the *washichu's* vacillation, his uncertainty despite his machines. *Washichu* man would never solve the circle of *Wakan Tanka's* creation.

He checked his airspeed. The jet held its steep dive, screaming close to the speed of sound. A nudge on the rudder brought the artillery battery into the center of the gunsight. Somewhere, in another life, perhaps as a different creature, he had known combat. The emotions of combat were too familiar, too revealing to be new. He had done the dance of death before, under many bright sunlit skies.

He touched the ordnance release and the machine leaped as three-quarters of a ton of bombs left the fuselage. He pulled the control stick and pushed the throttles to full afterburner. The ground fell away in a green-brown blur as gravity fought against his G-suit, squeezing his middle, thighs and calves, countering the rush of blood from his brain. His brain touched gray fog as he pointed the plane at azure, blue safety. He stepped harder on the rudder and leaned to look into the rearview mirror for anti-aircraft fire as the afterburners bore him away.

He climbed fast and high to where the shellfire couldn't reach, waited, and then danced again through the death web. He found another artillery site and made his run, then returned to the sky a second and third time. One last time he rose for his final pass, intending to make the last run toward the sea. The flak was heavy. It was the first day after a truce and the North Vietnamese were well supplied from free access to the Haiphong docks.

The guns were silent, waiting, and then came alive again to reach up for him as he approached the final target. 'Dance,' he thought. 'Dance through the maze.' He laughed as he dropped like an eagle, held the control stick in the forward position, pressed the bomb release, rolling in a touch of forward trim he then pulled back to bottom out low over the enemy. He slammed the throttles forward and felt the surge from the afterburners. "*Hokahey!*" he yelled as he leveled the craft. He did an abrupt victory roll, then another and another. It was spectacular, but also a safe place to be, because he was but a blur to the enemy and required far too much of a lead for small arms fire, such was his speed from the afterburners.

"Four. The magic number is four," he thought as earth and sky revolved around the cockpit. Beyond the speed of sound he began his fourth roll, still low over the enemy positions. He was careful to apply a touch more of forward trim as he slowly rolled upside down. Careful to keep the nose above the horizon, he held the inverted position, skimming over the blur of earth below while twin jets of orange-red after burner flame roared from the expanded, wide open exhaust ports. His nose now wanted to rise as he held the plane for a long moment upside down. Screaming in his earphones pierced his mocking laughter. It was his radar man. "Chief! Chief! Chie-ee-ef!"

Contempt surged through him. He let the pressure of the trim raise the nose of the upside down airplane to a slight climb, then abruptly slammed the control stick half way over. Rolling upright and relieving the down trim, he streaked toward the South China Sea in a shallow climb before pulling the stick back hard, the power and speed sending him upward at a high G rate climb. The acceleration and G pressure silenced the backseater, as he was subdued into unconsciousness.

Within minutes the coastline passed as he climbed to a patch of billowing clouds to follow the beach line south. The old imperial city of Hue appeared through the late morning mist. The radar officer checked in with radar control and gave an account of the bombing passes and heavy flak.

The pilot's anger faded when he heard fear in the other's voice. He laughed loudly, and as he laughed, he thought of the prophecy that night in the holy man's cabin. Fifty missions. Fools Crow was right. Now he had counted coup for Fools Crow and the spirit people. Charging Shield threw his head back against the ejection seat and laughed aloud. The more he thought about the operator's fear, the harder he laughed. Rolling over the enemy position, with no ammunition, they didn't know the significance of the low victory roll over the enemy. How could they understand counting coup? The *washichu* in the rear seat had never heard of any such act among the armies of Europe from which the Americans were so influenced.

Counting coup. Dash in and touch the enemy. If the enemy is touched, he is considered dead and must be retired from the field of battle. The enemy would return to camp in sorrow, but his family would rejoice that he lived and within a short time, he too would appreciate life. Counting coup had its danger though, since the enemy was free to deliver a death-giving blow while a warrior was in the act of touching. The victory roll was Charging Shield's coup. He laughed again. Only *he* understood the meaning of his victory roll.

Not all of the radar operators were afraid during combat maneuvers, but too often, too many showed fear in some way. Most didn't laugh with the pilots about close calls. 'Pilots, fighter pilots,' he thought, 'now, they were warriors.' Most of the ones he knew weren't afraid to die. He wished he were flying the Douglas A-4, a single seater.

When the mountain range north of Da Nang passed under the Phantom's nose, he trimmed his control stick to begin the descent for Chu Lai. As he drew closer to the sprawling base, he slowed to drop his landing gear. "Yankee Echo Eight, cleared to land. Traffic, a C-130 on final." The runway was straight ahead. When the cargo plane was turning to a taxiway, the Phantom F4 left a wisp of smoke as its wheels touched the runway. The drag chute billowed out of the tail to slow the machine and at the end of the runway he turned off to a taxiway, the engines reduced to a lowering whine.

Survival gear made his step heavy as he dropped to the ground. He considered a contemptuous glance at the radar operator still fumbling with his harness straps, but he knew the man was new to combat missions. Also, he didn't have a wotai or a Red Man's beliefs. Charging Shield pressed the stone in its buckskin sack. "*Pilamiya aloh Wakan Tanka. Pilamiya Wichoni hey.*" He thanked the Great Spirit for his life.

He had worn the small stone faithfully according to Fools Crow's instructions. His wotai was his protection and he was thankful.

It was nearly noon when he left the debriefing room at the operations Quonset. A helicopter gun ship buzzed low across the distant row of tin-roofed huts sitting on a sand dune. There was little to do at Chu Lai but wait for the outdoor movie, wash clothes and clean the hut. The endless boredom of shifting sand and dreary shacks made him yearn to go home. He had resigned from the Marines to attend the university, but had first requested a combat assignment. In a few months, school would start, and his orders were due. Any intention of remaining in the service had ended with this war. The Marines had allowed him to rise from enlisted rank, but a warrior's role in a war like this one had proved too frustrating.

His grandmother's advice echoed in his memory, "There will always be a war, Grandson. If they can make a business out of their religion, war can be a collection plate, too." But the war, despite the frustrations, had provided the way to reach for what he must. Even Fools Crow, a pacifist, never objected to his involvement and had helped his warrior's role with the coming of the wotai.

Later, Charging Shield would learn to contend that the war was mostly political and economic, no different than most, where the poor were rallied for cannon fodder through a sense of patriotism and, especially in this war, the higher realm, those in control, the elected and economic leaders, strove to keep their warrior-age sons out of combat units, taking no share of the direct and deadliest exposure. In but a short time, Charging Shield would set his course upon another path and would leave the warring to politicians.

*   *   *   *

The high-finned Phantoms circled like a pair of tiger sharks above the South China Sea. Two electronic laden Grumman A-6 Intruders orbiting off the coast of North Vietnam were contacted by the F-4's. The Grummans took their positions, holding a separated, lengthy, racetrack orbit, their missile surveillance scanners sweeping inland. The mission's target was located in SAM territory. It was Charging Shield's hundredth mission, no doubt his last mission. He was due for discharge and new pilots were checking into the squadron. If his orders would not arrive, he would receive a mandatory R and R in Japan or Okinawa, at the completion of one hundred missions.

The cruising fighter-bombers turned inbound. The thin beachhead giving way to beige landscape, looked little different than South Vietnam, except for monsoon-flooded rice paddies casting mirrored reflections of false tranquility. The late summer storms were saturating North Vietnam, Laos and Cambodia further inland. Meteorology predicted that Chu Lai would receive heavy rains by noon.

EAGLE VISION

Charging Shield glanced at his watch. His main gyroscope for instrument landing had turned faulty and he didn't want to make an instrument landing at Chu Lai in heavy rain. The pilots had noted the cloud buildups west of Chu Lai. All Laos and Cambodia missions had been cancelled. Charging Shield hoped to leave Vietnam before the monsoons; emergency missions were launched regardless of weather and more than one crew and their aircraft had disappeared in the torrential downpours.

He unzipped the top of his flight suit, pulling the braided cord at his neck. He tugged to bring the small lump of buckskin from underneath his survival vest. He fondled the buckskin. His orders were due.

"Where are my orders?" he asked as he clutched the wotai pouch.

Square coastal rice fields thinned away to rising piedmont, the rice paddies climbing with the terrain, narrowing to stepped radial bands ending at mountainous, dark green, almost impenetrable jungle. Yet, fifty miles further, somewhere under the thick foliage, a North Vietnamese truck battalion was hidden and protected by surface to air missiles.

The first warning tone issued by the patrol planes crackled like scrambled eggs across his helmet's receivers. His muscles flexed like a prizefighter circling an opponent. The voiceless tones meant North Vietnamese, or more than likely their Russian advisors, had activated radar sets and were no doubt tracking the Phantoms. Both pilots tensed on their flight controls, their feet poised to jam down the rudder pedals in coordination with a sideways slam of the control stick to full aileron.

Any further warning beginning with the spoken code word for the sector, in which they were flying, he would do an abrupt split "S" maneuver to his right, at the same time igniting both afterburners. Fritz, the section leader, would roll in the opposite direction.

The split "S" maneuver was the most expedient means of losing altitude and changing direction. The plane would roll over on its back like an upside-down turtle before it dropped its nose straight down in a dive. In theory, the launched missiles would be radar locked to a computed destruction point out ahead where target and missile were calculated to converge if evasive action had not been taken. Below, the enemy controller would attempt to alter the missiles' course into the targets. Fortunately, for the fighter pilots, the missiles' smaller steering surfaces made the projectiles awkward and clumsy in comparison to the fighters. Too much correction and the SAMs would tumble and cartwheel futilely. If the early warning surveillance aircraft detected the upward-bound missiles in time, the fighters usually had a high survival rate... if the fired missiles were detected in time.

Pilot error jeopardized the pair of fighter-bombers from Marine Fighter/Attack Squadron 115. The lead A-6 surveillance aircraft, having flown north longer than the uneasy pilot had wanted, suddenly banked seaward before signaling their counterpart. At this point, the surveillance radar was blind and it was now the mission of the second A-6 patrol plane, trailing further south, to scan the enemy areas inland.

Precisely at this moment, the experienced Russian missile technicians fired a salvo of three missiles.

Fortunately, an alert radar operator in the second A-6 had anticipated the lead aircraft's turn and was already sweeping his scope inland to locate the Phantoms, while three ascending blips were off the bottom of his screen for a few long seconds. When the three ascending dots appeared, the operator's eyes went wide. He punched the emergency warning indicator without a moment's hesitation.

"Q-B Seven, Q-B Seven!" The code word for fired missiles was shouted out across both pilots' helmets. Q-B was their sector by latitude, Seven by longitude. Both pilots reacted to the code word as instinctively as if their own names had been yelled in alarm. The lead plane rolled left, his wingman rolled right. The inverted pair hung suspended for a long, precarious moment before the black noses dropped, hurtling down, down to the green jungle, miles below.

A flash of gray, like a gigantic telephone pole, roared ahead and past the wingman's window. It was the second missile. The first missile had been directed at the section leader's plane and was now tumbling wildly out of control. Preoccupation with the lead missile caused the enemy controller to err, detonating the second missile too late. The shock waves reached out with a solid thump, but no damage was inflicted to Charging Shield's plane.

His machine was now screaming downward under full afterburner power when the last missile flashed from below like a giant spear, detonating much closer. The vacuum shock from this blast snuffed out his right engine, sending the machine spinning. Around and around the F-4 spiraled down, the dark jungle revealing a glistening silver streak bisecting the whirling circle, the peaks and valleys growing deathly sharper. The 'G' forces paralyzed his leg upon the rudder. He strained to release the pressure upon the rudder and pushed back on the control stick toward a neutral position. Down he whirled and he began to panic.

"Kola, Kola," a voice called in heavy Sioux. Then, it spoke again in accented English, "Little Brother, little brother, push back hard. Push, little brother. I will help you." It was the voice of Cross Dog.

The streak of silver transcended to a discernible river before the pilot managed to neutralize his controls, pushing the stick forward against the centrifugal force with all of his strength and pushing his foot with equal difficulty against the rudder pedal opposite from the spin. The stabilator, rudder and aileron surfaces responded, the spin ceased, the dive shallowed and, finally, the plane came under control. Smoke trailed from hot kerosene in the dead engine. He pressed the aileron and rudder controls to point the machine out to the safety of the South China Sea.

Charging Shield's adrenaline began to subside. He had been too excited to notice the loss of the right engine. The power of just one afterburner, coupled with the supersonic speed accumulated from the dive over ten thousand feet, concealed the loss of the engine. Now, as he brought the throttles out of afterburner, the sudden deceleration warned him of his situation. He checked the dead engine's RPM gage, relieved to find a wind milling turbine indicating that the engine wasn't frozen, decreasing the chance of battle damage.

At that moment, Fritz called across the radios, "Chief, where are you? Are you okay?"

"Feet wet," Charging Shield replied.

"C'mon back, Chief," Fritz ordered, disregarding radio formality as he glared down through his canopy at the tell tale smoke trails. "I got the bastards spotted." The vindication in his voice flooded through his transmission.

Charging Shield scanned the left engine instruments, satisfied with their readings. He double-checked the fuel flow, pressing the quantity indicators, calculating his reserve fuel. The Phantom was a flying kerosene tank: fuselage cells, wing cells and two external tanks fed the thirsty machine. Abnormal fuel loss would indicate battle damage. It was against Marine regulations to re-light an engine that had been knocked out of action.

He had adequate power to return to Chu Lai or Da Nang on one engine and could disregard the section leader's order. Another order, considerably higher, from Air Force Command, decreed that the destruction of SAM missile sites within the DMZ area, including the QB sector, required U.S. Air Force clearance. Even if missiles had been fired, a half-hour waiting period was required before attack. Fighter-bomber pilots were at a loss to understand this directive. Was it to allow the Russian crews time to escape? The tell tale smoke trail left by the SAM missile did not last a half-hour.

The regulation made Charging Shield's decision for him. He recalled, with disgust, proclamations made by dove senators on college campuses. It was his last mission, unless emergency missions demanded his duties. What would they do? Ground him and send him back to the States? He laughed aloud.

"Let's get the bastards, Chief!" the RIO's vehement voice encouraged across the intercom.

The right engine lit without incident. Satisfied, Charging Shield pointed the big machine back toward Finger Lakes. Fritz called out his altitude and position, boldly oblivious to enemy radio surveillance. Charging Shield lit both afterburners to scream back to the section leader, homing on a black orbiting speck. Within minutes, he was joined in formation.

They made only two passes apiece. The leader called for his wingman to bomb several hundred yards short of the napalm drop after Fritz had pulled up from his first pass. A flaming secondary explosion erupted from the jungle when the first load of six bombs detonated. "Right on, Chief," Fritz yelled with exuberance across the radios. The section leader expended his remaining napalms close to the fiery jungle, sending a ricocheting fire streaking a half-mile, obviously igniting a missile, like an

errant Fourth of July rocket. The last of Charging Shield's bombs scattered the diminishing fireball below with resultant lesser explosions.

After several victory rolls, the section joined back in formation, departing south across the mountains north of Da Nang. Out ahead of the monsoon, scud clouds were lowering below the mountains to the coastline, moving toward Chu Lai and Da Nang. Within an hour, the rains would be drenching both bases. At a thousand feet, both Phantoms streaked above the landing end of Chu Lai runway, the lead plane peeling away, breaking sharply to arc smoothly back to the touchdown point. The wingman held his course for several seconds more down the runway then rolled ninety degrees to the horizon, following in a wider arc to increase the landing separation from the leader. The drag chutes deployed as each aircraft landed.

The pilots offered little at the debriefing. They reported possible secondary explosion, presumably a minor truck depot. Possible ground fire was alleged; anti-aircraft fire was reported to be negative. The aviators were thankful they were not career men and that they'd both be rotating back to the States any day.

Charging Shield walked across the sand dunes with his RIO and Fritz, their conversation oblivious to the mission. Instead they laughed and reminisced about two attractive schoolteachers the pilots had dated in Okinawa. They stopped at Charging Shield's hut for a rum and coke, despite the time of day.

After Fritz and the RIO left, Charging Shield sat on his locker beside his bunk and mixed one more rum and coke. It had been a good mission. He languished, assured that there were fewer Russians to fire missiles at the fighter-bombers. He never finished the liquid in his canteen cup. The ever-present heat and the rum made him drowsy. He fell back on his air mattress and was soon asleep.

The combat missions soon faded. He dreamed; finding himself looking down on West River and riding in a pre-war sedan away from the city limits, pointing a plume of gravel dust at the growing town hiding in the darkening shadows of the Black Hills. The car followed a winding stream bordered by greening alfalfa fields, then crossed a shallow river to ascend a broad table dotted with winter wheat, sorghum and opening range.

At the end of the table, the road dropped to the desolate floor of a prehistoric sea. The car entered the Oglala reservation and the Badlands to deposit him on a dusty trail leading to his grandmother's cabin.

It was once again that occasional dream... the dream that would bring him back to his beginning. He would dream of the buffalo. The thundering herds, the shrill cries of the hunters, the open freedom of endless, unblemished plains where man was one with all-encompassing nature. Above it all, the overseeing eagle peered down from wide blue, depthless sky.

He slept for several hours. It was a soothing sleep. The rains came, thunder rolled distantly, sending a cooling rain shower that dispelled the heat. Heavier droplets began to fall. The wind increased, tearing off a piece of tin from an adjoining hut. He slept through it all. The thunderstorm rolled on, expending itself at sea.

"Captain. Captain," a voice called. "Captain Charging Shield. Wake up, Sir."

He looked into the youthful eyes of the corporal from the squadron administration section. "Wake up Captain. Your orders are in. You have to catch the milk run."

The corporal shook him again. "There's a C-130 out of Da Nang tomorrow morning. You'll get processed in Okinawa. Your orders are in, Captain. You're going home."

KAREN

CHAPTER SEVEN

On the Kadena flightline, a World Airway 707 waited to carry Marines across the vast Pacific. On board, the flight crew drank coffee and chatted casually about their stay in Okinawa. "Really, Karen, I'd be happy to front for you if you don't feel up to it," said the blonde stewardess as she studied her friend's tired eyes.

Karen Ray sighed with relief. She was tired. The thought of standing at the entryway with a pasted smile and feigning indifference to the stares and whistles of the boarding vets was just too much for her to take right now. She had a fitful night's sleep plagued by morbid thoughts of the war, the wounded and then, there was the reoccurring dream. Each time, she awoke with a sense of fear and foreboding that haunted her entire day.

That morning the dream began in its usual manner. She saw herself in the middle of a dying land. There were humans, for as far as the eye could see; one giant mass of gaunt and hungry people moaning and fighting over what little clean water was left to drink. From where she stood, she could see the entire country. To the West, the land thundered and avalanches of soil fell into an angry sea. To the East, the sky was purple; through fleeting clear patches of light she saw the infrastructure of an entire city collapse. Raw sewage flooded over houses and people, consuming in its wake the last remnant of land not already occupied by garbage or pillars of barrels oozing poison. The once-bountiful Midwest was desert; carcasses of livestock bloated for circling buzzards. The air was pungent with the smell of toxins. In her dream, she frantically searched for shade and plant life but the land was forsaken and cooked to a prickly brown.

In the distance she heard the beating of drums. She walked for a long time as the drumming sound grew. She spotted a tree on the horizon. She broke into a run for the green tree, never had she so appreciated a leafing tree.

She reached it, exhausted, thirsty, and trembling. Slowly she dropped to her knees and embraced the tree's massive trunk. A soft fall of footsteps approached, and she saw a hand holding a cup of water inches from her face. She drew the cup to her parched lips. From her kneeling position she could see an older Indian woman, in traditional dress, standing over her. The first words out of the woman's mouth made Karen smile. "Don't call me a Native American," the husky woman in a beaded buckskin dress said, with a mischievous grin. "I was called an Indian my last couple of circles down there and got used to it." Then the Indian woman threw her head back and laughed heartily. She extended her hand and looked with gentle eyes overflowing with warmth and acceptance.

She took Karen to a circle filled with people of various races. Their conversations were filled with amiable, almost musical laughter. Food was piled high on platters, water poured freely from wooden pitchers. The children were healthy with eyes that sparkled, just like those of the animals they played with: fawns, wolf pups, raccoons and bear cubs. The Indian woman smiled from across a large table, passing Karen a bowl of fruit before exclaiming, "What took you so long to get here?"

Her alarm went off.

Karen felt a hand on her arm. "Homeward bound," her friend said as she hurried to the entrance to greet the servicemen. "Here they come."

Karen busied herself in the galley with the beverage cart. Occasionally she glanced out at the men coming on board to offer a welcoming smile. A few days ago she was on the somber outbound flight. She had looked at the men - most of them boys - and wondered which ones would not be coming back.

The return flights held a spellbinding aura of relief. These men were the lucky ones for they were returning - alive. Beaten, maybe even broken, but they were survivors. The war made her feel fortunate to be a woman. She opposed her country's involvement in the war from the beginning. She wasn't sure she understood how it all started and why, but she did know that it wasn't the solution. She didn't grasp war mentality.

Yet ironically, she also noticed inside herself a strange feeling of envy. These survivors had tasted adventure. They had come face to face with pain and death, and they were forced to confront their deepest fears. It was a test many failed to pass, their eyes told her that much. But the ones who did pass the test... how could they ever be afraid of anything again? They would know an area within their framework that would allow them a freedom from fear. They would be strong, like tempered steel.

She went into the aisle to begin the safety check. One of the men approached searching for a seat. She noted the gold wings above rows of ribbons on his uniform. His eyes held hers as they squeezed past each other, exchanging cordial nods.

Unlike Charging Shield, Karen Ray's dreams were sharper and more focused, allowing an awareness of past circles of time to become closer to the surface of her subconscious. She was not a male and therefore lacked the ego that detoured, dominated and restricted those inner thoughts that probed into the teaching experiences of past circles. She had little trouble engaging the concept that she lived before, many times before, down through endless circles of time. Her pasts were much closer, and she was blessed with an association, a camaraderie of recognizable characters that returned to their life stage, sharing the amphitheater of life circles. It was why the woman in her recent dream was more than vaguely familiar. She did not choose to recall those lives, however, or any one of the cast of characters except for one.

There was that one figure of the past, her warrior mate. She could do without him for long periods if she was upon a mission, a high plane mission, for she had reached that state, and had continually added to it, down, down, over and over, through her evolution. But the one instinct always remained. She still preferred to have him nearby, even if it was a distant hovering in a far off background. She had been wandering too long in this circle, not set upon a specific purpose or mission and right now she missed him and did not want him to be a mirage far away in a lonely distance. She dearly missed the entwined completeness that nurtured the serene solitude of their mateship.

She had beseeched the powers, wondering out loud if she had a mate. She had even taken the pipe and pointed it outward, feeling rather awkward, yet knowing what she held could be powerful. It was on a cliff overlooking the coast of California. Her subconscious from the past had helped her. She had been reluctant, even afraid to take the peace pipe from the old leather container. 'Use it.' A husky woman's voice called out. 'Get on with it. Ask the forces.' The past had spoken. She took the pipe and asked for her mate.

Charging Shield took an aisle seat next to a former acquaintance, an Infantry officer, First Lieutenant Bill Polito. As the aircraft taxied, Charging Shield singled out the dark haired stewardess he had slipped by earlier and watched intently as she demonstrated the ditching instructions. When he placed his military blouse in the overhead compartment, she offered a polite smile. He sat down and leaned his head back. Before he closed his eyes, she handed him a pillow. Her pale blue-gray eyes gazed down as she offered a gentle adjustment behind his head. They were face to face like a pair of nested eagles for a serene moment. He noticed the broad shoulders, the erect, stately posture, and those strong, high cheekbones... for that feature alone she progressed from attractive to very attractive in his mind.

The 707 roared down the Kadena runway. The melody and verse of a familiar song seemed to play as the passenger plane ascended the bright rays of the late morning sun.

"Out on runway number nine
Big 707 set to go
There she goes now my friend
At last she's aloft
Hear the mighty engines roar
See the silver wings on high
She's away and outward bound
High above the clouds she'll fly."

He wasn't sure if he knew the exact words and began to compose his own.
"This old Vietnam has got me down
It's no earthly good to me
Been stuck here on the ground,
hot and lonely as can be.
Out on runway number nine
Big 707 set to go
Got my orders in my hand
And I'll be homeward bound
Here the mighty engines roar
See the silver wings on high
She's away and state side bound
Far above the clouds she'll fly

Where cannon shells are still
And the missiles cannot kill
Oh the liquor tasted good
And the women are so fine…"

Before the aircraft reached cruise altitude, he was asleep. The night before, he had begun his celebration at the Futema Officers' Club with several R and R pilots from his squadron. At dawn, he was heading for the Kadena terminal in a speeding taxicab waving farewell to his companions. While he slept, the stewardess kept busy. First coffee with a roll was served, followed later with lunch. That afternoon the jet pitched slightly. Charging Shield momentarily thought he was aboard a Phantom as he awakened.

Polito's elbow stirred him. "You had a long sleep, Chief. This out-standing airplane pussy is worth eyeballing. They got a blonde on board who has got a mean set of tits. Anyone who wouldn't eat that is strictly a vegetarian."

He looked around for the dark haired stewardess and gazed at her as she came down the aisle.

"You missed lunch. Do you want a cup of coffee?" she asked with a courteous voice.

He wanted a rum and coke, but accepted the coffee instead. "Did you fly in Vietnam?" she opened the conversation.

He nodded. Her voice seemed to carry a melody. It was a pleasant voice, confident and captivating.

"Can I ask what you flew?"

He stared at the cheekbones, noting the miniature ponytail that set above her shoulder-length hair. It was tied with a red, white and blue ribbon. The same as the squadron stripe across the tail of his Phantom. He named his airplane, somewhat shyly, lighting her eyes with an alert smile. He liked the way the ribbon swept her hair back. She was pretty, no question about that. Her tan, like her hair, was not as dark as his, but her features hinted that somewhere in her bloodline they may have had similar ancestors... except for her eyes, the pale blue bordered on gray. Such haunting eyes, seeming to reach back into his past.

She unconsciously looked at the gold wings pinned above his shirt pocket. "Are you getting out?"

An exaggerated grin accompanied his nod.

"I bet you'll be flying for the airlines?"

His eyes left her for a moment to glance at the forward section. "I'm going back to school. You never know, maybe I should try the airlines," he said a bit hastily. After a brief pause, he introduced himself and the lieutenant.

She offered a polite nod to the lieutenant, then fixed her eyes on the aviator. "Charging Shield, that's a beautiful name," she spoke emphatically without reservation. "Charging Shield," she pronounced each syllable with a quiet emphasis. His name seemed to roll over inside of her, repeating itself. The name answered his nationality.

The pilot was taken aback. He had never heard his name spoken so... it was as if she had conveyed some age old familiarity back into a past and yet her soothing voice seemed to touch upon a vaguely familiar, hidden melody.

They looked at each other, not knowing what to say. Karen hoped she hadn't embarrassed him.

Polito broke in. "What's your name?"

"Karen Ray," she replied, her eyes fixed on the pilot's. 'Those eyes... they are familiar,' she thought. The moment lasted a few seconds, but to Karen and Kyle, it left its impression.

Charging Shield broke his trance, handing his coffee cup to Polito. Her openness - and that look - dissolved his sense of shyness. "Here, why don't you sit down?" He took the pillow from his seat and put it across the aisle armrest. "C'mon, sit down and relax," he coaxed.

"Well, okay. I guess it wouldn't hurt for a little while." As she sat, her curvaceous legs projected into the aisle. Her ankles were trim, tapering gracefully toward firm calves. He noted that they were active, assertive and outrightly beautiful. She was tall, like a Sioux woman. He guessed that she was only three or four inches less than his height.

"Can you tell me about your missions?" she asked.

"There's only one mission and that's the one we're on right now... going home is all that counts." His eyes lingered a moment longer on her legs before he looked up at her. "I must have set a record checking out of Chu Lai." It had been a long time since he'd been next to a woman. Her close presence was disarming, yet he managed to sound casual. The strange magnetic aura was pervading but he managed to attribute it to her attractiveness... and yes, it had been a long time since he had been this close to a woman... an American woman.

"Didn't you fly off a carrier?" she asked.

He shook his head. "The Marine jets are at Chu Lai or Da Nang."

"Chief, that's confidential information," interrupted Polito, wanting to be part of the conversation.

They talked briefly, at first comparing notes on restaurants and shops in Okinawa. They exchanged hometowns. As he got more relaxed, he noticed the crystal dangling from a silver chain around her neck.

"Oh, I got this from a Cherokee man who was on one of my flights." she responded to his question. "He was very insistent that I should have it. I remember wanting to buy this little pipe stone turtle necklace that he had, and he said, 'No, this one is your necklace. It will protect you in these airplanes.' He was so serious about it I didn't dare turn it down. Now I wear it all the time."

"It's your *wotai*, then." Charging Shield remarked.

"*Wotai?*"

"That's a stone that comes to you in a special way - and protects you like the man said. I've got one too."

"Oh," Karen urged, "tell me how yours came to you."

Charging Shield looked at Polito and decided to downplay his experience. "It's a long story. I wouldn't want to bore you with it." He took a sip of his lukewarm coffee. 'Yes, it was a long time ago... the war, the missions.' he thought. 'God, she grew more beautiful the longer she sat close with those gorgeous legs sticking out into the aisle.' Polito cut in with his brazen comments, which Karen adeptly countered by turning suddenly crisp. Dispirited, the tall lieutenant groaned as he rose, offering up his seat to inspect a poker game aft behind the galley.

"Don't let us chase you away," she said, her eyebrow raised slightly as she stepped back into the aisle.

"I need to stretch," Polito answered, squeezing his companion on the shoulder.

She took the lieutenant's seat. He felt the electricity when she brushed by. "What are you going back to school for?" she asked.

A puzzled look came and went. He had enrolled in business to placate Ernie Hale, but right now, all that seemed to matter was returning home and the Sun Dance. He gave her his stock answer, the one that seemed most plausible to strangers when he was pressed to explain. "I want to make some changes, and I know I'll need an education. Lately, since I became a pilot, I'd go back to my reservation for the Sun Dance. The Sun Dance, that's part of our religion," he clarified. "Every time I'd hear the same complaints, mostly about the Bureau. You ever hear about the Bureau of Indian Affairs?"

She nodded.

"The B.I.A. has been milking Indians ever since it started. The B.I.A. - the reservation system." He offered a look of resignation. "I want to do something more with my life than bore holes in the sky." He shrugged his shoulders reluctantly. "I have been a long time in the Marines. Maybe I will come back in but without an education I will never go anywhere."

They sat quietly before he spoke again. "What about you? What made you become a stewardess?"

Her look reflected the same unsure expression he had just moments before. She erased it with a flippant laugh. "My office job was boring, the kind where the most excitement of the day is to eat lunch with the same old group and complain about work. I finally decided I was too young for that and needed adventure. Travel, meeting different people, being free, this is the perfect means for doing that." She attempted to sound nonchalant. "There are times when I'm tired, and the passengers get on my nerves, and I end up wiping chicken Kiev off my uniform, but it's a good job. It's perfect for now."

"What would you like to do next?"

"I'm still trying to figure that one out. I don't really know yet. At times it feels like I'm making it all up as I go along. You know, just doing what feels right at the moment. I do know that I want adventure, and..." her voice trailed off with a sense of discomfort.

"And what?" Charging Shield prompted.

"Well, I have sort of a long term dream. You promise not to laugh?"

"You have my word," Charging Shield nodded.

"I dream of building a cabin beside a lake or stream. Most of the girls I work with are hung up on luxuries. In my cabin, I'd like to see how many I could do without."

"You're really serious?" he asked with a bemused expression.

"You don't believe me, do you? At least you didn't laugh," she added, "most people do."

"I'm sorry," he apologized. "You startled me when you said you could do without luxuries. Most girls are impressed with how much coin a guy makes. More gold, more luxuries."

Karen reclined back into her chair. "C'est la vie," she replied with a haughty air. "I don't want to be tied to soap operas and new drapes. I want to be part of something with substance, like the cabin, and the stream."

"Just you and the cabin?"

"Not necessarily. If I could plan my destiny, it would include someone like, I don't know, ... a soul mate who feels the same way I do. The isolation of a cabin would be the perfect environment for our sameness, our appreciation of nature." She stopped talking and let out a sigh. 'Karen,' she said to herself, 'shut up while you're ahead.'

He was pleasantly surprised with what she said and relished the way her tone and words meshed so well with his own thoughts.

"So," she perked up, "what's your destiny?"

Her question startled him, but he answered without hesitation. "My immediate destiny is returning home to my tribe. That's all that matters for now."

She looked around with an engaging grin. "I'd say, everyone on this airplane shares your immediate destiny, returning home."

She conveyed a teasing laugh. Her manner reminded him of Eagle Feather. He remembered the sun dancers coming out of the sweat lodge, the early morning sweat lodge to cleanse and prepare them for the Sun Dance. Eagle Feather would usually joke and tease, especially to the newcomers. There was a method to Eagle Feather's easygoing manner, for it would ease the sun dancer's apprehensions, especially those who were enduring for the first time.

"How long were you in Vietnam?" she asked.

"Long enough for a combat tour. I volunteered. It got me out in time for fall semester." He darted his eyes toward the window. "I never expected you to say you wanted a cabin. My grandmother lived in a cabin."

EAGLE VISION

A sharp vision rocked through her as he ended his words. She envisioned a cabin with a gentle curving stream. In the distance, a trio of high projections rose against the skyline. They were unusual looking, like narrow spires.

"We used to live in a cabin too," he went on, "when we lived on the reservation, but I was too young to remember much about it. After we moved to West River, we lived close to a mountain stream called Rapid Creek. All summer long we played in that creek."

"Sounds better than a concrete swimming pool," she managed to respond casually, but her thoughts were focused on the image of a cabin and the stream, and the strange looking spires.

He offered an agreeable nod before he spoke. "We started out at a place called the Black Bridge. It was an old bridge where the creek was shallow. I used to mud crawl there with my two sisters. We'd build a little dam along the side and catch minnows. There was a marsh under the bridge, full of frogs and turtles. After we learned to swim, we'd move upstream to the Beaver Dam. It was barely over your head in the center, then it shallowed out. The older kids swam at Saddle Rock. We had a tree swing that dropped over the deep part."

The mention of the tree swing removed her from the cabin image. "I love tree swings!" She paused for a moment to return to her own childhood, then tilted her head toward him. "At least some kids still have decent playgrounds."

His expression clouded. "No, it's all gone," he sighed. "One day in high school, I walked across the Black Bridge and saw the bulldozers straightening out the stream. Beaver Dam and Saddle Rock disappeared. People built houses and put up 'No Trespassing' signs. They had the city condemn the creek, and we had to swim in a concrete pool." He took a sip of coffee, which was almost cold.

Karen remained silent, but her look evidenced displeasure with the ending of his story. "You mentioned the Sun Dance. What's that?"

"It's a ceremony," he tested her with a glance of caution, "a ceremony to the Great Spirit."

"Tell me about the Great Spirit," she said, eyeing him.

The strength of her tone made him give the kind of answer she was looking for. "*Wakan Tanka,*" he spoke firmly. "We call the Creator the Great Mystery. We also call him *Tankashilah.* That means Grandfather. The Grandfather made Mother Earth and Father Sky. We think of ourselves as the grandchildren."

A sharp smile parted her lips. "Do you think God needs a gender? Why couldn't you call It, Grandmother/Grandfather or Grandparent." She left an emphatic pronunciation on the word - 'It.'

Her question brought forth an uneasy look from the pilot. "It does sound somewhat chauvinistic." he answered sincerely. "Maybe we should say Grandparent. I'm sure the Great Spirit is like you say. It doesn't need a gender." He copied her emphasis with an agreeable grin.

"And the other tribes?"

"The northern tribes, they pretty much believe the same. Some of our ceremonies are similar."

Her eyes lit with added interest. "Your ceremonies, can you tell me about them?"

"Why do you want to know?"

"It all sounds so interesting."

He retreated, feeling suddenly mischievous. "We're not supposed to talk about them to non-Indians. You're non-Indian, aren't you?" he forced a sober look. He couldn't resist the temptation to tease.

"I suppose so. I'm adopted, so I don't really know what I am," she said as if she'd answered the question too many times.

"I hope I didn't say anything wrong. I'm sorry."

"Oh, don't be sorry!" She lightly squeezed his arm to reassure him. "This way, I can pretend I'm from a tribe somewhere way back."

Her quick touch on his arm erased any doubt in his mind that he was falling for this woman. It was an innocent gesture, but it conveyed a power, a good power, a comforting power.

She had felt it too, momentarily losing her train of thought. "Where were we? I wanted to know more about your ceremonies, and you wouldn't tell me."

He tried to shrug off the strange feeling welling inside. After all, he was now a combat warrior. He shouldn't allow himself to get so distracted. He managed to wink at her. "If you ask too many questions, you'll turn into a toad."

She laughed, her smile quickly melting to a frown as she noticed the other flight attendants preparing the serving carts. "Darn, we're getting ready for dinner. It's back to work." She rose from her seat; consciously aware of a mysterious harmony emanated by their discussion. "Will you tell me more later?"

"Be glad to," he said.

He thought about Fools Crow's *Yuwipi* ceremony as she stepped into the aisle. She'd never understand that, he said to himself. Their eyes met and held each other. "I enjoyed talking to you," he said. "Thanks for sitting down."

"I enjoyed it too," she replied, taking his half-full coffee cup.

The pillow fell to the aisle. He admired her figure until she disappeared behind the galley. He retrieved the pillow and pressed the reclining button, closing his eyes to fondle the pillow absentmindedly. His mind was filled with the girl's expressions... that voice, that serene, comforting, song-like voice... and her questions... no one had asked questions like that from the squadron. The squadron, it was the only world he had known for so long, it seemed. To survive in combat, it had to be. And before that, his girl from West River, she had always avoided those kinds of questions, and she was Indian. The light-heartedness within him suddenly dampened. She wasn't that much Indian, yet she had always been ashamed, maybe that was why she never waited. Maybe, if he hadn't joined the Marines, he'd be married now, probably living in West River. A distasteful frown formed. 'No, he would never trade his adventures for that!'

Traditionally the warriors of his tribe, the Dog Soldiers, the Akicitah, never married until they were well into manhood and most importantly had tasted life's share of adventure - rich, sweet adventures not available around the campfires. The older ones from the elite warrior societies laughed at the few foolish ones who married young. "Hang-around-the-tents," they called them. Combat, the buffalo hunts, the warrior societies, honor, - life was too rich to limit one's adventure to an early marriage.

Deep down he had always known his girlfriend from West River wasn't the woman for him. Now that he had again tasted the exhilarating, deadly adventure of combat, he knew for certain she was not the one. It seemed now that there was something in his past that demanded a special woman. That something was vague and uncertain, but it was there, like a salmon's instinct returning to a stream, one particular stream.

The retreating figure of the stewardess came back vividly. The pleasant feeling returned. He had never met a woman who talked that way. And she was attractive. He cautioned himself, he was too fresh from Vietnam. It would be too easy to be carried away. 'No!' he argued, she was extraordinary, damned extraordinary. He relished the fullness of her thighs, imagining her firm breasts hidden and subdued by the stiff serving garment. And God, her legs couldn't have been more perfect, at least for his taste. Her legs were those of an energetic, boundless woman. And those eyes. A sense of foreboding seemed to cast caution upon his spirit. Those eyes had a penetrating sweep... indeed they did remind one of a hawk or an eagle... or even a Fools Crow - Fools Crow was a human eagle! They probably have backed off most men, he surmised. Yes, an eagle! He remembered the eagle that his father had saved from a coyote trap. Even in temporary captivity the eagle's look was dominant, when he was a child looking into the chicken coop where the great bird was nursed back to health. For some strange reason she seemed to be some mysterious reflection of that very eagle. The long hours in the cockpit, the close brushes with death, the skies of Vietnam grew further and further away as he relaxed contentedly.

THE EAGLE
AND THE MEADOWLARK

CHAPTER EIGHT

At this point on the homeward journey almost everyone was sleeping. She took a seat in the area closed off for the flight crew. Within seconds she was asleep, dreaming of her own beginnings.

The old woman tilted the wooden rocking chair back until it touched the front porch wall. A gust of wind made her hunch her shoulder blades, and she drew the faded Indian blanket from her lap up to the soft folds of her neck. By now the brown grass around her tiny house was mostly covered with a crackling blanket of dry leaves. She breathed in deeply the smoky city air, coughing and sputtering uncontrollably as she reached into her pocket for a slip of paper. She unfolded the little square that by now resembled a piece of worn leather, the name and address scrawled upon it barely legible. Although her blue-gray eyes were almost clouded over with cataracts, she knew what the writing said. She had memorized it long ago. The old woman was more than aware that this was to be her final winter. It was time to put in order what few affairs she had.

The blue light from the black and white television threw a luminous glow around the living room. A couple in their thirties relaxed together on the sofa, satisfied amid the dolls and stuffed animals strewn across the floor. A knock at the front door yanked them from their early evening reverie.

"Are we expecting someone?" the man asked as he got up and stepped over the toys. He opened the door to find what he guessed to be a sixteen-year old boy and a frail old woman. They both looked Indian. The old woman studied his face and mumbled something to the boy.

"Hello," the boy said. "Are you the Rays?"

Before the man could say yes, the boy interjected. "We have come very far. May we come in?"

"What is it that you want?" the man asked skeptically.

"She has something for the little girl," the boy said, nodding his head toward the old woman.

"For... you mean Karen?" The man and his wife exchanged puzzled glances from across the room. The woman walked over to join her husband at the door.

"Who are you?" the wife asked. Stone faced, the old woman looked at her and then down at the boy.

"She is the girl's great grandmother," the boy answered.

The wife looked at her husband nervously and shrugged her shoulders. "I guess we'd better let them in," she said as she opened the screen door.

The boy picked up a shopping bag from the step and helped the old woman to the couch. She sat for a moment, staring into the television set. She then motioned to the boy for her bag, and she spoke to the couple while she fished for something inside of it.

"She says that you are the caretakers of a very special child; your child wears the daybreak star," the boy interpreted.

The child's adopted father could not help but interrupt, "I don't understand. What is she talking about and where does she get off thinking she knows all about Karen? We've had her since she was a month old."

The boy told the old woman what the man had just said. She spoke to the man while the boy translated. "She was present with the midwife when your daughter was born. Our tribe believes strongly in signs from the Great Spirit. She knows that you have doubts, but she is happy because she knows you love the girl and will provide for her well. What happens outside of that is left up to the Great Spirit."

The old woman paused and pulled out a white buckskin bag trimmed with colorful beadwork. She began to talk again.

"This belongs to your daughter now," the boy said. "The contents are valuable, and she asks that you treat it with respect." With a thin, trembling hand the old woman passed the bag to the younger woman and looked deeply into her eyes. "Your daughter may not appreciate it when she is young. She will not understand it. But in time she will. That's why you must take good care of it. It will become important when she is a woman.

The old woman caught a movement from the corner of her eye. She looked slowly toward the hallway and saw a small bare foot and the ruffle of a flannel nightgown disappear around the corner. She broke into a toothless smile. A warm, knowing smile.

"One more thing," said the boy. "Do not worry about your daughter. She will be healthy and grow up to be a beautiful and strong woman. Give her freedom and she will blossom like a healthy tree."

When the couple was alone again, they sat down and the woman loosened the drawstring of the bag. She reached inside and pulled out a hard clay pipe bowl and a wooden stem. "You know, I actually think I believe that old woman," she said as she ran her fingers across a hieroglyphic drawing carved into the red pipestone.

* * * *

The Boeing approached the eastern edge of the vast Pacific. 'Fasten Seat Belt' and 'No Smoking' signs were lit. The Marines buzzed with anticipation. Some would have relatives at the El Toro Air Station. He woke to the anxious conversations of men who had been long away from home.

After the aircraft landed, the Marines filled the aisle. A staff sergeant stepped aboard to call out processing instructions. Finally, the file of military men debarked from the plane.

He looked down at her as he was about to leave. "I hope I see you again. You made a long trip enjoyable." He wanted to ask for her telephone number but felt uncertain. Her eyes seemed steel gray with the light from the open door.

"I have a few days off, and El Toro isn't that far away," she surprised him. Her warm voice was reassuring.

"Can you write down your number?" he asked. She smiled and held out her hand to drop a piece of paper into his. "I'll call you," he whispered. "I hope we can get together."

The lieutenant sat quietly on the bus to the bachelor officer quarters. The spell of returning home had subdued his usual banter. They unloaded their bags at the BOQ and were assigned a room.

Polito unlocked the door to their quarters and threw his luggage on the first bed. "goddamn, Chief, I wouldn't have waited until the last minute to get her phone number."

"I know," Charging Shield agreed. "I didn't want her to think I was putting on the big hustle."

"Christ, Chief, the way she was eyeballing those wings. Goddamn stews spot every pilot that gets on board. I think I'll stick on a pair of golden leg spreaders next time I get on an airline."

The captain hung his blouse in the closet declining to comment as he removed his tie. Polito continued. "You got an edge being a pilot. Stews see guys like you as a potential airline driver."

"So what? I like stews. I like that stew," his answer was emphatic as he unbuttoned his shirt. "Shower's going to feel good," he said as he stripped to the waist.

Several days were spent at the discharge section. His time was occupied with physical examinations and paperwork. One morning he was sitting in a phone booth talking to Karen; that afternoon they rode together in a Kharman Ghia toward a Pacific beach.

She parked the yellow convertible and reached in the back seat for a duffel bag containing a pair of air mattresses. After walking about a mile, they spread their beach towels. His gaze appraised her legs as she removed her cotton robe. 'Her legs couldn't have been more perfect.' Her calves were strong like a girl who had trained in dancing or ice-skating. Her waist was trim, not too skinny, but trim, and her breasts were prominent but not oversized, and that was fine with him. He wasn't a breast man; not that he didn't appreciate them. 'Hers were okay,' he thought. He was glad they weren't more prominent. 'She had enough attractive features,' he concluded.

She caught his stare as she reached for the air mattress. She knew he was sizing her up, and she felt a twinge of self-consciousness. At least he didn't look disappointed. He wasn't so bad himself. His lustrous black hair, dark tan, broad shoulders, and strong legs appealed to her. More than anything else, it was his confident demeanor, natural and spirited.

They plunged through the pounding surf. After several efforts, they floated comfortably beyond the breakers, waiting to ride the rolling surf. The first wave started to swell. They paddled furiously in pursuit, but failed to catch the breaking crest.

"Better luck next time," she quipped.

"This beats Chu Lai only because the waves are bigger," he laughed, "and not because of some beauty in a bathing suit." He admired her lifted leg as she rested on her mattress.

"Captain Charging Shield, what are you thinking?" she gave him a scolding look. "You're supposed to see if Mother Nature will give us a breaker."

"I know," he answered as he stroked toward her. "But right now I'm engrossed with how beautiful Mother Earth made one of her daughters."

"And that makes us brother and sister," she pretended seriousness.

The air mattresses collided. He dropped into the water, putting his arm around her, holding his mattress with his free hand. "No way do I ever want you as a sister," he said, as a swell gathered its surge toward the invisible moon. Their heads bent toward each other to hold their first kiss while the swell lifted with great power then broke beneath them. As she tumbled into the water, her mattress shot toward shore. He placed his mattress behind her. Their bodies pressed together, holding again their embrace as they slowly drifted toward the beach. The couple breathed heavily and kissed passionately.

Charging Shield felt something slide by his legs. Frantically, he tried to rise, pulling down the air mattress.

"Kyle, what's wrong?" Her eyes widened.

He felt the same intrusion again... then laughed with relief. "Maybe Mother Earth doesn't want us so close. Damn, that scared me. I was brushed by seaweed and thought it was a fish."

"Something is hitting my legs," she sounded startled.

"A fish or seaweed?" he asked apprehensively.

"Seaweed, silly," they both laughed at her reply.

He thought about a reef off the naval base in Puerto Rico and the time a hammerhead had brushed against him out of nowhere. Fortunately, he was able to take refuge in branch coral until the shark decided to leave. "C'mon, let's get your mattress and catch some surf," he said.

Soon they were rising and falling in the foaming ocean. She squealed playfully when a breaker sent her tumbling. Over and over they rode the pounding surf. After awhile, he felt his chest sting as his mattress ground to a halt at the end of a wave. He looked down at his irritated skin beginning to chafe from the sand and the mattress. He glanced at the sky and yelled at her, "We'd better go in for awhile."

"Oh no, it's too much fun," she pleaded as she came up next to him.

"Okay, one more time," he relented.

She ran toward the surf. They bobbed in the sea, waiting for the last wave. Watching a swell raise then gently lower, she decided to ask him again about his ceremonies. "What happens at the Sun Dance?"

He stared at her, admiring her beauty. He wished he were a lion looking at his mate. 'Lions are so beautiful,' he thought, especially their faces. To have that freedom, especially a lion's freedom... he wished he were a male lion resting with his mate on the African veldt.

She repeated the question. "Can you tell me about the Sun Dance... Kyle?"

She brought him from his daydream. "Let's go in," he said. "I'll tell you." He turned toward shore to catch the crest of a wave and soon they were speeding onto the beach.

She wanted to ride the waves longer, but also wanted to hear about the Sun Dance. Ever since she had met this pilot, he had answered to the strange yearning that had been building within her. Somehow, he had bridged into a past that could have been. What that past was, wasn't clear, but when he spoke of his people's way, it satisfied that quest which was becoming more and more a part of her. The sea lapped at her ankles as she left the water to cover herself with a beach towel. A flight of sea gulls flew above the distant waves as they sat in the sand.

"Look!" she said. "Aren't they beautiful? We may fly, but we can never fly like they do. Maybe you could feel free in your Phantom, but I can't say that."

The gulls banked sharply toward them, their silhouettes growing larger. "Oh, to fly like a bird. I wish I could be a bird after I die," she wished aloud.

"What kind would you want to be?"

"Oh, I don't know. What kind would you want to be?" The gulls passed low over them.

"I've returned from war. Maybe it was right and maybe it was wrong, or maybe it was both. Only history will tell, but the combat is still in me." His eyes trailed behind the disappearing gulls. "I was a hunter and also the hunted. I wish I could be an eagle when I die."

"I could be an eagle," she commented lightly but her words held an earnest ring. "But maybe I should be a bird that could sing and wake up a little part of the world, even if it was just a meadow or a forest."

He laughed. "Meadowlark... that's what you remind me of. If I were an eagle in the spirit world, I would fly to your meadow to listen to you sing."

She envisioned a yellow bird, singing freely in a meadow. It was a pleasant thought, offering a secure serenity.

"A meadowlark. Good, I want to be a meadowlark in the spirit world," she agreed. "Tell me about the Sun Dance, Kyle."

"Years ago," he began, "a woman appeared to the Sans Arc band." He paused momentarily and recalled the story that his grandmother had told. "The woman was the Buffalo Calf Maiden... some say White Buffalo Woman." Before he reached the end of his story, he drew a peace pipe in the sand. She leaned forward to study the drawing that he made with his finger and grabbed his hand out of reflex.

"Kyle! I have one of those!"

"A peace pipe?" he blurted.

"I bet you can't believe it! I've had it ever since I was a little girl. It belonged to my great grandmother, I think. Anyway, she gave it to my parents to give to me when I was old enough. It's in an old buckskin bag with beads on it." She eyed him strangely and spoke in a slower, studying tone. "I even used it once, even though I really don't know how to. It always seemed so mysterious to me. I never understood why it was so important that this old lady should travel miles to drop it off. My mom said she didn't even speak English."

Charging Shield looked at her in amazement. He asked about her great grand-mother and wondered if the girl before him would ever know what tribal lineage still coursed through her.

Karen felt exhilarated, finally satisfied about the strange pipe that came to her, yet she managed to subdue any outward show of ecstasy while he continued to explain.

"We call our pipes our portable altars." He looked over his shoulder to the east. "The Buffalo Calf Maiden told them how to use the pipe and where they could find the red pipe stone." He drew a circle in the sand then divided the circle in quadrants, explaining the power of the hoop surrounding the four directions. "Our bodies, the trees, the moon, the world, they're round like the circle, unending and forever." At that moment, a lone seagull drifted behind the girl, to effortlessly hover on an ocean breeze. The seagull reminded him of her wish. "We believe life is like the circle. After this life, we'll come back, but maybe in another way. Maybe you'll get to be a meadowlark after all and I'll be an eagle." He smiled as he shrugged his shoulders. "Be better than having to live like a lot of people do."

She followed his stare to watch the seagull drop its wing and fly behind a sand dune. "I believe life is like a circle," she replied, to his astonishment.

He turned to the symbol drawn in the sand before explaining the colors that he had learned from his grandmother. "The four colors stand for the four races of man."

"And the four races of woman," she added to his explanation.

"And the four races of woman," he agreed with a smile and continued, "red, yellow, black and white."

BUFFALO WOMAN

He erased the figure in the sand. Next he told her about the Sun Dance and, this time, he referred to the same spirit woman as the Buffalo Woman who brought the tribes together for the annual gathering.

'A woman brought the teaching to the tribes.' She liked that concept. 'Now that's unusual.' She especially appreciated what he had to say about the Buffalo Woman.

He elaborated on the Sun Dance. "On the last day, the men pierce." He pointed to his chest that showed no scars. "They give their pain so the people, the tribe, will live."

Karen winced. "It hurts just thinking about it. Do women get pierced in the chest too?"

He explained. "Some women dance the Sun Dance right alongside the men, but they do not have to pierce. Because they bear children, they already suffer more pain than men do so that the people may live. In this way, the tribe recognizes and acknowledges that women give of themselves so all of us can come into this world."

"I never thought of it that way, but you're right. I like that, Kyle." She leaned forward. "Women have more power than they realize. They have the power to create life! Even women who never bear children, they suffer pain too, every month!" She felt inspired. "We really are powerful!"

He acknowledged her remark with a nod. He told her about the return of the Sun Dance and how Eagle Feather and Fools Crow brought the ceremony back. She asked about the holy men.

"Once a holy man acquires his power, he keeps it by fasting and praying on a mountaintop or a badland butte. The holy men say you have to be humble. When they go up on a mountain, they call it vision quest."

Charging Shield reclined to admire the sunset. It was red... 'The edge of the world,' he thought. The red sunset over the ocean cast an auburn tint to her hair. He stretched his legs out, suggesting they should soon be leaving.

"I didn't realize it was so late," she said, looking at the sun disappearing beyond the rim of the Pacific. "I feel so small when I look out there. Think how vast and powerful something, somewhere must be." The cirrus clouds high above still reflected a peach-red glow. "I like to watch clouds," she said simply, looking upward, but there was depth to her words. "I see so many figures... once I saw a buffalo... it was so real..." She looked at him shyly. Her statement had brought him to an attentive sitting position. She wiped the sand from her legs as she rose, avoiding his gaze, to look back at the sea.

The surf invited one last swim. The couple vanished in the breakers then swam to deeper water. After they returned, they dried themselves silently with their towels. He deflated the mattresses, packing them in the duffel bag. They walked quietly in the twilight. She was lost in her own reverie, feeling as though she had been allowed to reach into a preferred past. Her look was one of pleasured contentment as she watched the last rays of fading sunset arc to violet and purple. After awhile, they stopped and stood facing each other. He turned her head to brush several grains of sand that clung to her hair. When he bent forward to kiss her, he dropped the duffel bag as she looped her arms around his neck. They held each other in a long embrace. He reached down and picked up the bag before they walked slowly, their arms entwined.

He asked if he could drive. It had been awhile since he had been behind the wheel of a civilian car. She handed him the keys and soon he was entering the freeway leading back to her apartment. Time had darkened the skies and the night air streamed through the side windows.

"I can't get my mind off what you told me," she said as they drove away from the beach. "I wish I could see a ceremony."

He couldn't visualize her at the Sun Dance with him. He would be too busy, he alibied to himself. "Yes, they are interesting." he answered in a non-committing tone.

Karen broke a period of silence. "Kyle, why aren't you married, or have you been?"

"No one wants me," he laughed. His smile erased. "I was going with a girl from home. She married someone else."

"Was she Indian?"

"Yes," he answered with a curt nod.

"Did she ever go to a Sun Dance with you?"

He shook his head. "She wasn't interested." His answer was quick and cold. "Her parents preached assimilation. Like most Indians I know. They want to cut from the past. I have a brother and a sister like that."

"I'd go to a ceremony if I had a chance," she said testing.

He turned off the freeway to drive the short distance to her parking lot. "Why aren't you married?" he returned the question, avoiding her comment.

"I'm not grown up enough. I want to live first, find out who I am, have some adventures. My sister married when she was eighteen. I just can't imagine wasting my youth that way. Besides, I won't settle for any one but the right man, the one who wants to hang out in my cabin with me and listen to the birds sing." She sighed. "Marriage is a big commitment, and I plan on making it only once." She had found herself thinking more and more about the cabin, ever since she met this pilot with a culture so different from the dominating sea of humanity around them.

As they rode the elevator to her apartment he put his hand on her long loose hair. She gave him a slight, almost imperceptible nod when she turned to him. They embraced and kissed until the elevator came to a stop.

Karen laughed as she placed the key in the door, thinking about how their being together had stifled her appetite. "I don't know about you, but I haven't been hungry all day. Maybe you want a sandwich or something more?"

"I might have been hungry before I kissed you. You are doing wonders with my appetite."

She busied herself in the kitchen while he surveyed her apartment from the living room. A shoji screen, brass lamps and carved fruit reflected her trips to the Orient. Several paintings of beach scenes with seagulls hung from a wall, which he admired, especially her signature on the oils in a lower corner. A Japanese tape deck centered a set of bookshelves. After awhile, the hungry couple sat on the couch eating a pair of ham and cheese sandwiches. When she placed her napkin on the coffee table, he reached across her lap. At the touch of their hands, he thought back to when she was sitting on the armrest in the 707.

"I like to believe that the experiences we have and the people we meet - they don't happen by accident," she pronounced prophetically.

"And in regards to our meeting?" he asked.

She countered his question with one of her own. "What do you think?"

Her voice reminded him of his grandmother's. His lightheartedness left him, and he nodded with a serious look. "You are a very interesting woman, Karen. Completely different than anyone I have ever met since joining the Marines."

She laughed. "I hope I'm not too different." She stared out the window. "When do you have to go back?" she asked.

"I'm in casual company. I don't have much to do except wait for my discharge."

"When will that be?"

"It has to be soon. The Sun Dance starts next week. I have to be there. If my orders don't come, I'll take leave. I can always come back and get discharged."

"Could I see the Sun Dance?"

"Not many non-Indians... I mean people, who aren't familiar, see it."

She bristled for a moment. "I'm not exactly a non-Indian, Captain Charging Shield." Her voice lightened. "What would happen if I went to the Sun Dance with you? Let's say if we knew each other better, and I wanted to see it." There was a note of persistency in her voice.

He didn't like the way the question confronted him. He replied that if he took part in the Sun Dance, he wouldn't have much time to spend with her.

"Are you going to be in it?"

"You have to be asked by the holy men. After all the combat I saw, coming home in one piece, I'd have to do it if they asked me." His eyes rested on woven burlap suspending a vase from the ceiling. After a few moments of silence, he continued, "I know I'd be afraid to be pierced, but I promised Fools Crow I'd do it if he asked me."

"Fools Crow. That's an interesting name. He's one of the medicine men?"

"A holy man," he declared. "Holy man is a better word."

"I wish I could do things like you," she said, somewhat tormented. "You have a tribe to be part of."

He wanted to steer her away from the Sun Dance. He moved a couch pillow to tug gently at her waist. He pulled her closer and nuzzled his face into her hair.

She giggled. "What did you mean when you said you'd be afraid to be pierced? I wouldn't think you'd be afraid of anything by now."

He wished she would put the Sun Dance matter to rest. He placed his fingers close to her lips. "This isn't the time to be talking about that." He placed his hand around her shoulder and began kissing her neck.

"Kyle..."

"One more question and you'll turn into a toad," he whispered in her ear.

Karen slipped off her shoes and cuddled next to him, burying her head into his shoulder so he would have to stop kissing. Part of her wanted to surrender completely to his touch. Her body ached to be with him. Yet another part wanted to keep a firm reign on her passion, to keep it in check so she could stay in control. Kyle reached across her with his free arm, and gave her a hug. She tilted her body toward him as he slid his arm past her shoulder; his hand lightly brushed her breast and stopped to rest on her forearm.

A surge of frivolity helped him lighten the moment. He spoke quietly, "Karen, If you had been born Indian, perhaps I could predict your destiny."

"Really? What would you predict for me?"

Charging Shield laughed at her enthusiastic response. "I don't know." He placed his fingers on his temples, closed his eyes, and spoke in a low voice, "It's your destiny to make passionate love with a lonely Marine just back from the front lines of battle." He leaned forward and kissed her lips. She leaned into the kiss and placed her hands around the back of his neck. Charging Shield pushed his weight forward until she was beneath him on the couch.

"Kyle," she spoke as he undid the top button of her blouse and kissed her collarbone. Her upper back tensed. "Kyle," she said again quietly, putting her hands on his head. "I feel like this is all moving so fast. Maybe we should slow it down some."

He stopped kissing and looked into her eyes. He couldn't help showing his disappointment. "Okay... sure. You're probably right." He tried to sound composed. He sat up and put his hand on hers. The penetrating look of her eyes almost hypnotized him into a tired stupor. The jet lag and days of little sleep hit him suddenly. He let out a slumber bound yawn.

She nodded and couldn't help but laugh. It relieved the tension for both of them. He rested his head back, oblivious to the laugh, closing his eyes and, as he did so, she studied his sharp nose, wide cheekbones and tapering chin. She pictured him astride a pony, somewhere on the open prairie, glorying in life and the sky around him. 'How incongruous for him to be lying here in this Los Angeles apartment,' she thought.

He opened his eyes and looked quietly. 'I could study those eyes forever,' she said to herself. 'There's something mysterious about them, yet familiar. It's like they're a thousand years old.'

Their conversation at the beach echoed in her mind. Somewhere, somehow, she had been a part of the ceremonies. A meadowlark is what he said she would be. A trace of a smile touched the corners of her mouth. A picture of a cabin flashed through her mind. One with a tiny stream, hidden beneath clusters of wild plum and choke cherry bushes. 'The cabin with a stream in back.' There was a heavy hovering above the cabin. An eagle glided toward a tall tree, settling next to its mate. Her eyes focused on the huge talons, gripping the bark of the thick branch. One of the birds sprang from the branch and flapped down to the meadow. It grew smaller and fluttered as it landed. 'Yes... the eagle could change to a meadowlark!' The meadowlark sang.

The air conditioner clicked. "You've made me do a lot of thinking. It's a strange and beautiful thing to carry your people's culture in my thoughts but I think we should call it a night. You can sleep here on the couch or else I can take you back to the base. I would love to take you back in the morning. Maybe you can show me a Phantom jet." She spoke with a tired yawn, "I can barely keep my eyes open." She smiled, when she heard him issue a soft snore.

She draped a blanket over him and sat by the edge of the couch to kiss him once more. Only the monotonous hum of the air conditioner filled the apartment's silence. She looked down at him like a benevolent mate while he slept soundly. She gave him a gentle kiss on his forehead before she left for her bedroom. He was already in dreamland as she crept quietly away. He was an eagle resting on a badland butte and his mate next to him had just brushed her beak across the crest of his head.

FAREWELL

CHAPTER NINE

I will sing for you
I will wait for you
— Sioux Love Song

Polito yelled from his bed when he opened the door to the BOQ room, "Chief, you slick son-of-a-bitch, how is she?"

Charging Shield stiffened.

The lieutenant's wink accompanied a sly grin. "C'mon, you spent all night with the broad. I just got back from Tijuana... had a couple short times and a blow job. Might've paid for it, but it's cheaper in the long run."

"Polito, I don't pander fuck stories to be one of the boys. She hasn't been laying me or the troops. Okay?"

"Goddamn, Chief, you don't have to get so touchy. I just asked if you got laid. What's wrong with that?"

"Polito, some girls don't screw right off the bat. She's the kind you white folks would take home to mother."

"Bullshit, aviator, you got this white world pretty well psyched out. You sure as hell meet the broads."

Charging Shield glanced at his roommate as he removed his shirt. "Yeah, but you've been laid and I haven't, now that should make you happy."

Polito drew himself to a sitting position and slapped his leg with an accomplished grin. "Chief, you mean you haven't had any pussy? Holy Chrriist! Get laid! I've seen too many troopers wait for that hometown piece of ass and then wind up getting married. A hard-on can make you fall in love fast after a combat tour. Before you know it, you're in debt for a couple of rug monkeys and a ball and chain."

"Polito, you gross bastard, you just described your fate. You'll be pushing a lawn mower and your rug monkeys will be as ugly as you are. On top of that, you'll be dumb and happy like your future wife."

Polito glowered. "Love 'em and leave 'em. You better watch out Chief. This stew is going to play it cool and get you a ball and chain."

Charging Shield laughed. "Now that wouldn't be all that bad." He walked into the bathroom and opened his shaving kit.

"How'd you get back to the base?"

"Borrowed her car."

The lieutenant reached for his trousers. "Holy shit, Chief. No pussy, but you got her car. Just a matter of time now." He looked at his watch. "It's getting late. I'll call us in," he said with an envious frown.

"Find out what time the dental ward opens," Charging Shield called to the lieutenant leaving the room. He removed his clothes and stepped into the shower. As the warm water sprayed down, he thought about the girl. The smell of fresh coffee had awakened him that morning. He was fascinated by her legs when he walked into the kitchen... and that pleasant voice, such a soothing, lifting voice when she greeted him.

He savored their kiss just before he left. She was more responding, more relaxed. He was glad he had restrained himself the night before on the couch. He liked everything about her. She had occupied his thoughts as he drove to the base. He looked forward to the evening. The war was behind him and now he had met a woman, this woman, seemingly more and more a special woman. He tried to recall a vague dream that had come to him in her living room. He was an eagle in the dream, lifting from a fall-green meadow. Beside him, another eagle rose in flight. They were like a pair of Phantoms ascending a cooling wind rising above the Black Hills and the Badlands. In the distance he could see the Sun Dance grounds. A circle of vultures was slowly descending toward the centering tree and the people dancing. The pair attacked, scattering the ugly birds. After the fray, the eagles wheeled and circled in play before locking talons to cartwheel toward his grandmother's abandoned cabin. They broke their fall only a few feet above the earth. When he landed, the dark haired girl was beside him. She smiled and laughed. Her laugh was like one fighter pilot's laugh to another after a mission. He had the feeling of returning from war in that dream and now, a woman, this woman, had taken him in.

After he dressed, he spent most of the morning at the dental ward. He had decided to remain in the Marine Corps Reserves and was assigned to a Reserve helicopter squadron in the Twin Cities. The Reserve pay would aid his college expenses and he could fly extra weekends during the summer months when he was not in school. Noontime found him shopping in the Post Exchange, wondering about the Sun Dance. He was anxious to return home, yet wanted to continue his new relationship. He planned the evening. Before dinner he would take her to a squadron and let her sit in a Phantom. First he would have to get permission, he reminded himself. He would stop in at an F-4 squadron that afternoon. After he left the PX, he walked back to his room. A telephone message from the BOQ steward was pinned to the door.

"I have to go out on a flight," she said after he returned her call. "Scheduling has everything all mixed up. They put me on a reserve list."

"I'll be right there," he said with disappointment. He didn't bother to change his uniform and drove the Kharman Ghia onto the freeway.

She met him at the door with her suitcase. "I never thought I'd have to fly so soon," she said dejectedly as he opened the car door for her. "I made a trade but it didn't go through."

He turned the car from the parking lot. "I wanted to take you to the Officer's Club for dinner tonight."

She moaned and reached across to touch his forearm. "I would have loved that. Let's do it when I get back." She directed him toward the airport freeway. When he entered an approach lane, she turned toward him, raising her knee to cross her legs. He stole an admiring glance.

"You know," she said, "I've been thinking about you all morning."

"What a coincidence," he grinned. They both sat quietly for a moment savoring the newness and exhilaration of a blossoming relationship.

"I've been thinking about what we talked about last night," she finally broke in. "It baffles me that the Indians flourished on this continent for centuries, and then the white man came along and destroyed so much in just a short time." She glanced out the window and back at Kyle. "How did you manage to stay with your people's culture?"

"I had a Grandmother that I could listen to. But it goes beyond that." He paused for a moment to collect his thoughts. "The missionaries and the Bureau of Indian Affairs built boarding schools and all the children had to leave home. They never saw their parents most of the year. It's easy to destroy culture when you have a whole tribe of children locked away. I was lucky; I didn't go to a boarding school very long. My brother Lawrence... we ran away."

"Your parents?"

"My mom, my dad, all my brothers and sisters. They all went through the boarding schools. They didn't learn about our way." He paused to reflect. "My dad remembered from his grandparents, but kept it pretty much to himself. In his time, you didn't speak up. We moved off the reservation and the missionaries talked my mom into sending me back to the boarding school." A dark scowl turned defiant. "My dad... it was the only time I saw him tear into my mom and those priests, when they came up to get me. They couldn't take me back since we didn't live on the reservation. Schools in West River weren't a picnic for an Indian, but better than being away from Mom and Dad. My grandmother put me onto my Indian road."

A Lincoln Continental filled his rearview mirror. His thoughts returned to the boarding school. He remembered the brother's firm grip while the priest beat him with a leather belt. He was too small to remember much more but he did remember that it took three brothers to hold Lawrence. And the loneliness, the dreaded loneliness when the bus would take them to the boarding school. It was lonely was all he could really remember... and being away from his parents. Thank God, especially for Lawrence and Mildred, and even Hobart and Leona. He pushed the accelerator to dart around a semi-truck. When he changed lanes, the Lincoln sped by. The quick action turned his thoughts away from his past. He was concentrating on merging traffic entering from a crossing freeway, when he felt a moist kiss on his cheek. He turned, startled to see her close beside him. She gave him another quick kiss before she settled back in her seat.

"What was that for?"

"For running away," she said.

They parked the car at the terminal and walked to the flightline.

"You're going back to Okinawa?"

"Yes, she said solemnly, "We'll have Marines again on this trip."

"Unless they call out the reserves, I'll never make another tour. That was a year ago, but it seems like yesterday."

"I'll be back Sunday," she said, "but I don't know the time." She offered a relaxed sigh. "Then I'll have a couple weeks off. I'm going to interview with some other airlines."

"I'll check with base operations and meet you at El Toro," he replied. "You know something? We haven't known each other very long, but I'm going to miss you."

She reached for his arm. "I feel the same way."

"You're thinking about working for another company?"

She nodded. "After the war's over, these charter companies will be cutting down on personnel."

They walked along silently, finally he said, "I wish I wouldn't have talked so much. It was pretty one-sided."

"Oh no," she answered. "I wanted to hear what you told me. I wish we'd had more time together. You'll meet me when I come in?"

"I will, don't worry." His face flushed. "I really shouldn't be using your car. I can catch a bus back to the base."

"No, take it," she said as she shook her head. "I'm going to try getting off at El Toro since all the passengers will deplane there. If I can't, you can come get me here."

They walked down a corridor in the overseas terminal. At the departure gate, he gave her a brief kiss while the ticket agent unlocked the boarding ramp door. "See you at El Toro," he said as he turned away.

"Kyle," she called. She looked at him with anxious eyes when he turned back toward her. "I have something to ask you. It means a lot to me."

"Okay," he replied.

"Can I go with you to the Sun Dance?"

He didn't want her to ask the question. He tried to think, groping for a reason. "We're still strangers. We don't know each other that well."

"We're not strangers, Kyle," her tone was firm.

He threw her remark aside. "You won't be ready for it," he stammered.

"Ready for it; what do you mean?" she asked.

"Well... I may have to leave within a day or two after you return whether or not I get my discharge. What about your interviews?"

"That isn't any problem," she smiled. "I can do that later. Don't you remember when I told you I loved adventure?" Her determination made him uneasy.

"I like you a lot, Karen, and I want to be with you when you come back, but I may have to be in the Sun Dance if the holy men want me to. I really should be there by myself, except for relatives. Out there, I won't have time, even for you."

"But Kyle, I..."

His words cut into hers, "I'm sorry, Karen, it just won't work."

She lowered her head. The two stood in awkward silence. He reached under her chin and raised her head slowly. "It just seemed like a wonderful adventure," she said softly.

"Karen, I don't think you understand. If you were there and I was in the ceremony, it would be hard for me to concentrate on what I should be doing."

She crossed her arms. "Maybe you don't want a white girl on your home grounds..." her words trailed. Her sad expression reminded him of a shepherd pup he once had.

He watched her steps carry her toward the departure gate. He felt himself sinking into a lonely pit. "Karen, wait a second," he called.

She stopped and turned around. Her eyes melted him as he approached. "Please let me go with you," she begged.

His brain whirled in panic, rushing his words and thoughts. She threw her arms around him when he relented. "Alright, you can go." But the minute he spoke, he knew he was wrong. She was too excited from his answer for him to break his word.

When he unlocked the door of the convertible, he muttered to himself, 'You dumb son-of-a-bitch.' He hated himself all the way to El Toro. What would his relatives say? She would be one helluva distraction. It would ruin everything.

The days went by slowly. The thought of her being at the Sun Dance troubled him deeply. The ceremony and his relatives would demand his time. Worse, the contrast between the two would not go well with the Oglalas waiting to honor one of their own, who was returning from the white man's war unharmed because of the power of the Indian Way, the Natural Way.

Most importantly, he had called on his own traditions before going off to war. He was one of the first in the new movement starting to sweep the Native American world. He had explored the white man's way, yet preferred his own beliefs and now the Oglalas would want to see that preference demonstrated without distraction. 'Akicita, Akicita!' The words ran through his mind. 'Yes, a true Akicita would not allow any distraction.' Yet he wouldn't break his word to her. It was such a powerful feeling that he had for her. He shrugged his shoulders and resigned himself to whatever course he would end up taking. He wanted to see more of her, this was definite he knew. He would toss it out to the Six Powers, to the Four Directions or whatever mysterious forces there were that could act on such a matter.

Saturday morning his orders arrived. He would be discharged the following day. That same morning, he checked flight operations and was told that her World Airways flight had been grounded in Hawaii and would not be scheduled to return until after he would have to leave for the Sun Dance.

Karen slumped back to her apartment after her flight had landed several days later. She had read the emphatic note he had left taped to her door, telling her that her car keys were in the manager's office and explaining why he had to be at the beginning of the Sun Dance. The note also listed his mother's address. She grabbed a bottle of wine from the refrigerator to comfort her remorse and carried it to the couch. The first glass went down easily. She kicked off her shoes and peeled off her uniform before pouring another. She reclined on the couch and placed the glass on her stomach. 'So what if we are from different cultures?' She thought of the electricity she felt on the airplane during their first meeting, the passionate kiss in the ocean, their long talks about subjects dear to her. She swirled the wine around in her glass, watching the circles it made on the inside. "You and I, Captain Kyle Charging Shield," she said aloud, holding her glass to the ceiling, "are connected. Like it or not." As she raised her free hand to wipe off the makeup that was smeared under her eyes, she recalled their conversation about the eagle and the meadowlark. She placed the glass on the coffee table and smiled through her tears as she drifted off to sleep.

The despair, the sickness, the drumming, it all peeked back into her consciousness like a nosy neighbor who doesn't know the meaning of privacy. The tree, oh

DANCING EAGLES

the tree, and the jovial woman. "What took you so long to get here?" she said. "We've been waiting."

Karen shrugged her shoulders. "Where am I? What is this place?"

"Come, I will show you." In a whoosh the woman vaporized into a cloud. "Come, woman," she commanded, "climb aboard."

From where Karen stood she saw an image of a buffalo in the cloud. She blinked and shook her head. As she stepped onto the cloud she brushed a piece of hair from her eyes. She was surprised to find her hair tied in braids.

The cloud rose slowly. 'Such a dramatic feeling,' she thought, when her feet lifted from the ground. She was now clothed in moccasins and a fringed buckskin dress. She laughed at how light and natural she felt. The buffalo floated her above the tree where they first met, above the healthy people, feasting, playing and singing. Over the barren land she was carried.

"Look behind you," the buffalo instructed. She turned to see the tree growing, its branches lengthening, as if spreading out to shade the corners of the world. Small bands of people approached from the Four Corners of the Universe to gather and stand beneath the branches. Other small bands of people came from different points of the horizon to join them. The tree continued to unfold.

"It's time for you to get off the cloud now," the buffalo commanded.

"What? So fast? Aren't we going back to the feast?"

"Get off. Now." The woman's voice replaced the buffalo's.

"Now? But we're in the middle of the air! Aren't we going to land first?"

"You have more power than you think. I'm going to disappear soon. Take the leap."

"But I'm scared."

"Take the leap!" she thundered as the cloud lost its form and changed to rolling mist.

She closed her eyes and jumped off the cloud. The fear of falling overcame her as the hard ground zoomed closer. The cloud woman's voice echoed in her mind. 'You have more power than you think.' Just above the ground she extended her arms and felt a source of power that stopped the onrushing earth. Upward the force of her newfound thrust landed her on a high badland butte. She caught a glimpse of another time. She no longer had arms, for they were eagle's wings. It was such a profound contentment in another time. Was it in the past or was it really now and was she just in some other form? Possibly it was in the future, but it really didn't matter, she acknowledged to herself. Her feeling on the butte was such pure contentment. "This Charging Shield. Let him go. He has a mission to fulfill." The voice spoke silently yet it seemed to reverberate from every gully, crest and valley. It was more powerful than cloud woman's voice.

She looked out across the jagged badland spires and on the horizon was her eagle mate. He was flying away but he would return she sensed, because for her and for him there really was no time. As a pair of great birds they had transformed past that entity called time that had to be for the two-legged forms. She and her mate were in that ultimate design of the circle where form was endless. "Go on to your mission my gallant knight," she called out a verse that did not fit the time. 'Yes, indeed,' she thought, 'we have been upon many quests.' She stretched her great wings and drew in a deep breath of Badlands air. She would relax and wait and maybe even fly off to see what her mate was about, for eventually his mission was but the beginning of a more powerful quest of her own.

FOOLS CROW

CHAPTER TEN

Circular No. 1665   *April 26, 1921*

> *The Sun Dance and all similar dances and so-called*
> *religious ceremonies are considered Indian Offenses*
> *under existing regulations, and corrective penalties are provided.*
> *— Charles H. Burke*
> *Commissioner, Office of Indian Affairs*

Fools Crow tied his warbonnet to the tipi flap pole. The tall holy man was unusually muscular and agile for a man long past his physical prime. His tent had risen the day before on the eastern edge of the campgrounds. At the center of the encampment and a stone's throw in diameter was the Sun Dance arena. Pairs of pine poles, spaced about a car length apart, formed the perimeter of the arena. At the top of the cut off poles, at twice the height of a sun dancer, some nailed and some tied, thinner poles criss-crossed to form a flat platform for freshly strewn pine boughs and resultant shade. Gap, the foreman for the final touches made on the arbor bower, had made his report to Fools Crow, the Sun Dance Intercessor and was driving away in his battered pickup truck with a few unused poles in the pickup's box. It was Tuesday, the day before the cutting down of the Sun Dance tree and most of the holy men, sun dancers, singers, drummers and local traditionalists had arrived to select their campsites.

Several hundred yards away, as distinctive as Fools Crow's high, cream-colored tipi, a squat, silver, Air Stream camper trailer was parked. Inside, Mildred busied herself cooking while her husband, Ralph, a white man, unloaded water cans and folding chairs from a pickup.

Ninety miles to the north, Charging Shield rose from his mother's couch to drive his sister's car to the reservation. When he arrived at the sun dance grounds, he was greeted with an offer of fried prairie chicken. His mouth watered as he lifted the lid of the pan warming on the stove. Mildred set a plate of chicken for him on a small coffee table. His sister was a decade older then he and heavy set like her husband.

"Mom's coming down," her eyes furtively sought his reaction. "She didn't want to mention it, when you first got back. She doesn't want you in the Sun Dance."

"She said something this morning," he answered without expression. He wore new jeans over a pair of plain brown western boots. A short sleeve khaki shirt still bearing military creases was tucked into his jeans and under a wide leather belt. The only elaboration of his dress was an oval belt buckle covered with sky-blue beads and the silver and black outline of an eagle hovering over a prairie butte. The handmade beadwork had been a gift from his sister while he was in Vietnam. He took his seat on the couch behind the low table. Neither he nor his mother had sought a confrontation that morning. He passed over lightly her remark about the Sun Dance, answering that holy men would have to ask him first.

"She wouldn't mind half as much if those damned priests would quit stirring her up," Ralph growled. "Those Jesuits got your brother, Hobart, and your sis, Leona, working on her. Long as I been around, I ain't never seen those two at Indian doings."

"They tried to get Lawrence to side with 'em," his sister added. "He told both of 'em off. He said he'd done a lot of wrong in his day and most of it comin' out of a bottle, but one thing he'd never do is stick his nose in a man's religion. Hobart and him nearly got in a fight."

Charging Shield appreciated their consideration. He doubted if his sister would sound as firm had their mother been present. Mildred had lived too close to home for her first marriage. She had placed her parents and even her brothers and sisters before her former husband. Her only regret, brought on by her divorce, and that in itself weighed heavily, was the denial of Sunday Communion. She had endured twelve years of mission boarding school indoctrination, an emotional, pain-inflicted past that churned the haunting denial of church sacraments within her troubled consciousness. Paradoxically, Ralph had become a steadying harbor; more so as the years of their close relationship increased. The couple faithfully attended the annual Sun Dance and, each year, within Mildred, the meek and obsequious mold cast from the boarding school years slowly yielded to a rebellious spirit.

Charging Shield admired his good-hearted yet candid brother-in-law. The man made his living as a locomotive engineer for the railroad. He wasn't a churchgoer, but he was as guileless and unpretentious as any of the most unblemished faithful. Ralph had a reputation for fair dealing and the ability to size up one's credibility with a respectable degree of accuracy. In many ways, Charging Shield likened Ralph to his brother, Lawrence, except that Ralph was outspoken and confident, whereas Lawrence was most often reclusive and quiet except when he was alone with his youngest brother, Kyle or with drinking friends. Hobart had neither of the two men's characteristics. Hobart was selfish, determined and ambitious. Charging Shield distrusted Hobart's concern over his participation in the Sun Dance. The striving businessman had never expressed much interest in his activities before. Ralph's remark seemed to read his thoughts.

"Hobart ain't all that bothered about saving your soul, kid," Ralph was blunt. "He's got that store of his in hock to some bank. He's more worried what them big shots around West River will say. Besides, there's talk your friend Ernie Hale has got him interested in politics; city council or something like that."

"Alderman," Mildred corrected.

Charging Shield looked at his brother-in-law with disbelief, but as he recalled his arrival home, he began to believe there was truth in what Ralph had indicated. Ernie was almost like glue around the family when he had arrived at the airport, making a point of having both brothers pose together for the newspaper photographer and the elaborate reception which followed at Ernie's spacious hilltop home with a commanding view of West River.

Ralph interrupted his thoughts, "I know what you're thinking kid. You don't believe an Indian can make it in West River politics and I'd say he ain't got a snow-ball's chance in hell, but if you got Ernie and his money behind you, anything can happen. You sure as hell didn't hurt anything for your brother, coming back with all those ribbons on your chest."

No wonder his mother had avoided any discussion of the Sun Dance. After the reception, he had a private party with just Ernie and Lawrence, and his throbbing head was now paying the price. He pushed his plate back and sat silently.

"Only one thing in Hobart's mind, brother. He's going to make it in the white man's world come hell or high water. And you know your sister Leona. All she's ever cared about was passin' for white. Both of 'em trying to live too high off the hog for their own good." Mildred offered a disgusted comment. "Neither one's going to advertise bein' Indian."

Charging Shield studied his sister for a moment before addressing her with a direct question. "How come you and Lawrence... you're not like those two? You all went to the same boarding school."

"I don't know," she shook her head. "Lawrence and Hobart, them two always been different since the day they was born. In boarding school, Hobart went along with the priests and the nuns; Lawrence, he fought back. We always heard how good Hobart was, but when I think back on that damned school, all by ourselves, away from the folks, it was Lawrence that stuck up for me and Leona. Anytime he'd get something extra to eat, he'd sneak over to the girls' side and share with us. Hobart, he'd never do anything like that." Her voice carried a touch of vehemence. "Hobart always followed the rules," she looked up and added wearily. "After I left that school, I used to be like Leona. Ashamed as hell of bein' Indian."

Her confession brought a troubled expression. Her eyes settled on Ralph, dissolving her distraught composure. "Your brother-in-law there, he ain't like that phony bank clerk Leona's married to."

Ralph's questioning look made her elaborate further. She pointed a finger at her husband. "Ralph, you was the one that said we ought to go to the dances. And that was before they had these big crowds." She turned to her brother. "I'm lucky I got someone who understands. I guess I always had it in me... wantin' to know more... where we come from. I guess most everybody deep down in... they want to know, but that can get killed off in different ways. It ain't no good bein' ashamed, no matter how you cover it up."

"I was raised just across the Rosebud Reservation line, Kyle." Ralph put his over-sized hand on his shoulder. "Good thing I was big. Had to fight my way out of a scrap or two on both sides. Always a few got to shoot their mouth off about who a man chooses to run with. Back then, a lot of these little towns had baseball teams. Those days some good players came out of the reservations. The war came along and we all joined the service. After the war, I played ball with Lawrence and met your sis. Teams paid Lawrence good money to pitch." A smile crossed his face. "I got called a 'squaw man'... only twice that I can remember." He doubled his fist. 'Didn't take long for folks to learn not to make fun of Ralph and your sis." The heavy man pushed the plate toward his brother-in-law. "The way I see it, long as we don't bother anybody, we got a right in this country to go with who we damn well please or pray the way we damn well please, too." Ralph stopped abruptly with almost an embarrassed look. He wasn't used to making speeches. He pushed the plate of meat toward Charging Shield. "You better eat this prairie chicken. You get into that Sun Dance and you're going to wish you had some food in your belly." His voice lowered and was less emphatic.

Charging Shield's mood lightened. Ralph's words fortified his resolve. He picked up a drumstick, waving it in the direction of the arena. "If the holy men ask, I'll go through the Sun Dance," he replied stubbornly.

Later, he walked through the growing campground. He thought about the California girl as he drew closer to Fools Crow's tipi. He felt a longing for the stewardess as he stopped to survey the tents springing from the alkali dust and prairie sage. 'It wouldn't be right,' he tried to convince himself. 'Not now. Not if they ask me to do the Sun Dance.' He hoped somehow, however, some way he would see her again.

When he came abreast of the tipi with the warbonnet fluttering in the early evening breeze, he heard his name called out in an excited voice. Chief Fools Crow had seen him through the open tent flap and had called out his name as he emerged from the large tipi. He grasped the holy man's hand as Kate Fools Crow stepped from the tent. Tears came to her eyes as she walked on past him to face the south, extending her arms to sing a high tremolo... 'Le le le lah, le le le lah'... four times. The tremolo was a woman's honoring. She had to thank the power within her husband's medicine first, before she could greet their guest. After she was finished, she turned and hugged him. The tall woman was a few inches shorter than her husband and a decade younger. She smelled of campfire smoke and fresh coffee. While she clutched him tightly, his grandmother lived again for a brief moment.

Kate spoke in Lakota and started to cry. Her words were simply:

"A warrior has returned.
You have come back
with honor.
I knew you would."

Fools Crow and Charging Shield stood in silence. She was crying for those who would never return and for those who would only sing the tremolo at the burial grounds, and there were many who were buried from the white man's wars.

Finally, Kate was through, allowing the two men to visit. The holy man sat in a wooden chair and offered his guest an overturned wooden packing box that was long enough to sit several persons. Charging Shield noted the holy man's graying, thinning hair and the deepening wrinkles around his eyes. The holy man was into his seventies but his endurance, gait and alertness belied his age. Fools Crow's dark eyes were his most revealing feature. They conveyed a mystical penetration that reached a man's soul. Kyle tried to recall the language spoken often by his parents, as the old man spoke to him in fluent Lakota. He brought the *wotai* from under his shirt and held it momentarily, then made flying motions toward the ground as he attempted to answer in broken English and Sioux.

"*Maza soo*... bullets... ehh shells *wa-neecha*... 100 times, Grandpa. *Wakan Takan. Oh pah win gay won ze. Week chim nah Ah nak kek shin.* (The Great Spirit protected me 100 times)." He managed to convey in broken Lakota.

"Ho lela waste (wah shtay) *aloh... Wo peh la miye,"* Fools Crow replied. Very good, I am thankful." The old man sat back, confident of the *Yuwipi* Power that had been so accurate in the ceremony. A fatherly warmth emitted from the powerful eyes.

"Son, *Wacikiya wiwanyag wachipi?* You dance the Sun Dance?" he asked in English, aware that his fellow tribesman was not fluent in Lakota. Seldom did the holy man speak in English.

Charging Shield replied, *"Hau* (Yes)."

"Waste aloh. (Very good)." The old man exclaimed. *"Hihanna leh che."* Fools Crow pointed to Charging Shield and then to the ground with a cutting motion. *"Wagan chon kickaksah.* (Tomorrow we will meet here to cut down the sacred tree)."

"Waste aloh, Grandpa," Charging Shield bowed his head. He shook the old man's hand and started to walk away, stopping momentarily beside Kate who sat forlorn, her mind still absorbed with the many deaths the reservation had encountered over the past wars for the white man. He bent to hug the woman but was afraid she would start to cry again.

"You are back, Son. You must stay now. No more war. Go to school," she said in English.

"Yes, Grandma," he spoke obediently. "Yes, Grandma. No more warrior... *wichasta wa neech* (warrior no more)." He made quick hand motions of a horseback rider falling, then pointed to himself. He made another gesture with his hands of a man aiming a rifle and then throwing the weapon away. He then crossed two fingers over the pointing finger of his left hand and gestured a horseback rider riding away. Kate nodded her head as though she understood. "Tell Grandpa I will be here tomorrow. Tell him not to worry... I will dance the Sun Dance," he said to reassure the couple, sensing an awareness of his mother's feelings against the Sun Dance. He wanted to visit longer, but Fools Crow was the Sun Dance Chief and it would be impolite to occupy an excess amount of his time.

Hobart's late model car was parked beside the trailer house when he returned. He heard his mother and Leona's voice as he approached. The conversation inside the trailer made him uneasy; a confrontation, he knew, was soon to begin.

He noted Ralph's absence when he entered the trailer. Mildred offered coffee, attempting conversation in a timid voice. "Over fifty camps pitched today. By Saturday there'll be two, maybe three hundred." She added, "never had this big a crowd a few years ago."

Hobart was dark, swarthy, his stomach paunchy as he sat on the couch beside his mother. He performed his older brother's 'I told you so,' bullying scowl before greeting his younger brother coldly. Leona was lighter complexioned like his mother. She was even fair in comparison, for she fanatically avoided the sunlight. She was attired in a broad-brimmed straw hat, long-sleeved, high-collared blouse and fashionable slacks. Julie Charging Shield looked as tired as the rumpled cotton print dress she wore. Like many Sioux women, his mother was taller than an average white woman. She had a commanding face, fairly devoid of wrinkles for her skin had never known makeup and her hair was still as black as it was gray despite her age, which was approaching seventy. The older woman looked haggard and torn as she sat in the middle of the trailer house couch between Hobart and Leona. She started speaking the moment her youngest took a folding chair beside the door. "Well, Son, I've heard you're going to go through with this Sun Dance. You know I don't want that. If your father was alive... he wouldn't want it either."

He wanted to answer that his father would have been proud but declined to argue. He slowly sipped his coffee, staring back at his sister and brother. He avoided his mother's hard stare, but managed a glance before he finally spoke, noting she had aged considerably in just the year's time he had been away, her face paler than the day before when the family had met him at the airport.

"Mom, you were at the *Yuwipi* before I went to Vietnam. Everything predicted came true. I have to be thankful for being alive." His words gave him a sense of reassurance, dissipating his anxiety. "Mom, why are you so against it? Is it the priests or is it you?"

"Well, they don't want you to... ever since they found out these medicine men might have you in it. They say Fools Crow's *Yuwipi* didn't bring you back." She bent forward, firming her words. "You're not a full-blood. This Sun Dance and all this Indian religion, the priests tell us all it's going to do is bring trouble. You ain't an Indian, Son, least not like these full-bloods. They're reservation Indians, Fools Crow, the whole bunch of them. You've got no business throwing in with 'em."

Charging Shield sat passively staring out the trailer window watching a water tanker approach in low gear. Traditionally, the older an Indian woman was, the more she spoke with authority toward her sons, relatives and even to her husband unless she was approaching senility, and his mother was yet some distance, if ever, from that. She was a leader in West River, respected by both Indians and whites alike. He was afraid of the authority his mother commanded, but he was also afraid to break his vow, especially since the Sun Dance Chief had formally asked him.

The Bureau of Indian Affairs tanker truck drove past at a slow rate sprinkling the road with water to hold down the dust. "Well, how do you answer, Son?" his mother called out over the dissipating din of the truck's motor. "All my boys seen war and you were the last one. I worried all the time you were gone. I prayed to the Blessed Virgin every night. I didn't think you'd make it, flying that airplane and so many getting shot down, but my prayers were answered." She turned to look at her oldest son. "Hobart and Lawrence, they seen war without a *Yuwipi*. It wasn't Indian religion that brought them back."

He sensed she would cry at any moment. "I think I could be making a mistake if I don't fulfill my Sun Dance vow," he answered as he shifted uneasily in his chair.

"Your father and me, we left this reservation. All we ever wanted was our kids to get ahead. You was lucky goin' to school and staying home once we moved." She started to cry. "I don't want you in that Sun Dance. Those old ways, they're no good anymore. The priests have been on me night and day lately. Go on to school and thank God you're back alive."

He looked away from his brother's glare to Mildred for support, but she turned to face the stove. He stared at the floor, reluctant to face the three adversaries to his beliefs. After a long wait, he finally answered. His speech was slow and halting, "Mom, I know it sounds like I don't appreciate what you've done, seeing us through some hard times... but I'm no longer a boy now." He stared distantly out the window. "If I want to believe it was some of the old ways that brought me back, I have that right." His eyes shifted back and forth from the window to his mother, expecting her to comment, but she remained silent. "You say I'm not an Indian like the full-bloods." He shook his head. "Up in West River when I was a kid going to school, I sure as hell was called an Indian." A bitter frown crossed his face. "Full-blood, half-breed, quarter-breed, just-plain-breed, I was as much Indian as any full-blood in West River when it came to never being invited to a party or getting a date. Even some of the Indian girls were ashamed to go out with me." He glanced at his sister, Leona, then spoke with quiet resolve. "Thank God I wasn't brainwashed in the boarding schools and got the hell out of West River. Maybe that's why I can see the good of our way." His eyes settled on his mother. "I brought you sorrow because I was away being a warrior. I also brought you honor if you want to look for it. Fools Crow's wife, she sang me a tremolo. I heard you sing tremolos for my brothers and uncles, but you still haven't sung one for me. You're just as dead from Vietnam as you are Korea or World War II. It's worse if you're a P.O.W., the country will let you rot." 'P.O.W. - P.O.W.' The letters rang through him. The thought of pilots he had known wasting away in the prison camps turned his emotions to defiance.

The *wotai's* movement underneath his shirt momentarily startled him. He stiffened slightly. "No!" he shouted. "No... No, Goddamnit... I'm not a prisoner of war. I'm home and I'm alive. I was protected through our way!" He rose from his chair to throw open the screen door. He stalked out of the trailer, walking blindly across the prairie, away from the growing circle of tents.

Hobart yelled after him, "Kyle, come back here!" His overweight brother ran to him with puffing breath. "Look, Kyle, I want to tell you something for your own good."

"You always did look out for me," Charging Shield replied sarcastically.

Kyle, goddamnit, you got a chance to make it in West River, away from this goddamn no-job reservation. Don't fuck it up." Hobart, an inch and a half taller, glared down at him. Leona joined them at that moment. Hobart continued with an exasperated tone. "Lotta people... white people, came into my store when you were overseas. They was proud of you. When I told'em you was coming back to go to college, they was double proud." He pushed his finger at his younger brother.

"White people run this country. They don't like it when someone like you turns 'em down for feathers and witch doctors."

"Must be bad for your business," Charging Shield's sarcasm remained. "If their religion is so goddamned holy good, how come they got such a piss-poor record? When they first came here, we took care of them. Their religion didn't teach them to do the same to us. Their religion let 'em bring slaves. Ours taught us to set 'em free."

"I don't give a shit about the goddamned past, Fools Crow, or that stupid rock around your neck." Hobart shot back with a growl. "All I know is I'll knock you on your ass if you get wise, and you know I can still do it."

"Wouldn't set too well if you're going to be a politician," Charging Shield shot back. "I might have to campaign for your opposition and that wouldn't look very good." He added coldly, "I think that would really piss-off Ernie Hale!"

The words made Hobart almost buckle at his knees. He looked like a man who was about to have a heart attack. He turned his head momentarily toward the trailer house and took a deep breath. When he looked back his composure changed dramatically. He began to speak in a lowered paternal tone, "Now your mother... Our mother... has a weak heart. She had a couple of murmurs when you were overseas. She's too damned old to be watching this Sun Dance shit. You keep it up and you're gonna' be responsible for a heart attack."

"You don't have to live in West River," Leona chorused. "It's embarrassing if you do that Sun Dance. The newspapers will play it up."

"Newspapers in this state... Are you kidding?" Charging Shield snapped with a bitter laugh. "Horseshit and gun smoke newspapers. All they know is what drunk was arrested. They don't have the balls to tell the truth."

"They were at the airport on account of you." Hobart bellowed.

He swept his older brother with a knowing look before he let his eyes scan the horizon in the direction of the mission. "Did you ever read anything about the boarding schools, or the corruption in the Bureau and all the rest of the crooks that have perpetually fucked us over?" he responded evenly. His sister flinched, shaking her head with a disgusted grimace as he turned toward Hobart. "What's this about Mom's heart?"

"Doctor said she had a bad heart. She could go any time and she doesn't care either, since Pop died," Hobart answered. "I got better things to do than draggin' her around in all this heat and dust to talk to you."

"She enjoyed it when Grandma was alive. She gets to visit her old friends. Deep down in, our Mom is still very Indian." Charging Shield pointed his last remark at his sister. His gaze shifted to the Sun Dance arena. "Well, I'm sorry, Brother and Sister, my mind is made up."

Hobart glared back. "I would think damned hard. That's my mother too. If anything happens to her, I'll break your neck, Kid."

Charging Shield's reply was firm, "You try it, I guarantee I'll hurt you back, even if it takes a club to do it." He stepped back a few paces adding, "Anything else you have to say on behalf of your great white father and your white Jesus?"

"Yes," his sister came at him to spit into his face, hitting him with a hard slap. "You're possessed, you filthy-mouthed devil; you'll burn in hell someday. You don't insult God with your filthy Marine mouth. Stay away from my house and my kids."

Charging Shield felt the moisture despite the sting on the side of his face. He was bitter, but fought to regain his composure. He focused his attention on a lone sunflower; the deep brown center and the yellow orange of the petals, swaying in the light breeze. The buffalo grass in the background appeared bluish-gray with a touch of olive green. Somewhere a meadowlark sang while he continued staring at the flower. He fought back the tears, but soon the flower lost its vividness.

His sister and brother turned and walked away.

He sang the song tauntingly as they left, "... Jesus loves me, this I know, for the Bible tells me so..." He repeated the verse then yelled in anger, "I have only one sister left in my family, Leona, you fucking sellout!"

He watched them enter the trailer house for a few minutes, then drive down the dirt road with his mother toward the highway.

He turned from the Sun Dance encampment to cross a barbed-wire fence. He walked for miles in the blowing buffalo grass and sage. A meadowlark flew past to land on a choke cherry bush. The bird sang a short song before picking a choke cherry, then flew away.

* * * *

Wednesday morning, early, he gathered with the sun dancers outside of Fools Crow's tipi. It was an August day, the Moon of the Ripening Cherries, but the Dakota elevation provided a chilly temperature.

The sun dancers and holy men wore faded jeans, boots, and western shirts. A young girl stood among them. The girl was a virgin and represented the Buffalo Calf Maiden. After Fools Crow joined the group, they walked toward a stand of cottonwoods.

Fools Crow brought his pipe from his tobacco pouch to lead the procession toward a tree, fanning out in an attacking fashion. They proceeded forward, reversed and continued the attack and retreat movements until gradually they stood beneath a cottonwood tree. The Oglala holy man filled his pipe then offered it to the four directions.

The group stood silently while their leader prayed. He asked the tree to forgive them for cutting it down, telling the tree that it was selected to bring back life to the people. He then motioned for the girl to take an axe to deliver the first cut. A sun dancer followed the girl and soon the cottonwood was ready to fall. Several ropes were attached to pull the tree over, slowly, onto six pairs of bearers who bore six stout poles to bear the weight of the tree to the arena. They were careful to keep it from touching the ground. It was a tall tree, but not large at its base.

When the procession came abreast of his encampment, Fools Crow sent Blacktop, his adopted grandson, into the tipi. Before the tree was carried, he had made explicit instructions that no one from the felling party should precede the Sun Dance tree. Blacktop returned with a bucket of buffalo tallow.

When the party entered the arena, Fools Crow placed the tallow in a hole that had been dug at the center. Red, yellow, black and white flags were tied to the tree branches and a rawhide cutout of a man and *Tatanka*, the buffalo, were also tied near the top. Twelve choke cherry branches for the twelve moons were secured below the buffalo. A peace pipe bowl was buried at the bottom of the deep hole. When the tree was raised, a cheer rose from the gathered group.

That afternoon and evening, more tents and campers swelled the campground around the cottonwood tree.

REVEREND BUCHWALD, S. J.

CHAPTER ELEVEN

They will teach us to quarrel about God, as
Christians do on the Nez Perce Reservation and other
places. We do not want to do that. We may quarrel
with men sometimes about things on earth, but we
never quarrel about the Great Spirit. We do not want to learn that...
— Chief Joseph

Just before daybreak the male dancers filed into the sweat lodge, their towels wrapped around their waists. Fools Crow and Eagle Feather took their positions inside the entryway, sitting on a soft bed of sage covering the dirt floor, except for a shallow pit at the center of the canvas covered dome. Catches, the Oglala, held a narrow drum as he sat next to Fools Crow. Outside, the sound of crackling fire and an occasional popping cedar log broke the solitude of the morning air.

While the holy men offered a prayer, a man of medium build in his sixties, sporting thinning braids used a pitchfork to stir the red-orange coals surrounding a stack of granite rocks. At Fools Crow's call, John Lame Deer delivered a glowing rock through the lodge opening. The tines of the fork hummed a vibrating pitch when he dropped the first rock into the rear of the dishpan-sized pit. When seven rocks filled the pit at the center of the lodge floor, Lame Deer placed a bucket of water and a dipper beside Fools Crow. The Rosebud holy man served as assistant to Chief Fools Crow for the ceremonies, along with Catches. After the flap closed, water was splashed on the rocks. Charging Shield flinched from the blast of hissing steam. Hot mist settled, forcing his head low to inhale deeply what little air remained. The gasping of men sucking for air began the first part of the cleansing ritual. Charging Shield reached for a handful of sage to wipe his sweating body. The fragrant smell from the soft leaves seemed to aid his breathing.

More dippers were poured causing the huddled participants to cry out. Darkness filled the low, willow-framed lodge as the red rocks sizzled the water their red color fading away. One dancer pleaded through the billowing steam, *"Mitakuye oyasin! For all my relatives!"*

The flap raised. Fools Crow held the flap open to cooling air for a few minutes then spoke to Eagle Feather and Catches in Sioux. After the flap was lowered, the two men sang an honoring song accompanied by the beat of a small drum. At the end of the song, each man prayed. The prayers asked for strength to endure the Sun Dance.

Fools Crow made a final prayer, pouring the remaining water in the bucket onto the rocks. A closing song was sung by Catches, Eagle Feather, and Fools Crow. Their voices keyed a high pitched staccato chant, the drum seeming to vibrate the earth floor. When the song ended, the flap opened. Charging Shield felt clean and refreshed as he followed the sun dancers from the sweat lodge, their towels around their waists. Eagle bone whistles were worn by the sun dancers. Charging Shield bore a thin wooden whistle he had found in his sister's trailer. The wet buckskin pouch holding his *wotai* also hung from his neck by a leather thong as he walked bare chested in the crisp morning air.

The dancers entered the tall tipi at the edge of the arena to dress themselves in the shawl kilt skirts of the sun dancer. They remained barefoot, slipping sage wreaths around their ankles and wrists. A sage crown bearing a matched pair of eagle feathers adorned their heads, the feather shaft held firmly by the crown's tightly wrapped sage.

"Charging Shield," Eagle Feather commanded in his gruff yet gentle manner, "come here and sit beside me. Since this is your first Sun Dance, we will have to test you. Fools Crow is your holy man, so I will act as an adversary, although, if you pass the test, I believe you and I will become allies. I predict we shall travel some-place together, but first you must pass this test.

"The Sun Dance is no show, although, many come to see a show and there are many enemies of the Indian way. Some of our own people are the worst enemies. You know that if this ceremony dies, our nation will also die. I must know if you are committed, and will call upon the spirit of the rock people to help me. They have just cleansed you in the stone people lodge. You have been off to war and now you are clean and ready for them. They now want to talk to us." Eagle Feather grunted laboriously when he bent to retrieve an object from the buckskin bag that held his peace pipe.

"Now look down and when you look up I will be holding a rock... What do you see, Charging Shield?"

Charging Shield studied the crystal agate with the rainbow rim. "It's a man!" He paused and added, "The man is wearing a warbonnet. At first, I didn't see the warbonnet." He also saw a buffalo man and a woman; a strong looking woman with flowing hair. He had heard that Eagle Feather's *wotai* stone came to him after his first Sun Dance. He had gone to swim and relax in the Black Hills at the hot springs creek called Minnekata. A large snake had crawled across his foot when he had stood by the creek bank. The snake swam across the stream and the stone flashed four times from the streambed before the holy man reached down to pick it up. Few doubted the power within the stone.

Fools Crow and Eagle Feather exchanged appraising glances. "Now put your head back down. I will show you the same rock again... Now look."

Charging Shield spoke with innocent amazement, "The man with the warbonnet has turned into an eagle. He's turned into an eagle!"

"Hau, hau," murmured the holy men.

"Good, Charging Shield. The Stone Spirits say you will be allowed to dance the Sun Dance. Since you do not have a pipe and have been off to war, you shall carry a pipe for a visiting holy man."

"Yes, Uncle," he replied obediently.

"Next year you will be allowed to pierce if you have a pipe of your own. This year you will dance with a boy, Black Top, to the east of the arena. To fulfill a prophecy, you and the boy will greet the sun every morning."

Eagle Feather motioned to Catches who was standing by bearing a set of sage wreaths. Charging Shield stepped forward. Around his waist he wore the blue shawl borrowed from his sister. After he slipped a pair of wreaths over his ankles and a pair over his wrists, he was startled to see Bill Eagle Feather holding a sage wreath crown bearing two upright eagle wing spike feathers. Charging Shield dropped to one knee; his head upright. "Now you look like a sun dancer!" Bill remarked proudly as he crowned the younger warrior.

The Rosebud holy man addressed the dancers. "You all know this, but I must reaffirm it. Do not eat, and drink as little as possible. Before the white man, all across this land, tribes gathered to be thankful. Now only a few come together. The Great Spirit will be looking down on his grandchildren. Those of you, who have brought their mates, must not sleep with them. We must strive to show our attention to the one above." The calm assurance never left Eagle Feather's voice. He pointed

BLACK TOP

to the lodge opening. "Let us proceed. The sun is already up and we must greet him."

When the men filed out of the tipi, they were joined by an equal number of women. The holy men directed the participants to form a line. From the column of several dozen, six men would be pierced on the final day. All carried peace pipes with the exception of Charging Shield. Fools Crow led the procession to the ceremony grounds halting at the entrance to allow one of the women to be the first to enter. Before the ceremony could begin it would have to be opened by woman, for it is woman who is the beginning of all who are born. While she circled the arena with a sage hoop, a Yankton holy man offered Charging Shield a peace pipe to carry. The woman finished her circle and rejoined the column.

At the southern edge of the arena, gathered around a tub-sized drum, the singers began their chant. The throbbing drum pulsated out across the still prairie with the rhythm of a heartbeat to send the dancers clockwise around the tree of life.

Lame Deer, the wiry holy man from the Rosebud, wearing red velvet wrapped around his braids, took his place close to the singers to serve as acceptor for the pipes while the dancers offered their prayers to the four directions. Several hours would pass before most of the pipes would be offered and smoked by the singers and visiting holy men.

After Charging Shield had offered the Yankton pipe, he was taken by the sage gauntlet at his wrist and led toward the eastern edge of the ceremonial circle. Beside him, the boy, Black Top was placed. Charging Shield blew the dull sounding wooden flute whistle with an extended arm to the red dawn spreading on the prairie horizon. The pencil thin whistle lacked the size and shrillness of the thicker eagle bone whistles. The two bobbed to the drumbeat as the sun slowly rose. Occasionally the pair would return to the shaded bower when it would come time to rest with the other dancers. It was a long morning for Charging Shield and the dark, spindly, full-blood boy. Both faced eastward, dancing solitarily in one place while the sun slowly rose. Charging Shield's legs ached and his neck was stiff from gazing at the bright sky. The boy remained at his side; his head drooping lower as the hours passed by. Finally, before noon, Fools Crow returned the pair to the procession of dancers ready to leave the arena. The weary boy at Charging Shield's side momentarily erased his tired expression when they paraded through the entry gate before the admiring crowd.

While Charging Shield changed in the ceremonial lodge, a new camper van turned from the highway to the campgrounds. Eventually, a priest stepped from the parked van walking a straight line for the silver camper trailer. Charging Shield finished dressing about the same time that Mildred answered the knock on her screen door.

"Is your mother here?" Father Buchwald inquired anxiously.

"She wanted to stay, but Hobart made her go back to West River. Mom's not getting any younger, you know." The woman made a welcoming gesture. "Come in and have some coffee."

Buchwald took a seat on the couch while Mildred peered out the screen door at the new van. "My, that's a nice one," she exclaimed. Her tone was warm and laudatory.

"It's from a government grant. The mission is working on a study: the urban reservation relationship and alcoholism," added the priest.

"I think we've been studied enough," Mildred replied bluntly. She took several steps toward a coffeepot on the stove. "They ought to spend some of that money on the Indians."

"Now, Mildred. Indian secretaries will be employed," Buchwald chastised with a scolding air. "That bus is a research vehicle for field work. All in all, the grant will put money into the community."

At that moment, Charging Shield passed close to the trailer, stopping to listen through a side window.

"Field work? What you mean by that?"

"Well, ah... Extensive field work in the reservation and urban community. The van affords privacy for compiling research data. It's an encompassing project, Mildred, a feasibility study centering on reservation needs... and urban needs evolved from a culture still too rooted in the past." The priest's academic voice pretentiously lowered to a worried note. "And, of course, the devastating alcohol problem." A paternalistic smile lit his face.

"Well, you've lost me." Mildred's answer was blankly polite. "You always told us, Jesuits are the most educated ones. I hope you can do some good."

"We're the soldiers for the Holy Father," Buchwald puffed his chest, adding zealously, "the shock troops for the Lord."

"Your feasibility study is more money down the drain. After you're through, you'll milk another hundred grand to study us." Charging Shield sent a cold, commanding voice into the house trailer as he glared from the doorway.

Buchwald jumped at the first sound of his voice. Still somewhat startled, he stared in fascination at the Indian. 'So now he would confront this militant who had turned against the church.' His hunched stance made him look as if he were about to leap forward off of a diving board, or out to catch a real, live devil. 'Some said he was hypnotized by Fools Crow or Eagle Feather... and the old Badlands witch, the Grandmother. Her devil's influence was still alive. This militant had no business on the reservation. Her poisoned babble had brought him back to carry on the heathenry.' The priest studied the Indian's face intently. The cold-blooded look coming from Charging Shield's eyes unnerved him. There was nothing conciliatory in that look, 'why he was more vicious looking than his brother Lawrence.' Buchwald's hand unconsciously rose up to rub his temple. Buchwald noted that

Charging Shield lacked the mannerisms of a beaten, economically subjected people. Worse, he was outside of the priest's grasp, no longer a helpless boarding school child. On second thought, Buchwald decided to avoid a confrontation.

"Well, Mildred, ah, I'd better by going," Buchwald stammered, shrinking back from the low table.

"Finish your coffee. I want to talk to you," Charging Shield commanded.

"Now, Kyle, I'm not looking for trouble," Buchwald's voice quavered. "I've come in peace. I've been on this reservation longer than you, and I'm simply paying my respects to dear friends."

"Look, Buchwald, I know what you're up to. You want to pressure my relatives, especially my mother. You 'Soldiers of the Lord' are plenty worried about a lone, damn, swear-wording ex-Marine Captain taking part in a Sun Dance. If I go back, then the others might get ideas... and you and your kind would have to make a living off our reservation." Charging Shield dipped his head over his shoulder toward the van, lowering his voice to a whisper and raising an eyebrow with an exaggerated half-smile. "And if we go back, we might solve our alcohol gift from you people, without another worthless study." His voice mocked Buchwald's pretentious tone.

"Kyle, I didn't come to hear militancy."

"You didn't hear a word I said, Buchwald. Not one damned word."

Buchwald was spellbound. He managed a weak nod. Never had he heard an Indian or anyone talk to a Jesuit in such a brazen manner, at least not on a reservation.

Charging Shield leaned forward to speak again almost in a whisper and the same eyebrow raised, "Don't wait for a lightning bolt to strike me dead." He began by looking up to the ceiling. "You might have some of your brainwashed, boarding school products fooled, but not me."

"Kyle," Buchwald said with placation, "I've known you since you were a little boy. Why, your mother... "

"Hold it right there," Charging Shield interrupted. "I'll listen, only if you'll listen to me. Then maybe we can have some dialogue."

Buchwald's face flushed. His anger began to flare. "I'm not here to play silly games. Someday you'll beg to have the Blessed Sacrament, like your sister here and the Lord have mercy on your soul. The direction you're going is hopeless, son. You'd better return to the Lord our Savior."

"How about the Great Spirit?" Charging Shield countered as he pulled up a chair to sit facing the priest.

"The Great Spirit; *Wakan Tanka*; the Sun God; devil talk. They will all fall before the risen Son of God who was conceived by the Holy Ghost and born of the Virgin Mary." Buchwald stood up, his words recovering their aplomb; his customary, superior smile returned, covering his face like a mask.

The Indian stared at the floor and lowered his head. Buchwald stepped forward from the couch.

"Kyle, you can't fight the Lord... It's foolish to fight us. We Jesuits have a history of adversaries, but they all fell." He swept his arm like a flail across the room. "Kings, dictators, politicians... They've all fallen before us."

Charging Shield continued to sit silently in his chair thinking back to Cross Dog and his brother Lawrence and their strategy, planned before they entered Buchwald's office to be punished. "We'll go in acting scared," Lawrence had said. "It always throws them off guard."

Buchwald felt a sudden surge of power over Charging Shield who was beginning to slump in his chair. "It isn't your fault, son. Some of these old medicine men are the slickest fakers in the world. Why, they know sleight of hand, they have tricks and the power to hypnotize. You may have been hypnotized or drugged, you never know. We were shocked to hear your mother had gone to one of those *Yuwipis*. You could have been responsible for her soul, son, dragging her down to Fools Crow's, thinking you'd get protection for the war. If she'd died, her soul would have gone to the depths of hell." The priest pushed the flat of his hand out as if stopping some unseen force. "I had her come to confession and the sacrament of Penance, and the Blessed Sacrament of Communion removed the stain of mortal sin. Now should your mother depart, I'm sure the angels of the Lord and the Blessed Mother will welcome her with open arms." Buchwald pointed his finger at the slouching figure. "Your mother, Kyle, is no doubt our greatest missionary just through her example. Your parents worked hard, spent their money on their family and not on drinking. Your mother saw to it that her family followed the church's teachings."

Charging Shield's head hung lower. He brushed his eyes with the back of his hand. Mildred stood by the sink, staring in baffled astonishment at the sudden, subdued change displayed by her brother.

"Kyle, I know all about these medicine men." The man in black placed his thumbs in his front pockets while he slowly paced the tiny living room. "Why, you take Fools Crow there... The old faker does this thing simply for the money. You can't blame him, in a way. He feeds every Tom, Dick, and Harry that comes to his place. Yes, money, money is the root of all evil. That's why we in the Jesuit order have the vow of poverty." He grimaced, baring his stained teeth, as if the sermon was drawing to a close. "Now, nowhere have I ever heard Mr. Fools Crow take a vow of poverty like we Jesuits. Not only that vow but we also will not take up with a woman like he has. We truly can devote ourselves to the Lord's work without diversion."

Charging Shield put his head between his hands pretending to stare at the floor, masking the glint in his eyes. 'I will hear you out, Buchwald... And then you'll listen to me,' he thought to himself.

"Ah, yes, money... " Buchwald went on. "Money and Mr. Fools Crow. Kyle, as you get older you'll learn these old fakers are in this for the money game. Otherwise they'd be out doing an honest man's work digging ditches like your father did. Of course your father didn't attend church like your mother, but he was, nevertheless, a good man." A disturbed frown gave way to a benevolent smile. "That is why we allowed him the last sacraments and a Christian burial. Now, if your father were alive, he wouldn't approve of Fools Crow... or the Sun Dance. He'd ask that you listen to your mother." Buchwald continued his sermon with calm relish.

"We gave you the opportunity to gain eternal life. A confession is what you need. Now son... " He reached for the slumping figure's shoulder. "The true church can help in more ways than one. Many a B.I.A. college scholarship has gone to intelligent young Indians due to our efforts. I know you're on your way back to school. The Lord will provide for those that beseech him." Buchwald was the epitome of confidence. "Don't feel bad, boy. If you want, I will tell Fools Crow that you have seen the light and he won't be able to harm you." The Jesuit's face was covered with an accomplished grin. It was obvious to him that Julie Charging Shield had dictated to her son that he wouldn't be taking part in the Sun Dance. The trips to West River and the sessions with Julie had borne fruit.

"Mildred, your brother here," he said, as he clutched Charging Shield's shoulder and turned slightly as if to cast a dramatic paternal pose for some invisible photographer, "I'm sure he's seen the light. I'd better leave the two of you to your thoughts."

He beamed down on Charging Shield's awe struck sister, holding forth an anointing hand. "Someday you're going to be right behind your mother when it comes to working for the church." Buchwald reinforced his declaration with a sanctimonious spreading of his hands. He thought about reminding her about living with Ralph, a divorced man, only as brother and sister, and she might get to receive the sacraments but thought this subject needed another time and probably total privacy. "You get led astray like your brother here, but then Mother always brings her sheep back to the fold. I'm sure Julie will rest easier now... "

Charging Shield rose from his chair to stand in front of the doorway as the priest spoke. "Just a minute," he interrupted. "I want to tell you something."

Flush from his unexpected victory, Buchwald failed to note the abrupt change in the Indian's voice. "What is it, my boy?" His eyes stared in disbelief at the vicious smile. "Why, why Kyle. What's going on? What's the matter?"

"Priest, it's my turn now... "

Buchwald looked for a moment in disbelief, then remembered something unconsciously from the past. His hand went instinctively to his temple, massaging his head for a moment. The sharp elbow thrown by Lawrence, long ago. It all came back to him. His face began to get red as he flushed with anger. "No, I won't be intimidated. You won't speak to me that way." He attempted to push the Indian aside.

Charging Shield lost his balance and fell back against the wall. He managed to spring forward in time to lower his shoulder solidly into Buchwald's soft stomach sending the Jesuit staggering toward the couch.

Mildred ran to the narrow hallway to stand frozen as she watched the Jesuit still standing but doubled over, trying to catch his breath.

The priest's pained gasping left Charging Shield unmoved. "Missionary, that's nothing compared to what you did to us in that boarding school. When you get your wind back, sit on that couch. It's my turn to talk."

"You hit me, you militant!" The priest gasped fearfully. "I never beat children. I never... "

Mildred ran forward to shake her fist at the Jesuit. "Don't you lie!" she screamed. "You were one of the worst. All of you beat us; you and your God... damned... leather... straps. Don't lie!" Her voice choked and she began sobbing.

Charging Shield's eyes reddened when he saw his sister crying. Tears welled up for a brief moment when he thought about the boarding schools. The memory of Crow Dog made him wipe his nose on his sleeve and put his arm around his sister, turning her toward the rear of the trailer house. He set his jaw, as he glared at the missionary. "I heard your story, preacher. Now we'll hear what an Indian has to say." His words were slow and deliberate despite the reddening of his eyes.

Buchwald retreated toward the couch but refused to sit. "No, Kyle, I won't be forced. I'll have you arrested for assault and battery." His eyes widened when he saw the Indian reach for a rolling pin beside the kitchen sink. The crass tone of his words gave way to panic. "And intent to kill," he hastily added.

Charging Shield stalked the missionary. "Priest, you're going to hear my side," he said with bitter malice, raising the rolling pin. When the priest shifted his balance to block the impending blow, Charging Shield caught his adversary's shoulder with his free hand, slamming him into the couch. He brought the rolling pin down hard on the coffee table.

"Priest, I see boarding school all over your goddamned, wicked fucking face," he yelled. "Don't interfere with me! Understand?" He screamed loudly.

The priest stared back in disbelief. His face was white, his mouth open.

Charging Shield slowly regained his composure, but was still hot with anger. "My turn to talk," he began with a menacing stare. He waved the rolling pin in front of the Jesuit then threw it into a corner.

"You are a deceiver, Charging Shield. You are nothing but deceit. A true devil you are. You're possessed with an evil spirit. You pretended to listen. The real Indians would never deceive like you."

"Deceit... evil... devil... " Charging Shield threw his head back with harsh laughter. "We had to learn those words from you to survive." He paused for a moment then continued in a vindictive tone. "I told you I'd listen, if you'd listen to me." He began slowly and softly then with a raised pitch. "Missionary, we're going back. We're going back to the Great Spirit our way. We don't need you, priest." He drove his finger to emphasize his point. "You're interfering with something way bigger than your church when you try to stop our Sun Dance. That ceremony is a teaching from a culture that honed it for thousands of years. A real proven earth stewardship." His voice lowered and tended to plead... "The Buffalo Calf Maiden was sent to us by the Great Spirit. She told us to use our pipe in the Sun Dance. The Six Powers showed Black Elk that our sacred tree would return. Those are pretty big forces to meddle with, priest. I wouldn't think of trying to stop you from saying Mass in your chapel. Why should you interfere with what is holy to us? Don't you realize that you are nothing but a pitiful human being like the rest of us here on our Mother Earth? You don't know any more about God than I do and that's not a helluva lot." Less harshly he added, "I have always left you alone, why don't you leave us alone?"

"You are bullying me; uttering filth and slime... to me... a Jesuit Priest. Is that leaving me alone?" Buchwald shot back, "You can't know about God the way you swear, then mention your Buffalo Calf Maiden cock and bull in the next breath."

The Indian stepped backward. "Yeah, Priest, I swear. But I don't beat captive kids and I don't try and destroy another people's religion." He paused and added in a less defiant tone. "I'm sorry," he said, "but you wouldn't listen to me otherwise. Maybe I was too long in the Marines fighting your wars for you. Maybe you people exasperate the hell out of me."

"And I won't listen to any more of this witch talk. We brought God to you pagans, not this Buffalo Maiden cock and bull." The missionary shook his head at the floor... "And worse yet, so many of you heathens believe it." A wild glint sprang from his eyes. "It's the work of the devil. That peace pipe fairy tale... and you all run around a tree like possessed savages."

The manifest boldness of the priest's declarations left Charging Shield staring back at his adversary, unable to reply. The missionary closed his eyes with a supercilious smile. "I've heard you, Kyle. I don't believe you and never will. You can kill me, but I will not give up my faith in the risen Lord, the fulfiller of all religions. He is the fulfiller and the redeemer of even your sinful soul. Without him you are lost and a thousand buffalo women are worthless."

The priest stood up.

Charging Shield slammed him back into the couch. "Sit down! You fucking anti-Mother. I haven't finished yet! No one's asking you or anyone else to give up a damned thing. All we're asking is that you leave us alone... just leave us alone!"

Foam flecked Buchwald's lips as he yelled back in a frenzy, "This is false imprisonment, Kyle. False imprisonment! I'll have you locked away for years, you militant devil."

"You stand up again, anti-Mother priest, and you just may go to your reward," Charging Shield replied calmly. "They'll blow Gabriel's horn for you."

The priest sat, a blank stare was fixed on the coffee table. "Anti-Mother? Anti-Mother? Just what do you mean by that? What kind of a statement is that demented mind of yours trying to make?"

Charging Shield laughed long and with a wicked grimace. "You and all that you stand for have been letting our Earth Mother get thoroughly raped. The Negroes use the term 'Mother Fucker.' You know, missionary, I think that term applies to a whole lot of you so-called organized people, but in an environmental sense of the word. Your theologians could always look the other way anytime there was some more of Mother Earth to dig up or forests or indigenous people to be cut down. I think that the beavers and the buffalo would agree with me. Whatever the wealthy wanted to do or the Kings and Barons, you were right there to tell them it was okay to do it." He paused for a moment to let his words weigh. "Your motto was, 'Go ahead and fuck Mother Earth.' That is anti-Mother in my book. I hope it catches on. It's a perfect term for you kid-beating, anti-Mothers."

From the dance arena, the announcer called out the social dancing agenda. The afternoon's activities repeated across the loudspeaker displaced the icy silence within the trailer house. A pious grin began to grow on the Jesuit as if he had not heard his adversary's remarks. His head came back; his half-closed eyes were directed at the ceiling. "I'm willing to die for the Lord. Yes, die for Him," he exclaimed with fervor. "Jesus, is my Savior, and I will live for his name... To the very end." He rose slowly. In contrast to a few minutes before, he was now, devoid of fear. "My Lord, my God, my Savior. I will give my life to bring eternal light to my people, the Sioux... in His name."

"Why you hung up martyr," Charging Shield grimaced a pained scowl before he pointed at the doorway. "Get out, Buchwald. Get out," he said with an exasperated shake of his head. "You'd love to be a martyr, wouldn't you?"

The missionary's smile was triumphant. "And furthermore... He held his words until he had safely reached the doorway, "And furthermore, you pagan devil, I'll stop your heathen Sun Dance," he remarked with a smart smirk as he threw open the screen door and leaped out of the silver trailer.

Charging Shield held a hopeless look for a long moment before he dashed from the trailer to yell at the figure walking with hurried strides to the research bus. "Leave our Sun Dance alone, you bloodsucker," he called out with venom. "You've sucked my people white."

SWEAT LODGE

CHAPTER TWELVE

The second day of the Sun Dance was little different from the day before except that the pangs of hunger seemed to be more pronounced for Charging Shield. The pipes of just the six Sun Dance pledgers were offered on the second day, causing the ceremony to last but a few hours while a small crowd looked on. After the morning ceremony, Charging Shield took a long walk into the hills leading into the Badlands toward the northwest. It was late afternoon before he returned to the campgrounds. The afternoon was cool enough to allow him the sighting of two rattlesnakes emerging from their holes to start off early on their evening hunt. The fasting made him tire easily and his late afternoon nap lasted long into the night. That evening he never heard the new arrivals coming into the campground, many from long distances. The following morning would find the camping area doubled in size.

The third day, Saturday morning, the sweat lodge fire was tended by Eagle Feather. At the first hint of day, Charging Shield walked toward the bright blaze near the ceremonial lodge aware that the hunger pangs he had felt severely the night before were now no longer existent. Somehow, he felt as though he had been given a totally new and fresh body and this time one without an appetite. He huddled close to the fire covering his shoulders with his sister's navy blue shawl.

"Nephew, so far you have done well, but we still have two days to go." Eagle Feather said as he sat next to him. "I was the first to predict you would do the Sun Dance." The flames reflected traces of gray in the Rosebud holy man's close-cropped hair. "I predict you will see many adventures in but a short while," Eagle Feather continued in his matter-of-fact manner. "This Sun Dance and those airplanes behind you are only the beginning."

Charging Shield was pleased with the holy man's words. His eyes rested on the thin bark of a limb bursting into flame. The comfortable fire and the large framed man sitting next to him gave him a secure feeling. He recalled the return of the Sun Dance when Eagle Feather boldly brought back the piercing. He had sat with his grandmother that day, more than a decade before. Since that time, the old woman had fulfilled her circle of life. His mind drifted to the tall cottonwood tree guarding his grandmother's abandoned cabin and the shallow stream below. He remembered her words as they watched Fools Crow pierce Eagle Feather in the center of the curious crowd numbering less than a hundred. "Put your head down and pray hard, Grandson. This is a pitiful ceremony compared to the old days. You pray hard that these old ways come back."

"Nephew, so far our ceremony is going well," Eagle Feather's lowered voice interrupted his thoughts. "The missionaries haven't made their move yet. We'll have to be on the look out today."

"They already have, Uncle," Charging Shield answered. He grimaced at the fire before explaining the incident at his sister's trailer house.

Eagle Feather shook his head slowly. His tone was fatherly. "Nephew, it is good to fight for the return of our way... but you want to be careful around those black robes. He fell silent and looked into the fire. "I've studied the white man all my life. I guess I got a right to, seeing as how he's always been studying us. I've discovered the white man doesn't make a move against someone unless there's money behind it." He crossed his legs and glanced in the direction of the mission boarding school, several miles from the dance grounds. "That mission's a business more than it's a church."

"Money?" Charging Shield threw a perplexed frown.

Eagle Feather nodded with a blunt look. "That mission operates a big money getting 'pogram'."

"A money getting 'pogram'? You mean program?"

"There's a fancier name for it. You know, when they have the Indian students write up those plastic teepee letters and send out little salt shakers covered with Indian signs through the mail asking for donations?"

Charging Shield nodded, "You mean their solicitation program?"

Eagle Feather beamed and sounded out the word phonetically. "Yes, that's it. The so-lic-i-ta-tion pogram'. They get all kinds of money that way, mostly from the East. Lotta whites got guilty consciences about Indians. That 'pogram' supports more than the mission. It takes care of those priests' retirements, travelin', vacations and the head office down south. They own lots of land too." A disgusted look came and went. "That grave yard above the mission, they know how to work on those old people, you can bet your boots on that. Those last sacraments to get you in the spirit world has got them lots of land. And those Bureau superintendents are in cahoots with them, they take that 'last rites' land and switch it for the tribe's land surrounding the mission." He exhaled with tired exasperation. "Donations and land, it's all a big business, more money than we can imagine. This ain't the only reservation, either. That one up in Crow country makes more money than any of them." He looked at his pupil sternly, "Fight them, Nephew, but be careful. Be careful around those black robes," he repeated.

'Business'. The word left an indelible ring. He shot the holy man an appreciative glance.

"They'll try to stop you, Nephew. They don't want you in this ceremony. An old fool like me with little education, they can make fun of. You, that's a different story. I've heard that you ran away from that boarding school out there before they could break you. Now you've gone out and traveled the white man's road, yet you come back to the old Way... on top of this you're going on to college. They're afraid sooner or later someone like you could blow the whistle on them."

After more sun dance pledgers and holy men gathered around the blaze, a man with a weak heart was brought to the sweat lodge. He barely crawled to the rear of the domed structure for a curing ritual conducted by Eagle Feather. An honoring song to Chief Gall was sung and the heat within the interior of the lodge seemed more bearable than the day before.

Charging Shield was apprehensive about the condition of the coughing man seeming to grow paler each time the flap was raised. The ceremony concluded. All filed out except for Eagle Feather and the weak hearted man. Out of curiosity, Charging Shield remained close to the entry flap while Eagle Feather chanted a dirge sounding like a buffalo lowing in a lonely wallow. A pipe was brought inside of the sweat lodge and the flap left open while Eagle Feather and his patient smoked slowly. Eagle Feather reached into his medicine bundle retrieving several silver gray sage stems. The odd species of sage puckered the man's face with the bitter taste. After a short while, a healthy color flushed the patient to Charging Shield's astonishment. Before the man left the sweat lodge with a spirited gait, he was cautioned by Eagle Feather to return for added treatment.

Charging Shield followed the holy man to the ceremonial lodge with renewed awe to dress once again for the Sun Dance. After the dancers formed the processional line outside the tall lodge, Gap, the bearer of the buffalo skull was placed at the head of the procession followed by the holy men, Eagle Feather, Fools Crow, Catches and Lame Deer.

Red Bow, a young Oglala in his twenties, was to be pierced for his fourth time the following morning and was immediately behind the holy men. Several members from the Rosebud and Hunkpapa tribes were placed behind Red Bow. Charging Shield followed his cousin, Sonny Larvee, with Fools Crow's adopted grandson, Black Top, the quiet, shy boy in his first years at the boarding school, at his side.

The barefoot dancers entered the arena from the east. Again Charging Shield and the boy were placed with their backs to the tree to face the rising sun. The singers sang and the eagle bone whistles kept time to the beat of the drum. Charging Shield blew on the small wooden whistle that he had found in his sister's trailer house. Its sound was pathetic compared to the shrill eagle bone whistles. During the first recess period, after the peace pipes were offered, the pair rested with the other dancers under the circular bower. The dancers sat at a special recess place cordoned off by ropes under the shading bower's western side.

While he rested on a thick plank, a sturdy two by eight nailed to two sawed cottonwood logs; Charging Shield sat pensively, appreciating the shade offered by the bower. Coming down the road and approaching the eastern gateway to the arena he noticed a procession marching in a military manner. The marchers carried the American flag and the tribal flag at the front of their column. Each flag was flanked by a rifle-bearer carrying First World War, bolt-action rifles. Behind the color guard, a tall, warbonnetted man walked proudly. He appeared to be a decade younger than Fools Crow. As they drew closer, Charging Shield recognized the man as the tribal chairman. The man's name was Enos and was a close friend of his brother, Lawrence. Lawrence had remarked several times that their family was blood related to the tribal chairman.

Fools Crow and Bill Eagle Feather walked across the arena to greet the procession. The two holy men joined the parade of marchers immediately behind the color guard, each flanking the handsome chairman. The whole procession entered the dance circle to parade in a complete circle around the arena, bringing the crowd of onlookers to their feet, including the sun dancers. As the two flags passed by, members of the crowd held cowboy hats and baseball caps over their hearts while women sang out tremolos.

When the procession stopped in front of the sun dancers, Fools Crow motioned for the audience to sit back down. He then walked toward Charging Shield indicating for him to stand. Fools Crow then grasped the sage wreath tied around Charging Shield's wrist and led him to the announcer's booth near the south end of the arena. The tribal chairman followed close behind them. The announcer handed down a microphone to the holy man and the Sun Dance Chief began to speak in Lakota. Fools Crow paused and turned Charging Shield around to face the audience, then began speaking again. Several times the audience murmured and applauded. A few women tremoloed.

As Fools Crow continued to talk, the chairman stood next to the sun dancer and greeted him with a handshake. "You understand Indian, Kyle?" he asked while the microphone blared Fools Crow's voice.

"Only a little," Charging Shield replied. "Not enough to understand what he is saying." He added. "It's something about Vietnam, isn't it?"

"Yes," Enos replied with a raised voice. "He is proud that the spirits have answered his ceremony that he held for you. He's telling them that he will have an appreciation ceremony for you... to thank them... probably after you get started back in school." Enos continued to interpret for the combat pilot. "Now he is telling them that this Old Way is coming back and it will be good for the people." Enos surveyed the crowd. "With this bunch here, they already know that." He made a head motion behind them toward the town to the south. "The ones not here are the ones who should hear what he is saying. I'm a traditionalist like you, Kyle. I support these ways." A sour note crept into his voice. "But I'm outgunned right now. Too many of these 'church-Indians' on the council and I get outvoted."

Charging Shield felt surprised that he was considered a traditionalist. He assessed the chairman's words and reasoned that he, himself, probably could be called a traditionalist. At least he wasn't a 'church-going Indian' and he was in the Sun Dance. He knew though, that he understood very little, especially the language. Maybe he wasn't exactly a real traditionalist but he was moving in that direction.

Enos seemed to read his thoughts. "Don't worry about the language, Kid. It is what you stand for, that is what counts. I ran around with your brother, Lawrence, back in my day. I can't run too much anymore because of these politics but we are still good friends." Enos managed a smile. "Oh, I still get together with him when I come up to West River." His voice dropped. "We're related you know."

Charging Shield nodded in agreement, "My Mom, Lawrence and my sister, they all told me. They say it's on my father's side." He looked at Enos and noted his nod. In the background, Fools Crow's voice began to slow down.

"Sounds like you are going to have to say some words," Enos offered.

Charging Shield's eyes widened. "But I don't talk Indian."

Enos laughed. "They know that, Kid." He shook the eagle feathers of his majestic warbonnet. "Just get up there and tell them that you appreciate your life... And tell them that the Way is going to come back." The tribal Chief puckered his lips for a moment. "You believe that, don't you?"

"Yes, yes, ... I do!" Kyle answered awkwardly and began to clear his throat.

"Don't worry, Kid. Just tell the truth." Enos spoke assuredly. "Just remember. This crowd is on your side. Mostly older people are out there. Not many young ones, yet. We've got to get the young on our side. They're wandering around in the bars... or still brainwashed by that boarding school and these missionaries. This Way has got the power to get our young on the right road and out of those bars. Missionaries had their chance but their way ain't working. Tell it to em', Kid."

Fools Crow stopped speaking and handed the microphone to Charging Shield. As Kyle grasped the microphone he felt nervous and apprehensive about speaking out in public.

Typical of Sioux culture, there was no rehearsal... no time to plan and go over what should be said and what should not be said. Custom dictated that an important speech should come from the heart. Without being warned, a man or a woman reached into their mind and brought out the highlights of one's experience and wisdom, if it was there in the first place; wisdom and understanding from the richest of the experiences. The rest would flow as long as the speaker was truthful.

Charging Shield stammered his own introduction but gathered force as he talked. He began with Fools Crow's *Yuwipi* ceremony, even his mother's reluctance to attend. He then told about wearing the stone in combat and his belief that the Spirits had watched out for him. The crowd applauded and again the women tremoloed at that point. He ended by sweeping his hand in a semi-circle. "Look around us here. Look over at the sun dancers. How many of the young do we see?" He paused then yelled out, "It's time to go back... go back to the old Way!" He heard a call coming from the tribal Chief at that moment.

"*Hokahey! Hokahey!*" over and over, Enos repeated. The crowd picked up the acknowledging expression and chanted back.

"We must all return to the Way. The Missionaries have had us for too long. They have had our young for too long and have turned them into *washichu*s. I was lucky. I escaped their brain washing when my brother Lawrence and I ran away." He pointed to the Sun Dance tree. "This Way proved to be my protection." Charging Shield ended with a flourishing wave. "Go back. Go back... and get your young to go back... we have but one life to live... why not live it as a true Lakota?"

He handed the microphone to Enos while the crowd cheered and then he took his place beside Fools Crow. Enos removed an eagle feather that had been pinned near the chest pocket of his shirt. He signaled for one of the drum groups to begin a drum roll. At the sound of the drum he called Charging Shield to step forward.

"Kyle Charging Shield, my relative," he began, "you are to be honored for being a veteran and going across to fight an enemy in this war that is still going on." He looked around and held up the eagle feather in a pointing and fanning fashion. "All of you who are veterans out there and you who are related to veterans, all of you are also honored." He raised his commanding voice. "In the old days, a warrior was honored by his people. This is the backbone of our life as social people here upon our Mother Earth. When a warrior returned from a war party, or a defensive battle with the soldiers, so that our people may live, ... he was honored and respected... and appreciated." He paused with a long silence then began slowly. "Many of our relatives have never returned... the first great war, when we were not even citizens, yet we went across anyhow... then the second great war, the one which most of you were in, including myself... the Korean War which our relative here, Kyle Charging

Shield was in. And then this Vietnam, our relative was in that one too. And now he stands before us here and is truthful to proclaim that it was the power of the Way that allows him to be here."

Enos held up the eagle feather and presented it to the Marine pilot. "Wear this upon your Sun Dance rope, my relative, when you pierce."

In a few minutes, the color guard passed out of the arena and the Sun Dance continued. As the morning drew on, Charging Shield looked as close as he could to the sun without being blinded. The eagle feather was tied to his belt over the navy blue kilt. He blew the wooden whistle and danced steadily. The temperature rose quickly during the early morning. His neck ached and his mouth was dry. He wanted to sleep and felt as if he could while dancing in his place.

Looking through half closed eyes, he watched a cloud slowly drifting. A woman seemed to rise from the top of the billowing cumuli. Then the cloud became a buffalo head and then a man's head, then it was both... a buffalo man. The woman reappeared as the cloud parted. Her shoulders stood out prominently above the cloud. It was evident there was power within the woman.

The final song for the morning was sung when Fools Crow tugged on the sage gauntlet to lead him to the procession. The dancers left the arena and filed to the ceremonial tent. As he removed his kilt, Eagle Feather and Catches exchanged a low conversation with Fools Crow. "*Waste aloh*," he heard Fools Crow remark... (That's good).

Eagle Feather made the announcement. "Charging Shield, tomorrow you will be allowed to pierce. You will not have to wait until next year."

It was an honor, but the fear of being pierced stifled any exuberance that may have accompanied such an award.

"Do you take the vow to be pierced?" Eagle Feather's raised voice filled the tent.

"Yes, Uncle, I vow," his answer lacked hesitation. "It is but a small sacrifice compared to what the Great Spirit through the *Yuwipi* has spared me. I am not dead nor am I a prisoner of war. I shall be honored to pierce."

"That is why we have made an exception. We also wish to honor the request of our tribal Chief, who is one of us and has a hard road with those others. You have been off to war... far across the ocean and you spoke well today. You are not afraid to fight for the Way. You believed that the Way would protect you and for those reasons your people will honor you further by allowing you to pierce in your first dance. Do not forget what you saw... far across the ocean. Wars have been too much a part of those who have taken over this land. The Earth will need help and two-legged cannot be fighting wars. We pray that only peace will come to this land. But, since you have faced death many times, it is proper that you pierce tomorrow... to thank the Great Spirit for your life."

Chief Eagle Feather extended his hand to Charging Shield. After the handshake, Eagle Feather removed his eagle bone whistle from around his neck and presented it to the sun dancer.

Charging Shield was so impressed he was momentarily speechless. Finally he composed himself to decline the holy man's special gift. "I deeply appreciate your gift Uncle but what will you use for a whistle? I can not take such a gift while you have yet to Sun Dance."

Eagle Feather threw his head back and laughed heartily. "I won't be using that little pencil pip squeak you've been blowing on." He reached down and opened an old tin suitcase to select an eagle bone whistle from several others. "We found a rancher that's been poisoning coyotes... but the eagles got to the poison. I've got all I need for awhile." The holy man looked at his new whistle. "I don't like to see eagles get killed this way and we're trying to educate the rancher but at least he's listened to us and, of course, has given us the remains."

After Charging Shield finished dressing, he proudly draped his eagle bone whistle around his neck and carried his shawl kilt and the sage wreaths toward his sister's trailer house. On the way he stopped to blow several shrill notes on the new whistle. One of the wreaths dropped to the prairie grass and he walked on. Just before he reached the trailer a voice called out. He turned and was somewhat startled to see a young priest walk up with the wrapped sage.

Father Weitz introduced himself. Charging Shield was taken aback, momentarily at a loss for words. When he awkwardly reached out to accept the wreath, the priest spoke politely. "I saw you in the Sun Dance this morning. You're Kyle Charging Shield."

Charging Shield managed a weak nod. "And you're with the mission?" he replied back with a questioning look, staring at the trim priest's unusual attire: a beaded watch band, cowboy boots and jeans, contrasting sharply with the Roman collared, short sleeved, black shirt.

Weitz sensed the Indian's uneasiness. "I'm fairly new." he answered with polished speech then tilted his head toward the Sun Dance tree a short distance away. "It's a beautiful ceremony," he spoke warmly. "If I had a tribe, I'd want to be part of the ceremony." His spontaneous response left little doubt as to his sincerity. "I deeply appreciate the way your people honor their veterans even though I am against wars. After this morning, I realize that men and women who go off to fight should not be made to feel ashamed or alienated from their countrymen."

Charging Shield stared back dumbfounded, managing a puzzled, "Thank you", before he turned to continue walking toward the trailer house. He entered and placed his eagle feather on a shelf above the couch. When he sat on the couch in the empty trailer, his thoughts dwelled on the short exchange. He wondered why the young priest would attempt such cordiality but Eagle Feather's warning regarding the Jesuits outweighed the earnest look in the handsome priest's eyes. He couldn't trust any reservation Jesuit, he cautioned himself. His people's history was one of trusting and being deceived.

After awhile his mind drifted to the holy men. He had seen firsthand how costly a war could be. He hoped their prayers could avoid more wars as he started to doze. His legs were tired and as long as he slept, he wouldn't have to think about eating or thirst. He removed the eagle bone whistle from his neck and blew on it several times. The shrillness seemed to cause a moment of magical sound. He set the whistle on a folding chair and began to sleep; dreaming that his Phantom flew into the cloud which had appeared in his vision. The strong woman appeared in the cloud. A mist seemed to shroud the woman's features, yet he could see her black hair was braided, and she wore a buckskin dress. The buffalo man he could not find although he circled and looped the cumulus cloud. All this time the powerful woman looked on approvingly. He was afraid of her but as long as she appeared as an ally, he continued his search for the buffalo man. What he would do if he found the buffalo man, he didn't know. He wanted to see that vision again though. It had so much power. He circled once more before his Phantom hovered close beside the woman. The mist parted, revealing a face and posture like his grandmother must have had in her younger days. Her eyes were like a soft fire. The eyes became windows drawing him closer. He was no longer in the Phantom but was looking outward from the window of his Grandmother's cabin. In the sage-grown driveway an eagle pecked away at a lifeless jackrabbit while a meadowlark sang. He forgot about the buffalo man and the woman. Nothing else mattered anymore, except the two birds and the tiny part of the world around them.

SUN DANCE

CHAPTER THIRTEEN

The morning he feared most had arrived. It was the fourth day; the day of the piercing. He felt alone as he walked toward the tall lodge. The previous night, hundreds of pow wow dancers had pounded the buffalo grass nearly bare, twisting and turning to the pulsating throb of drumbeats, enthralling the crowd gathered for the evening social dancing. The Plains dance costume contrasted sharply with the sedate skirt and sage wreaths of the morning's ceremonial Sun Dance. Eagle feather, hawk and owl tail bustles were clustered with gay plumage. Bright beadwork, fringed breechcloths, breastplates and bone chokers comprised the Plains social dance regalia. Roach headdresses made up of long rump and tail hair of deer and porcupine, accentuated the face-painted dancer's exciting movements. The bristling hair roach also bore a pair of eagle feathers, which swiveled in bone sockets. Around the dancer's ankles, bells were worn to keep time with the quickened pace of the drums. The morning Sun Dance ceremony was far more somber.

The encampment was silent. He had watched the night's festivities but now his mind was only on the morning's ordeal. He feared that he might display a lack of courage at his first piercing. He wondered if he was worthy to take part. He worried about his mother's words; maybe she was right. The Sun Dance was only for full-bloods and he had been too long in the white man's world.

When he jumped across a ditch, the *wotai* bounced against his chest. A sense of reassurance momentarily dissipated his fears.

Eagle Feather's queried greeting awaited him at the sweat lodge. The rocks were still dark indicating the fire had not been burning long. He admitted he was afraid but would still pierce.

"You are honest, Nephew. I am confident you will go through with it." Eagle Feather's steady voice gave him needed assurance.

While they sat in silence, Eagle Feather recalled the previous Sun Dance. 'The Coming of the *Wotai* Sun Dance,' Eagle Feather always called it when he held his discussions alone with Fools Crow. "He has a mission, no doubt more important than this Sun Dance," Fools Crow's voice in Sioux echoed. "This Sun Dance is wakan and must be endured to overcome the force on the mountain but if he knew of this force, I doubt if he would vision quest... and I couldn't blame him." After the Sun Dance it would be Eagle Feather's task to prepare him. The Sichangu would steer him to a special one who could direct this new sun dancer's thoughts to a powerful vision. Eagle Feather studied the flames of the fire, for he now knew, having discovered the identity of the special one revealed in a strong dream. It was Ben Black Elk, the son of the departed visionary, Nicholas Black Elk. As the rocks heated, other dancers gathered around the fire, assembling for the last day to file into the domed lodge for the cleansing bath of steam.

Eagle Feather motioned to the pouch hanging from Charging Shield's neck. Charging Shield extracted his *wotai* from his pouch and handed it to the holy man. The Sichangu handled it with respect.

"Uncle, it was the mystery of the Great Spirit that allows me to be here and not be rotting in a prison camp," Charging Shield commented. "The mystery powers have been allowed to come through that rock."

Eagle Feather studied the stone for a long moment. Finally the Rosebud addressed his pupil, "We all know there's plenty of enemies who wish to keep us from learning our old ways." Eagle Feather looked meditatively at the stone then back at the anxious eyes of Charging Shield. "This *wotai* brought you safely back to stand up to one of those who would destroy our ways. Part of that mission is fulfilled, now another part is before you if you so choose."

Charging Shield felt helpless. Eagle Feather's foreboding manner and serious gaze made him nod half-heartedly. "Someday this *wotai* will leave you. There is another ceremony you must endure if you wish to keep this *wotai*. You will have to Vision Quest after this Sun Dance."

Charging Shield looked pensive.

"There is a saying about those who suffer the Sun Dance. A reward may come your way since your sacrifice was not easy." One eyebrow raised on Eagle Feather's heavy-featured face. "A wish can come true, maybe more than one, during this circle... from Sun Dance to Sun Dance. The holy man's tone grew ominous. "If you seek a strong wish, one that you might think impossible, then, you can give it great strength by going on the mountain."

The combat missions flooded through. That feeling of a warrior's life before and then what was it... an interlude of wolf, eagle, buffalo? That woman, the warrior would want to return to the woman. If a great reward were to come his way, he would wish in that direction without having to be definitive. How could one define something so recessed, yet was? The Sun Dance left little doubt about its force and power. He realized the annual ceremony was but a part of the overall force stemming from his cultural roots; his people's past, an underlying current waiting to sweep him back into its mystery.

"Be careful what you ask for after a Sun Dance, and always be thankful, Nephew. If you wish to keep this *wotai* a while longer, you will journey from here to a teacher- a special teacher. Rest up for a few days first. Afterwards, you will have to vision quest. Then we will ask you to endure another Sun Dance."

Charging Shield thought for a moment, 'Yes, if he could somehow wish for the freedom of the natural past and her with it. A life where Mother Earth was not bought and sold; a life where your dwelling could be shaped from Mother Earth and your clothing was natural as well... and definitely, her with it.' He returned a silent nod of acceptance. "I will do it, Uncle." A chorus of approval came from the dancers sitting around the fire.

After the sweat bath, the male dancers dressed in the broad-based tipi to the west of the arena. Eagle Feather reached under a folded blanket to bring forth a coiled rawhide rope. He threw it across the tent with oral instructions to obtain a braided rope if he planned to dance the following year. Then the Rosebud holy man gave him a sharp, hardwood peg. Charging Shield placed the peg in a Durham tobacco sack tied to his belt. Catches painted an eagle on his chest with a tube of red lipstick and drew a circle over his left breast. The circle marked the spot where he would be pierced. Catches turned him around to draw wavy red lines down the backs of his arms.

"Look here," called Eagle Feather, holding out an eagle's claw. "This is what I pierce with. It cuts cleaner!" His words ended with a morbid hooking of the claw into his chest leaving a fearful knot in his pupil's stomach.

The women who would take part in the ceremony stood outside the tipi, waiting for the men to dress in the ankle length kilt skirts. Rousseau, a tribal council member, approached one of the women. At that moment, Charging Shield stepped outside through the flap, overhearing the councilman badgering the woman. "What's so important?" he growled at the breed who sported a narrow moustache.

"Where's Fools Crow? We want the dance to get started. A camera crew has paid for picture rights." Rousseau growled back.

Charging Shield replied with an air of disdain, telling him the ceremony wasn't intended for a camera crew.

"Well, there is another matter." The councilman fingered his belt buckle nervously. "We have to get on with the dance because Father Buchwald wants to say Mass. This year he's been kind enough to step aside to allow the dance to go four days. The least we can do is to let him say his Mass."

Charging Shield threw a warning look like a wolf would an intruder over a piece of meat then turned towards the tent. "Get your priest," he snarled.

"He wants you to get started so he can have his Mass said before noon. He doesn't want to hold up the meal we got to serve." The councilman's words hurried, his voice raising at the figure creeping through the parted tent flap. "He's thinking about the welfare of the people, you know, otherwise we'll have to hold up the feeding of this crowd, depending on how long the medicine men delay."

Inside the tipi, the holy men filled their pipes with tobacco and red willow bark. After they finished, he informed them of Rousseau. As Fools Crow and Catches left the tent, Charging Shield turned to wait for Eagle Feather, studiously observing the buffalo horn headdress the holy man was adjusting.

The Jesuit was standing beside the councilman when Eagle Feather and Charging Shield joined the discussion. The priest threw both men a glance of contempt before he addressed Fools Crow and Catches in an admonishing tone, as if he were scolding children. "I want you boys out of there by eleven o'clock. I want to say Mass in honor of Jake Red Cloud. It's been almost a year since he passed away. In accord with your traditions, now is the appropriate time to honor him."

Fools Crow stood in silence. If Fools Crow had wrath for Buchwald it went unsaid, but the old man's burning eyes were protestation enough.

"Father!" Catches addressed the priest politely. "You have the other fifty one weeks in the year. All that we are asking is this one week to pray our own way. Why can't you say your ceremony this one week where you always say it... inside of your church? Why can't we have this day to ourselves? It is only one day. You have all the rest on this reservation."

The priest was unmoved. "No, I'm sorry. We made too many preparations. Red Cloud's family is here. People will be wanting to attend Mass." The missionary darted his eyes among the crowd drawing to the discussion. "My altar had to be loaded on my pickup. Think of Jake Red Cloud. We would dishonor him... especially his family. I have made plans with the family, they are obedient followers of the true church and are expecting to see the service held here." The blank, unmoved looks made him perspire. "I've given in enough." He continued with an air of exasperation. "I could insist to the council that only the Lord's service be offered on this holy day of obligation. It was not a tradition in the old days that the Sun Dance had to fall on a Sunday." His words carried an added forcefulness. "Now you people are insisting that you must interfere with our church tradition which is much older than your ways. You men seem to forget that I know more about your history than you do."

Buchwald threw an appraising look at the eldest holy man. "Why Frank Fools Crow here, and I say this with due respect, Fools Crow can't even read. There are many facts of history that he doesn't know and I'm sure he will be the first to admit it."

"Hold it right there, Buchwald!" Charging Shield could no longer contain himself. "You're playing the old government Indian agent game now. Pitting Indian against Indian." His voice was firm and steady. "Red Cloud's family against the holy men. Attempting to tear down the credibility of our Sun Dance Chief. You're trying to turn us against each other, priest. "

"Charging Shield," the missionary spat his name, "you're not qualified to speak for these older men. You young militants have a lot to learn when it comes to being an Indian." The priest's chin jutted outward and his chest puffed. "I've been on this reservation a lot longer than you. You should have the decency to remain quiet."

"Let him continue," Eagle Feather said with authority, his frame seeming all the more massive by the pair of horns projecting from the bison headdress. "Go ahead, Nephew," he said as he looked at Charging Shield.

Charging Shield turned to Fools Crow. Fools Crow nodded and so did Catches. At that moment Father Weitz walked up, unnoticed behind the crowd.

Armed with the assurance of his mentors, Charging Shield's words flowed with strength. He glared down at Buchwald. "You're facing a new Indian, priest. We've found out you don't have the answers that you've always claimed. You're facing holy men who have support from their people once again. We've discovered our way was right for us all along, despite the brainwashing we received in your boarding schools. Now you're trying to make us feel ashamed because of how you have schemed to break the power of our Sun Dance." He swept an arc with his arm. "These people didn't come from four directions to see your Mass. They came to be reunited with the tribe; to dance Indian; to give gifts to each other; to get away from the evil of your world, which has gotten more evil through the weakness of your religion, and weak because men like you do not understand what real humility is. You talk about Christ and Moses, but when is it that you ever went out into Mother Earth, the Creator's Creation... the wilderness you say, and fasted and prayed like what your black book claims they did?"

He pointed proudly to the wizened men around him. "Our holy men, every one of them do." He glanced eastward, then back at the priest. "Hell, your people wouldn't know how to come together like we do here and yet you want us to become like you. Too many of us have already." He looked at Rousseau with an air of disdain. "You aren't as concerned about the Red Cloud family as you are in attempting to stop our Sun Dance. Jake Red Cloud's family are mere pawns in your sneaky attempt to take away the last spark of life we have." He added with scorn. "You Jesuits have gotten away with your methods all around the world, but the Oglalas, the Sichangus and the rest of the Lakota that gather here, you will not destroy. You will not dilute our way that has been honed down through the time of our tribe."

"*Hau, Hau.*" The gathering of sun dancers surrounding the priest called out as the younger Indian spoke.

"Centuries ago, our way guided the Lakotas from the east, where the white man would have surely annihilated us had we remained." Charging Shield held up his *wotai*. "As for myself, the Great Spirit, through the ways preserved by my tribe, has allowed me to return safely from another of the white man's wars." He squeezed the *wotai* hard and said with finality, "Priest, we're going back and you can't stop us."

Eagle Feather looked down at the Jesuit. "Father Buchwald, you take your altar and go where you always say your Mass. We have our way and you have yours. Now leave us alone!" His bulky frame capped with the dominating horns lowered at the mission pickup. For a brief second, he was Tatanka, the bull buffalo, ready to charge the black truck holding the altar, sweeping its repressive symbol forever from the ceremonial grounds. He turned to take his place in front of the procession. Fools Crow joined Catches to form up the line of sun dancers. The crowd of Indians listening in on the discussion glared at the priest and the council member. Mary Bad Hand, a woman sun dancer was among them.

Not one bit undaunted, Buchwald yelled defiantly, "I'll stop this pagan ceremony and these pagan ways."

"Not today you won't," Mary Bad Hand yelled back.

"*Hau! Hau!*" roared the crowd.

From the rear of the dispersing throng, one drifted away, ambling aimlessly through the surrounding circle of tipis, tents and camper trailers out to the solitude of open prairie and sage, a setting more in tune with the lone figure's deep thoughts. Father Weitz turned Charging Shield's words over and over. 'You talk about Christ and Moses, but when is it that you ever went out into Mother Earth... and fasted and prayed like they did? Out into Creator's Creation. Our holy men, every one of them do.'

What was the harmonic mystery of this simplistic yet so deeply demanding way that had drawn him like a magnet to this reservation? This mystical culture that wasn't pagan or heathen despite the rantings and ravings of men like Buchwald. And now the words of one of them had begun a strange, restless stirring that would draw him deeper into their way. 'Vision quest, vision quest' - the words rang. Before he would ever permanently leave this reservation, he vowed he would befriend either Fools Crow or Eagle Feather. Someday, one of these men would prepare him for a vision. Like Christ... like Moses... he would go out into Mother Earth and fast and pray.

The dancers and the holy men entered the arena to circle the tree of life, then all faced eastward as the singers chanted the beginning of the Sun Dance song. An equal number of women dancers assembled with the pledgers among the men dancers. A small boy danced beside Eagle Feather. It was said that the heavy holy man had a weak heart and would use the strength of the boy to carry him through the long Sun Dance ordeal. After the sun dancers offered their pipes to the cardinal directions, the first song ended to signal their retirement to the recess area. Catches then walked across the arena to deliver his message to the people, after first thanking the Great Spirit for the day that was before them.

Catches spoke in Sioux only. The soft-spoken holy man described a vision that he had experienced. "My journey took me into the spirit world," he described. "Many drunks had to walk before me. They all reached out for a bottle which would always disappear. When it disappeared, the cries of children would echo. These were the children of the alcoholics that had called for them on earth but were never heard." The slight man's eyes swept the crowd. His words took on an added forcefulness. "It was cold and lonely in that dark spirit world. I also saw the women who had left their children. They spoke to me and told me to return and tell their relatives what a lonely world it is they're in."

Charging Shield looked across the arena. The men and women bowed their heads with apprehension as the holy man spoke. Catches spoke in Indian again. He told of the Buffalo Calf Maiden and the coming of the sacred pipe. When he finished, the middle song began. The dancers filed back into the arena to again offer their pipes. When the dancers faced to the south, Fools Crow positioned Charging Shield between Red Bow and Mary Bad Hand and close to the singers. The woman had introduced herself earlier and had invited him to join the Native American club at the University.

The offering song began as Lame Deer and Gap approached the three dancers with a tall Hunkpapa woman named Defender. Charging Shield stared at the stately woman who appeared to be in her early forties. She was unquestionably the most beautiful woman he had ever seen. Her features were delicately chiseled, yet conveyed a sense of strength and power. Her posture was straight and erect as she walked forward between the two men to accept the peace pipes. The woman's beauty made him think of his vision he had the day before. The woman in the cloud resembled the figure in white buckskin standing before him, reaching out to accept his peace pipe.

He lowered his eyes as he held his pipe to the woman. The woman was regal, confident, yet he sensed she was someone to fear if she was not respected. Twice he offered the Yankton pipe but she refused to accept it. He became nervous wondering if she somehow thought she was not respected. The third time he offered she still refused to take it. Charging Shield rubbed the *wotai* across the pipestone and acknowledged in his mind that he was afraid of the woman. The woman smiled as if he had nothing to fear and his pipe was accepted. Mary Bad Hand's pipe was taken by Gap, then Lame Deer received Red Bow's pipe. The drumming stopped and the dancers filed to the rest area at the western side of the arena. The three acceptors presented the pipes to the singers who in turn lit and smoked each pipe.

Three more times the dancers faced the four directions, and three more times pipes were presented. Traditional believing members of the audience helped the singers and drummers smoke the pipes and during this period of smoking, the dancers were allowed to rest, for they were fatigued from fasting and tired quickly. They sat quietly, preserving their strength for the final test yet to come. Charging Shield sat beside Mary Bad Hand asking her in hushed tones about student life at the University. The stocky, jovial woman had been a classmate of his older sister, who had died of pneumonia in the boarding school. For several days he had sat

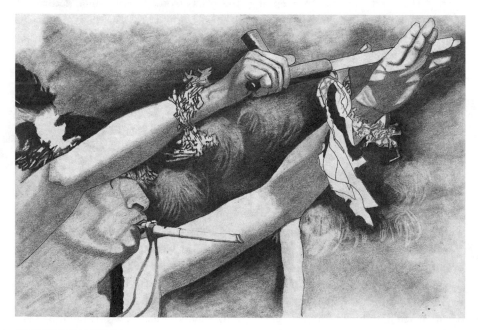

BESEECHMENT

RED BOW

SUN DANCER

beside the outspoken and dominant woman during the rest periods. She seemed to replace the sister he had lost and he now looked forward to their continuing friendship.

After the fourth presentation, the time of the piercing was finally before them. The sun was directly above and only a few clouds were in the sky far away on the southern horizon. Above the Sun Dance grounds the sky was bright blue. Fools Crow selected Red Bow as the first to offer his pain so that the people would live. While Red Bow was led to the bed of sage at the base of the tree, Lame Deer spread the dancers in a circle facing the center. Charging Shield, standing beside Mary Bad Hand, told himself to pray and not to watch the piercing. He blew the eagle bone whistle and looked toward the top of the tree... but his eyes drifted back to Red Bow, motionless on the bed of sage. Fools Crow bent over the prostrate figure to insert a narrow blade in and back through the skin of his chest, following the two cuts with a wooden peg. Red Bow's rope was tied to the peg with a buckskin thong. Four eagle feathers were spaced midway along the braided rawhide. The sun dancer rose cautiously, careful to avoid stepping on the rope then slowly backed away. His eyes were distant as he stared straight ahead. He stepped backward, then slowly eased his weight onto the rope. The four feathers attached to the rawhide bond stood out against the crowded background, one feather for each time the man had pierced.

Eagle Feather was next and an eagle's claw was substituted for the wooden peg. Fools Crow made only one slit with his knife then pushed the claw into the cut to force the sharp tip back out again. Like Red Bow, Eagle Feather showed no pain nor moved a muscle. After a leather thong bound the claw to the rope, Lame Deer aided the holy man as he rose to take his position to the right of Charging Shield. The massive body of the Rosebud Sioux danced in time to the drums. His head tilted back and his arms reached out as he blew on his eagle bone whistle. Charging Shield felt an added security and confidence because of the holy man's presence.

Catches then took the piercing position, electing to pierce himself. Before the beginning of the morning ceremony, the slight, quiet man had also had six eagle feathers sewn into his flesh; one on each arm and four on his back. A light breeze fluttered the feathers as he sat on the sage clasping his chest muscle before inserting a steel awl. The Oglala holy man's courage and willingness to bear pain was renowned throughout the tribe. He also pierced deeper than anyone. His chest bore wide scars from previous Sun Dances.

Lame Deer followed the two cuts from the awl with a wooden peg, then tied the end of the Oglala's rope to the peg with a thong. Catches appeared as though he was in a trance as he danced to the end of the rawhide.

Charging Shield followed Catches. Fools Crow's dark eyes were glowing coals as he led him to the blanket of sage at the base of the cottonwood tree. The holy man removed his sage crown when he reclined to lie on the soft cushion. The sun dancer looked upward at the colors of the four directions attached to the upper branches of the tree. The brilliant blue of sky emblazoned the colored cloths billowing from a slight breeze. Lying down he realized how tired his legs were. It was comforting to lie down. He was aware of his outstretched legs. He hoped he could concentrate to prevent any flinching of his body. He did not want to be afraid. 'Like Catches, like Eagle Feather,' he told himself. 'Like Buddy Red Bow," he added to give himself the resolve not to flinch.

Lame Deer knelt beside Fools Crow and held the braided rawhide rope provided by Eagle Feather. Both men were uneasy. Holy men worried about the first piercing. It was the time of apprehension. A beginner could easily faint, or worse, change his mind at the last minute.

Charging Shield sensed their concern. Pointing to the red circle painted on his chest, he tried to sound reassuring, "I'm okay, Grandpa." He looked up at the tree; it seemed like a leaning tower with bright colored wings. Should Charging Shield fail to pierce, Fools Crow, his sponsor, would have to pierce in his place. Two years before, Eagle Feather had two ropes attached to him because of a last hour change by a would-be sun dancer.

Fools Crow clasped the narrow-bladed knife and pinched the flesh of his chest. It became an excruciating, burning sting of a wasp as Fools Crow tunneled the knife under the skin in a twisting force to push the point back out again.

"Peg? *Took teh*? (Where is your peg?)." He asked. The apprehension of an initial sun dancer had caused the holy man to forget a most important element. Charging Shield reached for the Durham sack tied to his belt. He raised himself, avoiding a direct look at the knife pinned to his chest while he attempted to take the cloth tobacco sack from his belt. He clutched the sack and pulled hard, breaking the string that attached it to his belt. He handed the small sack to Fools Crow. "It's in there, Grandpa."

Lame Deer retrieved the peg inserting it behind the knife as Charging Shield looked back to the top of the sacred tree. The piercing was bearable but the pushing of the peg into the wound was far more painful. The sun dancer had a difficult task not showing the pain. After Fools Crow pulled out the knife and the peg was inserted, Lame Deer tied the rawhide rope onto the peg with a strip of buckskin. He now was connected once again to his mother... Mother Earth, from the buffalo tallow at the base of the tree to the rawhide rope and the wooden peg. The connecting rope was his spiritual umbilical.

Lame Deer reached under his shoulders to help him stand. His chest felt on fire but he tried not to acknowledge the pain. His sage crown was placed on his head after he put his eagle bone whistle into his mouth. He was aware of the drums despite the searing pain. He bobbed slightly to the music and blew softly on his whistle. He danced toward the end of the rope retaking his position next to Chief Eagle Feather, then eased his weight back onto the rawhide. The pain intensified then slowly subsided.

EAGLE VISION

"Ho, Nephew, look." Eagle Feather pointed upward and to his right with his eagle bone whistle. Out of the cloudless wide sky a lone cloud about the size of the Sun Dance arena seemed to be floating lazily toward them.

Charging Shield's thoughts were too shrouded in his pain and anticipation to pay much attention to a lone cloud, nor to realize any significance. He looked briefly and lowered his head. He did not want to be distracted at that moment. It was the time to pray.

Three more sun dancers were pierced and now seven leaned back against their rawhide ropes. The seven pledgers and seven women danced forward to touch the tree of life. Fools Crow, Lame Deer and Gap also put their hands against the trunk to send up their prayers, believing a supreme grandparent was looking down at that moment on its grandchildren, gathered in a circle near the barren badlands of North America.

Several times during the piercing of the last two dancers, Eagle Feather pointed with elation at the progress of the approaching cloud. By this time Charging Shield began to realize the significance of the lone cloud and watched its slow progression. He wondered if the cloud would actually float directly over the Sun Dance. After the last dancer was pierced and at Fools Crow's signal, all of the dancers danced slowly inward to touch the cottonwood tree. After the tree was touched they returned slowly, dancing backwards to the end of their rawhide tethers. By this time, Chief Fools Crow had noticed the approaching cloud and exclaimed with excitement, instructing the dancers to greet the cloud. All of the dancers blew strongly upon their eagle bone whistles then danced inward to touch the tree, their whistles shrieking strongly. When Charging Shield touched the tree, Bill Eagle Feather's powerful hand touched his hand and the tree actually let out a shrill shriek much like the sound of the eagle bone whistles, but with more volume. At that moment, rain droplets began to fall upon the dancers. The dancers touched the tree two more times in the same manner. By this time, the cloud was directly above and a strong murmur of awe came from the onlooking crowd. After the fourth touching, the dancers were free to break their bonds by pulling backward against the rawhide braided rope.

To his right he saw Eagle Feather straining against the rawhide. To his left the rope was taut. Catches, the quiet holy man, leaned back with outstretched arms and closed eyes. Charging Shield leaned away from the tree. The searing pain in his chest became an erupting, spreading canyon; widening and evolving as he hung balanced on his heels. The canyon opened to a peaceful meadow. The buffalo man and the woman flashed through his brain before he saw a warrior riding a sorrel horse to a dwelling. The sorrel and the lodge became all colors. A soft voice called to him from the lodge. The voice was mixed with the song of the meadowlark. He thought it strange they should be one, the voice and the song; but it was restful and comforting, so comforting, like a long journey's end.

Now, only the song of the meadowlark called to him. The sound beckoned from a branch of the cottonwood. He looked to see an eagle sitting on a topmost branch above his grandmother's cabin. The bird transformed into a woman, a woman garbed in a lovely, fringed buckskin dress. For a brief moment she stood there, then she grew wings and dropped down to the meadow to sing a meadowlark's song.

"Behold, Charging Shield," she spoke strongly. "Behold, my mate," she spoke, "I could draw you some pictures of faces I've seen in the clouds. I can make you hear the sound of water as it falls over the moss covered rocks. Someday, we shall have wings, my mate, wings to carry us away to tomorrows of beauty. We shall ride on our wings to soar like the eagles, and yet... and yet, I can do more, Charging Shield, and in that world I shall show you. Eagles, my mate, for mates must be alike, but I am woman, Charging Shield.

The pipe... the way of these ceremonies... all things upon this land... they are from woman. Ah, yes, my warrior mate... our Mother is powerful... for she is Earth." After a short pause she began again.

"Now, I must teach you, Charging Shield. I must reveal the gift of this tree, and all trees throughout our universe."

She lifted her head back as if to clear her throat. A meadowlark's song came from her lips, yet a powerful flapping from a pair of eagle wings accompanied in the background.

'What was she?' Charging Shield asked. "Bird, woman... eagle?"

She winked at him knowingly and laughed brazenly before she began in a commanding voice.

"Behold, the gift of the Tree is what the Creator wants us to see of life.
Budding blossoms,
full lush greenery,
unclothing to nakedness.
Strength, endurance, beauty, peace.
All of this,
brilliant changing hues,
painted about us.
Touching us with their aroma of the seasons.
We are indeed One!"

The vision ended abruptly. The peg broke free, sending him skidding backward on his seat in the hot, dusty arena.

The sun dancers were placed in a line, standing side by side, after the last dancer broke free. The crowd gathered to pass by in a long file, passing from right to left in front of the Sun Dance pledgers, to shake the hand of each dancer and to acknowledge the holy men for their perseverance. An old elder uttered a proud, "Pilamiya, kola (Thank you, friend)," as he passed in front of Charging Shield. His wife followed beside him. When she came before Charging Shield, she shook his hand

and began to cry. She put her head onto the sun dancer's chest, wailing piteously for a few moments. She repeated the same sorrow filled moments before Sonny Larvee and Buddy Red Bow, who were to the left of the former Marine. Most of the older Sioux women cried when they came before the young sun dancers, because in the young men they saw renewed encouragement. Some boldly called out with instructions to fight for the return of the Way. Their lament registered deeply within the spirit/souls of the sun dancers.

EAGLE FEATHER

CHAPTER FOURTEEN

Some white men think their ancestors were monkeys.
Some of us Indians think we are related to the buffalo, the wolves,
eagles and the bears. It is all Mystery; really no one knows.
It is foolish and wrong to kill each other over conversions.
That is not the Indian Way.
— Thunder Owl
Mdewakanton Sioux

A lone eagle circled high to watch the long line of people shake the hands of the sun dancers. That afternoon he drove with Eagle Feather to West River, to arrive in time for an honoring supper his sister Mildred had prepared. He greeted his mother's attendance with pleasant surprise.

"Well, you did it, son," she said. "I guess I couldn't stop you."

"I'm not so sure it was you, Mom. I think someone else was putting on the pressure."

"They bothered me," she admitted. "Every word was about the Sun Dance, but that's all water under the bridge. The Indian in me can't help but be proud."

After several days' rest, the holy man and his new assistant drove eastward across the hot August prairie in a pickup borrowed from Mildred and Ralph. Eagle Feather sported a red bandana tied loosely, draping over the collar of a once yellow shirt so faded it almost matched the worn pair of surplus khaki trousers the shirt was tucked into. A long wide belt reached around the Brule (Teton Sichangu Sioux) ending beneath a flat, rectangular, beaded buckle almost hidden by his girth. The buckle was a gift from a Rosebud woman who had suffered a serious case of arthritis. A tea made from the lower stem and upper root of a prairie weed eventually reduced her painful swelling. The following day the holy man would take his traveling companion aside to show him an unobtrusive plant whose tiny flowers stained the skin purple. After several sweat lodges and a *Yuwipi* ceremony the woman's cure was complete. The belt buckle artfully displayed a buffalo headdress above a pair of crossed peace pipes.

The holy man paid little attention to the dry heat, seeming to enjoy the comfort of the spacious pickup and the company of his young driver and pupil. It wasn't long before he was queried about the old days - when the Bureau of Indian Affairs banned the Sun Dance and the missionaries were in the flower of their power.

"*Lela shee cha*, nephew. Lela shee cha," (Real bad, very bad) the answer came in emphatic Sioux.

They drove in silence while the holy man thought about the past.

"Years ago nephew, we had to do everything in secret and it was tough if you got caught. Those old holy men before my time suffered more that I ever did. Me and Fools Crow... we were protected it seems. Fools Crow had land that he had to sell and his first wife had land. After she died, the land went to him and this helped him through some hard times."

After a short period of silence, Eagle Feather continued in his authoritative, yet fatherly tone. "Myself, the Great Spirit gave me a trade. That is one thing that I have to say for the boarding school. Some of us learned a trade and this kept us from starvation many times.

"I can do all sorts of odd jobs... carpentry, mechanics, if I have to, but I learned how to be an electrician during the war. I started out with it in boarding school and when the war came along, they took anyone with whatever experience they had."

Charging Shield mused over how disappointed the Karma generation would be, discovering that a holy man could know electrical technology and even wire a house. He revealed his thoughts to his passenger, lighting an amused smile.

At an intersection, the pickup turned north, placing the setting sun to their left. Eagle Feather pointed northeast, "Those Hunkpapas up at Wakpala... the tribe is leasing this old Episcopal mission that went broke... they been holding these get togethers so that the old way won't be forgotten."

"Cultural workshops," Charging Shield volunteered.

"Yeah, that's what they call them. That's what they have to say when they fill out all them government papers." He toyed with the knot on his bandana before continuing. "Maybe this will be a way for our holy men to get around to these reservations where the pipe and the *Yuwipi* has been stamped out."

Charging Shield shifted into high gear before turning toward his mentor. "How did they stamp out Indian religion?"

"They had the army on their side," Eagle Feather's expression turned grave. "If you didn't do what the missionaries said, you'd be in trouble. Even after the soldiers left the reservations, we were always afraid they'd bring them back."

"I heard they had the army round up our peace pipes and medicine bundles. Is that true?"

Eagle Feather nodded his head. "That happened at Oglala... other places too. It was before my time but I know it's true. They gathered all the Indians camped around there and made them put their pipes and medicine kits in a pile." The holy man's clenched hand rose in the air and opened quickly. "They poured oil on it and lit a match."

Eagle Feather sat quietly for several minutes before continuing. "In the old days those priests would come right into your cabin. They'd throw out anything that was for Indian religion.

"There was a priest at the mission. A great big guy about as big as I am, I guess. I was trying to think of his name. It was one of those German sounding names." He paused... "Well, anyway, Black Elk was a healer and was having a ceremony for a relative that was sick and during the ceremony, this priest had gotten wind of it and they could see him coming. Boy, he wasn't wasting any time. He had a big mouse colored horse and was coming toward Black Elk's cabin."

"How could they see so well at night?"

"It was in the daytime. Black Elk would always hold his curing ceremony in one of those old white Army tents."

"The old Indian Grandmother tents?"

"Yeah, one of those kind and he would have the sides up in the summertime to keep it cool."

"How can you have a *Yuwipi* in the daytime?"

"Black Elk was powerful, nephew. Really powerful. I can't say whether or not he was strictly a *Yuwipi man* but the spirits were with him - that's all that matters. He could do things no one could and don't believe those missionaries didn't know it."

Charging Shield wanted to ask more about the daylight ceremony but the holy man continued.

"Well, this priest came up and jumped off his horse and ran right into the tent. He kicked the dirt altar apart and took the tobacco pouches, rolled them up and threw them out. All this time Black Elk was tied up and couldn't do anything since he was about to call the spirit people in. They say that big priest even threw Black Elk's peace pipe out of the tent. The Indians were afraid of him and they say he cussed the whole bunch out."

Charging Shield gripped the steering wheel and slowly shook his head, staring down at the white highway lines flying beneath the front of the truck. They both sat in silence. The heat waves from the asphalt formed water mirages in the distance. "Those were tough times, my boy... tough times and not much could be done to protect ourselves. Those days the missionaries could get away with anything. They were in thick with the government people. They could make it real tough on you if you tried to go against them."

"What ever happened to that priest?"

"Well, he got back on his horse and told them not to ever do Indian religion again. He said it was the work of the devil even though we don't believe in such a thing. The Indians there all saddled up their horses and hitched up their teams. After he was satisfied they were going to break it up; he lit out back to the mission.

"Well, at Black Elk's place, they said there weren't hardly any clouds in the sky, but before that priest got back to the mission, he got struck by lightning. It killed his horse and broke his leg real bad. I guess he laid there and was dead before anyone found him. It took a while before those mission priests ever tried to break up any more healing ceremonies after that."

"Well, at least them missionaries learned something."

The heavy man's voice was grave. "By the looks of the way this mission bunch tries to stop our Sun Dance, they didn't learn."

"That Buchwald, he's something else," Charging Shield moaned. "He said he kept my mother from going to hell. How can they know where someone is going after they die?"

"Nephew, it's bad enough to interfere with other religions, but a worse thing is to try to influence the Almighty. Those who think they control who can be forever lost in the spirit world..." he paused to shake his head. "That is bad. Awfully bad. *Lela shee cha*. Some of these people and their ways are crazy, son... crazy." He pursed his thick lips and blew out a whistling stream of air. "The more I study the white man, the more I believe that he should be learning a lot of our ways instead. He does not have that good a track record to be teaching others how to be like him."

"You know, Uncle, I don't like Buchwald for what he tries to do to us, but I could never wish that the Great Spirit punish even him, forever. He can keep his Mass; even the Indians that want to go his way. I just wish he'd leave us alone."

"Nephew, you are learning fast. The Sun Dance was good for you." A confident smile accompanied the holy man's gentle nod.

The sun had passed below the horizon when they bought gas in a town less than an hour's drive from their destination. They had coffee in a restaurant and soon were back on the road heading north to Wakpala.

"I have heard that old Black Elk was powerful, really powerful, Uncle."

"Yes, he was, Nephew. When you call the spirit beings in broad daylight, you are what they call powerful."

It was dark when they drove across the Wakpala Bridge. The moon was nearly full, reflecting from the water. They drove on, several miles, before proceeding up a hill to a cluster of dilapidated buildings that had once served as an Episcopal mission.

"This is the place," Eagle Feather announced.

A man and woman named Glenn and Irma Three Stars, the mission caretakers, bid them welcome, delighted that they had arrived before the end of the workshop's evening session.

After they were led into the community hall, Eagle Feather brought his pipe from a plain buckskin bag. He stood before a cluster of Hunkpapa Sioux, wetting the pipe stem with his lips, then attached the jade stone pipe bowl to load the pipe and offer the stem upwards. The people bowed their heads in reverence.

"Ho, Tankashilah. Grandfather, grant that these days may bring renewed life back to my Hunkpapa cousins. Have pity on us, oh merciful Grandfather. Give us good weather so that we may enjoy a sweat lodge. Allow my cousins here to learn well what I must teach. Ho, *hetch etu aloh.*"

When he lit the pipe, the Hunkpapas stepped forward. After the pipe was smoked, Eagle Feather spoke briefly. "Brothers and sisters, tomorrow I shall teach the way of the pipe. When the sun sets, a sweat lodge will be ready for those who wish to take part."

Irma Three Stars pointed toward a table set with an urn of coffee and a stack of sandwiches. The sandwiches consisted simply of homemade bread, U.S. Department of Agriculture Surplus Commodity cheese and canned beef. No lettuce, pickles, tomatoes or mayonnaise, yet, to the two travelers, they were delicious! The crowd of Hunkpapas gathered around the table to shake hands and exchange conversation with the Rosebud holy man. Many of the workshop participants had been to the Sun Dance. Their words centered on the annual gathering.

A man with a limp spoke in Sioux to Charging Shield. Eagle Feather interpreted, "This man had no way to get to the Sun Dance. He says he is proud of you for piercing. He has hope, now that he sees young men going back to the old way. He says, he too, was a warrior. He went across the ocean and fought in the first big war. He says he is proud that he volunteered to fight for this country, even though at that time the Sioux were not yet allowed to be citizens. He is proud that all of his sons volunteered and fought for Uncle Sam in World War Two. He said, two of his grandsons he lost in Korea."

Charging Shield shook the aged outstretched hand, studying the weathered face. One eye was clouded while the other squinted, wanting to focus closer. The squint subdued the old Indian's attempt to smile. Despite the pitiful expression, Charging Shield sensed strength and hope in the man's grasp. These were the people of Gall and Sitting Bull. But Sitting Bull was murdered and so was the Indian Spirit among the Hunkpapa.

After a long handshake, the man walked slowly away aided by a twisted cane. He spoke in Sioux as he left, "You must dance gazing at the sun and the other young men must dance beside you. We old ones will be with you." He held up his cane and leaned back to emphasize the Sun Dance.

Later that evening, the two travelers were led beneath a black starlit sky to a bunkhouse. The moon was hiding behind a bank of clouds when they opened a leather-hinged door. A kerosene lamp was lit. Charging Shield examined his chest when he removed his shirt. Strange, he thought, how the piercing wound was healing with only a slight scab; his only irritation, a dull, occasional ache from within, where obviously connective tissue had been strained. Otherwise, there had been only minor pain, no fever, nothing. Within a few days the scab would drop, leaving but a slight scar that Catches and John Fire claimed would recede with each passing year. He remembered Catches applying a pinch of badland dirt to each sun dancer's wound after all had broken free. "On this day, Mother Earth is truly holy. She shall heal all wounds for the Lakota sun dancer." Catches had spoken to him in a soothing tone, sensing his apprehension when he applied the alkali soil.

The holy man blew out the kerosene lamp. "Sleep sound, Nephew," he commanded. "We'll have to build these Hunkpapas a sweat lodge tomorrow. You'll be cutting willow and hauling rock. They asked me to do a *Yuwipi* ceremony up here too."

The following morning, the pair looked down on a broad river as they walked from the bunkhouse to the community hall for breakfast. The weathered barn board buildings cresting the commanding knoll faced inward around an elliptical, graveled cul-de-sac. The community hall, the bunkhouse and the caretaker's cabin had undergone a tidy renovation, contrasting sharply with a pair of dilapidated classroom buildings, a dormitory and a pitiful church, its one tall spire leaning back like a dunce hat, pointing downstream toward the river bottom. A corner of the church buttressed a corral holding several horses sipping from a stock tank. Behind the corral, sweeping away toward rolling prairie, sage clumps were thinly sprinkled on the richer grassland in contrast to the Badlands of the Oglala reservation.

After breakfast, the holy man held out his peace pipe before the workshop audience. "You must not forget that four has many teachings," he said after offering the pipe. "There are four directions from which the Almighty teaches. There are four seasons, which he uses to teach of the four directions. We are always at the center of the four directions." He pointed the stem toward the floor and continued with calm clarity. "There are four races of man. Man has four faces. His first face is that of a baby. His mother must take care of him like our Mother Earth cares for us." He drew an imaginary line with the pipe. "The second face is the in-between face. Now he must learn from the older ones and explore Mother Earth. The third face is when he is in his prime. He has to provide and share... and be a warrior if there are enemies." He looked around the room. "There are many here who have received your fourth face... the face of the old. Now you must look back. Before you leave this world, you must pick out those roads that were best." He swept the pipe toward two children sitting on the floor. "Pass your knowledge on before you leave this world."

EAGLE VISION

Eagle Feather halted his speech and held up four fingers. "Four - it is important to our way. At the Sun Dance we wish to thank the Almighty for his gifts. He has given us many things through four ways. We want to send our prayers to him in a way that he has spoken to us. That is why the Sun Dance lasts four days." He walked to a table and picked up four cloths representing the four sacred colors. Each cloth was attached to the end of a willow stick. A braided cloth, made up of the four colors, remained on the table. He waved each cloth separately and returned them to the table. He picked up the red cloth and tore a piece from it. "Each by itself is easily torn. Now let me have the cloths braided together." The braided cloths refused to tear.

"All men, all women together cannot be destroyed but, individually we can. You must learn that all men and women have good ways, all are holy and someday we will all come together."

*　　*　　*　　*

The noon meal was served outside to observe the quartering of a buffalo carcass. Charging Shield was in the shadow of the rundown church that overlooked the broad river coursing slowly below the mission when an attractive female approached him.

After she introduced herself, he made a sitting gesture, studying the girl's complexion, admiring the touch of oriental that seemed hiding in her features. He guessed that she was a quarter or half Sioux.

Rosalie Carlson was her name. "I thought we should get to know each other," she said as she sat beside him. "I'm a senior at the University," her voice was pleasant.

"How do you like the workshop?" he asked.

"It's worth a couple of easy credits," she said with a languid shrug. "Quite a few Indians are at the University. You'll have to join our club."

Their conversation dwelled on the college at the eastern end of the state. After a while, the girl helped several women carry the buffalo meat to the community hall. He studied her long, lithe body made slimmer by the tight-fitting western shirt and faded Levi's. Her round breasts seemed out of proportion to her small waist and long thighs. The single braid topped with a beaded comb reminded him of his mother's hair. His eyes followed the girl to the community hall anticipating her company at the University.

'My mother and Mildred, they'd like it if I would date an Indian girl,' he told himself. He found himself comparing Rosalie with the stewardess. A determined grimace swept his face. The Sun Dance was over. He couldn't have brought anyone back to the Sun Dance. The Sun Dance had power. It made him forget the California girl. He'd get to know Rosalie better,' he promised himself.

Eagle Feather's lecture argued with his thoughts. "Red, white, black and yellow. They are all the same. All made by the Great Spirit." Eagle Feather's words made

155

him reconsider. 'The holy men were like the old timers. The holy men weren't prejudiced.'

'The people aren't holy men,' he countered.

A television commercial flashed through his thoughts. The television commercials show the white man's mate - she's always white. The black advertiser - his mate is always black. He'd be better off with his own kind. Like it or not. White, dominating society had its subtle but rigid rules. But maybe... she... Karen... was his own kind. She said she was adopted. That look, she could pass for a quarter or maybe... even half. What does that matter? He argued back.

That day came back to him. The pounding surf, Karen's curvaceous figure, those beautiful calves and thighs when she removed the terry cloth robe. Kissing her the first time, that tantalizing body pressing closely while the Great Ocean rocked and cradled the two of them- the eagle and the meadowlark. He turned his gaze toward the river and watched the water lapping at a tiny beach. Oh, how he missed the stewardess. Yes, she was a city type, just like him. They both had succeeded in the white man's world. Just because he had now sun danced, did that make him more of an Indian? He wasn't a reservation Indian. Nevertheless, his mother and Mildred, they would prefer a "real Indian", like this Rosalie, if he would someday get serious over a girl. He jumped to his feet with a perplexed scowl. The holy man's wisdom, the red, white, black and yellow clamored against the television commercials - you never see the black advertiser with a blonde wife... both contrasts pulled inside of him as he walked away from the church.

WAKPALA
SPIRIT CEREMONY

CHAPTER FIFTEEN

Although there is only one Great Spirit,
there are different ways to talk to It.
— Thunder Owl
Mdewakanton Sioux

The afternoon sun looked on with the silent crowd watching the construction of the sweat lodge close to the river's edge. Eagle Feather bent peeled saplings while his assistant tied them together with thin strips of willow bark. After a domed framework was erected, Charging Shield gathered driftwood. He used one of the saddle horses; a blue roan gelding that belonged to the mission caretakers.

As he pulled the first load toward the lodge site, Rosalie offered her help. He answered with a smile, extending his hand and an open stirrup. They rode double up a beaten path to saddle a sorrel mare beside the steepled church. He noted her experienced manner when she slipped the bit in the reluctant mare's mouth. Soon they were riding down the bluff back to the river. She raced the quarter horse ahead, leaping across a washout. He admired the smooth gait of the horse as well as the effortless balance of the rider. As he chased after her he said to himself, 'Now this is the kind of girl my Dad would like for me. Mom would go for her too... as long as she turns out to be Catholic.' His deceased father had been renown for breaking horses during his ranch days and had roped and ridden in early stock shows long before they were called rodeos. It was exhilarating to be at full speed over thundering hooves as he gained speed down the bluff. It was like lighting afterburners and rolling upside down in the Phantom. He had always lived on the edge. The Marine Corps allowed him that feeling, now, once again it was so thrilling to return to that realm.

Eagle Feather called as they pulled a pile of driftwood with a lariat to the lodge site. "Better get some more loads, Nephew. I predict three or four go-arounds tonight. Get a bunch of rocks about the size of muskmelons. Make sure they don't have any deep cracks."

After the wood was gathered, he trailed a burlap sack across the slick prairie grass hunting for smooth boulders. The couple carried on a steady conversation while they worked. He discovered the girl was from a ranch and her father had been a tribal chairman. It was suppertime before they brought in the last load. The dust and the summer's heat made the river inviting. After the horses were returned to the corral and had their bridles and saddles removed, he waited in the dining hall for a sack of sandwiches and a jar of lemonade while she changed to a pair of cutoff jeans. "Get the fire going in about an hour," Eagle Feather instructed.

Soon the couple was splashing in the cool river. Charging Shield floated on his back relaxing his tired muscles. The water was a refreshing respite from the rock and firewood gathering chore beneath the hot prairie sun.

After a while they built a fire near the sweat lodge. He placed the rocks within twisted pieces of driftwood before touching a match to a roll of dry buffalo grass. While the flames grew around the stones, the couple sat with their backs against the lodge, quietly eating their supper.

"I heard that your older brother is going to try for politics in West River." Rosalie opened the conversation with enthusiasm in her voice.

Charging Shield nodded affirmatively, unable to speak because of a healthy bite of sandwich in his mouth.

"My Father is going to support him. He says it's time that Indians get into more than reservation politics." She absently picked up a stone and held it back by her ear as if she were intending to throw it into the river. "I hear it's that rich Jew in West River that's behind him." She threw the stone and watched it splash. She turned to him with a look of admiration. "I guess he's a good friend of yours too. Taught you how to fly, didn't he?"

Charging Shield swallowed and looked down at the scattered river stones at their feet. "I guess that's true. I was lucky that I met Ernie Hale as a kid. Course, the Marines and flight school taught me how to really fly."

"Well, the way I hear it, if it wasn't for that rich Jew, you wouldn't be a pilot and all. But that is beside the point. You could really go places in politics, Kyle." Rosalie declared as she shifted her position closer to the pilot and reached out to touch his shoulder with a delicate pat. "That's where that old Jew can help you."

He gazed at her attractive legs and then to her full breasts. He squirmed uncomfortably and looked around for members of the workshop. He reasoned that everyone was either eating and conversing in the dining hall or were retiring to the dilapidated dormitory for a refreshing nap before the evening's ceremony. He had never thought of his flying mentor and close friend as an "old rich Jew."

"I was surprised to see you traveling with a medicine man," the girl commented. He threw her an odd look but didn't answer.

"Why did you do the Sun Dance?"

"It's a long story," he replied with an upward turn of his head, admiring a hawk sweeping past the cluster of buildings sitting on the bluff.

"You really believe in that stuff, don't you?" She wrinkled her nose. "I can't get into the religion bit. These medicine men should teach the people to join the system if they're ever going to get ahead."

He wanted to avoid an argument by offering her a placating shrug. "They want people to get ahead but they also want us to live for the generations unborn."

"Generations unborn!" she laughed contemptuously and moved back away from him. "The white man runs the world. Indian ways are dead," she flatly declared. "I bet your brother knows that. Besides, what good can it do?"

Her statement spurred him but he managed to answer quietly, "Right now the washichu rides a crest. Someday... someday... maybe soon... too damn soon, he's going to wish to his high heaven he would have listened to our ways." His eyes followed a killdeer searching the parched cracks of the receding shoreline. He went on in answer to her suspicious look. "He doesn't know what living for future generations means. He does well to live for one generation." He frowned reflectively. "In the end, his own generation puts him in an old folks home."

Her features hardened. "Generations unborn. What the hell good is that?" She noted the look of chagrin cast by the down-turned pursing of his mouth. "Don't get so damn involved," she said pointing to the sweat lodge, "It could hurt your image."

"My image!" he replied sharply.

"Play the game. If you go too far on either side they can hang a label on you. You'll find that out when you get to the University. I don't have any problems there and I plan to keep it that way." An ironic truth hung in her voice.

"So I took part in the Sun Dance. What harm was that?"

"It's unnatural. It isn't like going to church."

"Unnatural? And you call a church... natural?" he questioned with a strained look.

She threw him an annoyed grimace. She stammered nervously before regaining her conviction. "You know what I mean. We don't live in tents and wear feathers anymore. Like I said, it's a white man's world. Follow your brother and get in with that old rich Jew. I heard he likes Indians."

'If a white man doesn't do it, then it's unnatural?' he wanted to say but he knew it would be a fruitless argument. Instead, he picked up a flat stone and sent it skipping across the river. "There's an old saying, Rosalie, one of ours. Respect your brother's vision."

An expression of mockery crossed her face. "Why do you want to be so... so Indian?" she questioned with a disgusted air. "You've made it in the white world. Don't ruin it for yourself."

Her word's echoed his sister's words, his sister Leona. "Why do you want to be so Indian?"

For a moment his past swirled before him. As a youth, he had watched the pow wow dancers in the arena and was drawn to their dancing. No Indians in West River ever danced in the pow wows like the reservation dancers did and then... even among the reservation Indians, only a few of the young people danced. It was mostly the old timers. Yet, somehow he wanted to dance. With the help of his sister Mildred he had assembled a dancer's regalia. Ralph had even helped. A pair of Mildred's brocaded couch arm coverings made by patients at the Indian tuberculosis hospital were soon changed to a flattering set of breechcloths sporting old time Sioux designs. Ralph returned one day with a porcupine head roach complete with swiveling eagle feathers that he had found at a pawnshop. He himself constructed a ragged, dyed, turkey feather tail bustle made from instructions found in a "Ben Hunt's Indian Costumery" book. An old breastplate, he had purchased at a rummage sale held by the West River Indian mission, filled out his dance outfit. Ben Black Elk contributed a pair of beaded moccasins complete with rawhide soles. He was ready to dance.

Mildred and Ralph were so proud. And then Leona came through the door just as he had finished dressing in his new regalia. "Why do you want to be so Indian?" she questioned.

'Strange,' he thought. 'Once he started to pow wow dance, the rest of the West River Indian students ignored him, except for Morris, Morris Shangreux, who was a breed like himself.' Morris had been raised by his grandparents and somehow had been able to cling to the old ways, despite attending the mostly all-white school. Neither he nor Morris was very popular with the rest of the Indian students and of course not with the white students. "Be white or become white," was the rule. Basically, both were shunned. One breed Indian girl did indicate an interest at a church social but once the girl's mother knew that he was involved with Indian dancing, the girl was forbidden to have any association with him. He had been 'stood up' by two other Indian girls on attempted dates and from a realistic and practical sense, he came to be attracted to only the dance and sports; they were much more dependable.

Morris and he were both drawn to the stirring drama of the dance. They were oblivious to any detours away from the alluring call of the dance arena. It was mainly the sheer artistry of dance that held them in thrall. They were like figure skaters among a bunch of hockey players- outnumbered but yet persistent toward their own bliss. Morris went on to become a gifted hoop dancer- a specialty of dance that few could master. He remembered well the whirling, twirling, dazzling display of beautiful solo performances mastered by Morris at the reservation dances. At the high school in West River, he would sit at the same table with Morris in the cafeteria, oblivious to the rest of the other students. Charging Shield was several grades ahead of Morris. His white friend Stan, the toughest kid in his grade, whom he spent many hours with playing basketball, was also attracted to Morris. Even Stan had become enthralled with the artistry and gift of hoop dancing. No one dared bother either of them at the cafeteria table because of the presence of Stan, who had been drawn to the warmth of his Indian friend's parents and of course the basketball. Kyle would come down the floor and feed the big center. Time went on and the two older boys joined the service. When he was in Korea he had received several letters from Morris but before he returned from war, Morris committed suicide.

He had been silent, lost in his reverie. "Kyle," she jarred him with her harsh, unfeeling voice. "That old Jew. He's behind your brother. Make the most of it." She added. "Stop being so Indian."

Her words stirred something inside. A sense of loneliness for Morris swept through him. The isolation from his own kind for dancing Indian added a touch of defiance. Now he had found a new satisfaction from his participation in the Sun Dance, causing him to answer in a standoffish tone, "Well Rosalie, maybe I don't have any choice."

A crowd gathered that evening for the sweat lodge. Eagle Feather managed to endure four ceremonies to allow the majority to take part. Charging Shield tended the fire and placed hot rocks into the lodge with a pitchfork when Eagle Feather called out. As he was staring at the fire, he was consumed by an old man's face rising out of the smoke. Upward, it carried the face. In the smoke the old man looked downcast. It was an old Indian's face and the rocks became peace pipes, medicine

PEACE PIPES & BUNDLES BURNED BY CAVALRY

bundles and buffalo skulls. The fire keeper envisioned a Cavalry officer directing a trooper to pour oil or kerosene upon the gathered medicine bundles. The officer brandished a saber. The people looked on in sadness. Gattling guns, Hodgekiss guns stood guard. Eagle Feather called out for more rocks. The vision vanished. Charging Shield looked at the Sioux gathered around the fire, eagerly waiting to endure the next lodge. They stood straight and tall, outwardly pleased to be going back, back to the Old Way.

Before the beginning of the final ceremony, two elderly women asked to remain in the lodge. "We waited a long time for this. We used to have sweat lodge when we were little girls and we're going to go through it again," one of the women spoke defiantly.

Bill laughed, "So be it, Grandma. You shall go through again if I can last that long."

Charging Shield walked with the holy man and Irma Three Stars after the final ceremony. When they reached the top of the hill, the moon's reflection across the water formed a man's face.

"Look! Look, Bill! It's the same face of the man that I saw in the sweat lodge fire tonight. It rose up in the smoke and looked down at me." Charging Shield spoke with astonishment, noting that in the water the face looked stern but not sad like in the fire.

Eagle Feather's reply was calm, "Yes, it is, Nephew. It is him. The sweat lodge was good. I look for a strong *Yuwipi* tomorrow night." The holy man stopped short, motioning for the other two to continue walking. When they were out of sight, he spoke in ancient Sioux to the figure in the water.

Charging Shield was stretched out asleep when the Sichangu returned to the bunkhouse. Eagle Feather's heavy body was fatigued from the long day, yet his mind was refreshed and contented. The man in the water had painted Spirit Mountain red and a sorrel horse with no reins was powerful on the mountain. The third quarter of the circle had begun. Within the next few days, the Sichangu was assured he would receive another strong sign; one that would direct his young pupil toward the vision sought by the holy men.

The following day, after the holy man described the Sun Dance to the attentive crowd seated in the community hall, he called on his assistant to explain the smooth rock that he had worn in combat. Charging Shield removed the buckskin pouch from around his neck. The Hunkpapas handled it with respect and awe. No one doubted the power of the *wotai* nor Fools Crow's prediction that it had protected him.

"Cousins, it was the mystery of the Great Spirit that allows me to stand here and not be rotting in a prison camp," Charging Shield commented. "The Creator has allowed some of his power to come through that rock."

Eagle Feather studied his assistant for a moment before he stared through the window at the gravel road winding away from the mission. The crowd remained silent; sensing the holy man had more to say. Finally the Rosebud addressed his pupil, "Nephew, someday this *wotai* will leave you." He turned toward the crowd and raised his voice. "We all know there's plenty of enemies who wish to keep us from learning our old ways." Eagle Feather looked meditatively at the buckskin pouch then back at the anxious eyes of the crowd. "This *wotai* brought my nephew safely back to stand up to one of those who would destroy our ways. Part of that mission is fulfilled, now another part is before him if he so chooses."

Charging Shield felt helpless. Eagle Feather's foreboding manner and somber gaze made him nod half heartedly. "There is another ceremony you must endure if you wish to keep this *wotai*. You will have to Vision Quest before the next Sun Dance."

Charging Shield looked reflective.

"There is a saying about those who suffer the Sun Dance. A reward may come your way since your sacrifice was not easy." One eyebrow raised on Eagle Feather's heavy-featured face. "A wish can come true, maybe more than one, during this circle... from Sun Dance to Sun Dance." The holy man's tone grew ominous. "As I said before, if you want to keep this *wotai*, a little longer, I will arrange a ceremony with Fools Crow. Afterwards, you will have to Vision Quest."

Charging Shield thought for a moment, then once again he repeated his wish. 'Yes, if he could somehow wish for the freedom of the natural past and her with it.' He returned a silent nod of acceptance. A chorus of approval filled the room.

That evening a stream of battered cars from the surrounding communities gathered at the mission grounds. Eagle Feather studied the growing crowd from the porch of the community hall for a few moments, then nodded his agreement to Irma Three Stars. It was decided that the *Yuwipi* ceremony would be held in the basement of the abandoned church.

As the people filled the old structure, Irma's husband overheard a conversation disputing the decision to have the ceremony in the bottom of a church. After the crowd had settled in their places, the Hunkpapa strode to the center of the room. "The missionaries have brain-washed the people. Everything is bad unless it has their approval. The spirits will enter this ceremony if we ask for their presence and not because of a piece of brick or concrete or whatever use this dwelling has had. We are praying to the same God. We call for power in a different way." He admonished the participants. "We do not accuse the *washichu*s of having evil present when they appeal to the Almighty. Why should they tell us that our way is evil?" A murmur of assenting 'haus' swept the room.

Bill sat in a corner holding a conversation with a tall Hunkpapa, Isaac Thunderhawk, who was the father of a young girl who had been killed, while walking with another Indian girl along a highway. The girl had been run down by a carload of white teenage boys who had been drinking. The two girls fled from the car into the ditch, but the Thunderhawk girl stumbled in a badger hole. The car left the highway and drove over her. The driver was held in an off-reservation jail awaiting trial, while his attorney contended that the girl had tried to commit suicide. Rarely were white men convicted for killing Indians. The *Yuwipi* would be held to reveal the true cause of the girl's death.

The holy man took a large abalone conch shell and a smudge stick made up of tightly bound sage plants. He lit one end of the smudge stick and had Irma Three Stars smudge each person attending the *Yuwipi* with the fragrant wisps. While Irma was smudging, Bill emptied a pail of earth onto the floor of the basement. He formed a small mound and patted the top smooth. He drew a round circle and crossed two lines inside of the circle - the symbol for the Power of the Hoop. He then drew a figure on the flattened surface. It was the same face of the man inscribed on his pipe stem.

Charging Shield held a bundle of loose sage plants, which he had cut into small lengths. He passed a piece to each of the participants. The closely packed bodies sitting on the basement floor caused the damp cement walls to sweat. No windows or ventilation circulated the air. He wondered how Bill's heart would take the conditions as he passed out the fragrant plant. "Put a piece over your ear or in your hair," he said as the Hunkpapas took the sage.

Bill placed a small red flag in an earthen container and set it at one corner of the altar area. The yellow flag, in its container, was placed at the adjacent corner. The black flag and white flag were placed at the two remaining corners.

The wife of Isaac Thunderhawk, Alvina Thunderhawk, unwound a long string of black tobacco pouches around the outside of the four flags, forming a large square enclosing the dirt altar and the area where the holy man would lay after he was tied. Eagle Feather stood up from the altar with his pipe and removed his shirt. His Sun Dance scars covered his chest muscles.

"Cousins, for many of you this is your first spirit ceremony. Do not be afraid of what you see here. It is only the old way that we are using to communicate to the powers that are beyond. Nothing will harm you as long as you show respect. If you are here only for a curiosity or some kind of show I hope that you will leave now before the ceremony starts. It will get hot, worse than it is now. Take a piece of sage and chew on it if you have trouble breathing." Eagle Feather reached down into his medicine bag for his *wotai* stone. He held the rainbow rimmed agate briefly before returning it to the fringed deerskin bag that also contained his peace pipe within a smaller, narrow red cloth sack. Eagle Feather withdrew the pipe sack and connected the green jade bowl to the sumac pipe stem. The pipe was offered to the four directions, loaded with a mixture of red willow, fall sumac leaves and Prince Albert tobacco, before being handed to Alvina Thunderhawk, who sat on the opposite side of the dirt altar, the place of honor position for holding the pipe."

"I'm ready to be tied," the holy man said to his assistant while pointing to a rawhide tying rope.

Charging Shield tied the holy man's hands behind his back with the rawhide cord then picked up the blanket of the *Yuwipi* and placed it over his head. The feather draped backward. "Say a prayer for me, cousins," Bill spoke in a muffled tone through the blanket.

YUWIPI MAN IN BLANKET

Charging Shield then took a longer rawhide rope, made a noose and dropped it over the holy man's head and drew it tight. He wrapped it around Eagle Feather's body once and made a tie, then looped it again around the holy man and made a tie. He continued the procedure until there were seven loops around the holy man, ending at his ankles with the final tying.

Isaac Thunderhawk stood to help lay the massive body of the holy man, face forward towards the west, and directly in front of the dirt altar.

Eagle Feather had received his powers through Fools Crow and the similarity between the two men's ceremony preparation was noted by the holy man's attendant. Charging Shield observed that the buckskin rattles, placement of the flags, and *Yuwipi* blanket were almost identical to Fools Crow's ceremony. Only the peace pipe bowl and the designs on the stem lacked conformity. Eagle Feather's pipe, which had a green jade bowl, was different from everyone's and no doubt reflective, to some degree, of his personality and manner. The stem bore four strange designs. Red pipestone was the customary material which Sioux pipes were made from. No one had a pipe like Eagle Feather's.

The two kerosene lanterns that lit the room were blown out. Charging Shield groped in the dark and sat down. Two Hunkpapa men sang the calling song to the beat of a cowhide drum. The high-pitched song was concluded and Eagle Feather called out for them to sing it again. At the end of the second song, Bill spoke out from under the *Yuwipi* blanket.

"Ho, there are some here that do not believe this way is for them. The spirit people will not enter until those persons leave. I will help those persons identify themselves. One is sitting with her back against the north wall and is resting her left arm against her knee, which is bent. One leg is straight out. There is a piece of sage lying on the floor beside her that she threw away and she is sitting close to someone that I have traveled with."

"Ho, Charging Shield, reach behind you on your right side. There is a woman behind you. Tell her she must leave so we can get on with the ceremony."

Charging Shield turned to place his hand behind him. He felt a rough textured boot. He then reached up and placed his hand on the woman's arm resting on her knee. He felt the broad turquoise bracelet that he noticed she wore when they had hauled the wood and rocks.

"Rosalie, you'll have to leave. I guess this isn't for you," he said.

"I'm sorry, I guess I've got too many doubts," she whispered as she rose to leave.

"There is a couple, a man and a woman near the doorway," Eagle Feather murmured from the blanket. "You do not believe either. You have planned to move away from here soon, where a job is waiting for you. You have come here for curiosity and think this is the work of a bad spirit."

The door opened and Rosalie and the couple left.

The drumstick hit the rawhide drum and the calling song began. Midway through the song the spirit beings manifested themselves, entering as blue lights dancing in a frenzy across the ceiling, bouncing off the walls, as if in a whirling ball; yet keeping steady timing with the rapid beat of the drum.

The buckskin rattles were equally active, dashing back and forth within the square enclosure formed by the tobacco offerings. The room was stifling hot and nearly suffocating, causing Charging Shield to reach for the sage. He chewed several leaves and worried about Eagle Feather. Suddenly, a cool breeze flowed through the room. A flapping sound came from the center, as if a large bird were actually flying before them. The cool blowing breeze caused a stir among the descendants of Gall and Sitting Bull. The singers burst into Gall's war song, joined by the Hunkpapas, proudly aware of the power of the *Yuwipi*.

The fanning breeze blew strong as the singing drew to a close. The room was almost cold as the drum ceased beating and the song ended. "Ho, *Tankashilah*. Ho *Tankashilah*. Thank you. Thank you for allowing us all to be here tonight," Eagle Feather's muffled voice called through the blackness.

"Grandfather, we are here to ask for the return of the old ways of Gall and Sitting Bull. Bless a family here with the strength and wisdom that Sitting Bull had through his medicine.

"We also are gathered to call on Thelma Thunderhawk who was killed before the Sun Dance. We hope that some word or sign may be sent concerning the daughter of the parents who sit here mourning the loss of their loved one. Ho, *Hupo*, *Hupo*." Bill called for the middle song.

The bluish lights returned and paraded around the room in a circle at a marching pace. The breeze again returned and Charging Shield felt the floor shake as if horses abreast were marching in the center of the room. He could hear the clopping of hooves through the loud drumbeat and chanting of the singers.

Isaac Thunderhawk cried out, "My daughter is here! My daughter is here! She's talking to me." The singers ended the song but Bill urged them to continue. All joined in a loud chorus leaving Isaac Thunderhawk to converse with his daughter in the way of the *Yuwipi*. The song ended; Isaac and his wife could be heard crying to themselves.

Bill called on each participant to pray, commencing with the first person at the left of the place of honor.

The Hunkpapas expressed appreciation for the ceremonies, beseeching special blessings on behalf of the holy man's health. A measure of comfort was sought for the Thunderhawks. It took more than an hour to hear the petitions, sending the temperature rising. Finally the bearer of the pipe prayed and the circle was complete.

Bill called for the untying song. The cooling breeze accompanied the spirit people's final entry. A buckskin rattle danced before Charging Shield, shaking itself furiously, emitting sparks at its base. The dim flow tempted a closer observation. When he bent forward, a cold sponge-like finger poked him in the forehead, sinking itself with a numbing projection. He jerked back in fear, his heart thumping against his ribs. Suddenly an eagle screamed. The breeze grew stronger, then stopped abruptly. The blue lights whirled over the holy man, hovered, then disappeared into the ceiling at the song's end.

Eagle Feather's strong voice instructed the crowd to light the kerosene lamps. Matches were struck.

Bill was sitting up untied, and without his blanket when the soft glow from the glass chimney lamps illuminated the room. The long rawhide tying rope was wound in a tight ball beside the buckskin rattles.

After the pipe was summoned from Alvina Thunderhawk, it was lit. Awed whispers accompanied the passing of the green stone pipe to each participant.

Bill was the last to smoke, when he finished he asked if Isaac Thunderhawk had any comments.

"My daughter appeared to me tonight. She said that she was run down by the car. It was like we all knew." The tall man began sobbing.

Bill broke in. "You have seen the power of the Indian way. Treat this ceremony with respect and it can become a great blessing. Your hearts prayed for power and we experienced a lot of it. It is an honor to be with you, my Hunkpapa cousins. Gall and Sitting Bull are proud of their grandchildren gathered here tonight."

BEN BLACK ELK

CHAPTER SIXTEEN

Knowledge prepares you for the Spirit World.
You don't want to be with those who have not sought knowledge...
in the Spirit World.
— Thunder Owl

Sandwiches were served with gallons of Kool-Aid and coffee at the community hall. The Hunkpapas clustered around the holy man discussing *Yuwipis* and powers of holy men, most of whom had long since been deceased. Charging Shield noted Rosalie's absence from the hall.

Later, he walked with Bill back to the bunkhouse. The kerosene lamp was lit and soon they were sitting on the edge of their beds, ready for a welcome night's sleep.

"Bill, don't you ever worry about your heart in a situation like tonight?" Charging Shield asked. He looked in the direction of the church. "It was hard to breathe in there."

"Oh, I must admit I worry a little. At first I am what you say - 'apprehension'."

"Apprehensive," Charging Shield volunteered.

"Yeah, that's a good college word," Bill laughed. "You're going to have to teach me some more of those smart college words." The holy man's humor brought a smile from his pupil.

"I worry a little, Nephew... it's plenty hot under that blanket all tied up but, once that drum starts and the spirits come in, I don't feel a thing," the older man explained.

Charging Shield knew that he was hearing a privileged explanation.

Eagle Feather went on, "All that I can say is that I am simply a man out there like anyone else. The Great Spirit is using me to bring in the spirit people. It is his power, not mine. I don't worry about my heart, though. If I did, I wouldn't have much faith, would I?"

"No. No, I guess not, Uncle."

Eagle Feather crossed his leg to untie a shoe. He watched his assistant remove the soiled buckskin pouch from around his neck before hanging it on the bedpost.

"Your *wotai*, Nephew. It has a power. My *wotai* has a power. If you wouldn't have believed in your stone's power when you was flying that airplane, maybe you wouldn't have come back. If I don't believe in my *wotai* or the power allowed in the *Yuwipi* ... then maybe I could get a heart attack." He dropped his shoe onto the floor. "Maybe that helps you understand."

It was the first time Eagle Feather had mentioned his own *wotai*. Charging Shield was aware that the unusual stone was seldom displayed and then only at the Sun Dance. He guessed that warriors' stones were temporary and holy men's *wotais* were more permanent... especially such an elaborate agate like Eagle Feather's. The rainbow agate, its crystal center, the powerful faces within: the warrior chief, the buffalo man, a strong woman with flowing hair and even a bearded man... a bearded man? Yes. He remembered the distinct image. It did resemble the white man's version. Yes, indeed.

Strangely, Father Weitz entered his thoughts. The young priest had seemed sincere when he returned the sage wreath that had been dropped. He sensed that Weitz would play some part in his mission. The vision quest and Spirit Mountain engulfed him strongly.

"I guess I should tell you how my *wotai* came to me." Eagle Feather interrupted Charging Shield's thoughts.

He related to Charging Shield the unusual circumstances leading to the possession of the stone... the water snake gliding across the stream, swimming directly over the stone, the bright light flashing up from the stream bed.

When he had finished, the Sichangu summarized his feelings, "I believe that the Great Spirit meant that I should have the stone. There is no question who made that stone and placed within it those powerful faces and signs. Even to this day, I find new signs, but the powerful ones always remain."

He held his palm upward in a cautionary gesture. "The white man, no doubt, will say we worship such a stone but, as usual, he is wrong about our way."

Eagle Feather's voice deepened with added conviction, "We recognize only the Creator as the highest power. But when the one above allows us such a symbol of his own creation and gives it a power to help us then, of course, we show it great respect."

Charging Shield propped his back against a pillow. The kerosene lamp began to sputter, its undulated glow seeming to animate the pouch at the foot of the bed. He spoke slowly, "I am grateful my *wotai* helped me in combat, Uncle. Now you say I have fulfilled only part of my mission. Obviously, the vision quest is another part of my mission and, if I make a wish between my sun dances, it may come true?"

Eagle Feather threw a stern look across the aisle separating the two beds. "I've been thinking about what I told you. Usually, that is the way it is, but you are still on your mission. Maybe your wish will have to wait until after the next sun dance. Just be careful what you wish."

The holy man thought for a long moment before continuing. "Your *wotai*, staying with you right now, is more important than a wish. Your *wotai* came to you in Fools Crow's *Yuwipi* ... it will have to go back through Fools Crow's ceremony... if it is meant to help you for vision quest."

Charging Shield fixed his stare on the pouch. The morning's vows to sun dance and vision quest had left him apprehensive. The pain and fatigue of the Sun Dance he had endured, but the mystery of the vision quest loomed like a fearsome wall on a dark rainy night.

At that moment, his grandmother's words came clearly. "You will have to do what the holy men say. You may have to help the foretelling power and fight for our way. If you show that you are not afraid, you might get your choice to come back... when you get older you still may not understand but it will be in your heart. It will be what you really want after you have been a part of the white man's world."

"Is that the way of the Mystic Warrior?" he remembered asking as a youth.

"Yes... yes, in a way. In the old days, before the white man, they lived for the Way so that they could be allowed to come back."

Charging Shield looked in the direction of Eagle Feather's bunk. Despite his vivid recall of the old woman's pronouncement, his words were halting. "For what I have to do... I will need my *wotai*. Will you talk to Fools Crow?"

"I will make arrangements with Fools Crow." The holy man sounded reassuring. "You've got some more things to do yet. You're going to need a *wotai*. After awhile, it might leave. Then you can go on... where you want to go. You go off to school and think about all of this. In the spring, when school gets out, you can vision quest."

Eagle Feather blew out the kerosene lamp. Only the sound of the crickets could be heard from the open cabin window. Eagle Feather turned his head to look over his shoulder. "I bet you're afraid to vision quest," he said matter-of-factly.

"I suppose I am," Charging Shield answered calmly, "but if I have to do it, I guess I can." He raised his voice, trying to hide a sense of fear. "After combat and the Sun Dance, I can vision quest," he added aloud, trying to convince himself. He wanted to ask the holy man about what his grandmother had said. 'You can come back.' The words haunted the silence. "Bill, what about coming back? What does that mean?"

"And where did you hear that?" A touch of irritation could be detected in the holy man's voice. Obviously, he was wanting to sleep with no more interruptions.

"My grandmother... and the Mystic Warriors," Charging Shield replied.

"Some day you may not want to be part of this world, if you are a true Mystic Warrior. A true Mystic Warrior comes to realize that a better life waits beyond." Bill answered and rolled over to face the wall. "Don't worry about it. You won't be disappointed if you keep doing what we are telling you." There was finality to his words.

He slept soundly, but late that night he dreamed vividly. He was at the crest of Spirit Mountain. At one side where he sat, a cliff was behind him; the vertical drop giving way to a sharp slant of loose shale with scrub pine sparsely rooted in the shale.

A vicious figure, by the sound of its guttural snarl and scratching claws, approached from below out of the enveloping fog at the top of Spirit Mountain.

He stepped back to the very edge. The figure crouched. Charging Shield was aware of a peace pipe in his hands, yet the peace pipe was also a warrior's axe. He was too afraid to defend himself with the pipe. The figure sprang from its crouch. Charging Shield turned and jumped in retreat off the edge of the cliff.

The fall seemed to take an eternity... combat in Vietnam, a chorus of warriors... Fritz and his squadron chattered on intercoms. Sioux words drowned out the pilots'. Strong Hearts, Kit Fox and Dog Soldier warriors called out, "*Hokeahay, hokeahay.*" They repeated over and over, "Take courage, take courage."

He was a lone Marine with casualties in a bomb crater, at the crest of a hill in Korea. His company had been overrun and most were dead except for the wounded beside him. He was about to die with the wounded but he still had two cases of hand grenades in the crater. He kept pitching grenades up over the lip. Bugles blared, flares lit the sky, the Marine observers on the next ridge called in artillery. Howitzers and heavy mortars rolled in like hail as a battalion of Chinese swept through. He kept pitching grenades and waited to die while the earth churned and shook. The next morning dozens of Chinese soldiers lay strewn around the crater.

A lone voice spoke to him that night during the heat of battle. "*Hokeahay, hokeahay*. It is a good day to die." Cross Dog's voice echoed Chief Crazy Horse's battle cry.

Now, once again a chorus of warrior voices repeated the words of Crazy Horse. Lightning flashed, thunder peeled, drowning out all. He fell through red fireballs blossoming in the sky. Blackness and sheets of flame, yellow and red alternated like gigantic salvos of anti-aircraft bursts.

When the crashing crescendo rolled inward, a new chorus called out, this time in English, but the English was difficult to understand. His warriorness could sense that they were words of encouragement, but the English was ancient and thickly accented. There was the sound of men straining at oars, the crashing of surf and an ancient voice barking commands. The rhythm of the oars matched the rhythm of the ancient words. It was an old man's voice, but far from feeble.

The boat grounded onto the sand and rock-studded shore. The occupants spilled out, their anxious and awed expressions denoting an arrival on a strange, new shore.

The old voice took command. The voice was so powerful it had to be that of a seer, a mentor. In old English it spoke, yet strangely, the voice was a replica of Fool's Crow's. The words conveyed a deep perception, a foretelling perception bidding Charging Shield a welcome into his ancient past. "Take courage, take courage," the old mentor called out to him.

Loose shale and the solid whack of a scrub pine broke Charging Shield's fall. His peace pipe hooked the pine, wrenching his shoulder painfully, but he managed to maintain his grip on the pine. He slammed to a stop like a Phantom jet engaging its tail hook on a carrier deck. Above, out of the shrouding fog, the figure appeared blue on the mountaintop. It had human extremities and yelled blasphemous obscenities. It leaped, snarling angry hatred. The fog parted, and the blue flaming thing blotted out the full moon.

Charging Shield woke, bathed in sweat. The full moon radiated through the cabin window. Bill's snoring afforded a sigh of relief. It had all been a dream! He reached for the *wotai* and tied it securely around his neck.

The following morning, after breakfast, the Hunkpapas pressed around the pickup. Their enthusiastic farewells expressed appreciation. Charging Shield waved to Rosalie, who was standing on the porch steps, before turning the pickup out of the driveway to head south toward the Rosebud Reservation. They drove for several miles toward distant rain showers scattered on the horizon.

Eagle Feather eyed the clouds, then turned toward him with an amused grin. "Looks like things kind of cooled down between you and that girl you was riding horses with. When you was waitin' for them sandwiches, I was wonderin' if you was going to start the right fire."

Charging Shield pursed a troubled frown. After he related the discussion at the sweat lodge, Eagle Feather swished his hand through the air at a harmless miller fly trying to make a hopeless escape through the pickup window. "So she didn't like the generations unborn talk." He said with a grim laugh, "Generations unborn... how do you know about generations unborn?" He rolled down his window and swished the miller out through the opening.

"My Grandmother... " Charging Shield offered. "My mom didn't like it, but she would tell me things anyhow."

The conversation settled on events at the Sun Dance. The holy man shared a vision he had experienced during the piercing. "I saw the earth heating up, Nephew. And it was hard for people to breathe; just like it is when I stay too long in them big cities. Them cities getting smokier, that's going to have a bad effect on them generations unborn. I do a lot of travelin' come winter. I go around and do ceremony when people call me. I can not be prejudice. I even do ceremony for the white man." The big holy man exhaled a gasp of air. "Actually, he is the one that needs the most help when it comes to this word... environment... that's a word we are beginning to hear." Eagle Feather held up his hand for emphasis. "Never exclude anyone because of the color of their skin. You will lose your power in ceremony if you do."

Charging Shield nodded in agreement even though, deep in his thoughts he doubted if he would ever conduct a ceremony. He preferred being a warrior. He would fight for the way and would certainly help the holy persons but ceremony... he would leave that to the holy men.

"*Mitakuye Oyasin, Mitakuye Oyasin.*" Eagle Feather repeated in deep seriousness. "If the *washichu* does not learn how it is all related, the earth will keep on heating and the generations unborn will suffer." The big holy man extended his arm out of the window and sat up straight and tall as if he was addressing an assembly of nations, instead of a pair of magpies lifting from a sun-bleached cow skull on the empty prairie. "In my opinion, this is a teaching which is the most important for all *washichu*s to learn." He called out long and hard to the magpies, "Mitakuye Oyasin. We are related to all things." As an afterthought, he looked at his driver and added, "Put that in your environment."

Charging Shield noted the bleak landscape, parched and bare in the August heat. An ominous truth toned Eagle Feather's words.

Ahead in the distance, a rain shower blotted out the highway. Lightning flashed from the cloud base as the pickup drew closer. A soft "Oh huh," from Eagle Feather greeted each flash. When the first droplets struck the windshield, the windows were rolled up. Charging Shield turned on the wipers. The rain was pouring across the cab when two bolts struck, almost simultaneously, seeming to straddle the pickup. Eagle Feather yelled his acknowledgment in rapid succession. Within a mile the shower ceased. A chastising smile settled on the holy man's face. "Those were West power *Heyokas* in that lightning, Nephew. Allies. They're nothing to be afraid of," he assured loudly. The blasting cracks left their ears ringing.

"*Heyokas?*" Charging Shield answered in a shaky voice. He looked at the holy man sheepishly, relaxing his tight grip on the steering wheel.

"Those are good signs, Nephew. Good signs. We didn't get killed, so I interpret what I just said was pretty powerful. "*Mitakuye Oyasin* - We are related to all things." Eagle Feather thought for a long time. The blast of the paired lightning bolts made him recall the pair of spirit men who had appeared in his Sun Dance vision. He recalled the old prophet, Black Elk, lamenting on Thunder Being Peak. The Sun Dance tree, the red stick, the sacred pipe hurled to the tree's base by one of the spirit men. A sharp realization of what he knew of Black Elk's vision made him sit very erect.

"They are power Nephew. Power." The tone of his voice prevented any further questioning. "If you vision quest and see lightning, *Heyokas* might be looking out for you. Trouble might come, but the *Heyokas* are watching to help out." He rolled down the window to let the cool smell of fresh rain fill the interior. "Don't ever worry about *Heyokas*, Nephew. The Almighty doesn't make anything bad. Sure, we laugh at things that are funny and some things even play tricks, but in the end, the Almighty is so powerful, it has no need to make something like this devil that the white man has invented." He paused then added, "Now, most of our people are believing in this devil. Those tribes that have spent a lot longer time than we have with the white man. They have picked up that devil and keep their own people scared with it."

Charging Shield noted that Bill was one of the few holy men that referred to *Wakan Tanka* as the Almighty before he asked bluntly, "Is the Blue Man something like a devil?"

Eagle Feather waved two fingers at the fence posts flying by. "Oh hunnh. That is a good question." After his customary pause he replied. "The Blue Man is what is happening now. It is a prediction by Black Elk and it makes sense." He looked at his pupil. "What is a good word for something that stands for something."

Charging Shield searched for awhile before he answered, "Symbolic?"

Eagle Feather's eyes lit. He liked finding new words. "Ah haa," his tone smacked with relish. "I like that word as much as I like that word ap-pre-hension." He hunched his posture to convey a serious air. "This Blue Man is what we could call - sym-bolic. The Blue Man is what is happening today. It is humans that are doing it." He stopped to think for a few moments. "It won't come in the middle of the night and get you." He looked strangely at Charging Shield. "If it would, don't worry, it is only a dream... and maybe it is just a message that must be delivered."

"That would be one helluva dream." Charging Shield remarked.

By the halting, thoughtful manner, in which the holy man spoke, Charging Shield could sense something else was on his mind. Eagle Feather held up his hand to quiet any more conversation. A mingling of satisfaction and meditation blossomed on his broad face. "Now I see," he wondered aloud. His hand rose higher as if to still any interruption on Charging Shield's part.

"Now I see," he repeated. "Oh-huh," he gave an Indian expression to his English. His eyes glistened while he deliberated for a long while.

"This vision quest of yours... and that *wotai*, it's had me puzzled. Now I see where it fits in. Last night I had a dream. I dreamed about Black Elk. That medicine man that did the healing." Eagle Feather leaned forward with an expression of intense seriousness. "That was him in the water and in your sweat lodge smoke. How well do you know the name - Black Elk?"

Charging Shield answered the name with reverence, "Old Nicholas Black Elk. I heard he was a prophet... and a holy man and of course his son Ben. Ben is a good friend of my parents."

"The old man Black Elk. I never called him Nicholas. That was what the missionaries made him go by. He was both, a prophet and a holy man like you said. He had vision, vision into what's ahead. That was his power. Last night he talked to me."

Charging Shield settled back, anxious to hear more.

Eagle Feather continued, "Back in his day, his medicine was strong in predicting. Black Elk got sick when he was a young boy. He took a trip to the spirit world and, after he came to, he was powerful. He predicted we'd see some hard times. He said our spirit would almost leave us but the Sun Dance would come to life and bring it back. He told about his spirit journey and predictions to a white man before he died. His son, Ben, served as interpreter since he'd been away to Carlisle school and could speak English pretty well. The white man wrote it all down but so far the authorities or who ever it is that controls books..." Eagle feather looked perplexed. "Whatever was written isn't getting out to the people." His voice carried an air of suspicion. "Maybe it is the Church... or maybe it is the Blue Man." His serious, contemplative composure lightened. "How well do you know Ben?"

"My mom and dad knew him pretty well. He used to come to see us when I was a kid. What happened to what was written?"

"The white man made this book that Ben talks about and went away. Black Elk's family, they still live in the same old cabin. Nothing much has changed for them, except Ben spends most of his time in the Black Hills." Bill looked west in the direction of the Black Hills. "He talks about his Father's book. 'My Father's book,' he is always saying, but no one seems to pay him any attention." The holy man paused. "Myself, I have never seen it." Eagle Feather let out an angry hiss. "You can bet your boots those missionaries are going to keep the lid on it. They've spread stories that Black Elk is a *Heyoka* and not to be believed," He hissed through his teeth again, "lots of damn fool Indians believe everything those missionaries say."

"What the hell is a *Heyoka*?" Charging Shield spoke bluntly and impulsively, then wondered if he should have tempered his question.

Eagle Feather showed no expression and answered with a nod back down the road where the thunderclouds were still rumbling. "You just saw them, Nephew. Lot of arm chair Indians out there believe they are some kind of bad." He looked at his pupil. "Do you think a *Heyoka* is bad?"

"If the Creator made it, it cannot be bad. That is what my Grandmother used to say."

"Oh hunnh." Eagle Feather grunted with a relaxed smile.

A paved side road bordered by buffalo berry bushes appeared in the distance. To break the monotonous pace of prairie landscape, Charging Shield slowed the pickup. The spot looked as good as any to stop and enjoy a biscuit with beef roast and a thermos of coffee.

They were greeted by bright red warning signs and a fenced enclosure. "Keep out - U. S. Air Force Property," the signs warned. The truck braked to a halt, backed up and turned around, leaving the intercontinental missile silo site behind. Charging Shield reached for the thermos bottle. The hinged doors of the missile silo had subdued both men's appetites for the time being.

"Nephew, I guess you know better than I, there's a lot of power back there," Eagle Feather said tersely as they continued on.

Charging Shield nodded in agreement. He knew a little more about atomic weapons than the average citizen. Some of the Marine pilots had been sent to Naval Atomic Weapons Delivery Training and he had been one of them. The training focused on aerial loft bomb delivery... releasing the bomb from a reversing, lofting pull-up to allow the fighter-bomber time to escape the nuclear blast. "Do you think the world could be destroyed by atomic weapons, Uncle?" Despite his specialized training that consisted of nuclear capability lectures graded 'Top Secret'; he placed more faith in what the holy man would say.

Bill shook his head. "No," he answered. "No, the white man will not be allowed to destroy the world. Do you think the Almighty, *Wakan Tanka* the Creator, would let mere man destroy His creation?" Bill groaned, repeating slowly, "I hardly think so... I hardly think so." His words trailed off. "Not that those things down in the ground don't have a lot of power. I'm not saying that, but, if it ever happened, this atomic war that people are getting rightfully worried about, if it happens, it will be a time the Indian will be thankful he's, he's..." The holy man stammered for a moment then asked while he swept his hand over his crew cut, "What's a good college word for being out there pretty much all by yourself?"

"Isolated," Charging Shield volunteered.

"Yes, isolated, that's what I want to say. Isolated," Bill repeated proudly and went on. "I got that environment word down first time I heard it. It was a natural, now I got to learn some more of them college words. Well... The Indian will be thankful he's isolated on a reservation if those 'big bangs' come. If it happens while I'm still here, I'll be glad I'm out on the Rosebud and thankful I've learned to do without."

"Uncle, what do the prophecies, our prophecies, say about my generation or the ones after me? The generations unborn? What will we see?" Charging Shield pressed.

"Well, you're asking a question that goes back to Black Elk, Ben's father. Actually, his vision was more worried about the Mother Earth getting pretty sick, more so than he was a big war. If that's true, then we are all wasting our time with all this war stuff instead of doing things, big things for this environment." The elder man paused to throw a head motion back at the missile site. "According to his vision, people are supposed to gain wisdom and knowledge from a four rayed herb cast down to the earth, but by the looks of things it hasn't arrived yet. He said a Blue Man would come over this land. Way back when he was a little boy he saw this Blue Man harming Mother Earth. They say the old man lost hope after he got older. I lost hope myself, but then when our Sun Dance came back, I guess I can say... maybe... maybe. You are the fourth generation after the conquest, Nephew." Bill's voice turned blunt yet remained prophetic. "Your generation could see big trouble, or it could see good times if people can get together and have some understanding."

"You mean war or peace?"

"One way or another, they are going to have to kill this Blue Man," said the holy man.

"You don't believe that this Blue Man can be killed in a peaceful way do you?'

Eagle Feather ignored his question as if it should not have been asked. "First I want to talk about war. Always remember, the white man is a European. He has a history of warfare, way more than what they like to accuse us of. They had their Caesars, Napoleons, Hitlers, their empires. The British, Spanish, Germans, French... the whole lot of them took over the world when they had their chance. All of it for power and greed. Way back... there was one of them called Alexander - The Great. I guess he was 'Great' because he conquered so much. They say he even cried because he ran out of places to conquer.

"An old fool like me isn't supposed to know these other things. Do my sweat lodges and sun dances; that's all I'm supposed to know." Bill spoke with an amused grin. He offered a mock laugh to the horizon. "When I was workin' durin' the war I got sent to the shipyards way out by the ocean. It got pretty lonely at times but the war was on and I was proud to be patriotic. I had lots of time on my hands so I'd go to the library and read during my time off." He paused, "Most of us always got bad things to say about the boarding schools but I have to be honest. They taught me how to read."

Charging Shield offered a reluctant nod and the holy man continued.

"Yes, us Indians had war, but we were more like the animals. We had flowing borders that we would fight over, like the wolves do, but never was there an Indian Caesar or Napoleon who had to take over all the rest of the tribes. We never had a bunch of marked lines that we claimed. When the white man pushed us back on top of each other we had wars. Everyone tried to stay alive. If we were so warlike, then how could we let those first white men, those Pilgrims, come into the country and instead of killing them off we kept them alive, even teaching them how to plant our corn? Sure, when the white men tried to take everything, we had to draw the line. When the white man pushed us back on top of each other, we all had to fight to survive. Course the white man calls us war-like and always fighting, never admitting he is the one that started everyone fighting.

"You take the *Ha Sapas* (Black people). The white man brought them over here in chains to do his work. They tried to make slaves of us before that, but they had about as much success with that as trying to tame an eagle or a wolverine. They couldn't do it to us so they brought that poor black man over in chains. He had no way to get back to his tribe. Those days, the Bible didn't teach white people that we are all relatives from the same Earth Mother. No, their Bible didn't say that the Great Spirit made the Earth Mother to bear all of us equally and that we were all equally *Wakan Tanka*'s grandchildren.

"A lot of those *Ha Sapas* ran away from the plantations. They ran out into the swamps and forests. The Indian tribes out there, they took them in. The tribes rescued a lot of *Ha Sapas*. There are a lot of *Ha Sapas* in this country who have Indian blood, and they don't know it. Those southern tribes believed just like we did. They knew that all things made by the Great Spirit were holy. We are all brothers and sisters."

"What color was that four rayed herb of Black Elk's, Uncle?"

"Red, yellow, black and white; same as our four directions and of course the four races of two-legged," Eagle Feather replied.

"There is a strong part of our way that is missing in the white man's way," Bill paused for emphasis. "The woman! She keeps the man side what I'd call... even sided." He held his hands up, palms upward, as though he was weighing on a scale. "Even sided... one side taking care of the other... " He spoke as if he were searching for a word.

"Balanced," Charging Shield offered.

Eagle Feather smiled broadly. "Bal-ance. Yes, that's the word I want, balance. The woman in our ceremonies, the Buffalo Calf Woman, Mother Earth... It's the woman power in our way that made us be good to those Pilgrims and *Ha Sapas*." The holy man eyed his pupil with a strange look. "Maybe it is the woman power that will finally kill the Blue Man."

Charging Shield ignored the subject of the Blue Man, instead he interjected strongly. "If we could be decent to strangers like the Pilgrims and the Black people, and we respected our Mother Earth, then why in the hell didn't the Great Spirit protect us?"

Bill frowned. "*Wakan Tanka* did in a way. You must admit, the white man could have wiped us all out, but something stopped him from doing it."

Charging Shield scowled but nodded his head in agreement. The holy man continued. "You have to give the white man's religion some credit for that, Nephew."

"He killed a lot of us, Uncle," Charging Shield responded with a stubborn tone.

"Yes, I'm not denying it... but there was a lot of the whites, there was a bunch of them that spoke up for us. Them Quakers have got to get some credit. *Kolas*, friends they call themselves and walked their talk. Somehow they got through to those big shots in Washington. I still say it was a lot of his religion that helped us out."

"Maybe so, Uncle, but I choose my Indian way. The *Yuwipi* power helped me in Vietnam. I thank the Great Spirit I am allowed to be a *Lakota*." Charging Shield threw a resolute look out to the rolling prairie. "I don't want anything to do with *washichu* religion."

Eagle Feather held up two fingers; his features portrayed both understanding and a reluctant caution. "Yes, our way is good for us, but the white man must stick to some of his own way. He needs more womanpower in his way but there are some good signs for him. He has a hard time letting others believe in the Great Spirit in their own ways. He keeps himself pretty ignorant when he doesn't see the good in all ways, but you have to admit, he could have wiped us all out.

"Oh, he still needs a lot of improvement, but that other white man with the rockets across the ocean has got me worried. The whole shebang' is making the whole bunch forget about the environment." It was the first time Charging Shield had ever seen Eagle Feather grit his teeth. "This world is heating up and more and more two-legged are being born every day. Your generation could see some bad times, but then there are always miracles.

"If the people can get together and pray together, real hard, I mean a big ceremony clear around the globe, I know that things could happen. Those people over there are just as scared as we are of those bombs and one good thing - the big shots on both sides can get blown away as soon as the rest of us." Eagle Feather scratched his chin. "Hmmm," he pondered. "You asked about the prophecies or what some of our holy people have predicted. Well there is one real strong prediction that is even shared by some of the other tribes that managed to keep their way." The Sichangu took a deep breath. "They say that a new people would come out of the *washichu* and the rest of them colors in that herb. These new ones would be what you call a good spirituality. They would all work together and get along because they would be allowed to know more things." Eagle Feather turned to deliver a stately pronouncement to an audience of one from his podium in the pickup truck. "There is also this prophecy about the Blue Man of corruption and greed. Nephew... don't ever give up hope in miracles. Our tribe is a good example. We lived because we beseeched the Almighty as a tribe. They say that this new bunch, mostly *washichus* and mostly women, they are going to learn how to beseech to the Great Spirit and think like an Indian and then they will take on this Blue Man."

After some long moments, Eagle Feather murmured, "Nephew I want you to see Ben Black Elk after you get back to West River and rest up for a few days. Tell him he should come to the Sun Dance. He should bring his father's pipe. Mention generations unborn, and his father's vision about the Blue Man, and hear what he has to say."

The crack of paired lightning bolts seemed to re-echo in Charging Shield's ears as he answered obediently. "I will. I'll do it for sure." For a moment during the crack of the lightning he imagined that he had seen the face again, the same face over the pile of medicine bundles and peace pipes but he was too startled to admit that it briefly reappeared. He wondered. 'So that was old Black Elk? No doubt he had suffered that devastating experience.'

Eagle Feather's expression became grave. "It's strange, Nephew. In my Sun Dance vision and in my dream last night I saw a flowering tree, but neither of us was there. In a way you were there, but it wasn't you in the way I know you now. You were with a yellow haired, a golden kind of hair, - a good-looking woman. She had two symbols, a meadowlark and an eagle."

Karen came to Charging Shield's thoughts, but he was puzzled. 'It had to be Karen. The meadowlark was yellow breasted. Karen's hair was the color of a golden eagle, dark but at times with a golden light when the sun hit it.' A sense of dread overcame him. 'No! She wasn't blonde or yellow haired.' A touch of loneliness prohibited him from asking about her. Instead he asked politely, "Is your health good, Uncle?"

Eagle Feather exhaled a soft rush of air. "I know my health." His answer carried a reproachful touch of irritation to brush away his pupil's concern. "I am a *wichasha wakan* (holy man). We know when to go." Eagle Feather thought for a while. 'The paired lightning bolts... the four-rayed herb, the power of knowledge and understanding.' He wondered if there would come a time for the earth to heal up through knowledge and understanding. The rainbow in his Sun Dance vision... that was a powerful sign for peace and coming together. Peace would have to come first so the people could put their attention on the earth. The woman with the two symbols, the eagle and the meadowlark. She was blonde headed. Maybe the color of her hair was like that new word Charging Shield came up with. Maybe she was symbolic that some of the white people were going to come over to the Indian way of thinking. It might be another time after many have passed on. Maybe in this new time the womanpower will reach into the white man's way after all! That would be a good way for the white man to wake up! But first this warrior has a mission,' he thought as he eyed his driver. "It's important that you see Ben Black Elk. That's all that I want you to be worried about," he commanded.

Charging Shield nodded before he spoke. "If Ben's father was a prophet, why didn't he become a holy man?"

"He had the chance. The old man left him his pipe. A lot of the old man's power settled in that pipe. Some say Ben had the power to call *Yuwipis* after the old man left. Lots of times power can stay in a family. When his father was alive, Ben helped out as interpreter. He learned a lot. People from all over came to their place... Indians from other tribes, even white people. The old man could look into the future, and word got around." Eagle Feather's face darkened. "Word got around to them missionaries, you can bet your boots on that. They gave the old man a hard time. Ben, he got married after he got his education. The missionaries worked on him through his wife who was part Mexican. And you know Mexicans. They're mostly

Indian but always denying it, always claiming to be Spanish. On top of that, I never knew a Mexican in these parts that wasn't anything else but Catholic." Eagle Feather pointed southwest, in the direction of the Paha Sapa. "After the old man died, Ben worked up in the mountains; winters he'd come back to the reservation. That bunch at the mission... one time they had Ben dress up in his beadwork. They had him kneel in front of their altar holding his father's peace pipe. They took his picture and printed up a bunch of pamphlets. They sent them all over asking for donations. We didn't like that, especially with the old man's pipe. That pipe needs to come back, it still has strong medicine." He tilted his head backward. "After that dream last night, my Sun Dance vision and now these *Heyokas*, I know that Black Elk's pipe should come to the Sun Dance." He craned his neck to take a good look at his pupil. "Yes, the way those *Heyokas* acted up, maybe the old man, Black Elk, is trying to tell us something. You ask Ben if he figures the Blue Man can be beaten. It's very important that you listen carefully to Ben Black Elk."

They crossed the reservation line. "Go see Fools Crow after you visit with Ben. Your *wotai* came through his ceremony." He left the holy man in a tiny community then drove northwest on a gravel road. Eagle Feather's farewell dwelled on vision quest. "Charging Shield, you will be tested... and then you will have your vision. Your vision quest can be important to us," he ended with heavy emphasis. The Sichangu's parting words played over and over for endless miles.

Later that evening, he was in West River. After several days rest, he purchased a used car and drove into the Black Hills. Close beside Black Elk's dwelling a narrow trout brook gurgled through granite and quartzite, sprinkled with flashes of mica and fools gold. He knocked on the door of the log cabin. The soft moan of rustling pines stirred the air as he was warmly welcomed by a slight, graying Oglala. Black Elk shuffled to a wooden bench beside an empty pot bellied stove in the center of a dimly lit room. He placed two cups of coffee on the flat-topped stove before he settled back into a pillowed rocking chair. The aging man had a strong face that conveyed congeniality, yet an aura of detachment. He was anxious to hear about the warrior's exploits, both in combat and the Sun Dance. He pointed to the bench and quickly steered the younger Oglala's conversation, after satisfying the customary amenities of the health and welfare of tribal relatives. Charging Shield sensed a touch of pride in the old man's eyes as he related his first Sun Dance.

"I heard that Fools Crow's *Yuwipi* ... they protected your airplane when you was fighting for Uncle Sam." A scholarly flavor carried the older one's words. Black Elk remained silent when he was apprised of Eagle Feather's request. Charging Shield sensed Black Elk might reply with an offended note. "Eagle Feather was most critical when the missionaries took my picture with my father's pipe."

"Don't you think you were being used when your picture was taken like that?" Charging Shield took his mentor's defense.

BEN BLACK ELK

"I had to lead two lives, Nephew, and maybe I still do," Black Elk's answer was tired. His spent frame seemed to cling to the rocking chair. "I was always sought after by the missionaries, and it seemed the easier thing to bend over to them."

"They say that my father was a great catechist. They say that he became a good Catholic. The priests are always telling me that." Ben pursed a tired frown. "They never tell how they took him and strangled him, and then drug him down to the mission and did one of their own ceremonies on him." Ben's voice carried a rebellious anger. He offered a queried look. "How do you say that when they do a ceremony that is supposed to take the devil out of you... if... you believe in a devil?"

"You mean, exorcising... an exorcism?"

"Yes, that's it. They drug him down there... they threw him in a wagon after breaking up one of his healing ceremonies. This German priest came right into the ceremony and scared all the Indians who had come in for a healing. My father had strong medicine." Ben Black Elk took a cup from the stovetop and settled back to sip his coffee, then leaned forward to set it on the bench beside Charging Shield. "After the big fight at the Battle on the Greasy Grass, after we wiped out Custer... my father's band went up to Canada. That is where he started to do his medicine. He was a strong healer and lots of people came to him. When they came down to Oglala, his reputation for healing got around and people came to get well from different kinds of sickness and ailments." Ben paused to take another sip of coffee. "The first priest that came along to break up his ceremony had the Cavalry backing him up. The Cavalry was stationed right here on the reservation in those days. This priest did pretty much the same thing that the exorcising priest did, later on. He came in to the lodge and grabbed up my father's pipe and medicine bundles and threw them outside on the ground. Only thing, that first time, the spirits stepped in. After the Indians all cleared out, that priest headed back to the mission. A lightning bolt hit his horse and killed the horse and the priest."

Ben looked over at the younger Oglala to see the satisfied grin breaking out. "For a few more years the priests stayed away from my father's healing ceremonies. By this time, times were getting pretty hard. He lost his first wife and his rations were getting cut off. I remember long hungry times. Those days if you were a holy man and didn't go along with the *washichu* way, you could be in big trouble.

Black Elk thought for a long time. "Everything seemed hopeless. It seemed what my father said could never come true. If an Indian stood up for the old way, the agent and the missionary would go against him. Your children suffered in the boarding school; your rations would be cut off or maybe you couldn't get into a rummage sale they controlled, to get some decent winter clothes. We even had to have passes to get around on the reservation. You could be cut off from seeing your relatives if you didn't bend to the *washichu,* especially their religion. Most of the holy men got scared and gave in. The priests made them say that the old ways would no longer work for an Indian. When they can come in and choke you and haul you away for one of their scary 'ex-cersizes' or however you say it, then you know they could get away with anything."

"Exorcism." Charging Shield offered again.

Black Elk nodded and continued. When I went away to school at Carlisle, we had to give in. Our hair was cut. We wore military uniforms, learned how to march and you can bet your boots- we learned *washichu* religion." He raised his head dolefully. "Those were tough times. Yes, they were tough times." He reached into his shirt pocket for a sack of Bull Durham. "It wasn't hard to lose hope, but now our *wagachun*, the cottonwood, has come back to the center of the nation. I wish my father would have lived to see it." He rolled a cigarette, placed the tobacco sack next to an ashtray and lit the cigarette with a wooden match, smoking slowly while he rocked in the chair.

Charging Shield sat spellbound weighing his elder's words. "I understand now about your father becoming a catechist, although I have to admit it's a helluva way to get indoctrinated... being drug down to the mission, choked and exorcised. Those priests must have scared the hell out of him."

"My father was a slight man, a small man, smaller than me. Those priests, none of them talk about what they did to him." Ben frowned. "He had to join up with them to survive." Ben looked hard at Charging Shield. "You are a young man flying those airplanes around and I bet you have chased some good looking girls." A smile came briefly and went. Somberly, Ben spoke, "When you settle down and have kids, if hard times come, you'll do almost anything for your kids to see to it that they survive."

Charging Shield reached for his coffee cup and nodded in agreement.

Ben continued, "He was always curious and he figured there had to be some kind of power in the way of the *washichu*. He studied it for awhile but it didn't take long. He came back to his vision."

Charging Shield added, "He must have. He told his story to that white man who wrote it all down."

Ben held up his hand. "I interpreted every word for my father and after it was all said and done, he did ceremony and he gave John Neihardt the name, Flaming Rainbow. 'You are a wordmaker... a talk sender. I see a rainbow and from it flames fall... and where the flames land... flowers grow.' These are the words he said." Ben Black Elk looked east, in the direction of the reservation. "My father was satisfied that his story would now be shared with the whole world. He was happy that day, like a big weight had been taken from him. He even gave names in ceremony to Hilda and Enid, Neihardt's daughters. Enid, she took every word down in short hand, after I would interpret what my father had said." Ben took a short puff from his homemade cigarette and blew it with an air of confidence, like a scientist in a research lab. "I think I can say that I know the book pretty well. Every word had to come through me."

"And Neihardt's questions back through you," Charging Shield added. "Yes, I would say that you probably could be assumed to know it... quite well." Charging Shield's voice was tart but Ben understood fully what message his listener was conveying. So used to living in a world of detraction, both men were well experienced with detraction from the dominant society, when it came to Native concepts of history and religious belief, even when first hand experience was often the source.

Ben continued to talk about his father. "He had John Neihardt take him over here in the *Paha Sapa* (Black Hills) for another ceremony after the whole story was given. He held up his pipe and prayed to *Wakan Tanka*, up on the mountain. It was powerful. A cloud came out of nowhere. It rained on all of us."

"You mean he did not pray to the *washichu's* version after he had been a cate-chist?" Charging Shield interrupted.

"No," Ben answered flatly.

"Doesn't sound like he was much of a catechist." The younger Sioux raised an eyebrow.

Ben looked surprised. "You know, what you say rings true, but we are so used to being owned by these missionaries... we forget to see what is so obvious." He was silent for awhile then added bluntly, "When Neihardt came to take down the story, the old man (Black Elk) made sure that the missionaries were not invited. The only ones there were his trusted friends. Old traditionals."

Charging Shield wanted to be clear. "You mean when he was about to impart his sacred vision to the world... through Neihardt's written record?"

"That's right, Nephew." Ben answered then repeated. "That's right."

Charging Shield took pride in being called Nephew. He did not want to offend his fellow Oglala but to comply with Bill Eagle Feather's directive he had to change the subject. "Do you think you might come to the Sun Dance?"

"What else did Eagle Feather tell you to say?" Ben's eyes held him squarely.

"About the Blue Man, and your Father's vision and the generations unborn," Charging Shield blurted. "I have to vision quest before the next Sun Dance. I have to ask you about your father's pipe and what your father predicted about the Blue Man," his words tumbled out.

"Vision quest," a vibrant change seemed to come over Black Elk's voice. "My father spoke of the black, white, red, and yellow. He saw them as horses in his vision," he said carefully and obviously not offended. "The four races of man, the four races of woman, that is the four rayed herb, Nephew," his words were loaded with power. "They're going to come together and right here out of this land... but that's still down the road. The generations unborn, they'll see that time." He spoke with conviction. "The white man, he doesn't live for the generations unborn, and the others are becoming like him, even our own people." A sour expression swept his features. "The generations unborn are going to curse this bunch here now because they could only live for today. They will have little remorse for what's going to happen to this bunch. There was a Blue Man in my father's vision. The Blue Man lived inside all this selfishness and greed. The Blue Man caused everything to get sick and dirty. The Blue Man was dangerous. He created a lot of narrow-minded-ness. He puffed up men's egos. Their pride made them build their own little kingdoms just like the ones they had back where they came from. Everything is made for sale by the Blue Man, including his religion. War is a big business for him too."

"Do you mean that something bad is coming?" Charging Shield inquired anxiously.

"It's already here," Ben Black Elk's answer was cold. "Look around us, right here in the *Paha Sapa*, the Black Hills. That treaty we won didn't mean anything. They discovered gold and their word on the treaty, this land, it was all up for sale. I've traveled to those big cities and all around them. The smoke gets pretty thick," Black Elk answered in a caustic voice. "This nation's history is only a few centuries old, Nephew. It's a history of taking, but now the taking part is going to be short-lived." He met the question squarely. "Yes, something's coming. What and how, I don't know for sure, but a lot of bad sickness for our Mother Earth and all the rest of us is here already. The Blue Man of greed and lies is running this country. He gets richer from taking and the poor get poorer. Generations unborn could have it worse. Mother Earth is going to give us some powerful signs. Drought, bad water, cities getting hotter. That's what Eagle Feather wants you to find out. It's so bad I don't care to know, if you want the truth. My father killed the Blue Man in his vision, but that hasn't happened yet. When you go up on the mountain, maybe you'll find some of this out. You might not understand it, and be thankful for that but you bring it back to the holy men, if that is a question they want you to seek."

"The Blue Man?" Charging Shield felt forced to ask. "How did your father kill the Blue Man? Bill Eagle Feather mentioned it. What is this Blue Man?"

Black Elk puffed several times. He closed his eyes, and after a long moment of contemplation his words grew deep and resonant. "My own opinion is that the more that knowledge gets around and two-legged can communicate the truth, that is what will kill the Blue Man. The Blue Man was making the Earth sick and was killing off all the winged and the four legged way back when my father had his vision."

"Sounds like the *washichu*." Charging Shield growled.

In the vision," Black Elk went on with an agreeing nod, "this happened after the Six Powers spoke their knowledge to my father. The Powers tried to kill the Blue Man on their own but they had to call on my father."

"I still don't understand how he killed the Blue Man?"

"The Blue Man was killed only in the vision. It was to show how it could be killed. It is very much alive, no question about that. The Powers gave him a bow and told him he would have the power to make live and to destroy. The bow turned into a spear when he killed the Blue Man but this happened only after he received the Six Power knowledge. I think that means two-legged has to know what my father knew to stop what the Blue Man is doing to the Earth and all the living things."

"The *washichu* doesn't have it in him to learn anything from us." Charging Shield's reply was coldly pessimistic.

"I have to admit. The rulers of this land don't know a damned thing about the Blue Man nor do they give a damn." Black Elk shook his head. "When this Earth gets hotter and they keep on getting more crowded together, then a lot of bad things will start to happen. The *washichu* will have no other choice."

"How do you explain the Six Powers, Uncle?"

Ben Black Elk drew a long breath as if to prepare for an often delivered dissertation. "The Six Powers are with us every day. Unlike the white man who has to wait to see his God, we can see ours every day." Black Elk placed his hands on his hips and puffed his chest momentarily. "Actually, I believe that we two-legged are represented by the Six Powers."

"You mean we manifest the Six Powers?" Charging Shield's question was supportive.

"Definitely," the older Oglala concluded. He reached to touch his fellow tribesman's arm and spoke as he held a finger above Charging Shield's wrist, "You are made of three of the Six Powers. You are part Mother Earth, the last power to speak to my father and you are also made of the life giving rains of the West Power, the first power to speak to my Father. Ben Black Elk made a rising sweeping motion with his hand over Charging Shield. "You are also made up of the energy from the Sun in Father Sky, the fifth power." He paused to summarize. "Earth, Water and Energy, these are all forces that allow you to be here as a Two-legged."

Charging Shield nodded to indicate his agreement.

"The other three forces are a little harder to understand when it comes to relating yourself to the Six Powers of my Father's Vision, but it is these three powers that we must use to fight the Blue Man." Ben Black Elk went on, "The North Power, the East Power and the South Power are different in a way from the other three, but I say they are what make you a two-legged; one who is allowed to make your own decisions. If you respect what these powers stand for then you can become a strong two-legged that the Spirit World will work with, and you can go on with a higher respect for yourself. In the end, the whole world will be better off if they come to understand and follow the meaning of what these forces represent and how they were revealed to my father in his vision.

Black Elk pointed to the north. "The North Power is being clean, truthful, having courage and endurance. Those are all things that we think of when we consider the cold winter. Our people lived close together in lodges to endure the long winter. All of those values are easier to understand when you are out in nature. Truth, as I said before, is what is missing in this country. The white politicians, judges, teachers, preachers, lawyers, all of them, they have to learn real truth and quit sneaking around it.

"The South Power has a different knowledge. It is a time of growth, warmth and also healing. All of our medicines come about when the summer sun keeps rising higher and makes all the plants that feed us and heal us. We have to appreciate the

South Power. All bounty comes from the South Power. If you need provisions to live, then beseech to this power."

The elder Oglala pointed east, "I think that the east is a great power that we two-legged are finally getting ready for. Each new day comes when the sun rises on the eastern horizon. Everyday we get new knowledge. We can criticize all we want about the white man's inventions but a lot of them help us to communicate and understand one another in a way that never could happen in the old days." He paused and added with a smile. "Got to give the Japs a lot of credit too. Seems they are inventing more than the white man." He laughed momentarily then continued, "Those of us who look for knowledge can blend it with the knowledge of others. That effort can become wisdom and through wisdom we can find peace and under-standing. These are all things that we can learn and be a part of by being aware of what the Six Powers can show us."

"There is starting to become more communication in this world. I see the spreading of knowledge as a powerful force upon this planet," Charging Shield added. "What the hell. It really... All of this communication is an allowance of the Creator in the first place."

Black Elk beamed a smile then indicated his pleasure with the statement by offering a pleasant expression. "Yes, I think that the East Power, the power to learn and communicate has been given to us by the Great Spirit. I think that the four-rayed herb of understanding is this time. It will be the power that can bring a lasting peace to this planet. It will have to happen, otherwise humans will keep on making arms and bombs instead of working on all this polluting and poison waters and eventu-ally the earth will suffer."

Charging Shield recalled Eagle Feather's thoughts on prophecy. "They would all work together and get along because they would be allowed to know more things."

Black Elk looked north in the direction of Spirit Mountain. "You're going to Vision Quest. You will gain a new knowledge once you do that. Always put more new knowledge into yourself, everyday if you can. You will never regret it." He shut his eyes and spoke as if he was reading an image. "The *Heyokas*, the lightnings will watch over you. I have a feeling you should look for horses when you vision quest. Look for red, buckskin, black and palomino. They will be the colors of the first four powers of my father's vision." He pronounced the colors carefully. Black Elk visu-alized a rainbow and a pair of eagles and a woman; a powerful woman, who could be an eagle or a yellow bird, a meadowlark, he guessed. 'That woman, she was going to be a part of the flowering tree but maybe in a time span just around the corner. These things he would not tell about.'

After a long pause, his voice heightened, "My father was one of the last with the foretelling power." Black Elk stared deeply then looked abruptly to the ceiling. "Stirrup had *Yuwipi* power passed to him by my father, and Fools Crow was next. The power was passed to Eagle Feather by Fools Crow. The key to all of this power that they held was that they were all very truthful, like the way the Great Spirit runs this planet through the Six Powers." His gaze dropped back to his guest. "They say I should have been a *Yuwipi* man, but that is not the way it works. If it does stay in your bloodline, it skips a generation, grandfather to grandson, at least in my blood-line. I have been criticized, but they do not know that." He shrugged sadly, "Unfortunately, my son is an alcoholic. I hope my great-grandchildren will seek the power when they become older. There is no way Fools Crow or Eagle Feather would return that power back into my bloodline." He tilted the rocking chair forward. "Fools Crow and Eagle Feather are the only ones left now with real foretelling power. I don't know of many young ones coming up. Possibly, the Chips people. Maybe there are others. I hope so."

"You mean when they die, it might be gone forever?"

"Uh huh," Black Elk answered bluntly. "Yes," he added as if to clarify. "There are still some of the old traditionals, Chips, Runnings, Plenty Wolf; hopefully their offspring will keep it going. The Chips people. Their young are powerful and are strong on healing and foretelling. So strong that it does not skip generations in their line. Hopefully there will be new blood like Eagle Feather. Those who will go out and earn it with their bravery and of course know what being truthful really means." He drew deeply from a newly made cigarette, exhaling the smoke slowly to the ceiling. "My father's power was in his vision. My power is in my dreams," his voice carried a haunting vacancy. "Your power is in that stone you wear and in what you must fulfill. It is not for you to worry about what happens to the *Yuwipi* or what-ever else. Generations unborn, Mother Earth signs, the horse signs and the Blue Man. That is your concern." His voice was final as he settled back to rock, staring at the lifting smoke. A hideous face in blue appeared momentarily. "There was a Sun Dance tree in my father's vision. That has come back. The Blue Man is all-powerful now. There was a flowering tree and that four-rayed herb of understanding. Be sure to pray hard when you see the daybreak star." The ugly face in the smoke mocked at him as he spoke. "Knowledge and wisdom and truthful people of the four-rayed herb can kill the Blue Man; it can win over the selfishness and greed. It can even win over those that say they don't have a religion and even those who are too narrow-minded about their own religion. It can win over those who see the shal-lowness of the middleman. The Buffalo Woman, she will help. Mother Earth will help too, like was promised in my father's vision." A rainbow crossed over the blue face. It looked startled and disappeared.

Black Elk altered his conversation. He knew better than to mention what he saw. It could scare away the young man's vision quest. 'This one is a Mystic Warrior, a throwback,' he mused. Mystic Warriors had lives of adventure. If they succeeded on their missions, they were well rewarded, but seldom did they come out of it alive.

After he ground out his cigarette, he began again on a lighter note, "I was like you back in my day," he reminisced. "I went away and got a white man's education.

They always told us to get an education. The missionaries don't want young men like you to return to the Power of the Hoop. You have seen their way and still prefer your own. They are afraid the Indian way will return if young men like you go back." He placed the cigarette in the ashtray before leaning forward to peer with unblinking eyes. "All over I hear that young people are speaking out. This must be the beginning of what we hear is called communication. This Vietnam, there's a lot of them that don't want any part of it. There's an outfit getting started called the Indian Movement that is standing up to the BIA. Now some of you are going back to the ceremonies." He paused. "Uh huh," he said with a relieved sigh. "Maybe my father's words will come true, even in my time. The Sun Dance tree is back now. Maybe someday it will flower. We'll do our part, Nephew. Maybe I'll see you at the Sun Dance with my father's pipe."

FOOLS CROW'S YUWIPI

CHAPTER SEVENTEEN

"Specific defenses may be available as to specific torts. For example, truth, as a defense to an action in defamation." A law professor's lecture came from an open window on a hot day in early fall.

As he cut across the campus, he heard someone call his name. He turned to see Mary Bad Hand. The heavy set Hunkpapa woman, in her thirties, waved to him. "I'm going to see Schmidt."

He nodded to her invitation and soon found himself listening to a squat, pink faced man, Lothar Schmidt, the Indian Studies Director. Several oil paintings hung from the walls of the anthropologist's plush office. One picture depicting the signing of the Sioux Treaty of 1868, caught his eye. Behind a mahogany desk, an autographed picture showed Schmidt presenting the State's governor with a peace pipe.

After awhile, Schmidt turned with a pretentious smile, "I've been waiting to offer you a job." The chubby white man removed his oversized glasses. "If your grades are satisfactory, we could use a part time pilot."

Charging Shield's eyes fixed on the gravy spots dotting the man's tie. Schmidt bent his head. "I imagine it's been quite a change for you. That Vietnam, I'm against it like most professors should be, but that shouldn't keep my department from hiring an Indian pilot."

"Before I went overseas, everyone seemed to support it," Charging Shield answered condescendingly, pausing for a moment to study the balding professor's sanctimonious expression. 'What the hell am I ashamed of?' he chastised himself. His eyes narrowed. "At the time, I felt I owed it to my country." His words firmed. "If it turns out to be a wrong war, then I guess I can alibi I didn't know it was a wrong war." He tossed a glance at the oil painting. His tone was brisk and cool. "Maybe I'll feel guilty someday when the whites feel guilty enough to do something about all those broken treaties."

Mary Bad Hand gave him an assuring wink. Schmidt offered a disparaging shrug at the historic painting. "Now we can't live in the past, leastwise treaties made a hundred years ago." His words were mechanical. He pressed his hands to dismiss the discussion. A fatherly smile accompanied his change of tone. "I hope both of you are considering graduate work. I'd like to see the day when a master degreed Indian or a doctorate could sit in my position." He sat back in his chair and patted the armrests.

"What specific field?" Charging Shield tested the man's statement.

Schmidt was startled by the question, but managed to compose a tight smile. "History, anthropology, or possibly a sociology degree would be preferred. Those are fields more in tune to the problems of the Indian." He toyed with an ash tray for a moment, "Knowledge of the customs helps, but it takes more than that. I dance Indian myself, you know. Been dancing for years. I don't care about the non-traditional regalia these modern bucks are wearing. The old crow bustle is what I prefer." Schmidt pointed to a photo on his desk. "Sometimes I have the only authentic dance outfit on the floor. There I go again, straying from the subject. Can't help it when customs or dance is mentioned. To be honest, I'm not so sure a Sioux could handle this job. So many factions you know. If you had an Oglala in here, then the Brules would complain or the Hunkpapas. The Yanktons would probably complain the loudest since this is their former territory."

"I see," Charging Shield pretended to agree.

"Yes, factions are pretty important when you're dealing with Indians." He grinned complacently at the two students. "Sometimes it takes a white man to do an Indian job. The tribes get pretty jealous, you know. I get along with the tribes. I grew up with the old timers and know more about the old ways than most men do; know more than the Indians do."

Mary's cough interrupted Schmidt's classroom monotone. "I've got to catch my class," she said. The two walked out into the hallway and down a flight of stairs. "I didn't really have a class," she confessed. "He gets so sickening."

"It's a good thing we left," Charging Shield's words were vehement. "Anymore from that degrading son of a bitch and I'd have gone across his desk. Goddamn! How in the hell do these Indian students put up with that bigoted bastard?"

"They know Schmidt's a loser, but there's nothing we can do when student aid and our club funding has to come through his office," Mary answered. "This whole state. It's always been that way. They don't want to give an Indian a chance. I'm surprised he offered you the pilot's job."

They left the building and walked across the campus toward the Student Union. "If you ever sat in his class and heard his insults, you'd be madder yet," Mary spoke. "All the summer jobs have to go through him, besides the research grants. This damn university won't let an Indian direct any of the projects. The faction thing is their excuse. It's all politics and money. Indian grants have brought in a lot of money and don't think this school doesn't rip off its overhead. Keep the Indian students quiet is the rule." She looked around cautiously and warned, "I wouldn't speak up too much, Kyle."

They entered the Student Union building to drink coffee at a table. "That damned Schmidt flies all over the country and gets his friends employed in the Indian programs," Mary said. "He's got a real creep running the oral history grant."

"What's that?"

"There's a woman back east who wants our history recorded straight from the Indian, without any white man in the middle altering what they are telling. She gave the university a bunch of money to go out to the reservations and interview. It sounds simple, but old Schmidt has got some screwball anthropologist in there deciding what questions to ask. He doesn't know a thing about us and won't hire any Indians to do the interviewing."

"An anthro?"

"Yeah, a funny looking little guy. He bounces around the campus in crepe soled shoes and wears them big round glasses, just like Schmidt. Makes him look like a goddamned owl trying to get off the ground. He's from Formosa, name's Win Yin Lee. The guy barely talks English; claims he did research in the Philippines."

Mary chuckled. "They flew Win Yin Lee to West River and rented him a car before they found out he couldn't drive. Now he's back here taking driving lessons." After they finished laughing, Mary remarked. "You should take that flying job, maybe you could keep an eye on that oral history grant."

"I could use a part time job," he answered.

*   *   *   *

The first semester exams were behind him as he flew the airplane toward West River. The door of the Cessna 180 bore the University seal above the lettering, INDIAN ACTION PROGRAMS.

Dr. James Howard, the University Museum Director, sat in the front seat. A smile swept the pilot's face when he turned and looked behind Dr. Howard and down at the crepe soled shoes of the slight Oriental sitting next to Lothar Schmidt. Win Yin Lee, the Director of the Indian Oral History Project, had been aptly described by

Mary Bad Hand. The two anthropologists in the back of the plane planned to survey Indian families in West River for future interviews.

The pilot squeezed the pouch beneath his neck as he sat at the controls of the single engine plane flying across the snow covered prairie. Fools Crow's *Yuwipi* ceremony would be held that evening at Mildred's and Ralph's. The holy man would pay homage for the combat protection in Vietnam and then beseech the spirit powers further for the warrior's vision quest.

Dr. Howard also looked forward to the ceremony having received Fools Crow's permission. The sandy-haired professor, in his late forties, was tall and gangly. His deep hazel eyes projected an amiable manner that seemed to heighten as the plane flew westward. The scholar was an authority on Indian history and was well received throughout the Midwest by the tribes. At the University, the Museum Director conveyed a contrasting impression. He was a man alone, isolated among his peers. Howard respected Indian customs to such a degree that he was ostracized by many faculty members, including Lothar Schmidt. No white man could equal the professor's particular background, but due to Lothar Schmidt's influence, the heavily funded oral research project had fallen to Win Yin Lee, whose only experience had been with a boarding school in the Southwest. The anthropologist had written a research paper on Navajo students, qualifying him as an Indian expert according to Lothar Schmidt's standards.

While the landscape drifted beneath the plane, Charging Shield's thoughts rambled. Since the Sun Dance he wasn't sure his decision to leave the Marines was entirely his. Some force, possibly the *Yuwipi's* seemed to be directing him, or maybe it was a spirit guide. Maybe it was Cross Dog, he mused. The way they had to fight in Vietnam and now the campus demonstrations spreading across the country, causing politicians to restrict the military more than ever. No, he didn't regret leaving the military. It was too confusing fighting for the white man. The force, or whatever it was, seemed to convey a message... he was still a warrior. The Sun Dance and his journey with Eagle Feather had expanded his senses. There was an unsettled mission of which he was becoming a part, but his warrior role would be in his own world, what little was left of it. Fools Crow's *Yuwipi* would reveal more if he was allowed to know more. A smile creased his mouth when he thought about the *Yuwipi* at Wakpala and Rosalie having to leave.

He had dated Rosalie, attending a few movies and a dance but their opposite values had resulted in little more than a casual friendship. He shrugged his shoulders and listened to Howard explain a historic Mandan site on the windswept prairie.

When they crossed a broad river bordered by tall cottonwoods, Howard elaborated, "The Mandan tribe, there are theories about their origin. Ever been around them, Kyle?"

The question opened a strange stirring. The river passing by added to his uneasiness. He shook his head. Below the plane, a draw, thick with cedar trees dropped down to a meadow, divided by a rivulet fed by spring water. A high stand of old trees to the northwest providing a windbreak, an obvious winter campsite, held him spellbound.

"Their Siouan language is similar to your tribes. For example, Four Bears. They would say, *Mahto Dopa*. Your people say, *Mahto Topa*. No doubt, both tribes came from the same area, way back, when your people lived close to the Atlantic."

"I thought we were from the Carolinas."

"Before the Carolinas, a Siouan speaking people lived in what is now New York and the surrounding area," Dr. Howard went on. "These people were the Kansa and Arkansa. They have shells from the Long Island area in their medicine bundles and their old chiefs claimed that they were from that place. It is a strong possibility that the Sioux were in Long Island before they moved on to the Carolinas. When the main body of Sioux left the Carolinas and went up the Mississippi, the Kansa and Arkansa went downstream. The Mandans went up the Missouri, as did the Omaha. The Mandans had eyes and hair quite unlike the rest of the plains tribes. They had gray, even pale blue eyes, lighter hair and complexion. Some believe they may have Celtic or Viking blood." Howard reaffirmed his declaration by adding, "I will show you when we get back- a startling collection of old pictures taken of the Custer battle veterans. Years later, in the thirties, photographers held a reunion for them in the Black Hills." He brought a pipe from his shirt pocket and pointed it at the prairie for emphasis. "I believe the Sioux came from the east. And like some of the northeastern tribes, they had very pronounced facial features, were taller and slightly larger and lighter than most tribes - much like the Iroquoian people." He pointed the pipe again. "Pictures of those old-time Little Big Horn warriors don't lie, Kyle."

Charging Shield shot the Museum Director a startled look. 'The woman with the strange eyes. Karen had those eyes, gray and pale blue.' The stirring feeling from the bombing duels came over him. The campground passing below seemed to catalyze a power of transcendence into a past life. 'He had been before, on that spot of earth,' it seemed to tell him. He wanted so much to return to that world again. 'Nomad, warrior, buffalo hunter and of course, that woman with the strange eyes.' The haunting spot below.

'Did he live before? Dog Soldiers, Strong Hearts, Warriors of the Eagle Circle? It would be a past he would always want to come back to. Those vast, spacious plains where buffalo grazed from horizon to horizon, where the wildlife was virtually unlimited and man, too, had once lived that freedom. The enjoyment of that past was too convincing.' The Cessna droned onward. The land below was now devoid of ranging game, altered by fences and squared strips. 'His adventures and the airplane gave him freedom,' he argued with his thoughts. Abruptly, he rocked the wings to convince himself, startling the two passengers in the rear seat. Despite the airplane, he felt restricted. He knew he would have to change, change like the land below, if he wanted to fit into the white man's world. How could he ever return to

the freedoms of the past when it was all gone now?' The impossible question haunted him as the plane sped steadily westward.

'What was it, Bill had said? Be careful what you wish after a Sun Dance or something like that? He had already used a wish after the Sun Dance. He wished for Karen and nothing happened.' He cautioned himself. 'If he wished for Karen then maybe someday he would meet her. The Indian way wasn't on a timetable,' he reasoned hopefully. The bare outline of the Black Hills grew slowly on the horizon. He pretended to see herds of buffalo on the rolling grasslands. Darting in and out, mounted warriors harvested a winter's supply of meat. 'Such freedom! Even with a sun dance wish, how could he ever taste that freedom?'

Dr. Howard removed him from his thoughts. "Your people's religion strongly portrays the circle. The Power of the Hoop. The unending circle of life. The Celtics had the same symbol as the Four Directions." Dr. Howard joined the tips of his index fingers and his thumbs to form a circle. He then crossed his index fingers to make a cross: the crossing of the four directions inside of the Great Circle. "This symbol has been found on old Celtic shields and in their religious art."

Charging Shield recalled the symbol that Eagle Feather and Fools Crow had drawn on their dirt altars. The Power of the Hoop symbol. It was indeed interesting that the Celtics had the same symbol. He began to respect his passenger's knowledge.

"Also, Celtic beliefs are very similar to eastern tribal religions." The professor continued, "I've often wondered... it's possible, a lost or exploring European band could have joined one of the smaller tribes along the northeast coast. A smaller tribe that desperately needed an ally for defense against the powerful Iroquois." Howard reached for an empty pipe in his shirt pocket. "I'm not so sure you Dakotas or Lakotas, at least some of you could be from the remains of the Round Table."

"You mean Camelot lives?" The pilot replied.

Howard tapped his pipe on the ashtray at the bottom center of the instrument panel. "Your people's pronounced facial features, your height, the Mandans, their lighter complexion, even your word for water - *minne*- is similar to the Celts-mehde." The professor hunched his shoulders, indicating he felt that he hadn't made much of an impression upon the Oglala 'Knight' sitting next to him. "Anyway, it's an interesting theory."

'The Knights of the Round Table?' Charging Shield questioned within his thoughts. Just when he was about to warm up to the initial suppositions offered by Dr. Howard, now this 'Knights of the Round Table' came across as too extreme. He thought the professor's theory was just another example of the white man's paternalism. But the Power of the Hoop symbol continued to leave its impression. With Lothar Schmidt in the back seat, the atmosphere was conducive to native suspicion. 'The Lakota had developed their own natural truths, they didn't need another white man telling them some band of immigrants gave it to them. Immigrants that couldn't make their own system work for them back where they fled from.' The drone of the airplane played back a haunting echo, however. 'The Knights of the Round Table, The Knights of the Round Table. The Power of the Hoop.'

He turned to briefly look at Schmidt. Schmidt issued a glazed smile. 'Strange,' he thought. 'Strange, how quiet Schmidt had become after they had boarded the airplane.' Unknown to the pilot, Professor Schmidt had taken a powdered substance while the plane was being pulled from the hangar and now, the professor was mellowly flying in more ways than one.

Schmidt's lethargic look erased the verbal echo from the droning throb of propeller and engine but his mind wouldn't let go of Howard's theory. 'King Arthur, Merlin, Camelot... Fools Crow was as powerful as Merlin.' Prince Valiant came into his focus. He recalled dressing for Halloween as Prince Valiant, the comic strip character that portrayed the days of King Arthur. Not once but several times he had masqueraded as his childhood hero. The last time his sister, Mildred, painstakingly curled and cut his hair in the knight's pageboy style. With his black hair, he even looked like Prince Valiant. His parents had laughed until they cried. It was his favorite comic strip, that, and Red Ryder. He would always read those two first when the Sunday comics would come. He liked Little Beaver in the Red Ryder strip; Alley Oop and Dick Tracy, too. He let his mind wander. Passing time as the landscape unfolded, recalling comic strips of his childhood. He had treasured his Prince Valiant costume. He had a cape, a leather belt and a cowhide scabbard and wooden sword his father had made for him. He didn't mind the dress-like tunic he had to wear. Mildred had made it to look exactly like what his hero wore. She even had Ralph make a helmet covered with tinfoil. 'The great warrior's tunic couldn't be a dress. He had slain too many dragons, ogres and just plain bad people for it to be a dress. And then there was the beautiful Aleta. Someday Charging Shield, the boy, someday he would meet and rescue a beautiful Aleta.'

Charging Shield laughed at his boyhood fantasy. How ridiculous he must have looked. He should have dressed up as Little Beaver not Prince Valiant of the Round Table. He almost laughed aloud.

Dr. Howard brought him away from his past. "The Knights of the Round Table, they had high values, high standards, chivalry, like your people, Kyle."

'Don't tell me they had a natural religion?"

"Since you mention it, they were indeed, close to nature. The Druids of Britain, they were of that same time span, their ceremonies were out in nature. They had foretelling power not unlike the *Yuwipi* that we'll be experiencing."

Charging Shield's childhood reverie had softened his attitude. 'Was there ever a real King Arthur, knights like Prince Valiant, Druids and Camelot?' He did like the Museum Director's manner, so far. It was totally opposite of Schmidt's when he talked about Indians, their history and their culture. Howard lacked the paternalism and patronizing stamp that most professors exhibited when they came to study a people's spirituality from a scientific, objective, mechanically warped ego.

Dr. Howard had loaded his pipe and in afterthought asked the pilot if smoking was allowed. Charging Shield nodded his approval; liking the aroma of the professor's tobacco. He did not like the taste of tobacco but he certainly liked the smell of most pipe tobaccos. "I think a very mystical people did exist in the British Isles back in the time your people lived close to the Atlantic," Howard spoke after he had the pipe smoking well. "Of course, the organized church, the Roman Church that had come over from the mainland was brutally destroying all systems of spirituality that spoke to areas of thinking and communication that they couldn't come up with or dominate."

"Not any different than what they did to us on the reservation."

"Sometimes history repeats itself," Howard elaborated, "I can't help but believe that the Knights knew that something very destructive was coming and they realized they didn't have the force to stop it. Their foretelling power no doubt warned them, no different than the *Yuwipi* power warned your people to leave the Carolinas and head west. No doubt, the *Yuwipi* told the Sioux of long ago to avoid the Iroquois and warned of the treachery of General Custer. The Battle of the Little Big Horn was one of many battles they won over the U.S. Cavalry."

"Killed eight soldiers for every warrior we lost," Charging Shield answered proudly. "Least that is what I read from a writer who researched Army casualties." He was glad that the drone of engine noise kept the two passengers in the back seat out of the conversation.

"They were great warriors," Howard added. "They had a cause, they had spirit and knew how to train their horses. Their circular religion allowed them little fear of death." Howard paused to let his words have their effect.

"Kyle, you've heard of the Great Inquisition, have you not?"

"Not from the Jesuits," the pilot answered with cold sarcasm. "Wasn't that when they killed a lot of people all over Europe for not going along with the church?"

"It was much more than that. No one knows for sure. Thousands suffered and were put to death, maybe tens of thousands, possibly hundreds of thousands over a long period- many centuries in fact. Thousands of innocent people were burned at the stake. Mostly women; even children were tortured, drawn and quartered, maimed or burned to death just for the slightest trivial suspicion of not going along with organized religion; a religion that didn't want humans to see God in nature, themselves and the God-made relationship all around them. The Druids, the Celts and your people believed that Creator could be observed all around them. Your people say, '*Mitakuye oyasin* - For all my relatives.' Literally, meaning we are related to all things made of Nature."

"*Mitakuye oyasin*," Charging Shield echoed his Lakota pronunciation with emphasis on the T sound. "It's an important saying in our ceremonies," he agreed.

"I just have an overpowering theory that your people and the people that saw their God in nature linked up back there in the past. But I guess, I'll never live long enough to prove it. I just can't believe that those Knights with all their honor and spiritual insight didn't realize what was coming and got the hell out of England and sailed west, taking Merlin's wisdom and the Druids with them."

He could almost hear the straining of oars, the crashing of surf, a longboat grinding on a sand and rock-studded shore and an old, powerful voice. A voice so strong it was seer or mentor, a voice like Fools Crow's, especially when he was in ceremony. "Take courage, take courage," it had called out to him. Charging Shield liked the feel of Dr. Howard's theory. His senses tuned well to it. His people did have considerably different features than the western tribes, especially the contrast between the Sioux and the Navajos or the Pueblos. Sioux were as different in appearance to many western tribes as Nordics were from most Italians and Spaniards. And then there is the Symbol- the Power of the Hoop.'

As the airplane cruised westward, the Black Hills became pronounced on the horizon. Soon they would be landing at West River. Dr. Howard proposed an interesting theory, he concluded, but Fools Crow's *Yuwipi* ceremony and the return of the Sun Dance was his immediate reality.

After landing at West River, he taxied the Cessna to the tallest hangar on the field. Ernie Hale jumped up from his desk when he strolled into his office. "Kyle, you wild Indian!" his loud voice vibrated the room. Within a few moments the burly man walked out to the airplane with his arm draped around the pilot. "Goddamn, Kid, you must be studying. I saw more of you when you was in the Marines. I bet you miss those jets." At the airplane, Hale barked orders to the professors, sending them scurrying like chickens in a farmer's driveway. The scholars clumsily pushed and pulled the plane to a trio of tie down rings, each fumbling with a rope that Ernie had to retie.

After the aircraft was secured, Hale pointed the passengers to a waiting room then turned toward a hangar. "C'mon, I got a bird that'll make you forget those school books."

Ernie led the way to an adjoining hangar. They entered a side door to walk down the darkened enclosure. At the end of the hangar, bathed in a shaft of sunlight from a dusty window, the red biplane waited, isolated and alone, as though it could take a passenger back through time. Charging Shield felt suddenly subdued, as if some mysterious force was waiting for a particular moment to fly him away. The suggestion of a life before merged with a life beyond flooded over him as he stared, mesmerized by the red Grumman Ag' Cat.

"She's almost mine, Kid," Ernie exclaimed with a wry smile. "I traded that old Piper Cub. Guess I told you about this crop sprayer in town who's going broke." A vindictive grin spread across his face. "Poor fellow, I knew him back in grade school. He was sort of a bully then," Ernie spoke with feigned compassion. "People wonder why I always had a favorin' for your brother, Lawrence. Well, after Lawrence got through with this guy at the swimmin' hole, I was no longer bothered." A hard glint came to Ernie's eyes. "He's been having a string of bad luck and the bank had to foreclose." Ernie burst out with a vicious laugh. "Yup," he added, "poor bastard is going broke."

Ernie's words broke the enchantment cast by the Grumman. Charging Shield stepped back to admire the rugged frame.

"When I get that baby, we'll trim off those spray nozzles and make an acrobatic job outta her. Then you can take her up and wring her out." The Indian's acknowledging nod made the businessman continue excitedly. "That cockpit is pretty wide. I'll fix it so we can sit side by side. Wait and see."

The short wing span won the fighter pilot's approval. He studied the cockpit of the single seated craft. It seemed forbidding, yet inviting. He stroked the side of the fuselage. A close feeling for the machine overcame him.

"You got a funny look on your face," Ernie interrupted his appreciation. "What's the matter, you lonesome for that Phantom?"

"Been too damn busy to get lonesome," he shook off the Grumman's mystique with his answer. A mischievous smile erased his serious composure. He reached for the wing strut and rocked the aircraft. "Never could do that to a Phantom," he said, enjoying his friend's frown. "I'll take her up someday, Ernie. See what she can do."

"Flying will never get out of your blood," Hale remarked as they returned to his office.

Charging Shield turned to look back at the hangar and did not disagree. "How about a lift into town, Ernie? I'll tell you how we jinxed those missile sites," he promised, throwing a mock punch at his flying mentor.

Hale's eyes lit like a child being asked to play. "Great, Kid. Get them professors."

Hale left the two anthropologists at a motel and drove on to a modest, two-bedroom frame house close to the foothills of the Black Hills. "Give me a call next time you're in town, and remember," he jabbed a finger forcefully before driving away, "you got a job with me this summer."

Julie Charging Shield embraced her son before welcoming Dr. Howard into her tidy home. Mildred greeted them also at the doorway. It wasn't long before Howard was discovered as a gifted storyteller and could even sing the old Sioux story songs in Indian. The professor put Julie in such a jovial mood singing rabbit songs; she invited herself to the evening's *Yuwipi*.

After coffee was offered in the living room, Mildred returned her cup to the kitchen. "I'd better get home," she said. "Lawrence went down to get Fools Crow and Amos Lone Hill. They'll be coming in pretty soon."

"Where's that postcard you had for Kyle?" Julie called out.

"What card was that?" he asked.

"Some girl sent you a postcard or was it a letter? I told your sister to mail it on down to the University."

He queried his sister from the living room. Not receiving an answer, he confronted her in the kitchen. "Was it from California?"

He felt a rush of blood as she nodded smugly. He had told his sister about the girl that he had met returning from Vietnam. Her answer didn't surprise him.

"I lost it," she said. Her voice hardened when her eyes met his.

"What did it say?" he asked with a scowl?

"Said she was going to be flying for another company and she was moving."

"And you lost the card, or was it a letter?" he shook his head grimly.

"You should marry an Indian girl," his sister spouted.

"What the hell's that got to do with my mail... and reading my mail?" he yelled.

"It don't look good... you and some white woman."

"Jesus Christ, Sis, you didn't marry an Indian," he countered.

"That's different, they're used to Ralph. You in the Sun Dance and all, it just won't look right."

His mother's quick entrance from the living room ended the argument. He picked up the telephone and called information in the major California cities, to no avail.

That evening, Lawrence arrived at Mildred's home with his two passengers. While the Oglala holy man and his son-in-law, Amos rested on a broad sofa, Mildred cut tobacco cloths into small squares to make the tiny pouches that would be attached to a long string. Lawrence and Ralph busied themselves in the basement covering windows and moving furniture.

Just before they finished, Mildred descended the stairs instructing them to leave an oval braided rug in the center of the room. "I don't care if it is a *Yuwipi*, that old man is going to lay on a rug, not on any hard floor in my house. He's getting old. Bad enough he has to go through these ceremonies. If them spirits don't like it, they can blame me."

Charging Shield warmly greeted his brother, Lawrence, when he entered the house with his mother and Dr. Howard. Kyle was surprised his brother wanted to attend the *Yuwipi* and was foregoing his social life at a local bar.

"The old man, there. He didn't say much on our way up here from the reservation at first, but we got to talkin' about the Cross Dog folks. Long ago, I remember those *Yuwipi* men that came to Cross Dog's place. Fools Crow, he knew them. Said they were pretty good." Lawrence looked down. "I got to thinkin' about all of you and this ceremony you plan to do. I think I'd be a damn fool not to join you. Maybe it will help my drinking."

As Fools Crow was descending the basement stairs, a taxi's headlights illuminated the driveway. Lothar Schmidt knocked on the door. "I heard you were going to have a ceremony and thought I'd drop by. Mr. Lee chose to remain at the motel." Schmidt began his words to invite himself to the ceremony.

"I'm afraid you'll have to ask Fools Crow," Charging Shield answered coldly. His refuting tone was obvious.

"I respect Indian customs. Where is the holy man?" Schmidt asked with glazed eyes.

Charging Shield gave a disdainful nod, pointing to the basement door. His sister's loss of the postcard had left him in a sour mood.

Howard spoke up, "Schmidt, this is a family ceremony. You really should be invited."

"What's wrong with my attending?" Schmidt postured an innocent look. "I'm a Director of Indian Studies. I intend to employ Indian students in our summer history program."

"You think just like that University," Howard replied sarcastically. "The white man has to run the whole show with a few token jobs thrown out as covering."

Schmidt started to reply but Charging Shield interfered, "This ceremony can't have animosity in the house. Fools Crow will decide. Doc, you tell him why you don't feel Professor Schmidt should attend."

"No, Kyle, I won't object if you don't. Let's go ahead and ask Fools Crow's permission."

"I must confess I've never been to one of these spirit ceremonies, should be interesting." Schmidt adjusted his glasses with a nervous gesture.

Fools Crow was sitting on the basement rug preparing a dirt altar when the men entered the room. The holy man nodded his approval without expression. Charging Shield noticed the design that Fools Crow drew on the flattened earth with a stick. It was not the man design that Bill had used but was simply four staggered lines and four dots. Fools Crow then drew the Power of the Hoop symbol. The design seemed to speak out that possibly some truth resided in Dr. Howard's theories.

Mildred unrolled the tobacco pouches tied together to form the square boundaries of the *Yuwipi* area. The cloths were red for blood that was spilled in war. She left an opening at the opposite side from the altar which Fools Crow's attendants would have to use to enter the spirit area.

Charging Shield lit a braided stem of sweet grass and handed it to the holy man. He shook the stem slowly, fanning the small embers in the grass and soon a pleasant odor filled the room. Fools Crow blessed the altar, his pipe and the ceremonial area with the smoldering grass and handed it back to Charging Shield. Fools Crow then stood to load his peace pipe. He offered it to the Four Directions, down to Mother Earth, up to Father Sky and then to the Great Spirit above.

He capped the pipe with a few sage leaves by placing them in the pipe bowl on top of the fresh tobacco. The capping would remain until the end of the ceremony when the pipe would be smoked.

Charging Shield waved the braided sweet grass under the pipe to allow the pleasant smelling smoke to rise around the pipe. He then circled the holy man, waving the braid. He continued the same procedure around each participant in the ceremony. When he came to Schmidt, the smoldering grass braid went out.

After Howard re-lit the grass, Charging Shield waved it around each participant, then snuffed out the glowing sparks with his fingers before handing a sage stem to each individual.

Howard instructed Schmidt to place the sage in his hair or over his ears. Fools Crow handed the pipe to Mildred, motioning her toward the place of honor at the head of the dirt altar and outside of the tobacco pouch boundary. The holy man then placed Charging Shield's *wotai* in front of the dirt altar, leaving the stone tightly bound inside the pouch by a buckskin thong. The old man's hands were tied before the blanket was placed over him. Fools Crow gave a shrill cry, somewhat like a tremolo. Charging Shield dropped the noose over his head and drew it down tightly, then wrapped the old man six more times, tying at each wrap.

Lawrence helped him lay the bound figure on the rug in front of the mound of dirt serving as an altar. The two buckskin rattles without handles waited at the right side. Charging Shield pulled the blanket from around the old man's mouth, before closing the spirit area exit with the last portion of the tobacco pouches.

The lights were turned out after the telephone had been removed from the receiver. The house was locked to insure that privacy would be enjoyed. Amos Lone Hill sang the calling song to the beat of a small drum. After some hesitation the spirit beings entered. The rattles shot across the room and shook fiercely as the tempo of the calling song progressed.

The blue lights and the swift movements of the rattles fascinated Charging Shield. They seemed to accelerate instantly and stopped just as quickly; yet always kept time to the beat of the drum. After the calling song was sung, Charging Shield was called to pray for his *wotai*. Charging Shield thanked the spirit people for his safe return from war. He mentioned the prisoners of war and asked for their return. He thanked the Great Spirit for his mother's improved health. "Let the Sun Dance come back strong the Indian way."

"*Hau, hau,*" exclaimed his relatives.

"I'm taking a new road. Maybe my education will help me be a better warrior for the return of our beliefs. Maybe my *wotai* will help me combat those who would destroy our way. I have taken a vow before Eagle Feather and the Hunkpapas to vision quest. I ask the stone to remain with me awhile longer. If it will, I also vow to be pierced in the next Sun Dance."

A chorus of '*haus*' filled the room.

"Good Road, a holy man who knew Crazy Horse and Red Cloud is present. He has listened to your prayer for wishing to keep your stone," Fools Crow's muffled voice called in Lakota. Charging Shield's mother was quick to interpret.

Fools Crow called for the middle song. Once again the lights danced throughout the room and the rattles bounced upon the floor.

Charging Shield sensed the heavy pounding of hooves as if horses abreast were prancing to the beat of the drum. They sounded as if they were parading in a circle. The cement floor trembled and the vibration and clatter slowly faded.

"*Hehaka Sapa, Hehaka Sapa,* Black Elk, Black Elk," Fools Crow called out when the spirit of old Black Elk entered. Once again, Fools Crow saw the Sun Dance tree surrounded by the colored circle. The quartered circle began to turn. A warrior, clearly an *Ohuze Wichasta*, a Mystic Warrior, stood on the red quarter, the quarter of the vision quest. A pair of lightning bolts flashed, straddling the warrior. Eagle Feather had told about the *heyoka* bolts hitting so close to the pickup... just before they passed the white man's rocket places. Fools Crow conversed with the spirit of the old prophet in muffled Lakota then related his message. "Good Road and Ben's father, Nicholas Black Elk, have listened to your prayer, Charging Shield. You will be allowed to keep your *wotai* for your vision quest on the sacred mountain. You shall receive a pipe soon, and with this pipe you will go to the top of Spirit Mountain. Be alert and know there are forces to be watchful for. Your pipe along with your *wotai* will be your protection. Old Black Elk wants you to watch for horses. You may have a vision that you might not understand. Bring this vision back to me. *Ho hetch etu aloh*."

Amos Lone Hill served as interpreter for the small gathering. After the holy man finished he added, "Now each one of you shall pray and Good Road and Black Elk will hear you."

Mildred prayed first, "Thank you for our Sun Dance, my mother's health and my brother's safe return from war. Help us to bring the Sun Dance back as it should be."

Fools Crow's muffled voice spoke out. "Good Road told me to tell the woman who holds the pipe that he appreciates her prayer but warns that the people are yet weak in the ways of the Sun Dance. Look for confusion and enemies of the annual gathering next year but do not lose faith."

The prayers continued. Schmidt followed Ralph. "Go ahead and pray, Schmidt," Howard offered after a period of silence.

Finally Schmidt cleared his throat and snorted deeply before he spoke. "I have nothing to say."

Lawrence was last to pray, "*Wakan Tanka*, I wish to thank you for letting me see again, a part of our way. Maybe it is what we need and there will be fewer problems among us."

The untying song was sung sending the blanket flying through the room. Schmidt let out a startled yell when it draped itself around him.

The lights were turned on when the song ended. The holy man's rawhide ropes were wrapped in a tight ball. The rattles were in their original spots as though they had never moved.

Charging Shield looked down at the *wotai* stone resting on the dirt altar. The buckskin sack remained in its original position. The sack had not been untied. The pipe was lit and passed around for all to smoke. The ceremony was over.

Mildred busied herself in the kitchen serving the meal that had been prepared. A large slab of deer meat was the main course. She placed the first serving on a plate and presented it to Fools Crow. He instructed Amos to take the plate outside to leave as an offering beneath a towering cottonwood tree. He thoughtfully placed a portion of tobacco mixed with the bark of the red willow on the plate. Mildred then served the old man as he sat on the floor. Rich laughter flowed with the meal when Dr. Howard sang rabbit songs and a few that he had personally composed.

"Doctor, you are a *wah-shi-chu keeawks a sapa*," Julie Charging Shield laughed.

"*Wah shee chu keeawks a sapa*, that's a good name, Julie. I know what that means but there must be a story behind it. You say I am a white-black man?"

"Yes, there was a black man who ran away from the slave plantations. He came up the Missouri and the Oglalas found him. He was almost dead but our people took him in. He learned our ways and our language. He married one of us and had a family. He said the slave people told them the Indians would kill them and eat them but he ran away anyhow. He always teased the Indians though, and would make up songs about us. *Keeawksa sapa* was his name. He found a home with us. Now you are making up songs, Doctor."

"I've been told some big lies too, Julie." He paused reflectively, "In a way, I've run away like Keeawksa sapa. Now your people are taking me in."

Mildred gave him a warm smile when she filled his coffee cup. Howard sang another song before the conversation centered on the events in the ceremony.

Lawrence attempted to describe the lights that appeared, "They were blue or bluish-green and they looked like electricity sparks. It seemed they sparked at every beat of the drum."

Schmidt smugly interrupted, "Oh no, they were red or maybe red-orange. I never saw any blue lights."

Howard's mouth dropped. He shot a startled look at the anthropologist.

"What's the matter, Doc?" Charging Shield whispered.

Howard shook his head and continued to stare at Schmidt. Charging Shield sensed foreboding anger from the professor's manner.

"Later, maybe later I will tell you," he whispered back. "It's not good."

That evening a snowstorm covered the western half of the state. The snowfall continued into the next day. Schmidt called an airline to return to the University, but all West River flights had been cancelled. After supper at Charging Shield's mother's home, he pleaded to return in the University plane.

"Sorry, Schmidt, you don't take chances with light planes in this kind of weather." Charging Shield shook his head to emphasize his words. "Doc and I are borrowing my sister's car for a drink or two at a nightclub tonight. Why don't you come along? My mother's going to stay at my sister's. You can stay here with Doc and me if you like."

A twisted grin came and went on Schmidt's face, indicating his assent. Later that evening they were sitting in a nightclub discussing various ceremonies. Schmidt dwelled on the vision quest at length. After he left the table for the rest room, Charging Shield took the opportunity to ask Howard about the red-orange lights.

"Well, I was worried when he mentioned them," Howard began. "It is a sign that the person doesn't believe what he is seeing and could in fact be making fun of it. You noticed that Schmidt didn't pray like the rest of us? I think he's on dangerous grounds."

When they returned to his mother's house, he fixed the couch for the anthropologist. Schmidt was sitting in the kitchen writing when he bid him goodnight. During the early hours of the morning he heard the anthropologist talking on the telephone. It sounded as though he was talking to his wife, but Kyle drifted back to sleep.

Before daybreak Charging Shield awakened. On his way to the bathroom, he noticed Schmidt's absence from the couch. He also noticed that the professor's boots were beside the coffee table. After he went to the bathroom, he checked the kitchen. His mother's house was small, consisting of two bedrooms, a living room and a kitchen. In the basement there was a makeshift bedroom and storage space.

He walked down the concrete stairs feeling a fearful chill as he thought about the strange way that Schmidt smiled. He turned the basement light on and unconsciously looked at the ceiling, then opened the door to the bedroom. He returned up the stairs to look into Howard's bedroom. "Doc, wake up. Wake up. That crazy Schmidt has gone without his boots on. It must be twenty degrees below."

Howard leaped to his feet. "Did you check outside?"

"No, Doc, I didn't." He put his shoes and trousers on and zipped up his flying jacket. A garage was across from the driveway. The garage served as a spare bedroom in the summertime.

Charging Shield was afraid to open the door but forced himself. He turned on the garage light and again looked upward. The wind blew a blast of frigid air against his back as he scanned the room. He looked under the bed and behind two old trunks before he went back inside. Howard was dressed.

"You didn't find him?"

"No."

"How about the car?"

"Come with me, Doc. He has to be in there."

The fresh snowfall reflected the streetlights causing the elm trees to cast eerie shadows as they walked to the car parked in the driveway. Charging Shield's mind speeded with thoughts, predicting what he would see when the car door would come open. Both men looked in, expecting to find the anthropologist frozen, but the car was empty. Charging Shield ran for the phone.

"Hello, is this the police station?"

"Yes, this is the police department."

He gave his mother's address. "You'd better send some squad cars up here right away. We have an idiot running around loose without his boots on."

"Is he a University professor?"

"Yeah, yeah he is."

"They found him a half hour ago. Both arms and feet are frozen. He's at the hospital."

Charging Shield felt faint when he hung up the receiver. His legs wilted and his stomach tightened as he stumbled for the couch. "He's up at the hospital, his limbs are frozen," he gasped. "That stupid son of a bitch. Man, we're in deep trouble, Doc. At least I am, in this town."

The car barely started in the cold weather. They drove to the hospital in near silence.

Schmidt's feet were under a half round frame as they entered a hospital room. He offered the strange twisted smile. Charging Shield hated the man for the publicity that would surely follow after the news people found out. He noticed that Schmidt moved his arms freely as he propped his pillow. His exposed legs had dark blotches.

Howard asked to see the doctor on duty and the nurse led him to the resident's office. Howard introduced himself.

The medical doctor spoke, "He is a very lucky man. A dog saved his life and his limbs. I think that he will lose a small amount of tissue off the balls of his feet but nothing serious. He will be in some degree of pain, but considering the other consequences he is fortunate."

Charging Shield breathed a sigh of relief. He had to sit down again.

"I suspect he is mentally disturbed. He said he intended to Vision Quest on the hills west of town. He cut across some one's yard and was stopped by a fence. He sat down there to freeze to death, then apparently changed his mind. By this time, due to the cold, he lost the use of his ankles and wrists on down."

"He crawled on his elbows and knees to a house and the dog inside woke up the occupants. They opened the door and Schmidt crawled in. The people were somewhat shocked, to say the least, and called the police."

"Cold weather will bother his feet for awhile but he will be all right. He is extremely lucky."

Howard calmly agreed, "Since this matter could bring unfavorable publicity to the University and to the Indian community as well, I hope you can curtail any news releases that may arise from this type of situation."

"I understand very well, Dr. Howard. We can keep it from the papers. I'm a University grad myself."

The previous night's snowstorm turned to a blizzard by noon. The snow continued that evening, finally subsiding sometime the next morning. The Cessna 180 was completely covered with a drift, requiring several hours of shoveling. The runway remained closed causing them to spend one more night in West River. That evening the family gathered to discuss the near tragic event.

"Without you there to explain to the police, Doc, I bet all hell would have broken loose. We'd be blamed for that professor flipping his cork," Lawrence spoke.

"Goddamn, can you imagine what would have happened if that goofy clown would have frozen to death and you wouldn't have been there? I'd be behind bars right now," added Charging Shield. "Once they'd traced his tracks back to the house, I'd be blamed for throwing him out without his shoes on. Mom would have been sitting behind bars too." He imagined his mother behind bars. "Indians suspected of slaying professor. Indian ceremony causes professor to commit suicide. Man, I can just see the headlines."

Lawrence started laughing and soon the room filled with laughter. Only Indian humor could make light of such a situation. It was natural tradition to laugh at the worst that could have happened. Charging Shield laughed so hard that tears came to his eyes.

Lawrence's imagination ran rampant. "Can you imagine that goggle-eyed goof-ball making it all the way to the top of the hill? '*Hahn ba lay chee yah,* man. *Hahn blay chee yah,* (Vision quest, man. Vision quest,)' he'd say. He'd sit right down and do his thing. Then that blizzard would roll in and cover him and his tracks all up. Meanwhile the police, National Guard and even the Air Force would be looking all over hell. Old Kyle and Julie would be prime suspects, they'd have 'em under armed guard at the County Jail."

"We'd be lookin' all over and all the time that nut would be up there with that goofy smile and his glasses all froze over looking down on us."

Lawrence wiped the tears from his eyes and laughed some more. "And then... the spring thaw would come and that goofy son of a bitch would roll into Main Street, off of that mountain in a snowball, breaking open right downtown. Old Julie and Kyle would get double life sentences."

The room howled with laughter. Charging Shield's turn came next after the laughter subsided.

"Or else, after that first time he sat down, he would have gotten up and made it over to the schoolyard. Then he would have done his thing like they say, Hahn ba lay chee yah!" Everyone laughed even in the middle of the story. "He'd of stood there in the schoolyard and that blizzard would have drifted around him making a snowman out of him. Then, them little kids would have gone to school every day with old Schmidt out there in the schoolyard, covered with snow.

"By that time, the FBI and the hippies from the University would have joined forces looking for him. Here he'd be right in the schoolyard. Congress would have passed a law banning all Indian ceremonies. Fools Crow would be under grand jury investigation and shipped to Fort Leavenworth."

Lawrence broke in laughing... "And then them little kids would be patting that snowman every day. A big Chinook wind would come in while them kids was sitting in school and melt all that snow on their snowman, and recess time would come and there's old Schmidt standing there. The whole damn school would have took off."

"University Professor Found Standing in School Yard, Two Blocks From Suspect's House, Ending World Wide Search." Everyone laughed. "Grade School Kids Undergoing Psychiatric Treatment." They laughed again.

"Lawrence, tell that first one again," someone said.

"Snowman... Snowman," Julie Charging Shield called out. "Doc, you go back to that University and tell them professors we got a good name for that anthropologist or whatever he is. 'Snowman', that's going to be his Indian name from now on. He earned it."

BOARDING SCHOOL

CHAPTER EIGHTEEN

Hearings before a Subcommittee on Indian Affairs
Physical Abuse of Children, Pine Ridge, South Dakota
Senate, on S.R. 79, 71st Cong., 2nd sess., 1930, pp 2833-2835.

Examination by United States Senator Frazier
Q. What is your name?
A. Mrs. Rose Ecoffey.
Q. Were you ever employed in the Indian Service?
A. Yes; I was matron in the school, boys' matron temporarily; I was there in August, September and part of October. Mr. Jermark asked me to go up there and take the matron's place.
Q. And when they got a regular matron you went home?
A. Yes.
Q. Is that the only time you ever worked at the school?
A. I worked as a nurse in the hospital.
Q. What about the conditions at the school? How were the boys treated?
A. Not good I would call it; runaway boys were whipped and a ball and chain was put on them and they were shaved close to their head; that is the way they punished them for running away.
Q. Why did they do that?
A. Because they run away and played hooky because they did not like the school.
Q. Do you know of any specific instances where they done that?
A. Yes; there was one little one 12 and another one 10, and they put a ball and chain on them and put them to bed and locked the door on them, and when I went in there I wanted to change their bed and the disciplinarian refused to let me; and it was not fit for anyone to see. They kept them locked up there for three or four weeks or a month. I asked Mr. Wilson, the disciplinarian about them—he was not here very long-and he said to leave them there.

*   *   *   *

Several months passed. A warm friendship grew between Kyle and Mary Bad Hand.One day, toward the end of the second semester, Mary paid him a visit at his apartment. He placed a cup on the kitchen table before opening the refrigerator for a can of beer.

"Did you hear about Win Yin Lee?" Mary Bad Hand asked as he poured her cup full of coffee. She scanned his efficiency apartment. "When Schmidt was in the hospital, Lee went down to the reservation. Damned fool should've stayed in West River." She waited until he sat across from her before she continued, "Guess half the Indians in town was running up to the hospital to peek in on Schmidt." She slapped her thigh with a chuckle. "That anthro could've taken a bed alongside of Schmidt and got all the interviews he wanted."

"What happened to him?"

Mary started laughing. "After all that project money Schmidt spent teaching him how to drive, he rolled his car off a reservation curve."

Charging Shield's wide grin broke into laughter. "How bad did he get hurt?"

"Not bad enough to get back here and clear out. Guess he spent all night in the badlands with a bunch of rattlesnakes before someone came along. He was one scared anthro." She reached for a pack of cigarettes on the table. "They're going to replace Schmidt," she said as she searched in her purse for a book of matches. After she found the matches she spoke with tongue-in-cheek. "For medical reasons, of course. Damned University would never admit how fouled up he is, leastwise to us 'skins'." A hopeful look crossed her face. "Some of the students and a couple tribal chairmen will be part of the search committee for his position. Doc Howard is going to take over Schmidt's position in the meantime."

"That's a switch," he remarked.

After Mary lit her cigarette, she sat back in her chair to blow a smoke ring at the ceiling. She waited for the smoke to dissipate before she spoke, "I'd like to see some of that grant money come up with a study on the boarding schools. I say a lot of Indians are alcoholics because they were taught to be ashamed of themselves. These studies and grants are always theorizin' about the Indian problem but they never take a look at the damage the boarding schools and missionaries did."

"Those two have always been off limits for research," he remarked.

"I remember when I was six, a bus picked us up in the fall;" she continued, "we wouldn't see our folks for nine months. Can you imagine white kids in suburbia being sent off for nine months? And now they're bitching about busing. Hell, we had busing a long time ago, only it was a one-way trip. If you were lucky, you could go home Christmas vacation, providing your parents had money enough to come and get you or a round-trip bus ticket was sent in the mail. A one-way ticket, and they wouldn't let you go home."

Charging Shield turned his beer can slowly, studying the label with a disgusted grimace.

"Most research grants come from the government, through the B.I.A. or the Education Department. The grants are controlled by Non-Indians mostly, or Indians like that creepy Rosalie Carlson. She's been at this University longer than I can remember and she's attended every Indian conference in the country. If she ever graduates, she'll step into one of the B.I.A. positions and continue to do nothing except take care of her crony friends who are just as phony as she is. Rosalie wouldn't know what to do with a shawl at a pow wow, let alone know what a pow wow is. You'll never see her at the Sun Dance either. The sociologists, anthros and Indian experts work hand in hand with Rosalie's kind on the government grants. They aren't going to let the truth be told; hell no, because if you want to expose the truth, you don't receive the grant." She pursed a hard frown. "It's as simple as that. Telling the truth would put an end to their summer vacations."

He sat quietly, nodding his head to indicate agreement.

"Then there are the do-gooders that will give money to the church for research. That church won't tell what really happened. Hell, they're so damn blind and bigoted, they can't believe their boarding schools did any damage. How could it be detrimental they say, as long as the people received Jesus? What more could the Indians want? Give 'em Geesus, even if we take their kids from them. But you know something, Kyle? When you're six, seven or eight years old, lonely as hell, lying in your bed in a spooky dormitory with a bunch of black hooded nuns floatin' up and down the aisle, you cry. Goddamn, you cry. Even animals have a family. God made families but they stole us from ours and they gave us, *Jesus*."

Charging Shield took a long drink, avoiding the woman's eyes. He recalled the loneliness, especially the first nights away from home. When he finished he posed a sarcastic look. "They always offer that excuse - 'but they meant well.' "

Mary's reply was coldly emphatic, "Meant well! Hell, Hitler meant well for the Germans, they say. What the hell good was that for the Jews in the ovens and the concentration camps?" She continued with fervor, "A paper Jesus and 'meant well' can't replace human love, not when you're six or eight or eighteen, and lonely as hell in a cold goddamn institution." She paused to glance across the room. "You was lucky you didn't do much time in the boarding school. You went to school with the white kids. You came home every night to a mom and dad."

The woman's remark evoked his response, "Some of the West River kids made fun of us but I was fortunate. I played sports and had some baseball and basketball friends that stuck up for me." After a quiet moment of reflection he spoke again, "Had this big, tough white kid for a friend. He played basketball and didn't have much of a home life. He never knew what the hell a homemade cookie or a pie was until he came over to my house. Funny how a little thing like a homemade cookie can change your life." Charging Shield smiled. "This guy was as tough as Lawrence and he really liked my folks. They gave him the love that he never had at home. Before he came along I had trouble with some of the white kids at school." He frowned. "I knew some Indian kids a couple grades ahead of me, they were ridiculed so much they had to go back down to the boarding school."

"West River's getting better," she acknowledged, "but when I was going to school the missionaries had an iron grip. When September came, the buses would load up the kids, little ones and big ones and down to the reservations they'd go." She ground her cigarette into an ashtray before she continued.

"I was in grade school with your sister Rose when she got pneumonia. She was real bad off. Lawrence wrote back to your folks and told them how sick she was. You must've been pretty small yet cuz' they were still living on the reservation then. Well, in those days they even censored the letters at the boarding school and your folks never knew about it until Rose was almost dead. The Indian grapevine finally got word to them. When they did get there, she was too far-gone. She died two days later. Goddamn, even an animal gets comfort from its parent when it's dying. What was wrong with that little girl having her parents with her when she was sick?"

"Lawrence was never told about it until after she was dead. He was sitting in class and heard it from his teacher. 'Lawrence, your sister died. They buried her this morning.' He didn't even get to go to the funeral. God, talk about mean. Those frustrated things were cruel." She shook her head. "It wasn't just the missionaries that was mean," Mary went on. "Back in my time, they had a big federal boarding school just outside of West River. Some fourth grade boys ran away. They were headin' for their homes back on the reservation but they got caught on the railroad track by Creston. They brought those little fourth graders back and chained them together just like a chain gang, like we always hear about in the South."

"Fourth graders chained?" He looked at her.

"That's right...fourth graders! I hate to even tell about the boarding school. People think you're nuts or a big liar."

"I believe you. Go ahead."

"They had solitary confinement in all those schools, too. I did two days on bread and water, locked in a place as big as a closet and pitch black, too. Well, those little boys were chained together and they had to march off all the miles down to Creston and back, around the flagpole on the drill field. It was about fifty miles. They stayed chained together until they finished the fifty miles. They ate together, slept together and went to the bathroom together.

"They had a long punishment table and they would march in step. If one fell down, they all fell down. When it was time to feed them, they'd all sit down and the dining hall girls would bring their food over to them on trays.

"How would you feel if that was your little brother sitting there?"

He stared out the darkened window. Mary took a drink from her cup and continued.

"It took a long time to march off those fifty miles." She motioned with her head toward the door. "I wonder how that would go over if you did that to some fourth graders in this college town? Fourth graders, and then people wonder why the Indians got so many alcoholics!"

"You know Indians were always a clean people, but they really tried to make us clean. We had to scrub, scrub, scrub when we worked in those boarding schools. I scrubbed a lot of floors in my day. We even scrubbed porches in the wintertime. We worked either a morning shift and went to school in the afternoon or the other way around.

"The girls worked in the kitchen, laundry, dining hall, dormitories, sewing room or clean up details everywhere. The boys were in the dairy, machine shop, barns and in the kitchen too. Everyone worked half a day and went to school the other half. We always laugh about how we really got only half an education."

The older woman paused to push her cup toward the center of the table. "Government and mission schools, they all operated the same way. We got less education from the missionaries. At the mission we'd get up at 5:30 every morning, get dressed and celebrate a goddamn boring mass every damn morning. You got slapped or had to kneel on the floor the whole time if you fell asleep or whispered. We'd go to church in the evening too and sometimes during the day. Hell, we were always going to church. Boys were separated from the girls. If you looked at a boy, you'd have to tell about it in confession. You couldn't even talk to your own brother standing in a mess hall line. We didn't get much education from the boarding schools, but we got all the work and religion we could handle. When we tried to go to college and compete with the white kids that had gone a full academic day, we couldn't get the same grades. The sociology and psychology experts claimed we had lower intelligence."

"We never got to read any books telling anything good about our leaders. They wouldn't even let us make a dance costume on our own time, let alone go to a pow wow dance. If you spoke Indian you got your mouth washed out with soap. If you weren't a Christian you were a pagan and would go to hell. God help you if you was related to the holy men. Those kids really received a brainwashing. That's why so many of us don't know much about our ways. We never heard anything good about the Indian ways... only the white ways. Yet most of the white people at those boarding schools were cold and mean, and every morning we'd look in a mirror and still see an Indian." She rose to turn the burner on the coffeepot. She turned it to high then adjusted the controls for low. "We used to drill every day. Right flank, left flank, to the rear march. I know all that stuff." She managed a stifled laugh.

"Discipline, everything was discipline," she said as she sat back down. "When our men and women went into the war, we did okay in boot camp. We all knew how to march." She studied the blue flames under the coffeepot. "I didn't tell you everything. I couldn't. Even you wouldn't believe me."

"I believe you," he answered.

Mary thought for a long while. She stared at the stove, then turned resolutely, "Kyle, the last thing I'll mention about boarding school is hunger. You get so damn hungry that you'll do anything for just a little crust of bread. If you were smart or

EVERYTIME YOU'D LOOK IN THE MIRROR

lucky, you'd be a waiter in the head nun's dining room or the head priest's table. Those people ate good. Hell, we'd be so damn hungry we'd eat off their plates, once we got them back into the kitchen. They ate a helluva lot better than the Indian kids ever did. The government schools were the same way. The employees stole them blind. When we unloaded the supply trucks, we saw butter and eggs but it never showed up on the tables for the Indian kids."

"Kyle, you remember that old brother Herman down at Oglala?"

"Yeah, I remember him. You mean the one that limps. He used to hold us down when Buchwald would put the belt to us. Course, now, I believe he was just following orders like the rest of us. I always think of him as being real scared, like God was always watching him. He had that scared look, the last time he held Lawrence down and the big fight broke out... then we ran away."

"I heard it was Lawrence or you that made him limp." Mary queried.

Charging Shield shrugged, "When you are little you can't remember much." His response was matter of fact. "I remember being scared... and then the fight broke out. Cross Dog and Lawrence planned it that way. Everything happened so fast." He paused; trying to reconstruct what seemed so far back in his past. "I remember two big fancy stones that Buchwald had on his desk. I picked one up and crashed it down on a brother's foot. It took him out of action, so I reached for the other rock. It was a polished rock and flat on a couple of sides and big, like the other one. I took another brother out of action and on the way to the railroad, Cross Dog and Lawrence were praising me. I felt like a Dog Soldier and warriors were singing kill songs over my exploits. I never was so proud in my life." A sad look shadowed his face. "I remember Cross Dog praising me and I fell asleep. The next thing I knew, he was dead and the war started the next day. I was never separated from Mom and Dad again- not until I grew up. That's what I will always remember. No more boarding school."

Charging Shield stroked his chin in a pose of wonderment. "Damn. It almost seems like yesterday. I can still see that scared brother holding Lawrence and being bossed around by Buchwald. I've seen him a few times when I was dancing at the pow wows. He seems okay."

"Yeah, he is, now maybe he is. Back when he was young, your sister Rose and I served him his meals. We'd get so goddamn starved, we'd let him feel our legs and he'd always leave a piece of meat and an extra piece of bread on his plate. We were just little girls though. I'd get so damn hungry that I'd let that horny son of a bitch feel my leg then damn near go nuts because I was afraid to tell about it in confession.

"It really bothered your sister and I. It got so damn bad that we decided to tell the head nun, especially when he'd come to feel us and he wanted to feel more than our legs. We got scared and we went to tell the head nun. We were both going to go in but I told Rose to let me go first in case of a beating... 'No sense both of us getting beat up,' I told her.

"Well, I went in and told. I learned my lesson. I never was beaten so bad in all of my life. I can still see that nun. She called in two others to hold me down and she took off that big leather belt they always used to wear. That nun beat me and I can still hear her." Mary paused to look straight ahead at the refrigerator door. "Now you know brother would never do such a thing. You know he wouldn't. He's like a priest. He couldn't do such a thing. Tell us that you're lying.

"They beat me so damn bad that I said that I was lying."

The coffeepot boiled over. He jumped to his feet to shut off the burner. Charging Shield stared through the apartment window. "I wasn't there long, but that goddamn boarding school still gets to me. I believe you, Mary. Lawrence told me the same things." He shook his head, "Not many people going to believe you, though. Not a helluva lot."

The older woman carried her coffee cup to the sink. "I'd better go. I said enough tonight. You're right. Ain't nobody going to believe it."

VISION QUEST

CHAPTER NINETEEN

Second semester examinations were over. In back of Fools Crow's cabin, Mildred placed hot stones in a small pit within the sweat lodge, then lowered the door flap to close out the sound of a crackling fire. As she stepped back toward the fire, her pitchfork bumped a peace pipe sticking out of the raised ground that formed a minature altar. She repositioned the new pipe so that it was half-buried in the soil with its stem pointing skyward. It was her gift to her brother to use during his first vision quest.

Inside the lodge, Fools Crow poured a gourdful of water onto the rocks. The steam blasted full force into Charging Shield's face, causing him to lie down on the floor where the temperature was cooler. He prayed in silence while the old man sang the preparation song for *hanblecheya*, for vision quest. While he sweated, he wiped himself with soft sage. When the steam subsided, Mildred opened the flap to hand the new pipe to Fools Crow. She remained with them, watching the holy man fill and light the pipe.

She watched the aging Oglala remove the *wotai* hanging from Charging Shield's neck and suspend it over the bowl of the smoking pipe. He then held both items upward, beseeching the Almighty in ancient Sioux. He ended the ritual by chanting a dirge as primal and dateless as the mysterious rock within the buckskin pouch. Then he smoked the pipe in silence, finally cleaning it with a twig and tapping the ashes onto the rocks in the small pit.

EAGLE VISION

The holy man was well aware that Charging Shield was not as fluent in Lakota Sioux as his sister. "Mildred, tell him to go to Spirit Mountain tomorrow to vision quest," Fools Crow told her in his native tongue. "He should start up the mountain before the sun sets. Tell him not to be afraid, for he has his *wotai*. He must observe everything, especially the four-legged and the winged people. The winged one with the yellow breast will watch over him. I will give him four colors from my bundle and show him how to use them for *hanblecheya*." He held up his hands, making a circle by touching the tips of his index finger and his thumbs together. "He must stay within the four colors if he has reason to fear. Also tell him he should eat nothing, drink little and return to me if he receives a strong vision."

That night they stayed at Fools Crow's cabin, returning to West River in the morning. Charging Shield left his sister at her home and drove north in her camper pickup, skirting the eastern edge of the Black Hills toward the isolated butte called Spirit Mountain. The road turned east after he passed through a town. To the northeast, Spirit Mountain towered like a massive sentinel, rising several thousand feet above the surrounding plains. In the distance, a gathering of low, graying clouds produced the beginning of a rainbow that straddled the road from north to south. As he approached the rainbow its northernmost arc grew more brilliant and seemed to remain anchored in place. At a junction, the road divided, one pavement heading north toward the mountain, the other continuing eastward. As he turned north the rainbow seemed to move with him. He marveled at the rainbow, now on his right, which was almost neon in luminescence. It was capped in a brilliant electric red, which gave way to mandarin red and a healthy ripe-corn yellow, before merging into bright green... a green like spring meadow grass... followed by a harmonious blue, before bottoming out in a shade of purple. Never had he been so close to a rainbow.

Off to his left, on the west side of the road, a lake appeared as the pickup topped a slight rise. The coolness of the lake was inviting; it was still early evening and hot, and he decided to enjoy a refreshing swim. Before turning west onto a gravel road leading to the lake, he noticed a herd of buffalo to his right, grazing contentedly within a fenced enclosure at the base of the mountain. As he parked the pickup beside the lake only the plaintive call of a killdeer broke the silence of the vast space, punctuated by the occasional slap of a fish rising for early summer flies. Back across the north-south roadway he watched the rainbow move slowly toward the buffalo pen, the buffalo turning slowly to face the rainbow as they grazed. As the clouds above the rainbow moved toward him they lowered, growing darker.

Thunder pealed from the mountaintop, which was crowned by a separate expanse of dark clouds, from which four fluffs of white emerged, illumined by the late afternoon sun. Above the cotton-like fluffs, a burnished and bronzed shaft of weak rainbow colors rose heavenward. The fluffy clouds formed a diamond frame above the mountaintop; 'the four directions,' he thought. He moved his gaze from the powerful symbol above the mountain to the bright rainbow, which hovered above the buffalo. The clouds advancing toward him halted, seeming to be held motionless by an invisible air mass, or some mysterious force emanating from the mountain. Sheet lightning flickered high above; several cracks of sky bolts lit the western edges of the clouds. 'West Power *Heyokas*,' he thought, '*Heyoka* power.'

Despite the ominous appearance of the clouds close overhead, he was not afraid. There was nothing to fear. This was the *Paha Sapa* and it was all *lelah wakan, lelah waste,* real holy, real good. He was now a pipe-holder and for him these were all symbols. *Wakan Tanka* created and controlled all symbols. These signs appeared for the pipe-holder's perception, interpretation, and acknowledgement. For him, these were powerful signs of welcoming, permission from *Wakan Tanka* to seek knowledge on the mountain.

Sheet lightning flickered again, spawned by the West Power. *Heyoka* lightning bolts set off a resonant rumble, like the bellowing of a giant herd of sky buffalo. "*Heyokas*," he called out. '*Heyokas*, the lightning powers. Eagle Feather said the *Heyokas* would watch out for him.' Charging Shield was not afraid of the *Heyokas* despite the ominous rumblings. He stretched out on the grass to watch the violent action in the sky. He was now a veteran warrior, he reminded himself. After many brushes with death in Vietnam, he had a new attunement toward and fearless admiration for the mysterious forces of the Great Spirit, and the connection of those forces to the ways of his people. These things manifested beauty; therefore they were *wakan*; they were *lelah waste*, and nothing to fear. If the forces wanted him in the spirit world, they would take him; it was as simple as that. He laughed as he took off his clothes, all except for his undershorts. Siouxs were unconsciously modest. They were never really alone. He had no doubt that, this close to such a holy mountain, Spirits were watching. Several lightning bolts reached for the earth as if to test him. He laughed again as he immersed himself in the cooling water of the lake.

Within the embrace of the lake waters, he watched the rainbow. It faded slowly from view as the dark cloud dissipated in its attempt to move west and north around the mountain. When he came out of the water he saw a pair of horses... a sorrel and a palomino... behind a distant fence line. As they moved closer toward him, their tails switched like waving flags. The horses galloped playfully closer, nickering. Their friendly manner added to the welcome he had felt from the rainbow and other signs. He heard a neighing and when he looked in the direction of the call, he saw a blocky-built palomino calling from the fence line on the opposite side of the roadway. The lone palomino was beckoning to the pair of horses who seemed to pay no attention as they moved toward a watering tank, close beside the lake.

Charging Shield dried himself with his shirt, dressed and drove across the roadway onto the winding side road leading to the parking area at Spirit Mountain. Two iron cattle guards broke the fences enclosing the buffalo. The spacious area reserved for the buffalo contained plenty of grass. Before reaching the second cattle

guard he stopped the pickup beside a large bull buffalo. For a few moments they were two creatures of yesterday, contemplating each other with mutual respect.

After he parked the pickup, he used his pocketknife to cut four sticks from buffalo berry and choke cherry saplings. Carrying his peace pipe, tobacco pouch and the four flags which were now tied to the sticks, he started up the winding, pine-covered path. He set a brisk pace and by the time he reached the top, several hours later, the sun had begun its journey below the horizon. He sat at the western edge of the mountain's broad plateau, captivated by the sunset. A miniature sandstone cliff just a few yards in front of him dropped down thirty feet. While he watched the sunset, a golden eagle glided by majestically, diving down to skirt the rim of the cliff, disappearing into a clump of boulders sheltered by a stand of pine trees to his right.

He touched the buckskin pouch holding his *wotai*, secured by the leather cord looped around his neck. The *wotai* had protected him in Vietnam. It would protect him during his vision quest also, he told himself. He shrugged off a tinge of nervous uneasiness as he watched the top of the sun settle slowly from view. He was held spellbound by the expansive scene that greeted him, as he sat at the edge of the darkening mountain. The play of changing light on the straw-colored plains below caused him to forget about the tiny flags he had brought. He filled his peace pipe and offered it to the Great Spirit. A sage plant was close. He picked the dry leaves that had endured the winter and placed them in the bowl of the pipe. He offered the pipe again, turning his back to a sighing breeze whistling softly through the pine trees. Soon after he struck a match, the fragrance of red willow bark mixed with tobacco added a pleasant aroma to the evening. Not used to smoking, he coughed several times when he accidentally inhaled some smoke. He liked the fragrance but did not appreciate the bitter, acrid taste left in his mouth by the smoke.

As he sat smoking, he quietly admired the construction of the pipe. It was a warrior's pipe. An axe blade projected from beneath the bowl, with bowl and blade carved from the same chunk of red pipestone. The combination peace pipe/axe was bound securely to its sumac stem by strips of rawhide.

The fire in his pipe went out. He held its warm bowl in his hand as he relaxed in the soothing mountain breeze. After awhile, he noticed the excited singing of a songbird. Searching upward, he saw a meadowlark land on the branch of a pine. Using his pocketknife, he dug four holes in the hard soil, forming a square whose length was slightly longer than his height. In these, he placed upright, the fruitwood sticks bearing the four colored flags. He rolled a flat, brown sandstone to the western end of the square, propping it with several boulders, before sitting with his back against it, this time facing east. If he was going to wait for a vision, at least he'd be comfortable, he thought. He searched the pine tree; the songbird was gone. Darkness came swiftly, but only for a short while. A full moon was rising above the edge of the plains from the southeast.

Before long, the full moon bathed his surroundings. Awash in the moonlight, the sandy path leading down the mountain appeared as a silver ribbon winding among boulders and bushes. He sat quietly listening to the chirping of crickets which, except for the soft breeze rustling the pine boughs, were the only sounds to be heard. To help forget his thirst, he welcomed the approach of drowsiness as he leaned back against the sandstone.

He dreamed of the pair of horses that he had seen earlier by the lake. He was riding the sorrel along a pine and shrub-studded trail toward a meadow. A red roan, a buckskin, a black and a white-maned palomino horse came forward to greet him at the meadow's edge. At that point, the dream became less animated. He sat upon the sorrel for what seemed an eternity, looking out at the meadow, with the sorrel's companion behind them, yet never closing. He awakened, forgetting momentarily that he was on the mountain. His urge for a vision drew him back to sleep. His dream repeated itself, leading him again to the edge of the lush, green meadow. Cross Dog appeared to him. He was elated to see Cross Dog.

"Brother," Cross Dog began, "Take courage. I watched over Lawrence when he was off in the big war. And I came to you in Korea and then saw the spirits watching over you with your stone in Vietnam." Cross Dog pointed back down the path. "Take courage," he repeated. This time the meadowlark woke him.

Charging Shield wore a contented smile as he looked up at the meadowlark. It was so good to see Cross Dog. The yellow bird sang shrilly. Ben Black Elk's predictions came true; the yellow-breasted bird and horses he had mentioned were now part of his experience. It was a good dream with which to begin a vision quest.

The moon illuminated his surroundings as it poked its way through the clouds. Off to the south, exposed by sheet lightning but too far distant for him to hear the rumble of thunder, a storm was building. Distressed chirps replaced the meadowlark's melody. At first, Charging Shield was too entranced by the buildup of distant thunderheads to notice the bird, but its annoying calls finally won his attention. He thought it odd that the bird would appear at such a late hour. Never had he seen a meadowlark in the night, nor perched from trees for that matter. He checked the four flags placed according to Fools Crow's instructions, forming a protective square about him. The meadowlark called out again. As a child he had been attracted to these birds which always seemed to frequent the fields where he hunted rabbits. Toward evening, when the rabbits came out of their dens, the meadowlarks would disappear.

The yellow bird brought Karen to mind. A feeling of loneliness overcame him. He recalled Eagle Feather's words, "After a Sun Dance, a wish can come true." He wanted to see the woman again. Yes, that would be his wish. He wanted somehow to see her again. He remembered he had not emptied the ashes from his pipe. He broke a small twig and cleaned the pipe bowl. As he did so, the meadowlark flew down the path; sounding as though it was alarmed about something. Just before the path bent sharply to the right, the meadowlark disappeared behind a clump of tall bushes growing beside two boulders. It reappeared momentarily in the high branches of a nearby pine tree, but then disappeared from view again. The bird wasn't really singing, but kept up a nervous chatter.

Charging Shield was tired. It was difficult to follow the bird in the dimness of the moonlight. Soon, the bird flew back up the path and disappeared again. The excited chattering stopped further up the trail just beyond the clump of bushes. Then the meadowlark reappeared, landing in full view on a pine branch.

Charging Shield wanted to sleep. He stared lazily at the bird, and started to doze. Out of the corner of his eye he saw a man-sized figure leap from the bushes, crossing the path to hide behind a boulder which was partially obscured by a thick stump and a fallen pine tree. The figure was not Cross Dog. The movement was too quick for a man, yet it seemed to be two-legged.

The hair on the nape of Charging Shield's neck stood out, his hand frozen on the peace pipe. He dropped the tobacco pouch at the sound of a twig snapping. He was aware of a sudden movement, as if the two-legged creature had leaped over the boulder. He knew it was now standing behind the fallen pine. He strained to hear any sound that might give him warning, but his heart was beating so wildly he could hear only its rhythmic thumping. He tried to control his fear.

With his free hand he took the pipe by the stem and raised it above his head. It was no longer a peace pipe but an axe, as he held it upward like a club. He looked around for a stone, but changed his mind, preferring the axe. There was no retreat. Behind him, the cliff fell to a steep grade consisting of loose rock, shale and boulders, studded with scrub pine. The steep descent gradually tapered off near the base of the mountain. The moonlight was obscured by clouds for what seemed like an eternity of darkened moments. As the moon finally reappeared to illuminate the scene, it revealed a blur of motion as the mysterious figure moved stealthily closer, behind a sandstone boulder. It was not a man. It was too fast. Only an animal could move that fast. But it was a sizable two-legged. Maybe it was both… man and beast.

Without a moment's hesitation, Charging Shield clutched his peace pipe tightly and spun 180° to leap off the cliff. The almost vertical grade of the loose shale broke his fall, but his momentum carried him forward and downward. His frantic steps turned into uncontrolled leaps as he plunged toward a jagged granite boulder. A scrub pine slapped him solidly in the face, slowing his descent. He managed to dig his heels into the loose rock and shale before shooting his arm out to catch the wind-gnarled branch of a fallen pine. He managed to come to a stop just short of a disastrous confrontation with the boulder.

'It wasn't real,' he thought. 'Soon he'd awaken from this dream. It was only a dream… one hell of a dream!' He felt a momentary stab of pain in one ankle, but it disappeared just as quickly when he turned to look up at the summit, where the figure was growling grotesquely. The figure was surrounded in flaming blue light, turning a darker blue as if it were some fiendish gargoyle forbidding entry to its domain. His sweat chilled, for now the thing was coming through the night sky. 'It had to be a nightmare!' The falling creature blotted out the moon, clawing at space as it hurtled toward him.

Charging Shield ducked just before it hit the ground. The two-legged creature bounced off the scree slope, brushing the top of a scrub pine and bounding, crashing past him. Its carcass gave off a stinking, malodorous scent as it cursed in a strange but vaguely English-sounding tongue. Charging Shield's mind worked frantically as the figure tried to brake itself, digging into the sliding rocks. Carrying his peace pipe in his mouth and without looking behind, Charging Shield scrambled back up the scree slope, scrabbling at the broken rocks, pulling at the occasional stunted pines to increase his momentum. He made it back to the base of the cliff separating him from the mountaintop and the protective square marked by colored flags.

When he reached the cliff barrier, he glanced down at the scrub pine that had broken his fall. The creature was still well below the pine, pausing for a moment on its ascent as if it, too, was sizing up the situation.

Above Charging Shield, a narrowing chimney crevice, pocketed with indentations and several ledges, offered an avenue of escape. He could hear the rock sliding below, as he hastily surveyed his ascent. Halfway up the cliff, he reached the first ledge. Turning in fear, he sought the location of the blue two-legged figure.

The creature was now above the scrub pines, scrambling and snarling at the loose shale and sliding rock. Charging Shield looked up to estimate his climb to the safety of a higher ledge, but a glance downward revealed the blue figure fast approaching. He braced his back against the cliff wall, sweat-soaked hands holding his pipe-axe like a baseball bat. At that moment he was certain that, had he not been fasting, his stomach would have emptied itself.

When the blue figure reached the base of the cliff, it growled menacingly for a few moments before bounding catlike up the narrowing crevice. Charging Shield smelled the ugliness below him; it was worse than rotting flesh. It was acrid, heavy and poisonous. Despite his nauseating fear, Charging Shield managed somehow to control his panic. A cloud shadowed the moonlight, darkening the snarling, grunting face with its gas blue eyes just as it rose over the ledge. Charging Shield hurtled forward to catch the ugly face full force with the pipe-axe blade, cutting into it and knocking it back to the sliding scree slope, sending it screaming in painful agony.

When Charging Shield struck his devastating blow, it was as if an age-old fear had vanished... vanished like a puff of smoke. The anger and hatred aroused by his fear placed him at the lip of the ledge, cursing down at the moaning figure who was crawling painfully sideways across the shale, as though looking for another avenue to the top of the mountain. Although the figure was now crawling abjectly and its blue-flaming aura seemed diminished, it was still snarling its intent to return to the battle. Charging Shield knew he didn't want the figure above him. Hurriedly, he made his way to the second ledge and, from there, to the protective square on the mountaintop.

"Charging Shield, you will be tested," he kept repeating Eagle Feather's words, "and then you will have your vision quest." Charging Shield wanted desperately to believe he would endure the second assault of the ugly, blue two-legged.

Fortunately, the moon still bathed the mountain's summit, although the thunderstorm far to the south was steadily advancing. Charging Shield looked to the east for signs of daylight. Morning will come soon; he tried to tell himself. He took the *wotai* from around his neck, lashing it to the pipe bowl, hoping that somehow it would give strength to his battle instrument. He even prayed, but in his still-agitated state he could not think of suitable words, so he prayed the white man's prayers by rote: "Hail Mary, full of grace" and "Holy Mary, Mother of God" and "Our Father, who art in Heaven." The prayers came precisely as he had learned them as a child. He squeezed his pipe-axe, recalling the power of Buffalo Calf Woman. The Buffalo Woman had killed the bad warrior. Because of her, he told himself, his pipe-axe was powerful. He lapsed back into rote prayer.

Although his fear had vanished he was still agitated, and he ended his prayers with a frenzied challenge to his adversary: "C'mon you motherfucker! I'll kill you!" The scream, carrying like an alpine yodel, resounded down the mountain.

Soon the blue figure came boldly up the mountain path, not in stealth as before, but openly retracing its earlier route, issuing labored grunts as it passed the stump and fallen pine.

"Remember to stay within the flags. Take courage. Take courage." The cautioning voice sounded like that of Cross Dog joined by Ben Black Elk and seemed to come from out of nowhere. Charging Shield was too agitated to notice that the voices were really a chorus of many voices - his ghostly mentors. His legs felt weakened, his eyes uncertain in the dim light. He looked down to make sure he was in the center of the four flags as the blue figure closed in upon him.

Once more, Charging Shield confronted the creature, only this time he was face to face with ugliness that filled him with nausea. He had to confront returning fear as well as the vicious, demonic eyes peering at him from a swelling gash across its fanged and hairy face. Charging Shield's instinct took command; he tensed his body, gripping his pipe stem like a baseball bat. When the creature tried to reach out for the peace pipe, it entered the protective square. The *wotai* burst through its bound buckskin covering, flashing and exploding incandescently, charring the clawed hands like napalmed flesh. The brightness of the explosion blinded both adversaries. An electrocuting shock accompanied the blinding flash, sending Charging Shield to his knees still clutching his peace pipe. Charging Shield could see only the indelible stamp of the flash searing his sight. The flash faded from blinding white to yellow, and then slowly regained the darker hues of the spectrum.

Charging Shield knelt, defenseless, his face burrowing down into Spirit Mountain. Although he could not see, he heard his adversary fall, landing solidly beside him. He heard a strange thrashing sound followed by a tormented voice and familiar yelp. It was coming from the ground immediately in front of him. Charging Shield strained to see through his fading blindness. He could barely make out the figure of a small dog standing shakily before him. When he finally could discern an arched back, bushy tail, and sniffing lope, he knew he was looking at a coyote or possibly a brush wolf, like his father had seen in the Badlands long ago. He watched its silhouette slink away.

Charging Shield stood watching as the dog-like animal ran back down the path yipping piteously. He shivered as he huddled within the protective flags, clutching his pipe-axe in appreciation, trying to reassure himself that the thing would not return.

His *wotai*! It was no longer attached to the pipe. He searched frantically, repeatedly peering down the empty trail. He put his hand up to his neck and found that the *wotai* was still there, tied securely.

Was this only a dream? If it was, it certainly was the most vivid dream he had ever experienced. He placed his hand on his ankle. It was numb from being cramped and from lack of circulation, but there was no gash that he could discern in the moonlight. 'Only a dream,' he told himself, but he knew he had been tested. He had been tested for his vision quest.

Somewhere in the dark hours, he fell asleep. The dream returned exactly as it had begun earlier in the evening, only this time the dream continued.

He rode the sorrel up the pine-covered trail. Before he reached the top of the mountain, the trail opened into the wide meadow with a lake on each side. A well-marked Appaloosa mare galloped across the grass to give him a spirited greeting. Indians were camped in the meadow, children were playing, and some sat beside tall tipis listening to grandmothers telling stories. Men and women were in the corn-fields weeding with strange-looking hoes. Beans were planted with the corn, and small fish were buried with the seeds. The climbing beans tied themselves to the corn plants. He looked down at the hoes and saw that the blades were made of bone. As he rode through the encampment, the Appaloosa mare never left his side.

The meadow broadened, becoming a rolling plain, teeming with buffalo. The buffalo herd seemed to extend itself endlessly while high-spirited horses... sorrels, pintos and Appaloosas... wheeled in circles, prancing within the herd. The people gathered corn, laughing and bantering. When they secured themselves within their tall lodges, the laughing and talking echoed among falling snowflakes. Winter snows blanketed the grass. The scene repeated itself several times before it moved across the continent. He was aware that an eon was unfolding before his eyes.

When the snows disappeared, an awe-inspiring scene repeated itself with such clarity that he was overcome by sweet tears of joy. He was one of the warriors riding in among the buffalo herds, cutting out a yearling bull, sending an arrow deep behind a shoulder blade. He wanted to watch such a bountiful life repeat its stirring cycles, over and over. The vision was so strong and powerful that he was almost brought back to consciousness.

The rivers were blue and clear, the grass endless and the snow was white, pure and ever so clean, like a spruce, birch and spearmint-bordered mountain pool. Like the land, the people were clean; there had been no alcohol, no drugs, for centuries upon centuries. The elderly Indians appeared healthy, active and nimble - well into their period of aging.

The people called out to him, interrupting the spellbinding, changing scene. They gathered around him, sweeping him along. The Appaloosa mare stayed abreast of his horse, prancing along with the laughing, surging crowd.

As they approached one of the lakes, a beautiful woman with an erect posture, like the woman in the Sun Dance, stood at an opening to a large tipi, holding a peace pipe. She smiled, leading his horse and the thunder-hoofed mare along the lakeshore toward a cluster of tipis, bark longhouses and hogans. People came forward, waving to the crowd and joining them as if they were relatives. He sensed he was in a spirit world, yet there was little change from the lifestyle of contented crop planters he had visited earlier.

One of the dwellings, a pole-supported earthen lodge, like those used by the Mandans along the Missouri, was separate from the others. When he dismounted from the sorrel, the Appaloosa mare disappeared behind the lodge. Charging Shield waited for the mare to reappear but instead a maiden wearing a Mandan dress came out of the structure with her hands over her face. When she stood before him, the girl laughed, pulling her hands away. It was Karen, the mate of his past lives.

Thunder shook him. They laughed and played as if they were mates. An overwhelming sense of ecstasy came over him as he clutched her in his arms for a long moment. The thunder shook again. He tried to hold on to the maiden but everything began to fade. He fought to remain in his dream, but a bright flash, accompanied by a deafening crash, jolted him awake.

He looked up from his resting place to see a towering thunderhead reveal itself with sheet lightning and a thunderous roar. He gripped his *wotai* and prayed to return to his vision. He wanted that life back; he wanted to be a warrior and to be with her, in the freedom of another time. The power of that freedom, and of her presence, was overwhelming.

Despite the approaching storm, he drifted back to sleep. Once again he found himself overlooking the meadow, astride the sorrel horse. The beautiful woman with the erect posture appeared with his *wotai* stone. 'The Buffalo Calf Woman,' he thought.

The woman pointed to a cottonwood tree with sprouting leaves. Eagle Feather and Fools Crow were pruning the branches. They tied rawhide cutouts of a man and a buffalo to the tree and placed twelve choke cherry branches below the two figures. Roan horses joined by one white horse entered the circle made by the yellow hoop and pranced clockwise around the tree. The cottonwood grew tall and straight.

The wind blew strongly. The man-beast appeared in the distance, creeping toward the circle but as it drew closer it became more refined and walked upright. It changed to a Blue Man coming in with the wind. The Blue Man wore a sleek blue coat over a white shirt and a flaming gas blue tie. His trousers were striped gray flannel. Where the Blue Man walked, acrid gray smoke lifted to the skies. The tree trembled, shaking off most of its leaves and spooking most of the roan horses, causing them to bolt from the circle. Four stalwart horses remained, however... a black, a white, a deep red roan and a buckskin... forming a line abreast, waiting for the Blue Man. The Blue Man led two horses, two robust palominos. The horse under Charging Shield nickered to one, a well-muscled palomino with a flowing mane that began grazing contentedly in the meadow. The other palomino with a bobbed mane appeared at the edge of the meadow and began to graze. The second palomino was a hand taller and more mechanical in its movements. There was plenty of grass for both horses; yet, they eyed each other with snorts and nickering. The Blue Man went back and forth agitating the horses. Soon, the Blue Man raided the Indian corn fields, taking the grain to feed the horses and using corn stalks to build a fire. Lean faced, gaunt Indians tried to plant more corn but they were chased away by the Blue Man. He began to forge weapons and armor and shoed the horses with heavy iron shoes. Both horses were changed into war-horses and were clumsy and awkward in their movements.

The Blue Man continued to go back and forth and soon the horses were wearing coverings of armor. The two palominos ate voraciously while they tramped down great patches of grass, leaving deep tracks with their iron-shod hoofs. The worn grass turned to dust but both horses continued to graze upon the remainder of the lush grass, each growing fatter and losing its well-muscled proportions. Between grazing, they marched back and forth. Dust rose to blot out the sun while great heat parched the meadow.

The Blue Man attempted to coax the four horses standing abreast and protecting the cottonwood tree, to come to him. When they refused to move, he closed in upon the hoop. The four horses charged whenever he crossed the yellow hoop, trampling and grinding the devious man down into a prairie dog hole. A pair of eagles circled high over the prairie dog hole, daring the man to come forth. Eagle Feather and Fools Crow walked away, taking with them the symbols they had placed on the tree.

Mary Bad Hand and Karen appeared. They placed twelve apple tree branches on the cottonwood and then hung a rawhide cutout of a woman and a rawhide cutout of a dove above them. Charging Shield knew that the younger woman was Karen, yet, she had golden hair.

The wind blew and this time horses of all colors and from all directions came prancing. The tree flourished, spreading open vibrant green leaves. A bright rainbow arched high overhead. People of different colors, their numbers not many, danced to a slow drumbeat. It was a dance of ceremony and they locked hands to form a small circle in the meadow. More people came into the meadow to dance around the horses, tranquilizing the two armored beasts. Women came from the dance circle to untie the heavy horse-armor, dropping it to the ground. A wind blew and it began to hail, but the hail turned to cooling slush, stilling the dust and soothing the earth. Explosions lit the sky beneath the rainbow and petals of fire dropped to earth. Where they landed flowers grew. The sorrel horse under Charging Shield reared and snorted. Indians seemed to emerge from nowhere carrying corn plants and bean seeds. They planted the meadow and fed corn to the horses.

A pair of warbonnet-clad chiefs moved excitedly among the people, leading a string of horses and gathering up warriors. They called to Charging Shield before riding to attack the Blue Man, who appeared again at the edge of the meadow. They beat him back sending him fleeing down a path.

When the warriors returned, the cottonwood began growing into a mighty flowering tree. Birds came to sing in its branches. More people of all colors gathered to circle dance with horses of various colors around the tree. The rainbow arched higher and brighter over the meadow. When Charging Shield dismounted, he felt a gentle nudge on his back and when he turned to look, the Appaloosa mare was standing behind him. A rumbling came from the horizon, the resounding hoofbeats of an immense herd of buffalo. He felt another nudge, but the Appaloosa had disappeared. Now, it was Karen standing beside him.

The two walked arm in arm to a pair of pine sheltered boulders. The feathers of his warbonnet began to grow, forming a giant eagle wing. The feathers closed over them, enveloping them both, lifting them. They emerged, winged and plumed, and free to fly. She was a meadowlark and then she, too, became an eagle. They flew east, a pair of eagles heading toward a faint rainbow on the distant horizon.

The power of the Flowering Tree jolted him from his vision. He looked at the moon and then above to thank the Great Spirit for his vision. The seven stars of the Big Dipper were bright against a black sky. A wisp of a cloud covered one of the stars. There were now six stars shining. He felt as if the Great Spirit was trying to tell him something. 'Thank the Six Powers,' he thought and marveled at the symbol in the sky. 'The Six Powers and the Great Spirit were all symbolized in the Big Dipper.' Something was revealing more to him. 'The dipper pours.' It was a sign that even the ancient two-legged would recognize. 'Pour forth knowledge and natural truth to the whole world.'

He imaged the Six Powers as a set of forces left to watch over all that happened on this planet or, perhaps, in this particular solar system, while the Great Creator had to administer all that vast, vast, inestimable space. Were there millions of stars or had he heard some authority claim there were billions? The scene above him was but a tiny portion of what could be seen from all locations on the earth.

A shooting star angled down from the heavens. 'There was life out there.' he thought. 'Many stages of life in differing degrees of evolution. Some planets were probably in their 'trilobite' stage. Some were in their dinosaur stage while others might have rudimentary forms of free-willed two-leggeds. Maybe some planets had two-legged who were equal in intelligence and as technologically advanced as those on Earth. A parallel universe? Parallel Universes? Now, that would be an interesting theory.' He paused in his thoughts but then continued: 'there are probably some planets with life forms far in advance of humans. Maybe they have been on their planets in a rationalizing, computer-discovered stage for hundreds of thousands of years longer than earthlings.'

'People should sit on mountain tops and stare at space,' he concluded. He laughed. 'Millions, no, billions of suns out there. Billions of suns; many, maybe all with planets revolving about them. How pompous, how egocentric mere man can be to think that this world could be the only planet with life among millions or billions of planets.' The power of the great vastness along with the vision of the Flowering Tree gave him strong hope. There were more and more of the two-leggeds who were becoming free of age-old illusions based on fear of the unknown or outright denial of a spirit world. Technological development, worldwide communication, freedom of thought, all of the new advancements have permitted great strides toward overcoming ignorance and superstition.

'Billions of suns meant billions of planets,' he thought. 'There *had to be* free-willed beings far more advanced than those upon planet Earth. *Far, far advanced.* No doubt, they were *watching Earth*. Watching closely, especially since the first explosions of atomic and hydrogen weapons.'

The advanced ones could not allow any outer space testing of that sort. He imaged some planets having scorched shells, burned to lifelessness. No doubt they were once populated by free-willed beings who had succumbed fatally to the use of weaponry or who had exhausted their planet's resources.

It wasn't difficult for him to believe there were many more highly advanced beings out there in space who were very aware of planet Earth and its potential for imbalance. 'Earthlings would have to prove themselves,' he concluded. 'They must prove that they can find a true path to peace, and prove that they can keep Mother Earth in a state of natural balance.' He hoped they had the intelligence to take into the future the Earth-saving values of those tribal ones in his vision.

Rain began falling in giant-sized drops, and lightning flashed all around him, but he wasn't afraid. Sheet lightning high in the heavens made thunder, adding a distant basso profundo. It formed the background to a crescendo of progressive flashes, which added their own deafening roar. Nature's volume was so immense that it could not be duplicated by a hundred gathered concert halls. For the finale, a bolting crack scorched an aged, towering pine, bathing the scene in brilliant light. The rain increased and he was drenched by the deluge, Mother Earth's lifeblood, life-giving rain.

His vision quest was over. The sheets of rain subsided to gentle droplets. They, in turn, gave way to a soothing mist that sublimated under the influence of the rising sun reaching out from the east.

That evening, Amos Lone Hill, Fools Crow's son-in-law, served as interpreter. The holy man listened while Charging Shield revealed his story. He wanted to describe the young woman in his dream, but Fools Crow's eyes wouldn't let him remember the woman. He stared blankly at Fools Crow. He knew he didn't have to tell about the woman. He wanted to be lost back to that part of his vision, when the eagle wing had covered them. He had flown freely, rising up from the mountain, and his mate had flown beside him. Flying with her toward the rainbow is what he really wanted. He savored those moments until Fools Crow urged him to continue.

Several times, Fools Crow interrupted while the vision quest was related. At the conclusion, the aging holy man spoke in broken Sioux so he could understand,

"*Hehaka Sapa, lelah owanyanke, lelah ouye...* Black Elk's powerful vision." Fools Crow pointed in the direction where Black Elk's descendants still lived on the reservation. "Black Elk told us the Six Powers predicted our Spirit would first have to return. I think he meant the Indian Spirit clear across this land. They lived close with *Ina Maka* (Mother Earth). The *washichu* must learn that harmony. It is not just a lovely word. Mother Earth will show that she must be respected. I have the belief that these things will have to happen because there is no other choice."

The old man picked up the peace pipe that had been carried to the top of the mountain. "The horses in your vision are for the four races. The sorrel stands for the red people. The palominos are of the whites but of two different places. The white horse shares little and that only with his own kind or those who will get him in trouble. They have used too much of Mother Earth's gifts and wasted it on war things to steal each other's possessions. They should have been working on what is really harming the Earth and the people of this land every day. He studied the pipe with a long pause. His voice lifted to an optimistic note, "You said one white horse did join the circle to defend against the Blue Man. *Waste aloh*" he spoke in Lakota, then continued, "The white horse is beginning to awaken. Time will tell if enough of them will do so."

He waved the pipe again. "There is a new people that are now on this land. They are a different kind of *washichu* and will be better for the whole world. We Red People, we must help them. Our earth knowledge is not for us alone, it must be shared with all. When these new people go out into the Earth Mother and do ceremony they will be shown that all these things of destruction can be headed off. The destructive ways take up too much energy and the Blue Man of greed and deceit must be killed. It has to be, for Mother Earth is in great trouble. We can all perish if she cannot be healed. Destruction can come right out of Mother Earth. But if it does, it will be because the two-legged powers will allow the Blue Man to be their God."

Fools Crow drew a breath and blew outward as though he were smoking the pipe. "Maybe all these bad things can be prevented or at least be slowed down until the two-legged with vision can get together and get a hold on it all. That last part of your vision gives me strong hope. It will be those of the Flowering Tree against the Blue Man people. There were two women at the Sun Dance tree. Woman power will have to become strong."

"The Blue Man people," his tone grew ominous, "they will spend their time in distrust of each other and while they do so, the grass will be fading away and yet they won't see it." Fools Crow handed the pipe back to Charging Shield. "This land will suffer if they don't change their ways. Mother Earth will warn us," he paused. "She will warn us pretty strong, then this land will suffer... suffer bad. The longer the Blue Man and the distrusting ones have their way, the worse the land will suffer and the generations unborn, they will be harmed the most." He held up a finger, "Remember the Buffalo Maiden Woman, she killed a man... one with wrong intentions... when she first appeared to us. I think that she and Mother Earth are related. *Ina Maka* (Mother Earth) might even have to kill off many of us if she is to survive. Earthquakes, falling stars (meteors and asteroids); too hot, too cold (temperature change) and great hunger can happen. Too many people... that is happening right now. Our people have been here so much longer than the *washichu*, yet we allowed ourselves way more room. Now the land, a two-legged's freedom with it, is disappearing. Our children suffer the most when they cannot have their beginnings, their youth, at play within her streams, her lakes and among the animals. When you take the Earth Mother away from our youth, serious trouble happens. When Mother Earth makes her changes, it could get so bad that everyone who is left will have to learn to live like an Indian. They won't have any choice."

The holy man placed his hand to his forehead, sitting silently before he continued. "The blue two-legged tried to chase you off the mountain to keep this message away. Fortunately, you paid attention to my instructions."

A rare smile formed. "You even took a good whack at him." The smile dissolved as Fools Crow continued, "The Blue Man fears knowledge and he fears that our people will return to their old ways of knowledge which comes straight from the Great Spirit, most of it through the Earth Mother. The Blue Man can be beaten but you have showed us, it is not through the old way of the warrior. You have fulfilled a goodly portion of your mission and, so far, you have done well." He paused for a moment before adding: "You have an ally."

He repeated, "You have an ally that gives us hope. Maybe it is she that will have to kill the Blue Man." He waved his open palm in an arc. "The rainbow... before you started up the mountain... that rainbow gives us powerful hope. And at the end of your vision you were flying toward it. It is a powerful symbol of hope made by the Almighty. Never make fun of what the Almighty has created and put here right before us. All you have to do is just look at it to know how powerful it can be. That is all that I can say for now. *Hetch etu aloh waste aloh.* It is so. It is good, indeed."

THE NEW INDIANS

CHAPTER TWENTY

There is a longing among the young of my nation to secure
for themselves and their people the skills that will provide
them with a sense of purpose and worth.
They will be our new warriors.
— Chief Dan George

The Cessna buzzed the waving figure standing near the General Aviation hangars. Lawrence waved his ball cap and watched the plane land at the West River airport. The two brothers hugged each other with deep grins before the pilot logged a loose door complaint inside one of Ernie Hale's hangars. Lawrence then drove his new station wagon to the main terminal and helped his brother unload several ore canisters for an outbound flight. Kyle Charging Shield was enjoying his summer job flying for Ernie Hale.

At the terminal he was surprised to meet Father Weitz. The priest had attended an education conference and was with two members of the Indian Movement. He offered the trio a ride into West River. One of the Indians, wearing a red headband and sporting braids, was introduced as Lehman Horn Chips, a Hunkpapa and his barrel-chested companion in a ponytail was a Chippewa named Leaf. He guessed both to be in their latter twenties, noting the strong resemblance between the husky Hunkpapa's sharp, angular face and that of Gall, the famous Hunkpapa Sioux chief.

On the way to town, Kyle discovered the group had met at the education conference. The topic of conversation centered for awhile on civil rights progress. The Hunkpapa was articulate and strong willed but also observant. Horn Chips interjected his opinion at times but Weitz carried most of the conversation. The Jesuit reminded him of a campus minister at the University, an energetic advocate and organizer of student protest against the war in Vietnam. Charging Shield learned that the priest had an off-reservation assignment for the summer to work for the bishop and was quartered at the West River Mission. The two militants were planning to resume their journey in a few days to the West Coast, where a meeting for a possible takeover of Alcatraz Island was to be held. Like Lawrence, the burly Chippewa remained silent, except for an acknowledging grunt now and then whenever Horn Chips would nod to an important point brought up by Weitz.

Charging Shield sensed he was being studied by the Hunkpapa. Like himself, he guessed Horn Chips had been city raised, but the roots of their ancestral past had been strong enough to spill over and resist the assimilating attempts of modern upbringing. Since both were Lakota, the blueprint within the DNA of those very roots made both sense that it would be culturally impolite to fire a barrage of questions at each other upon first acquaintance.

Charging Shield invited Horn Chips and Leaf to attend the summer's Sun Dance before leaving them at a relative's home. Their parting words wished both him and the priest well. They proceeded on with Father Weitz, Kyle's thoughts dwelling on the Indian Movement. During the school year a national news agency had credited the growing organization for exposing land lease corruption in a Bureau of Indian Affairs office. The Hunkpapa's strong face focussed in his thoughts. Deep within the recesses of his memory, he felt he had known the man before, somewhere... possibly in another time.

"Would you have time for a glass of wine?" the priest invited, as Kyle drove to the West River Mission.

Kyle threw a nervous look at his brother, which was countered by a wave and a laugh from Lawrence. "Don't worry about me, little brother. Ernie Hale has got me on a cocktail circuit for your brother, Hobart. Gives me a chance to talk about my ball playing days and the state Hall of Fame." Lawrence could not subdue a slight frown when he mentioned Hobart's name, then added quickly, "I'm doing this for our Mother," he said in one breath. "Others drinking, doesn't bother me, providing they don't go and make fools out of themselves."

Out of curiosity he accepted the invitation, glancing at his watch knowing he could not be late for a political cocktail party Ernie Hale was having later that evening. At Ernie's intercession and for the sake of his mother, he had made peace with Hobart. His brother was campaigning for Alderman and progress was surprisingly successful. His truce had bought him a reprieve from his mother. She would no longer interfere with his Sun Dance participation if he would let past differences rest and of course appear congenial in public, especially at Ernie's political gatherings.

Charging Shield felt an uneasy nervousness within the priest's quarters, although there was nothing monastic about a converted suburban home staffed by three Jesuits. Just being that close to priests brought back memories of the boarding school. The mission rectory was empty when Father Weitz unlocked the front door, which opened into a front room furnished with a couch, end tables, several easy chairs and lamp tables. Charging Shield was also curious why a priest, and a Jesuit at that, could be so friendly to two obvious militants, Horn Chips and Leaf.

Lawrence spotted a television set in a meeting room and asked to be excused. "Yanks playing Chicago today. Got to watch my baseball on my days off, if you two don't mind." After pouring a glass of ice water from the refrigerator, Father Weitz turned on the television set and started to leave Lawrence to the room.

EAGLE VISION

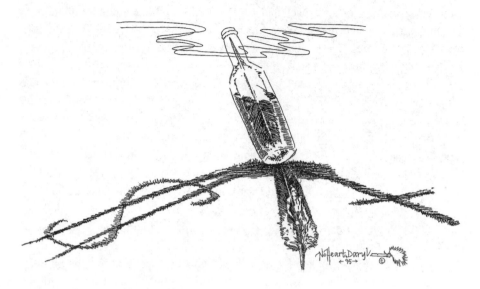

HOW TO GET THE "WARRIOR" OUT OF THE BOTTLE...

Lawrence looked at the glass and held it up to the light. "I used to be a warrior in the bottle, Father Weitz." He pointed the glass to the front room with a soft smile. "My brother there... he doesn't know it, but he has gotten the warrior out of the bottle." He held up his glass to make a toast while the priest nodded a silent affirmation.

"I admired your courage in the Sun Dance." Weitz said as he offered a glass of altar wine in the living room. He continued after his guest took a seat on the edge of a stuffed chair and acknowledged the compliment. "What are your plans after college? I understand you're a senior now."

The priest surely knew from his mother that Ernie Hale was pushing him for law school, even arranging a meeting with the Dean. It was Ernie that influenced his major in government and business. In time the priest would come to what he really wanted to know... but what knowledge did he have that would be of any value? They wanted him to act, get out of the Sun Dance... as simple as that. Surely they didn't believe he could be coerced into turning against the holy men. Now Horn Chips and Leaf, there is where real trouble could begin for the missionaries, not just the Jesuits but all missionaries. 'Ah, maybe they think I'm a militant... a possessed militant at that. I guess I am, in their eyes. I'm no doubt a heretic also or whatever else they wish to label me.' His thoughts made it difficult to suppress an amused smile.

Charging Shield's contemplative stare made Father Weitz restate his question. "What are you going to do with your degree?"

He didn't want to say that he knew Ernie Hale was planning politics for him. The thought gave him a queasy feeling. Ernie's words haunted and echoed, 'You're goin' to have to get out of these fool Indian things, kid. You'll learn, like your brother. You can do more for Indians... and for yourself, of course... by gettin' into politics. What with all your medals and keepin' your nose clean like you have... Damnit Son. We can go to the moon in politics.' Kyle shrugged off his reverie and looked at the priest. "I guess I could always work for the B. I. A., " he said, offering a half-hearted shrug.

The statement made Weitz wince. "Do you really want to work for the Bureau of Indian Affairs? It's quite bureaucratic you know." The priest knew full well that it was regarded as one of the most inept agencies in the federal government.

"The Bureau is upgrading their educational requirements. An Indian will have to have a masters degree for a decent position," Charging Shield volunteered.

"Precisely," Weitz added with a suspicious raise of an eyebrow, "That gives the white man more time to shift to other government agencies. All the incompetent bureaucrats will bail out in droves once the Indian Movement gets started." Weitz looked rueful but there was wisdom in his words. "When the Indian finally gains control of the Bureau, Congress or the Administration will abolish it."

"Eliminate the B. I. A.?"

"If they don't eliminate it, they'll take most of it away."

"Well at least we'll get rid of the boarding schools."

"Not just the boarding schools, Kyle, in time the reservations will go too. I'd think twice about a career in the B. I. A."

'If the Jesuit was being congenially deceptive by offering a mutual analysis of the Bureau he sure as hell was doing a good job of it...' Charging Shield looked puzzled and offered another shrug. "The Marine Corps... 'errh - they always told us in the Corps if we ever wanted to make field grade rank, we'd have to have a degree. I took quite a few college courses in there when I could."

Weitz pouted a genuine frown. "By the grace of God, man," he admonished harshly, "You don't want to waste your life back in the military!"

Charging Shield was taken aback by the priest's response. It sounded too sincere, as though he really meant it. 'The military would be the best place for you missionaries to have me.' he almost answered. He couldn't believe the priest meant it. The Roman collar beneath the handsome featured face made him realize he was still talking to a Jesuit.

"I wouldn't want to see you back in the Marines," the priest re-emphasized, "such a waste."

'A Jesuit but not a Buchwald... but still dedicated,' he cautioned. 'Their vows, you'd have to be damned dedicated. The vow of chastity. With looks like that, he wondered if the priest had ever slept with a woman... and they think our customs are strange.' He'd rather go through a dozen sun dances than take the vow of chastity.

"I'm against the war, you know," Father Weitz swirled the wine in his glass. His guest's mute nod to his statement wasn't surprising. Most reservation Indians were reticent and withdrawn in the isolated presence of a priest. 'But Kyle Charging Shield was no ordinary reservation Indian,' he would have warned himself, were he not so elated over his success at the National Indian Education Conference, and better yet, befriending two of the leading militants. It was exciting, the same excitement found in the civil rights marches. He took just a sip of wine. Change had become an elixir, moral change an opiate. There was substance to the emerging times, not empty pulpit sermonizing. 'The success in the south, the Vietnam War itself was being forced to its end and soon he would be a focal point of that force, for the reservations could be next.'

"It's an unjust war, we have no right to be over there." He paused for a moment, side tracked with other thoughts. 'The conference had been well attended, the atmosphere electric, civil rights had hung like silent smoke on every meeting. Blacks, Chicanos, liberals, clergy... and Horn Chips was no less articulate and he himself had coached him, winning his respect. Tomorrow he would report to the Bishop and Father Superior would come up to West River, wanting to attend.' Kyle Charging Shield's probing stare brought him back to the present.

"It's a civil war between north and south. We'd save thousands of lives if we'd just get out."

'A receptive change had overcome the Father Superior ever since the meeting - the day he had openly conflicted with Paul Buchwald. It wasn't easy serving as assistant to Paul Buchwald but the reservation was immense and the mission understaffed. There were more than enough duties to keep both men busy. The Father Superior did not regret assigning him to West River for the summer and of course, sending him to the education conference. They would be wise to make early concessions; avoiding the damaging publicity that would surely follow. It was only a matter of time before the militants would force a confrontation. And Paul, Paul will drown in the trouble he creates... this time I won't say a word if he wants to interfere in the Sun Dance.'

"Vietnam, you were there Kyle, I wasn't. I should respect your feelings about the war but there are other issues we should devote our energies to; issues where I'm sure we share the same opinion."

The mention of war no longer stabbed at Charging Shield. He was tired of the campus confrontations. 'Priest,' he thought, 'I should tell you about my vision. I wonder if you could interpret it as the prelude to something disastrous, if all nations don't start working together.' Instead, he decided to test the priest. He offered a vigilant look. "We're going to Sun Dance this summer... for the full four days. Do we share the same opinion on that issue?"

Weitz surprised him with an accepting nod.

"And Buchwald? I'm sure Father Buchwald has been doing his usual manipulating of his church members on the tribal council."

"I can't speak for him, Kyle," Charging Shield's hard stare and ensuing silence made him add. "I have no control over Paul Buchwald. I hope you believe me."

"And if you did have control?" he probed.

The priest's voice rose to make his point. "He's intruding on constitutional guarantees." He turned away to stare at a brass lamp. "Freedom of religion," he emphasized. "He wouldn't interfere if I had my way." Weitz made his words soft and final. He had a thought but didn't speak, 'But he will, and if you knew better, Kyle, you would hope he interferes, for it will be his undoing,' he said to himself.

"You're different, Father," Charging Shield took a sip of his drink before he held up his glass to the priest. He looked at him squarely, "I can't believe you'll last very long at Sacred Rosary Mission."

Father Weitz offered a shadow of a smile. "I may last longer than you think," he calmly hinted, returning a lighthearted salute with his glass.

Charging Shield did not fail to register the priest's assessment of constitutional protections but his people's history had taught him to downplay it. The treaties were much more explicit than the constitution and all of them had been broken. His thoughts raced back to the previous Sun Dance. "Buchwald," he spoke without thinking, "it was meant that I should oppose him."

"You mean fate?"

Charging Shield shook his head thoughtfully. "Maybe spiritual fate... yes... maybe spiritual fate," he said haltingly for he felt the words were still inadequate. "Buchwald has made me a warrior here in my own land."

"Combating Father Buchwald is a far cry from drop - from what you had to do in Vietnam," Weitz chastised.

Charging Shield wasn't offended and instead retorted calmly, "Vietnam allowed me to be a warrior." The words of Eagle Feather in reference to the communist system focussed in his mind. '... And that one does not respect the Great Spirit. He won't allow the Almighty to reach his conscience. He even punishes his own people that put the Almighty before him.'

'You mean the State as God?'

'Uh huh, ...that's the one I'm worried about...' the conversation with Eagle Feather played on.

Charging Shield knew any statement he would make regarding the war would be rejected. Masses of humanity had fled from repressive regimes, blatant totalitarian governments subverting even a man's beliefs... and there would be more masses of refugees when this war would be lost. How ironic for this priest to be swept up by the intensity of the times! He fixed his gaze on an empty vase placed precariously at the edge of the lamp table next to his chair. He lifted his stare to Weitz, asking hopefully, "Do you think we can stop wars? I'm all for it if we can."

"We have to stop them, Kyle. This one is leading toward an incredible confrontation," Weitz's voice raised in alarm. "Right now, you warriors have the means to wipe out civilized life in one horrible conflagration."

"No," Charging Shield disagreed, "In my culture, a true warrior had to be willing to sacrifice himself for the people... offering his life if he had to. If my people were led down the path of war, their leaders would have to be in the front with their sons - they were true warriors." He pictured the missile sites. 'The politicians on both sides were responsible for the intercontinental missile silos,' he contended to himself. "No, Father, it is the politicians who will start the lunacy of doomsday, not the true warriors."

The cutting truth of his guest's remarks perplexed Weitz. The younger Indian's statements took him back to the Sun Dance. "At the Sun Dance, last summer," he began with an anxious voice, wanting to change the subject away from the apocalyptic atmosphere that hung like a darkening cloud, "your words left quite an impression." He read the puzzled look and went on. "Before the piercing, when Father Buchwald was about to interfere, you gave a meaningful speech."

Charging Shield blushed slightly. He had forgotten most of what had been said. The confrontation forced Buchwald to retreat. *That* was what he had found worth remembering. Nevertheless, he appreciated the priest's compliment.

"I was moved that day, Kyle, by something you said," Weitz paused, "you said, 'we Christians talk of Moses and Christ, and that they vision quested not unlike what your holy men do...' and yet we no longer do this."

Charging Shield smiled but remained silent. He no longer felt mistrust for the priest. He sensed that the priest would like to keep him all afternoon with interesting questions but he knew that he would have to leave soon. He declined another glass of wine and looked at his watch. Only a little while and he would have to leave with Lawrence for a political rally at Ernie Hale's.

"I would like to ask one more question, Kyle." Father Weitz said as he returned with a full wineglass, "What are your views on forgiveness?"

Kyle smiled. It wasn't the first time he was asked the question. His smile remained as he began. "I think we will have some very different views on that subject." He paused to accept a nod from the Jesuit. "I don't put much stake in forgiveness." His words were flat and direct without emotion then went on in an unbroken monologue, "When I think of forgiveness, I think of trying to undo something that already has been. In the Indian way, you can not undo what the Creator has created. What you have caused or done or spoken, you really cannot undo." He waved his palm outward to emphasize. "The *washichu* believes that he can go through life and do what he wants to do and at the end simply ask to be forgiven. Me, I am an Indian. I do not see in Nature where this act or belief has any proof whatsoever. It is why the track record of my people was so exemplary." He leaned forward as if to emphasize. "They lived their life today for the life that they would live in the beyond. It sure as hell produced better results for the planet and for the people while they had to live together on their particular portion of this earth." He swept another arc with his hand. "Look at what their belief system did for this hemisphere and their generations unborn. Over and over, each generation had the same freedoms, the same resources and all the room that they wanted or needed. Year after year, generation after generation, centuries following centuries, for thousands of years." He rose up from his chair for emphasis. "Truth as the basis of our belief system versus this forgiveness thing of the *washichu* has let all of you Europeans off of the hook - up until now, regarding resources and room." He carried a look of dejection. "It... the resources and the spaciousness of Mother Earth is starting to vanish now." He knew the priest would not and could not fully understand and added to clarify, "Truth to an Indian is more important than forgiveness. Truth exists. It is the Great Spirit. To me, forgiveness is but a word. It is invented by the *washichu*. It takes away how serious every act and thing you do down here in this world, really is." The clock chimed out the hour. Kyle glanced again at his watch and added hurriedly, "You Europeans, you have even carried your fairy tales into your religion. The handsome prince rescues or marries the pretty princess... and everyone lives happily ever after. Even your movies are made that way." He studied the priest's face, not expecting him to understand. "Nature does not forgive. It does not always provide a rosy ending. If you hunt too big an animal with too small a weapon or you do not put away enough meat for the winter or a buffalo herd unexpectedly turns your way at full speed... it is not a happy or rosy ending." He added with finality, "and all of this is a creation... a happening made by the Great Spirit." The priest's mouth was agape as though he could not grasp Charging Shield's emphasis.

"I cannot believe that you are forgiven for your acts... especially those grievous wrongs that have caused painful agony to another. We believed in living every day for the life beyond. There was no fairy tale magic potion like forgiveness, that allowed the people to cheat and bend their lives around and away from a truly honorable and ethical standard of honest living."

At that moment, Lawrence entered the room. "Yanks won. 6 to 4." The big man quipped as he walked toward a chair. "We got to get over to Ernie's, pretty soon," he said, trying to sound polite while sitting down.

Weitz looked disappointed knowing the discussion was at an end. "I would like to be your friend, Kyle." He turned to Lawrence to repeat politely, "And yours too, Lawrence." He looked back at Kyle and spoke with an air of closure, "I understand your people believe that when a gift is received, the recipient should return one of equal value. I would like to return a gift for your words at the Sun Dance. They seemed to hold something for my future. Possibly I may seek out a holy man and ask to Vision Quest."

Charging Shield withdrew the *wotai* from under his western shirt before handing the buckskin pouch to the priest. "I sense that you have something to tell me.

Maybe you could hold my *wotai* and tell me."

Weitz held the pouch, his mind centering on the word - warrior. An overpowering feeling engulfed him. Within a few minutes he knew Charging Shield would drain the almost empty wineglass, set it beside the glass vase and accidentally brush the vase. It would bounce on the hard floor yet somehow would remain undamaged. The Indian would rise from his chair, pick up the vase, and exchange it for the *wotai,* then leave. Weitz was dead certain he had received a foretelling vision, nothing significant, but it was some kind of sign; some indication of a broader power that could be. He clutched the pouch firmly and then he spoke, "Kyle, would you mind if I quoted a biblical verse... from the Old Testament?" His guest's polite nod told him to continue. "Isaiah, a prophet, said long before the Christians, 'Nation will not lift sword up against nation, neither will they learn war anymore'." The priest's eyes searched his guests. "What does that mean to you?"

Charging Shield had hung on every word. He asked the priest to repeat the verse slowly. When Weitz was finished he wanted so hard for it to be a true verse, and if so, he would no longer be a warrior even though within his circle of circles, that lot had satisfied instincts of a thousand years past, a past that never left the unbroken line of one's genes. A serene feeling engulfed him. Woefully he knew it would only be temporary like the brief soothing of a lifting song, but for those few fleeting moments he believed the warrior days were numbered. He hoped there was power in those words, a power like a true holy man's vision.

The depth of the conversation made Weitz forget he had asked his guest for comment. "This man-made Armageddon, this horrendous atomic arsenal poised at each other when we have the most modern means of open discussion and communication available is utter madness," he spat disgustedly.

The emotional charge of the discussion made Charging Shield look at his watch and then toward Lawrence. He drained his wineglass and set it beside the glass vase, bumping the vase off the table and onto the floor. He rose from his chair to retrieve the undamaged vase. When he exchanged the vase for his *wotai,* he explained that it was time to leave, but for days afterwards he heard the voice of Father Weitz echo the words of the prophet Isaiah.

As they drove away, Kyle asked his brother for an assessment regarding the young priest.

Lawrence grunted as if to clear his throat. "Little brother," he began somberly, "you remember back when we ran away from that mission?"

"You know, I'll never Goddamn forget it. Especially Cross Dog," Kyle replied staring straight ahead and seeing nothing but road; so locked on to the past were his thoughts.

"Well... " Lawrence spoke with a long pause, "this is the first time I've been this close to one of them missionaries for that long a time and under their roof again. It was a pretty creepy experience for me." He took a deep breath. "I actually thought about having a drink." He exhaled sharply with his admittance. "Not even in the war, when I was pushing bodies with a bulldozer, and we had last rites with all them chaplains... I never got close to 'em." He hunched his shoulders and gripped the steering wheel tight. "I didn't hear all what you two were saying and I have to admit, this guy Weitz ain't no Buchwald. He sounds a helluva lot different than what we saw at the boarding school." Lawrence paused to let out a low groan. "The way I see it... they're all fundamentalists."

Kyle threw a coarse look at his Brother. Lawrence went on with a laugh, "Don't worry about me drinkin', little brother. The Yanks won." His face grew serious. "Fundamentalists want to hate. They want to feel superior to something. Those priests are fundamentalists, not a helluva lot different than Jesus freaks coming around and preaching at your door. It's easy to hate something that isn't exactly like yourself. Course they ain't ever going to admit that they hate or feel superior. But they hate that we keep our own views, our own ideas. Might say they're trying to save us from their devil but deep down in, they want power over us and if we don't give in, they can get pretty mean. We saw that in the boarding school. That's why I stay away from them and their religion. Even Indian religion has got me worried." The big Indian glared and held out a scarred fist. "Sure, it's the reason why I quit drinkin'. That was one helluva powerful *Yuwipi*, Fools Crow did and I have to thank you for that. Only a goddamn fool wouldn't be influenced." He held up a finger as they turned down the road that led to Ernie Hale's mansion. "You watch, brother. Once Indian religion gets on its feet. Indian fundamentalists who don't know a goddamn thing about the Great Spirit will move in on that too. Maybe they will become instant know-it-alls and fuck it up, just like this outfit this priest has got himself into."

*   *   *   *

Almost a month passed when he received a phone call at his mother's home from Eagle Feather. Usually affable the holy man's tone was serious. "You know that the Sun Dance is going to have a carnival and a rodeo this year?"

"A carnival? I can't believe it."

"One thing I never liked about the Sun Dance, Nephew, mainly that priest trying to take it over, but this carnival thing is the limit. Lately I've had a bunch of Indian Movement members come to see me. They want to hold a Sun Dance at Trading Post a week before the one at Oglala. I'm calling to ask if you'll take part with us."

Charging Shield was stunned by the request. He had always admired the holy man's bold defiance of the missionaries to revive the Sun Dance over a decade before. Now Eagle Feather was asking him to defy the tribe.

"Shouldn't there be only one Sun Dance, at least until we get our spirit back?" he queried.

"Maybe so, Nephew, but it should be a prayer, not a show," Eagle Feather paused. "I'm calling from the Trading Post. The owner says he'll feed all the dancers and can put up some lodges. If you'd come back, maybe more dancers would take part."

"The Trading Post owner?" Charging Shield replied, feeling uncomfortable that a white man would sponsor the Sun Dance. "I don't know. I feel uneasy about having more than one coming together... especially right now when we are just starting to get back our ways. Yet, I don't care for that carnival thing."

"We expect some trouble from the tribe," Eagle Feather's words broke a brief silence. "No doubt they'll try to stop us. I might be right, I might be wrong, but this is my way of saying I don't like this carnival thing."

"I hate to hurt your feelings, Bill, but I'm afraid I can't. There should be only one Sun Dance; at least right now... is my feeling. I'd better stick with my tribe. If I don't, I might have a lot of bad luck." He hoped his last words would soften the holy man's disappointment.

Later in the summer, after Ernie assured he could return in time for the beginning of the forthcoming Sun Dance event, he was assigned a charter flight, transporting a geology team surveying mining claims in the Southwest.

One morning while he waited in a desert terminal, he called the meteorology station and was pleased with the weather forecast. He hoped to return to West River in the next few days, for the Sun Dance was less than a week away.

A rental car stopped in the parking lot. He waved to his passengers. After preflight they were soon taxiing toward the runway. As he taxied, he noted an annoying rattle near the rear door. He turned the high-winged Cessna into the wind, then flipped a switch to cycle the flaps. At that moment, one of the passengers opened the door. The flap motor whined as it strained to lower the flap against the door. He heard a snap near the wing root and the motor ceased to whine. He taxied back to the flight line with the door jammed open.

"Goddammit, Kyle, that ain't the first time that's happened to those models," Ernie Hale's gruff voice came through the phone. "There's a micro switch, supposed to cut out that flap motor when the door opens. How long you figure it'll take for repairs?"

"I don't know, Ernie. They might have to get some parts from the factory. I went ahead and rented a plane so we could finish up the contract."

"Yeah, that's a good idea. Tell you what, kid. Stay down there with that airplane. Let me talk to the mechanic and I'll see what I can do to help you get her fixed."

The spare parts never arrived until the middle of the following week. He wouldn't be back for the beginning of the Sun Dance.

SUN DANCE COMMITTEE

CHAPTER TWENTY ONE

*We are told that your religion was given to your forefathers and
has been handed down, father to son.
We also have a religion which was given to our forefathers,
and has been handed down to us, their children.
We worship that way. It teaches us to be thankful for
all the favors we receive, to love each other, and to be united.
We never quarrel about religion.*
— *Red Jacket*
Seneca   1790

It was Saturday, the third day of the Sun Dance, when the Cessna's shadow approached the Black Hills from the southwest, darting through the dew-covered sage. He had spent the night at a tiny airport, waiting until morning for the operator to open the gas pumps.

The Cessna hugged the ground closely to avoid head winds aloft, skirting through the southern foothills of the mountain range before following a tree-lined creek leading to the reservation and the Sun Dance grounds. An opening between two knolls offered a brief glimpse of the encampment. The plane rose out of the creek bed, up and over the cottonwoods at the edge of the campgrounds. The Sun Dance circle captivated the pilot for a brief moment until the corner of his eye caught the Ferris wheel bearing down on his wing tip.

He jerked back on the yoke and turned the controls to full aileron. The plane rolled to the left, narrowly missing the Ferris wheel. 'A goddamn carnival. Bill Eagle Feather was right.' He couldn't believe what he saw as he kept the airplane in a tight turn, to glare at the carnival and rodeo grounds south of the Sun Dance arena.

The adrenaline from the near collision accelerated his heartbeat. His hand trembled when he lowered wing flaps for the Oglala airport, cutting the throttle as he sailed over the edge of the runway to bounce the aircraft on the dirt airstrip. He spotted a trio of tires in the buffalo grass at the end of the runway and parked the plane between them. After he tied the aircraft, he walked on the airport road that led toward the highway to catch a ride from the first approaching car. Soon he was walking through the ring of tipis, tents and campers.

The Sun Dance was in its final stages as he entered the crowd. He marveled at the number of dancers offering their prayers. He counted ten men and ten women, not including the holy men: Fools Crow, Lame Deer, Gap and Catches. One of the women was Mary Bad Hand. He found himself looking for Eagle Feather. The Rosebud holy man was noticeably absent. It was the first time he was at a Sun Dance without the huge holy man.

He took a seat close to the drummers and recalled the return of the ceremony; when he had sat with his grandmother as a young boy watching Eagle Feather's bold defiance of the missionaries and the government officials as he stepped into the arena to be pierced. Charging Shield glared at the Ferris wheel in the distance, bringing to mind the Rosebud holy man's words on the telephone. "One thing I never liked about the Sun Dance, Nephew, mainly that priest trying to take it over, but this carnival thing is the limit."

He watched Lame Deer test the rawhide ropes hanging from the Sun Dance tree. The Rosebud holy man leaned back against the braided rawhide and tugged several times on each rope. When Fools Crow spread a bed of sage beneath the tree, Charging Shield knew that a piercing would take place. 'The holy men know what they're doing,' he assured himself. He told himself to concentrate on praying and not to worry if someone decided to pierce on the third day of the ceremony.

When the sun was high overhead, the dancers rested while the drummers smoked from three peace pipes. After the pipes were smoked, they were placed on the buffalo skull pipe rack at the western edge of the ceremonial grounds. Fools Crow gave a signal to the drummers, then lead the file of dancers back into the hot sunlight, placing them in a circle facing inward around the cottonwood tree. One man was led to the bed of sage at the base of the tree. He removed his crown and took his place on the sage, lying face upward as Fools Crow reached for the flat-bladed awl from his medicine bundle.

Charging Shield failed to recognize the man but admired the courage that he displayed. Not a muscle moved when the sharp blade was inserted. The man continued to remain motionless when the wooden peg was skewered under the skin, following the initial cutting with the awl. The man rose from the sage blowing his eagle bone whistle with intense fervor as he danced toward the end of his rope.

Charging Shield lowered his head to pray for the return of the power of the hoop. At the end of his prayer, he expressed his gratitude for the knowledge he had received from the holy men.

After a while he raised his head and saw another dancer being pierced. Sonny Larvee was led to the bed of sage. Red Bow was pierced after Larvee. The culmination of the Sun Dance was taking place on the third day! He clenched both fists in dismay. He had vowed in Fools Crow's *Yuwipi* that he would pierce... what about the Sun Dance wish to be made... what about last year's Sun Dance wish? Would his failure to fulfill his vow dissolve that wish also? A half-hour went by, finally the last of the sun dancers was pierced. Despite his personal dilemma, he could not help but admire the majestic procession surrounding the annual Tree of Life. Six ropes

EAGLE VISION

SONNY LARVEE

trailed up toward the top of the cottonwood from six sun dancers. The prayers of the large crowd now carried upwards to the tree and on beyond, to the One above. It was not the time to question, he chastised himself. It was the time to pray. While the people prayed, the dancers moved slowly inward to pause at the base of the tree, then retreated slowly to the end of the rawhide. Again they danced forward to join together. After the fourth beseeching they were free to break.

Catches was pierced deeply as usual. Mary Bad Hand danced close by him. He leaned back against the rope; his hands were outstretched as he offered his pain. Six eagle feathers were sewn to his back and arms. Catches was regarded as the bravest of all for enduring pain, yet seldom had the gentle man uttered a harsh word. Not even the missionaries could make the holy man angry. Charging Shield reflected upon the words of Catches at the previous Sun Dance, "Father, you have the other fifty-one weeks. All that we are asking is this one week to pray our own way."

The time that could offer a vision had arrived. A low rumble coming from the cloud buildup far to the west stirred the dance grounds. A light breeze rustled the feathers sewn to the Oglala's skin. Catches's vision was brief. A woman appeared in the distant clouds. "There are four races, four seasons, four directions, four faces," she spoke to Catches. The cloud darkened, blotting out the woman. The vision ended. The other dancers strained at their ropes, while the holy man lowered his gaze to the bottom of the tree. Separately they broke their bonds to Mother Earth by leaning away from the rawhide umbilical. They had been privileged to be nourished spiritually by their true Mother and would carry this strength for a full cycle, until once again the seasons would return to the 'Moon of Ripening Cherries'.

Catches was the last to break. He strained against the rope, his skin stretching a hand's length as though refusing to release the wooden peg. Again he leaned back sawing with his body against the rope bringing a murmured gasp from the crowd. Finally, Catches danced slowly toward the center. He paused momentarily, then turned and ran away from the tree. When he reached the end of the rope, the peg tore free jerking his body around, sending him rolling across the edge of the arena. The recoiling rope shot the wooden skewer toward the tree and the crowd groaned as one, as if they too felt the sun dancer's sharp pain.

Peter Catches rose. Mary Bad Hand retrieved his sage crown from the ground before he danced humbly toward the gathering dancers. His attached eagle feathers fluttered with his motions.

The sun dancers kept time to the closing song while Fools Crow returned each pipe to its owner. The ceremony was concluded. Charging Shield was so impressed with the dignity of Catches that he briefly forgot about the carnival and the fact that it was the third day. He rose to join the crowd forming a long line to shake the hands of the dancers.

"Cousin, where were you? We thought you were going to pierce this year," Sonny Larvee asked as they shook hands. Mary Bad Hand was next to Sonny.

"I was, Sonny. I had trouble getting back. What's going to happen tomorrow since everyone pierced today?"

Mary lowered her head motioning toward the cottonwood. "Buchwald will say Mass," she murmured darkly. "The Sun Dance committee made a ruling. They say he had Rousseau introduce the idea last winter at a meeting."

After Charging Shield shook the last dancer's hand, he walked to his sister's trailer house with a sour look.

His mother and sister, Mildred, were waiting at the trailer house. "Where were you, son? You should have been out there," his mother exclaimed with a nod toward the arena.

He briefly explained his delay.

"That's too bad. I wanted to see you dance," she surprised him with her enthusiasm. "Now I have to wait another year, and I'm not getting any younger. I've done a lot of thinking lately. I guess an old horse can't switch in midstream, but I know that our own ways are good. The teachings of the Buffalo Calf Woman held us all together and we were too good of a people for me to believe otherwise. I knew too many of the old ones who believed that Old Way. They set better example than what I've seen out here in this world. I can't argue with truth, even though the priests try to patch it all over and have given me a hard time over your doings. You go your way son. I'll never say anything anymore. I'm thinking there is more than one messenger from the Great Spirit. No matter how you believe, be good to people on this earth and you'll be okay." She motioned again to the arena. "Well, daughter, let's go down and get in that line. I want to tell those dancers we're proud of them."

Charging Shield sat on the couch with a brief glow after they left. He was pleased with the morning ceremony itself and especially the change that had come over his mother. For the moment he wanted to set aside the mounting demand - somehow, someway, he would have to perform his vow taken at Fools Crow's *Yuwipi*. Maybe he would have to go out alone in the Badlands and find a cottonwood tree... maybe the towering cottonwood shading his grandmother's abandoned cabin. Would he have the courage to pierce himself? He fondled his *wotai* while he perplexed over his dilemma. He was tired. He rested his head on a pillow and started to drift away. He slept and he dreamed.

"Charging Shield, you have a Sun Dance wish," voices called to him from a darkened room.

"Don't I know it? I wished for my mate," he replied angrily.

"Yes, you wished for her," he now recognized the voices of his ancient mentors. "A Sun Dance wish; respect your Sun Dance wish," they chorused.

"What do you wish for this Sun Dance?" they asked.

"I have not pierced. I have no wish."

"What do you wish for - THIS Sun Dance?" they demanded harshly.

He considered their question moot, but offered an answer to appease them. "I wish we could have four days." His answer was blunt.

In the background he could hear Fools Crow, Eagle Feather and - oddly, Dr. Howard, scolding him, urging him to listen to his mentors. "What do you mean? The Sun Dance is over," the chorus of mentors taunted. Lightning bolts cracked all around, dropping him to his knees.

"Okay, it is not over," he relented. "If I do this Sun Dance," he called out, "then I wish... I wish for the freedom of the buffalo warrior. To ride freely and hunt upon Mother Earth."

"The past - you wish for the past," his mentors sang in a critical tone.

The walls of the room closed in; just at the moment he thought he would be crushed, he escaped through a tiny door. He found himself in Fools Crow's cabin, kneeling before a shrouded figure sitting on a blanket. Behind the figure, which now resembled Fools Crow, three other figures sat on high stools. The three became Eagle Feather, Mary Bad Hand and Dr. Howard. Strangely, the three wore judicial robes, although Eagle Feather wore a buffalo horned headdress and the braided hair of Mary Bad Hand was adorned with a sage crown. Her black robe also bore eagle feathers sewn to the sleeves. The three figures conversed among themselves with occasional looks cast in his direction. Off to the right of the trio stood two silent figures, standing close together as if they were observers. One of them was an Indian in an old dancing regalia. His face resembled Ben Black Elk but it was not Ben. The other man was a short white man with a heavy brow and a keen perceptive look.

The shroud dropped from Fools Crow, his face illuminating. "It is the Eagle Freedom that you seek," the holy man proclaimed.

"Is that what you wish?" the trio demanded.

"Think back upon your Vision Quest. Did not the eagle wing descend upon you and your mate?" Fools Crow coached. "It is within the eagle, you shall find your freedom. The buffalo are no more, not like they used to be. The eagle, *wanblee,* the eagle is still free."

"Is that what you wish?" the trio again demanded.

The lifting feeling of that vision was too powerful to resist. "Yes," he answered with vigor, heeding Fools Crow's words. "Yes, I wish for the Eagle Freedom."

"Do you wish for the past," the trio tested him.

"If that means the woman of the Mandan lodge, the woman in the lodge in my dream on the mountain - my mate of the past. Yes, I do wish for the past."

"You wish for both?"

"Yes, I wish for both. It is my past."

"*Hau,*" the chorus of mentors joined with the black robed tribunal, their anxious enthusiasm revealing their satisfaction as if they had boxed him in where they had wanted him. "Then you must pierce during the piercing day. If you fail, you shall lose both wishes," the tribunal spoke its edict.

"Question?" a stranger's voice called out. A Caucasian, meticulously dressed in a gray business suit, white shirt and striped tie, entered the cabin which by now had expanded to resemble somewhat, a rough boarded courtroom. "You wish for the past, are you not rejecting the white man's world? Were you not a warrior in his war... therefore you are not proud to be a warrior?"

Charging Shield rankled under the man's attempt to put words into his mouth. He recognized the man from a recent picture on the cover of a national news magazine. The stranger was a politician, a senator and a leading proponent against the war effort. "I don't regret combat, I do not regret fighting for my country," Charging Shield fired back hotly. "I was not a coward," but his strong words suddenly faltered. "But... the white men... they do not respect their own warriors. I will no longer fight for one who will not respect those he sends into combat." He pointed an accusing finger. "The chiefs of the white men, they hide their own sons from battle... you white men chiefs... you send other men's sons to face death, wounds and disillusion. These men who are too poor and cannot afford to be hidden by their fathers... the poor whites... and the red, black and yellow... They are the ones who have to fight in this war. "Worse," he yelled, jabbing at the senator, "You send us into battle then tie our hands. Your meddling grants favor to the enemy. Your truces get us maimed and killed." The anger of Vietnam, the senators, the college campuses welled up. "Put your sons in the front lines like our chiefs did and we won't have any more wars!"

"Then you reject our 'civilized' world with its special privileges?" the senator asked with a smirking smile.

"I definitely reject it," Charging Shield shot back.

"You wish for the past," the tribunal called out.

"How about it, Warrior?" the senator interrupted rudely.

Charging Shield's anger made him ignore the tribunal's question. He jerked his *wotai* out from its pouch. He held out the stone, pointing a beam of light on the politician. "A proud warrior - you misguided turncoat. A warrior, a mystic warrior of the past..." He held the stone higher. "My people's way protected me in your war. And when I returned, my people gave me honor. Because I fought for my country and was not afraid, I was allowed to pierce in my first Sun Dance."

"You call that an honor?" the senator sneered. "You are the one who is misguided..." The senator continued to speak, but a whirlwind boiled out from the stone, drowning out the politician's words and driving him from the room.

"How about your sons, Senator? What graduate school, what college, where are you hiding them?" Charging Shield yelled vehemently after the fleeing figure. In the background, an acknowledging refrain in Lakota came from the two figures that had stood silently. "*Wahste aloh* (real good)."

"Charging Shield, enough of the *washichu*'s war," the tribunal admonished. "Do you wish for the past?"

"My mate and the freedom of the Natural Way," he proclaimed.

Fools Crow spoke, "The past for two-legged can no longer be brought to this time. Only the winged, the four legged and the finned can taste the past, because for them there is no change. On the mountain, did you not sweep away with the eagle and your mate?"

"Yes, Grandpa," he addressed Fools Crow.

"Then know this. The eagle's freedom is highest."

"But my mate?"

"The eagle's freedom is highest," the chorus echoed into stillness. The walls closed in and he was back alone in the darkened room.

He had slept for several hours when his sister woke him. A card table brimming with food was set outside. He was hungry; the table was tempting but his dream overpowered the tantalizing food. He hadn't pierced for this Sun Dance and he had taken the vow. He turned toward the dirt road that led to the highway.

"Where you going?" asked his mother.

He made a motion toward the graying sky to the west. "A storm could come up," he alibied. "I should check my plane," he said over his shoulder before he disappeared behind two camper trailers. He spied Sonny Larvee's tent and headed straight for it. Off to his right, he noticed a cluster of tents. Several red headbands caught his attention. He recognized one of the wearers, returning a casual wave to Horn Chips.

"The line was really long today. The people are always so happy to shake our hands. I thought my legs would give out. It gets longer every year," Sonny spoke from a slouched, sitting position beside his canvas Army tent. His heavy frame was tired and spent like his speech. His wife placed two coffee cups between them when Charging Shield asked about the piercing.

The Oglala sat back to sip his coffee. "There wasn't anything we could do. It was all set up last winter. They elected a new Sun Dance committee and the missionaries saw to it that it was stacked with their own kind. We didn't know this would be the last day until this morning. The committee told Fools Crow they made a ruling and Buchwald would say Mass tomorrow instead. You know the holy men, they been pushed around so much and you were not here to speak up like you know how to do." Sonny picked up a handful of dust. "Enos, the Tribal Chairman, is in Washington and Bill Eagle Feather was gone too. This gave the Sun Dance Committee and the priest more courage." The powdered alkali sifted through his fingers bringing a dejected look. "You can't blame anyone, Cousin. That church has got too much organization. Too much power," Sonny said dejectedly as he watched a pair of blocky-built Navajos wearing red headbands walk by. "And the carnival...

the rodeo... that was part of the meeting too," he said sadly. "It's all their way to bring down the Sun Dance."

Charging Shield propped his back against one of the tall tent stakes that supported the old cavalry tent. His eyes followed the Navajos. He spoke with resolve. "What we need is an organization that protects our ways. Maybe the Indian Movement could become that organization, but, right now, we're going to have to take on these missionaries by ourselves."

"You know," Sonny responded wearily, "You read in the papers, the *ha-sapas* (blacks) are sticking up for their rights. They want to go to colleges down south like anybody else and get on a bus, sitting like anybody else."

"What the hell," Charging Shield interrupted, "they're getting shot just like anybody else over in 'Nam and most of them don't have rich Daddies or politicians to get them out of the war. No reason why they shouldn't be treated equal. They're carrying more than their load in 'Nam."

"Now they even got white people helping them. We got a right to believe our own way - don't we?" Sonny finished.

Sonny's question struck a responsive chord. The advice from Father Weitz lit his eyes. "Damned right, Cousin," he answered. "Since they finally let us be citizens." He leaned forward. "Not many whites are coming forward to help us for our cause, instead they keep sending money to these missionaries. But there's a freedom of religion clause, provided by the Constitution." He thought for a moment, then spoke forcefully, "That's one thing the Sun Dance Committee is overlooking."

Sonny's puzzled expression and faltering voice lacked encouragement. He looked down at the coffee cup. "Better drink your coffee."

Charging Shield shook his head. "I can't, I might be in a Sun Dance tomorrow."

"What are you going to do, Kyle?" Sonny's worried voice was hesitant.

"Fulfill my vow tomorrow or get put in jail. I'll have to borrow your Sun Dance rope." His eyes narrowed, revealing his determination. Charging Shield reached for the tall tent stake to rise from his position and walk toward the arena.

On the way, he offered a boy several coins to deliver a message to Fools Crow's tent. He paid several more boys to run through the campgrounds to summon the people.

"Mr. Rousseau and Sun Dance Committee members please report to the announcer's booth." The call went out across the public address.

He stood beside the announcer's booth at the entrance to the arena, while the curious crowd gathered. When Fools Crow appeared, Charging Shield looked out over a portion of the campgrounds and swept an arc with his hand. "Most of you have come here to take part in the old way," he began. "Traditionally our people gathered during the circle of seasons to thank the one above for the life of our nation. We are no different than other tribes in this world. We too have customs which we follow to send up our prayers to the one above." He sensed approval from the Oglala holy man's solemn stare and spoke with renewed confidence. "We all know that four is an important part of our way. Traditionally our people gathered for four days, not three, to thank the Great Spirit. In the old days we were one people with one faith and one Sun Dance. We were like a circle, all bound together with one bond. 'The power of the hoop'. Now there are many of the white man's squares pulling us in different ways. Many of our people have gone to these different squares and we have not tried to stop them. Nowhere on this reservation have we burned the white man's books or stopped him from praying in his temples. The reason why we have not interfered is because we are Indians.

"The white man has not respected our way, however, despite the fact that he has a very important piece of paper that tells him he must treat all men equal. That piece of paper is the Federal Constitution. The Constitution is like an Indian. It says that everyone must respect the other man's vision."

"Hold it right there, Charging Shield," Rousseau, the Sun Dance Committee chairman commanded. "Our committee didn't stop your Sun Dance or anybody from praying around here and we didn't make any agreements with anyone about the Sun Dance lasting four days." His words brought a rising murmur. "Times are changing. There ain't no buffalo anymore." He halted for a moment to point toward the cottonwood tree behind his adversary. "The church is changing too. Father Buchwald... he uses the peace pipe in his Mass. He'll be standing out there tomorrow by that tree in the hot sun... and he'll be praying with a peace pipe."

"We never asked him to use our peace pipe," a woman spoke out. Charging Shield recognized Mary Bad Hand's voice.

"He's got his own place to say his Mass... And his bingo games," another voice yelled.

Rousseau studied the growing crowd nervously.

"We don't have to make our way into another religion," Mary Bad Hand stood before Rousseau and asserted, "Especially one that is so intent on destroying our beliefs."

A supportive young voice cried out, "If we put the Sun Dance in their cathedral we'd be in jail."

Charging Shield threw the committee chairman a frozen smile, lacing his words with a courtroom formality. "The Constitution protects our religious expression. My freedom of religion is being threatened by the Sun Dance Committee and one Reverend Buchwald, whom I have reason to believe is a conspirator with the committee to deny my constitutional right to practice my religion by dancing in the Sun Dance."

He paused to glance over his shoulder at the tree, "Enough of the white man's talk. I'm going through with my vow. Tomorrow I do the Sun Dance even if I have to pierce myself. I will go before the tree of life and restate my vow to the Great

Spirit. You can try to jail me but I intend to bring a lawsuit against anyone that pulls me away from that tree."

"Wait, wait, Charging Shield," called Rousseau. "Let us talk a little more. You put us in a bad position. What about Father Buchwald? He has made plans for the Mass."

"I made more preparation than he. He's got a square church that he always uses the whole year. He won't be breaking any of his traditions." Charging Shield turned to walk toward the tree. Mary Bad Hand was right behind him.

Rousseau commanded the announcer to call for the tribal police. "No, if you want them, call them yourself. My son was pierced this morning," the announcer replied.

The crowd of Indians stood silently. Their eyes shifted back and forth between the two antagonists and the committee members milling in a group offering arguments.

An old man limped toward the isolated figure at the base of the tree. Charging Shield recognized the Hunkpapa from the trip with Eagle Feather to Wakpala. The man stopped midway and turned to the crowd. "I am a Hunkpapa but I will stand beside this Oglala tomorrow when he is pierced. Get your police," he glared at Rousseau. "Get them if you want but if you put this boy in jail, you'll have to get past me." He snarled with his squinting expression, raising his walking stick defiantly.

At that moment, Catches appeared beside Fools Crow. The two men held a huddled conversation. A murmur rose among the elders standing closest to the discussion. "Topa," (Four) the older ones urged. Fools Crow turned toward the committeemen with fire in his eyes. "I will pierce him," he spoke in Sioux. "I will pierce him." He made a cutting motion across his chest. At that moment, Mary Bad Hand put her hand on Charging Shield's shoulder and issued a shrill tremolo.

The Sun Dance Committee retreated toward the announcer's stand. "They're going to call the police," someone yelled.

Rousseau pushed the announcer aside and picked up the microphone. At that moment, two men wearing red headbands vaulted across the wooden railing behind the announcer's booth. A muscular arm reached out and jerked the microphone away from the committee chairman. Rousseau stared open-mouthed at Horn Chips, the Hunkpapa, and his Chippewa companion, Leaf, before he was forcefully shoved from the booth.

Somewhere in the crowd a woman burst forth with a shrill tremolo to echo Mary Bad Hand and was joined by another. "*Hau, hau,*" cried the crowd, as they joined behind the holy man approaching the tree.

The man with the headband handed the microphone back to the announcer. "Make the announcement. There will be a Sun Dance tomorrow," Horn Chips instructed.

"A Sun Dance will be held tomorrow morning. There will be a Sun Dance and a piercing tomorrow," the announcer complied.

The committee members dispersed quickly and left the arena.

THE LONE SUNDANCER

CHAPTER TWENTY TWO

See I fill this sacred pipe with the bark of the red willow,
but before we smoke it you must see how it is made and what it means....
And because it means all this and more than any man
can understand, the pipe is holy....
— Black Elk

Later that afternoon, Fools Crow called a meeting to plan for an evening sweat lodge. Charging Shield met the Hunkpapa man with a cane on his way to Fools Crow's tipi, discovering that his name was Loon. As he drew closer to the campsite he fixed his gaze on a cluster of white men visiting with the holy man and his interpreter in the shade of the pine bough arbor. The men spoke with British accents. They offered a bundle of tobacco and presented Kate Fools Crow a blue, trade cloth shawl with knotted fringe work.

Catches joined the gathering. Charging Shield spoke with one man in particular and learned that the Englishmen had saved for several years to travel. When it came time to leave, the visitors asked if they could watch the morning ceremony. Catches conveyed their request to Fools Crow in Lakota.

Fools Crow, the Sun Dance Chief gestured his permission with a nod and a welcoming wave of his hand. "It is for all, you are welcome," he answered in Lakota and Catches interpreted the message to the visitors.

Fools Crow briefly halted their departure with a motion of his hand and spoke in Lakota to Catches. Catches pointed to one of the Englishmen. "Select one of your men and send him to the Sun Dance tipi tomorrow morning. You have come far to honor our way. You are not like the white man in this country who does not respect our ways. One of you will be allowed to stand at the Sun Dance inside the circle tomorrow and he shall pray for your country and your safe journey home. Fools Crow says to take back the fine shawl that you have presented his wife. The man you select will wear it like a sun dancer." He paused, then added, "This evening the one you choose will join us in the sweat lodge."

After they left, Charging Shield queried Catches, "Should we allow white people into our ceremonies?"

"If they respect and are not there for show or curiosity, it is not wrong," Catches answered in his usual mild manner, then continued in a cautioning tone, "These men will be tested tonight but I have a feeling they are sincere. They have come a great distance and are working men, not rich men looking for something amusing. Charging Shield, you must learn that all men are holy," Peter Catches' soft voice rose slightly to admonish him. "Not all white men wish to destroy our ways. There are good men among them as well as bad. There are also bad men among us. The good from both ways must prevail."

Toward evening, the sweat lodge was prepared for the Englishmen. Included also for the evening ceremony were Horn Chips and his Chippewa companion. Charging Shield walked to the creek bank with Horn Chips and the Chippewa to gather firewood. They started back with armloads of wood, when suddenly three vultures wheeled overhead in lowering circles. One came so close it almost brushed Horn Chips with its wing tip. The ugly birds landed beside the path on three fence posts staring at the wood carriers.

The Chippewa was the first to drop his firewood to detour around the path back to the Sun Dance grounds. Charging Shield and Horn Chips were close behind. After they told of their encounter in Fools Crow's tent, the holy man sent an alarmed summons for Catches and Gap and the Hunkpapa named Loon.

When the older men arrived, the Sun Dance Chief took his pipe to start in the direction of the three birds. Catches walked to his left, carrying a tobacco pouch. Loon and Gap trailed behind them. The rest followed at a respectful distance.

The three vultures sat watching from the fence posts, refusing to fly, as Fools Crow drew closer. Fools Crow halted, motioning for all to remain in their positions. After Catches stepped forward with the tobacco pouch, Fools Crow loaded the pipe.

The holy man aimed the pipe stem before he spoke in a guttural, unintelligible sound. A single force seemed to pivot the trio of convoluted ugly heads as they swept the onlookers spread out behind the holy man. For some long, eerie moments they stared back at the man holding the pipe then fanned their wings to lift themselves before their awe-struck audience. Their ascent was a slow spiral, low over the campgrounds before they finally flew to the north, turning to black specks as they disappeared into the Badlands.

The group returned to start the sweat lodge fire. Fools Crow and Catches were deep in thought. No questions were asked by the younger men. The grotesque image of the scavenging birds seemed to prevent any questioning of the scene from the younger participants to the holy men.

After Charging Shield had retired for the night and the sweat lodge embers had cooled to powdered ashes, a thunderstorm came late in the night, followed by lowering temperatures. It was still dark when his sister called out, "Brother, wake up. You'd better get your things together."

He was tired, but the realization of what was before him jolted him from his stupor. It was cold and the wind howled while rain pelted the trailer house.

"I've been awake for an hour, brother. I had a terrible dream. I dreamt the storm floated us to the Sun Dance grounds and everything was slick and slimy. The Sun Dance turned into a Ferris wheel and people held on as it turned around. Then it dropped everyone into a sea of mud. That was one helluva dream. I woke up and it was raining hard. I thought that dream was going to come true the way it rained."

"That's not a good dream, Sis. It's as bad as the three buzzards that we saw yesterday."

The campground was agitated by the sighting of the three birds and their abnormal manner. They were wild birds staying deep within the Badlands. Never would they come so close to human... unless it was for a reason. But the holy men had remained silent as to their meaning.

"I don't know, Sis. Maybe I shouldn't go through with this Sun Dance. Maybe I'm not supposed to."

"I don't know, Brother. It isn't good. That dream was too real for me. I'm really afraid and I'm afraid for you, but you'd better go down there and see what the holy men say. If you don't want to dance, do what you must... but go down to the lodge at least."

He reached for his trousers. The three vultures made him more afraid than any dread of the pain of piercing.

His sister sat quietly on a folding chair while he dressed. "Take my shawl," she said. "You can wrap it around your waist... if you decide to dance." She watched him fondle the buckskin pouch hanging from his neck.

"This is all I have," he answered. "Never had time to stop by Mom's."

His sister opened a compartment above the couch and handed the wooden whistle to him. "It isn't eagle bone but it's better than nothing."

He brushed the Englishman when he entered the ceremonial tipi and was surprised to see Ben Black Elk. The old man sat with Fools Crow and Catches who were listening intently to a man who had taken part in the Trading Post Sun Dance.

"It was cold. We all shivered and nearly froze in the morning. We had the Sun Dance there for three days, then the Tribal Police came and said that it was wrong to hold a dance beside a highway and by the white man's trading post. The Indian Movement and our young people were there. They wanted to fight the police. Finally they decided to pierce at Rosebud. The frost on the ground was a sign that it was not good to have two Sun Dances. That is why I am here. I pierced yesterday on the third day but I still do not feel right. I wish that I could dance here today on the fourth day beside this young man, Charging Shield."

Charging Shield gave the man a worried stare before he replied, "This may be the fourth day, but it is also the third Sun Dance. Three separate piercing days will have taken place if I pierce today. I don't know if I should go out there." He looked at Fools Crow then turned toward Black Elk. "Uncle Ben, did you hear about the three buzzards?"

"I heard, Nephew," Ben Black Elk answered. "How were the buzzards sitting and which way did they come from?"

"I don't know. They circled in on us. The three of them sat facing the same direction, to the west. Each one sat on the top of a fence post."

"They were birds of death," Black Elk muttered to no one, shaking his head disconsolately at the tent floor.

Charging Shield explained his sister's dream. "I'm afraid to go out there, Uncles. I'm afraid."

Black Elk huddled with Fools Crow and Catches. The three spoke in low tones while everyone waited quietly for their decision. The wind rippling the tent and the rain lightly pelting the covering set an ominous din over the muffled Lakota discussion.

The Englishman sat near the entrance of the tent. His expression revealed a state of bewilderment. Never in his wildest dreams could he believe that he would sit in on such a discussion, and see the son of old Nicholas Black Elk come forth at such a crucial time. The Sioux, the mystical plainsmen, masters of communication to the spirit world, yet here in the heart of Lakota country, the Oglala holy men were worried and deeply disturbed by the strange signs and spiritual warnings.

After awhile, the three men indicated they had reached a decision. They nodded their heads in unison when Fools Crow made a cutting motion across his chest. Black Elk reached for his pipe bag and brought out his father's peace pipe. "Charging Shield, do not be afraid, do the Sun Dance," he said.

Charging Shield's voice was reluctant. "I am afraid, Uncle. I am not a holy man, but there are too many signs that are bad. Even I can tell that."

"Yes, they are bad signs," Black Elk answered calmly. "They are warnings to us but you will not be harmed. We have been told our tribe should have but one Sun Dance, not three... and it must last four days... and no carnivals or rodeos should be part of it. You have nothing to be afraid of." The howling wind dampened Ben Black Elk's words.

"I can't help it, Uncle. This is one time I am truly afraid," Charging Shield spoke with a tense, fearful look.

"Nephew, I had a strong dream last winter. I'd been sick for about a week. I thought I was going to die," Black Elk paused to listen to the wind. "I saw the young people coming to the Sun Dance but the tree was covered with rattlesnakes. I got out my father's pipe and the snakes fell off the tree and crawled away. The young people came forward and danced around the tree. At the end of my dream, there was lots of them and they were all colors." The elder Oglala rocked his head slowly as he peered into the younger man's eyes. "Nephew, you must do this Sun Dance so that the tree will live."

Charging Shield stared back, mesmerized by the look of Black Elk. He was cast back briefly into his dream on his sister's couch in the trailer house. The dream of Fools Crow, Eagle Feather, Mary Bad Hand and Dr. Howard... and the two silent figures. Ben's eyes held the look of the aged seer that had stood silently with the white man in his dream. Charging Shield now knew that the figure must have been Ben's father, old Nicholas Black Elk.

"Here!" He handed Charging Shield his peace pipe. "This is the pipe of my father. It still has the tobacco inside. He called for his pipe just before he passed on. He said that the Old Way is what he really believed in. Even after the missionaries made him take a look at their way. He smoked only a little of it before he left us to enter the Spirit World. You shall carry it into the Sun Dance and nothing shall harm you."

The pipe of Black Elk; the pipe of Fools Crow's mentor who predicted the people would gather around the tree and their spirit would revive.

"Afterwards," the frail man continued, "You will be rewarded. Before the next Sun Dance, you will do what your heart wants."

Half-heartedly, Charging Shield took the pipe. Ben Black Elk was convincing but his knees wanted to unhinge, his stomach felt like it did earlier that summer after he had faced the force on the mountain. 'Maybe his mother was right. He was not a full-blood and he had been too much in the white man's world.' The force on the mountain... his confrontation flashed through him. He was a warrior, he tried to tell himself. A surge of power seemed to emanate from the sumac stem of the pipe while he tried to convince himself. The handle jolted him, scaring him into answering. "Yes, Uncle," he said obediently but his mouth was acid-dry and his forehead beaded sweat when he said it. "I will pierce. We shall have the Sun Dance."

"*Hau*! Waste-aloh!" (Yes, very good!) cried Ben Black Elk. His chest swelled with pride for a brief moment before he offered a stern warning to the gathering within the tipi. "Let this be a lesson for all. The daughter of the Great Spirit told us we must gather together for four days as a tribe in one Sun Dance, not two or three. As the spirit returns, other reservations will gather around a tree, but we, as Oglalas, in this beginning time, we can have but one gathering at a sacred area selected by the holy men, not by a white man or trading post man.

He waved his hand with an encouraging flourish. "Get dressed, Charging Shield. My father's pipe is yet powerful. You have nothing to fear."

Charging Shield complied by reaching to the tent floor for his sister's shawl. At that moment, he felt nauseous. A fearful anxiety worse than the most intense of hangovers swept through him. A sharp-edged, suffocating grip reached inside his chest to throttle his lifeblood, driving him down to one knee.

His companions mistakenly reciprocated, kneeling down also, all bowing their heads, believing they were joining their comrade in prayer, all except Fools Crow. Fools Crow's eyebrows raised. Charging Shield was a mystic warrior. Mystic warriors prayed standing. They prayed straight up, to their concept of a Creator that they respected but were unafraid of.

A stinking, decaying darkness crushed in on Charging Shield. Worse, the loathsome figure on the mountain peered through the blackness of Charging Shield's void. Its power was so immense that he could no longer breathe. An excited clamoring of all of the subconscious mentors called out to him. "The *wotai*, the *wotai*," - their din becoming a mob's crescendo. Charging Shield struggled but was helpless to find the stone, even though it was hanging from his neck. His lungs were paralyzed and his body screamed out for air while the world seemed to fade away. The evil came forward ever so close, snarling its strange ancient curses.

Fools Crow leaped over a bowed figure to jerk the sack from Charging Shield's neck, snapping the leather cords. He retrieved the bare stone, crushing it to Charging Shield's chest. The holy man jabbed his knee into the dancer's back and with his free hand, grasped the underside of the dancer's throat, bringing forth a cursing, rattling rasp as he straightened Charging Shield to his feet. The holy man crushed the *wotai* deeper into Charging Shield's chest seeming to curse back in ancient words.

Charging Shield's darkness receded to gray twilight, the fearful force howling its retreat, a vicious snarling receding to pitiful yelps as though it would never return, at least to this warrior. When Charging Shield opened his eyes, Fools Crow looked at him... a yellow pair of eagle eyes. The holy man's grasp felt like a spring of mountain water to a man dying from thirst. He was the strength of the Buffalo Calf Maiden, a warbonnetted sanctity and love itself, for the briefest but strongest of moments.

Charging Shield could say nothing. Fools Crow released his grip, his widened eyes returning to their normal perspective appearance. The holy man nodded without emotion at the shawl on the tent floor.

Charging Shield attached the tightly bound sage wreaths around his wrists after he wrapped the shawl around his waist. The sage wreaths had been worn the day before by one of the dancers. A rawhide sunflower was hung from his neck while Fools Crow mended the broken pouch strap and reinserted the *wotai*. The pouch was tied to the backside of the rawhide sunflower cutout that hung from his neck. Fools Crow then handed him an eagle claw. Charging Shield tested the sharpness of the point then secured it in the wreath of sage on his wrist. He reached into his folded trousers for the wooden flute. When he blew on the whistle his face registered dissatisfaction with the tone. 'It will have to do,' he thought.

Gap placed a sage wreath on his head while Catches painted the eagle on his chest with red lipstick, drawing wavy lines down his back and on his arms. Black Elk came forward to insert two spike eagle feathers in the sage crown.

"I am ready, Uncles," he said wearily, as though his ordeal had never been. It was as though a storm had passed; a fever had broken; life would move on and the piercing of the Sun Dance an imminent storm too arduous to worry about the storm just past.

The procession began to file from the tent out into the drizzle, past the Englishman. As Charging Shield approached the exit, the Englishman spoke a word of encouragement.

The sun dancer stopped in front of the man to whom he had been speaking the night before. He noticed the eagle bone whistle hanging from the Englishman's neck. The whistle hanging from a buckskin thong mesmerized his eyes.

The English man reached behind his neck, as though he could read the sun dancer's thoughts, and untied the buckskin.

"Would you... could you use my whistle? It would be proper wouldn't it?" he spoke with a crisp air.

Charging Shield gaped dumbfounded. The inner wing bone of the eagle bore a fluted notch and was even decorated with old style, porcupine quill work.

"Please take it, old boy. You would honor us. Please..." the Englishman held out the whistle.

Charging Shield removed his wooden whistle to exchange. He was too perplexed to speak. He turned and walked silently toward the pitiful procession that was forming outside the tent. 'Where in the hell would an Englishman get an eagle bone whistle?' he asked himself.

Gap carried the buffalo skull at the head of the procession. Behind Gap, Catches and Fools Crow were paired. Charging Shield, the Hunkpapa named Loon and the Englishman were then placed in single file. Mary Bad Hand, Mary Pat Swift Hawk and Julie Bug followed the men sun dancers. Kibbe Ghost, an awkward young girl from Standing Rock, carried a braided, circular sage wreath and marched with Fools Crow beside the line of dancers.

As they made their way to the dance grounds, Charging Shield held the Black Elk pipe and noted that the designs were similar to those on Fools Crow's and Eagle Feather's pipe stems. The dancers waited outside the arena to allow the young girl to make her solitary walk clockwise around the sacred tree. The cold drizzle blew across Charging Shield's bare chest, adding to his apprehension. Never had such bleak weather been at the Sun Dance. The presence of Fools Crow and Ben Black Elk strengthened him, but the blowing wind and gray skies appeared far more powerful.

Surrounding a rawhide drum on the opposite side of the arena, the chanting singers began the opening song of the Buffalo Calf Maiden when the Standing Rock girl circled the tree holding forth Fools Crow's pipe. "Have courage, Nephew. My Father's spirit will be with us today," Ben Black Elk encouraged as he left the procession to join the singers.

When Black Elk was seated beside the drum, a rapid beat signaled the procession to proceed. As if from some supernatural cue, the wind stopped blowing and the drizzle ceased. Before the participants had taken the first recess, the weather was comfortably cool and not a breeze stirred. Charging Shield was no longer afraid as he cradled the pipe. Loon stood beside him throughout the morning - proud and defiant; waving his cane occasionally.

Cars and pickups continued to turn from the highway onto the damp road leading to the Sun Dance grounds. The surging crowd lined the entire arena, growing to three and four deep beneath the shade offered by the circular bower. Word had spread like wildfire throughout the reservation and to the Indian communities within the border towns and beyond. There would be a Sun Dance on the fourth day and a piercing.

An innate stirring had been kindled, the smoldering ember from the flame that, were history to predict, would have been extinguished but a century past, yet the ember refused to die. Now it reached out beyond the unfaltering traditionals, touching that deep subconscious circuit of the ancestral lineage, drawing them back as clan, lodge, band and tribal being. Yes, once again, they would cycle back together to petition the Beginning of All Creation; satisfying, meditating, finding - reliving centuries-old concepts; honed, sifted and spawned from their lineage. Concepts born out of the soil and the natural revelation of which they were still privileged to be a part; cultural ties so deep that for many, they could not be dispensed with. They looked on, saturating themselves with that living past which allowed them to pray with reverence to the same God, Force, Power, Mystery that most earthlings worshipped. At the end of the day the circle would release, some would even be seated in white men's services in the following weeks, but this day would live on in their memories for a lifetime, and they would recognize a Creator with a calm dignity that offered few avenues for disharmony.

The Oglala community was a ghost town, yet Reverend Paul Buchwald doggedly served the first of three Masses to a sprinkling of government employees and a handful of Indians within the wood framed church, close to the crossroads where the highway turned west to the Black Hills. Most of the Indians were anxious for the priest to conclude the Mass, for then they too, could steal away to the Sun Dance. The sharp featured priest lacked his characteristic energy. He was unusually listless, performing the Mass with the lifeless mannerisms of a rejected lover. The evening before and even that morning he had been reprimanded; harshly ordered by the Father Superior to remain away from the Sun Dance.

Out at the mission, behind his desk, the Father Superior was troubled. Father Weitz had warned that the Indian Movement would be at the Sun Dance in numbers.

'He couldn't risk a confrontation brought on by his parish priest,' he cautioned. 'Enough alienation had already poisoned the air, running the risk of retaliation or demonstration from the Indian Movement would be disastrous. The councilmen were worried, some had changed course overnight, even planning to attend the morning ceremony brought on by that ex-marine, whatever his name was. The councilmen would demonstrate their traditional colors, if not for religious reasons at least for political survival. The ex-marine... Paul, always claimed he was a militant. No doubt he was. No man would dare take on the whole reservation single-handed if he didn't have backing of some sort.' The old priest chuckled to himself. 'Yes, he had seen through it all; some day in the retirement community, when all this died down, he would tell them how he himself had foiled them all, seen through their scheme.' He may never have been as zealous as Paul, nor have the background of Weitz, but he was no fool. 'No, far from a fool,' he laughed exuberantly. He would admit he never stood out, but when it came to situations as this day would see, 'Well,' and his chest puffed, 'Yes, it was a damned lucky stroke for the Jesuit Order, that he had kept Paul in check and that he, the Father Superior, was at the helm. He could see through it all. That ex-marine was smart, you could give him credit for that; a front man, pure and simple, a front man for the Indian Movement. How else could they have such success?'

'Was the Indian Movement backed by Communists? That Protestant Council of Churches was giving them money and anyone with an ounce of brains knew who was behind them. The ex-marine, the fighter pilot in far away Vietnam. Ha! You never know where he went on his R and R's. Why would a man come back to this God-forsaken place when he didn't have to? There had to be something in it for him! Sure, I'll admit I'm concerned, damned concerned. Hell! I'm driven by that retirement fund and don't kid yourself. That washed-up pilot is expecting a lot more from this old world than being stuck in the chest every year. Smooth, yes, they are smooth, that Indian Movement, this front man, the whole lot of them. Why, hell, they're all nothing but a bunch of goddamned communists! Poor Paul, he'll never beat them with his religious threats, not anymore. He's as superstitious as those old medicine men, Fools Crow and that oversized bear, Crow Feathers, or whatever his name is. And Jim Weitz, I'll admit I have to respect him. In time he could see through it all too, these facades, the whole damned world is a facade. He's still naive and could get taken in by these communists, but he'll find out if he has the sense to learn from a man like me.'

The old priest breathed an uneasy sigh of relief. 'No, I'll be gone,' he told himself as he rejected the thought. 'Weitz will have to learn like I did.' His face soured with a look of chagrin. A cold, distant expression crossed over. 'He'll lose that liberal streak, he's smart enough, give him time.' His confidence and exuberance welled up to overflowing. The dam of hopes, dreams, failures, frustrations, isolation and all began to spill over into the shallow contentment of his reserve. A lifetime of emptiness flooded forth, pressuring, forcing, and then finally breaking the containment of a decayed and worn resolve.

The thought of the Indian Movement chilled him with a fearful anxiety. 'Zealots, like Paul, except at opposite ends. Worse, they were beyond the control of the mission. Jobs, politics and religious persuasion; they were immune. No religious fear, he desperately admitted, for he was groping for some sort of measure, but he knew nothing from the past would have any effect on the young militants. 'What was it that had turned this world so topsy-turvy?' the old priest asked himself. 'Colored and Negroes, demanding to be called black; Vietnam, demonstrations more radical each day on the six o'clock news; the campus sit-ins, protests, marches, draft card burning. God help us. Priests and nuns forsaking their sacred vows, leaving the seminaries and the convents, getting married, marrying each other! Who will look after us in the retirement homes?' He shook his head. 'And now this mixed up world has even reached out to this desolate reservation. Was there really such a thing as the Indian Spirit... or was it the Indian Movement? No, it was the times. Yes,' he consoled himself, 'Even this isolated reservation was swept up in the times.'

He looked at his watch and rose from his desk to start for the mess hall. He would breakfast with Weitz, then they would journey to West River for a meeting with the Bishop. An article from a magazine sent to him by a contemporary caught his eye. The article extolled the Indian Movement's exposure of corruption in the Bureau of Indian Affairs. His hands shook. The article was ironically lying on the latest compilation of mission land holdings, lease rental income and cattle sales. He clawed at the article, balling it up for the wastebasket. His jaw shot out. 'No, this mission was too lucrative to let a bunch of radicals destroy it! Thank God for Weitz,' his hand reached up to rub away the worried creases of his brow. 'The man could keep the Indian Movement at bay. At least for the time being.'

Before mid-day, it was the time for the piercing. Few pipes were offered, allowing the dance to proceed at a faster pace. The sun refused to shine on the event and the gray skies remained, although the temperature had warmed. No breeze stirred. The pipe of old Black Elk was presented but not lit, due to respect for the departed holy man. Nevertheless, it was passed around to the singers and the drummers who touched it in respect. When the pipe was returned to Charging Shield, he placed it on the buffalo skull pipe rack, pointing the stem upward and westward. "Thank you, old prophet," he spoke as he looked down on the pipe. "Your wisdom has helped keep our sacred tree alive." When he turned to face Fools Crow, he was led to the base of the tree.

He handed the eagle claw to Fools Crow as he took his place on the sage spread on the ground. Fools Crow bent over him with the sharp steel awl and made only one slit in his chest about a quarter of an inch long. Charging Shield stared at the light gray skies. The rawhide cutout of the buffalo tied to the tree's upper branches

LONE SUN DANCER

turned slowly. The rawhide man suspended above the buffalo also turned slowly. The cut pained but he concentrated on the turning buffalo and rawhide man, and he felt less apprehensive than the year before. Fools Crow pushed the eagle claw into the cut, and the pain knifed its way through his concentration, for it was a searing fire, spreading, tearing, erupting as the claw was pushed harder; in and back out again through the skin of his chest. Such grabbing, twisting, flashing pain! Fools Crow tied the claw to his borrowed rope with a buckskin thong, then Gap and Loon helped him to his feet.

Loon and Mary Bad Hand danced beside him as he moved into position away from the tree. Charging Shield held the rawhide above the incision to lessen the weight of the rope. He reached the end and slowly eased the rope's weight onto the throbbing pain.

"*Wahste* (wah-steay), *Wichasta. Lela wahste!* " cried the old man beside him. (Good, Warrior. Very good!)

"I'm proud of you, brother," Mary Bad Hand encouraged.

Four times he danced inward to touch the tree and at last he was free to break. "Tankashilah Ounchi," he called out as he looked toward the sky. "Let our spirit return. Let our ways come back, Grandfather/Grandmother." He felt more comfortable with a broad reference to gender in reference to the Creator. His eyes were drawn toward Black Elk's pipe leaning against the buffalo skull. An aura seemed to grow around all of the pipes resting with their stems pointed skyward. For a brief moment, he felt reassured that his prayer was answered. He also had the feeling he wouldn't have to Sun Dance anymore. Refreshing rest came over him as though it was a prelude to something better. He danced backward to break his bond with his true mother.

His skin was drawn outward and the rawhide rope also stretched, as he pulled away from the center of the nation. He leaned further away. When his full weight was on the rope, the eagle claw cut cleanly through the piercing. The chugging sound of an engine, Karen's laughter, the fall green meadow, grandmother's cabin... all flashed as the talon shot across the arena, propelled by the stretched rawhide to land beside the Englishman.

Charging Shield danced back into position still blowing the eagle bone whistle. The final song was sung. Fools Crow returned the peace pipes to the dancers before they were placed in a line to receive the handshakes and warm embraces of the people. The dance had lasted four days.

CANNON RIVER

CHAPTER TWENTY THREE

You may go
on the warpath.
When your name I hear
having done something brave.
Then I will marry you.
— Sioux Song

The figure clad in a bathing suit, stood on the beach, her feet implanted in the warm sand. Above her, almost within reach, a number of seagulls swirled lazily about, looking like brilliant alabaster porcelain figures come alive. She clasped a crystal attached to a fine silver chain, 'Oh, you winged beauties,' she thought, 'soaring and diving, feathers flared, wingtips extended into the wind as you move effortlessly on the currents... scanning the seascape, calling to lovers... forever one with the sea and sky. I feel your spirit reaching out to me. I can almost touch you. As a child I dreamed of flying... I know there is a part of me that lives in the sky and can fly. I think you feel that kinship with me too."

Their wings teased at her fingertips. Their calls spoke of freedom, the freedom of the wind. "Come fly with us," they seemed to say. "We'll feel the misty spray of the sea as we ride ever so close to the waves, tasting the power of the sea. Set your spirit free and come fly with us... come fly with us."

She reclined on the sand. Gently they settled close, speaking in whispers about the magic of the sky. Their cooing sounds echoed into words of promise, speaking as if they were one voice. "You will converse like us someday. You will be feathered and winged and have a fine, handsome mate." The drumming sounds of the sea pounding against the shoreline, the penetrating sunshine, and the feel of the warm sand lulled her into a dreamy trance.

'A new vision... but is it really new?' Something inside told her what could be; maybe a long forgotten dream had finally surfaced, reminding her that no matter where she traveled, no matter what she 'thought' she knew, in the end the heart is the ruler...

Unbounded joy exploded in her heart as she recalled Kyle's words. A deep sense of knowing she had no need to explain, calmly spread. In that moment, she understood clearly that in their short time together, he had opened a door and shown her something very dear and lovely that she was sure she didn't want to be without.

Love is an elusive thing she had decided. Her heart told her one thing and her head spoke to her differently. She had written him a letter, telling him of the new airline she was flying for and her new address; and another letter, but they had brought her nothing but disappointment.

"Those who are whole make no demands." Where had she heard that? 'I am whole, and I will ask him for nothing,' she told herself. 'I must fall back on my reserve, my own inner strength. Oh, but I only want for him to know that I will always carry him in my heart, and in the end the heart is the ruler. A part of me is with him now and I will not leave him.'

'Those who are whole make no demands. You know where you've been. You are now traveling with a new vision.' She rose from the sand with her back to the sea. 'Those who are whole...' kept echoing. Firmly, she resolved she would trust and depend upon that inner strength that had managed to carry her through the normal ups and downs of life.

Yes, she would fall back upon her reserve, that fierce independence instilled in her from childhood. She had loving, caring parents who had given her a stable background which helped her remain strong, single and independent. However, since his leaving, she felt confused about that independence. 'How can a person I hardly know have such impact and importance in my thoughts, in my life?'

She had been raised in the foothills of an eastern mountain chain not far from a lovely place called New River. Her outdoorsman father had given her a deep appreciation for the beauty of nature. When Kyle told her of his childhood enchantment with the waters of Rapid Creek, she understood well the intrinsic memories only a natural playground could impart.

Water does convey a powerful spirituality. The sweat lodge is a spiritual cleansing, a purification. She had known about the sweat lodge, but Kyle never talked about it much. His focus was the Sun Dance. The Sun Dance was the fire element coupled with the earth - Mother Earth. The dancers went out before the sun, its powerful energy burning down upon them. They in turn were attached to Mother Earth - their spiritual umbilical. Karen had the depth to perceive that. Their spiritual life had to be reborn. Their Sun Dance tree had to come back. It was a powerful symbol, and it was his mission.

"There are no accidents. For those who seek, the forces are working and we are always in the place we should be," she found herself saying aloud.

She felt tempted to put it all aside. But there was a nagging within... something that seemed incomplete. What was it she had thought so profound? Ah yes, the fire and the earth. Fire and Earth signs. It began to click.

'Fire, Earth, Water and...' her mind searched for the fourth. 'Fire, Earth, Water...' The seagulls circled above her. 'The atmosphere, the oxygen... of course, Air! Fire, Earth, Water and Air. There they were, the four elements. The Sun Dance is fire and earth. The return of the Indian Spirit.'

Her thoughts continued, seemingly led by unseen forces. Whatever was talking to her was leading her by the hand. 'Therefore, and I hate to be scientific about this, that leaves water and air.'

'Okay, but my intuitive brain, my intuitive self must solve this little mystery.' She felt smugly elated that she could throw out science, especially its non-spirituality, in total. 'Where was I before my ego got me off track? Ah yes, water and air. The Sun Dance... Fire down to Mother Earth. The tree springs forth. The Indian Spirit is reborn. What's that, but a natural spirit springing forth, nurtured by natural living peoples. Nature is the reflection of that Ultimate Power that, after all, created it. That power is much more present in nature than in concrete and steel. The nature people lived for centuries with nature, speaking and beseeching to It through their nature-based ceremonies: the Sun Dance, the Vision Quest, the *Yuwipi*, the Sweat Lodge and the pipe ceremonies.'

'... The sweat lodge and the pipe. There it is... water and air. The sweat lodge is water, the pipe is air.'

'The Sun Dance is for the rebirth, but something is telling me... the sweat lodge and the pipe are for something that lies beyond.' A glimmer of light flashed from the crystal hanging around her neck. When she pulled the stone out from her chest, she saw colors reflecting inside the crystal. 'The rainbow!"

"Rainbows," the seagulls spoke to her again. "Someday you will be with rainbows. Water and air and the rainbow. A rainbow and a tree. A huge tree with spreading hoops like ocean waves. A rainbow and a tree. Kyle helped bring forth the Sun Dance Tree. You will help bring forth a different tree... a tree of balance and harmony. You will bring forth the Flowering Tree." The seagulls flew away.

This three day trip in Florida was to be a mini-vacation for Karen and her red-haired, green-eyed friend, Sue, who had been working overtime to get Karen's mind off Kyle Charging Shield. Sue prided her matchmaking and was dating a pilot from another airline who 'happened' to be in town with a friend who wanted to meet Karen. Arrangements had been made to have dinner at an elegant restaurant a short distance from their hotel. Karen scowled, realizing she should be at the hotel, getting ready.

The sun was just beginning to display its setting colors. When the oranges receded to red, a bit of anger began to stir and she realized she resented the whole situation. "For your own good." Sue had said. Karen scowled again. 'She used our friendship to force me into this so-called date. I resent that most of all. If she were my friend, she would understand that I really do need this time to swim and just do some relaxing on the beach. I want quiet time! I don't need some smoky restaurant filled with strangers asking all sorts of dumb questions. Hell, I don't even drink anymore!' She looked at the skyline of tall apartments and office buildings. Her alcohol consumption was fairly frugal in comparison to most of her friends. At social gatherings she wanted to avoid being branded as a prude. Now that she had developed a closer feeling for the natural world around her, she could care less what people thought and had declined alcohol totally. In her opinion, alcohol inhibited her attempt to associate her spirit closer to Nature. The skyline reminded her of the crowded bars and restaurants that were starting to fill with customers. 'When we first planned this trip, Sue was going to spend it with her pilot friend and I was going to be free to be by myself. All of these extra plans are Sue's idea, she's determined to see me dating.' The figure on the beach gathered her belongings in a waning light of red-tinged dusk. "Well, I'll go tonight to be polite, but tomorrow is mine alone," she mumbled to herself as she spun on her heels to take hurried steps, angry that she had to break the enchanting spell cast by her surroundings.

Back at the hotel, Sue was too busy planning the forthcoming social events to notice Karen was a bit sullen and withdrawn. Karen paid no attention to the excited chattering about late breakfast on the patio, shopping, tennis and Sea World. She cared less about the new Italian restaurant with outstanding Fettuccini Alfredo. Wishing for the night to end quickly, she showered and dressed in her black silk dress which gave her a rather sophisticated look, but did nothing to change her irritation with the interruption.

The restaurant was elegant as advertised. Only upper income was welcomed by the menu with no prices, a pretty good indication of how much elegance the place had. Sue's date was her usual type, overtly smooth and a New Yorker. His friend, Jason, was younger by several years and quiet. Karen admitted there really wasn't much she could criticize regarding Jason. Her observation was limited, however. Sue and her date made it difficult to enter the conversation. Karen's vacant lapses back to the beach did not help the situation. Possibly, under other circumstances, she realized, he would be more talkative and less reserved.

Sue gave Karen several eye-rolling looks that were supposed to convey wordless messages, which Karen ignored. Finally, Sue accompanied one with a kick under the table. They excused themselves to go to the powder room.

"What is your problem, Karen? I go to the trouble to get you a date, in a really nice place with a really nice fellow and you act like a toad stool... like he is diseased... and worse yet, like he isn't even here."

"Sue, you know I wanted to be able to have some time to relax and not have to be... "

"You can't keep pining away for that Indian guy, Karen. He is gone... out of your life... if he had wanted to see you again; he would have answered your letter. Have a drink... several... and forget him."

Karen nodded, wanting to agree with her friend. Consoling herself, she looked forward to a trip she had bid. One that the senior flight attendants avoided. The trip was an 'up and down' with more work than usual, but it made several stops in Dakota country and at least she could be somewhere near him.

EAGLE VISION

The campus maples were turning September gold when Charging Shield handed a college newspaper across the desk to Dr. Howard. The professor leaned forward to glance at an article captioned: 'Dr. Howard Chairs Indian Studies Director Selection Board.' Dr. Howard pushed the newspaper aside to point at his desk calendar. "Some of the holy men want to attend a conference in the Twin Cities. How'd you like to get away for a few days?" He read the student's interested look. "If you'll get some interviews for the history project, I'll cover their travel costs."

Howard circled a date with his pen. "The urban Indians are behind the conference. They're hungry for the old beliefs."

At the West River Airport, the Western 737 waited to board the Twin Cities bound passengers. Karen looked on in fascination as the stern faced, black hatted man in graying braids ascended the boarding ramp ahead of his younger companion who sported a crew cut. After she helped Eagle Feather hang a garment bag in the forward compartment, she stared at the elderly man sitting in the forward section. The hoop symbol made of porcupine quills attached to Fools Crow's black Stetson held her attention. She recalled the day at the beach when Kyle drew the four directions symbol in the sand.

After take-off, she busied herself serving the aft section. When she was finished she walked forward, choosing her words to open a conversation with the two men. Fools Crow was gazing out the window when Eagle Feather nodded politely to her smile. Her question asking their destination was countered by another nod.

"Are you from West River?" 'He'll have to answer that,' she thought.

"I'm from Rosebud," said Eagle Feather blankly. Fools Crow looked up but showed no expression on his solemn face. The silence mounted.

"Would either of you know Kyle Charging Shield?" she decided to plead directly.

The question raised an eyebrow as Eagle Feather turned to speak to Fools Crow in Lakota. The elderly holy man's eyes lit when he returned his answer to his companion.

Eagle Feather interpreted for the stewardess "He said if you are a friend of Charging Shield's, he's glad to know you." The Sichangu holy man's reserve changed to a friendly manner.

Fools Crow warmed to a smile, then laughed, speaking in his native language. Eagle Feather interpreted, "He said when he was young, he was much more handsome than Charging Shield."

The aircraft pitched slightly as she joined in the laughter.

"How do you know him?" asked Fools Crow, startling the girl because it was directed to her in precise English. "Did you meet him when he came back from war?" The question was asked as if Fools Crow already knew the answer. The dark mysterious eyes held her, flickering when she returned an affirmative nod. He studied her for a long moment before uttering a resonant "Oh huh," then held out his hand.

She grasped the wrinkled hand firmly. At that moment the intercom blared out the pilot's rough air warning. The call, "Fasten seat belts. Flight attendants return to your seats," erased her fixation. She frowned at the cancellation of their visit before offering a cordial nod, then turned toward the rear jump seat.

Fools Crow shifted to the edge of his chair to follow her movements down the aisle. He spoke to Eagle Feather bringing forth at first a surprised look, then a knowing expression. The Sichangu peered at her retreating figure then leaned closer to speak in an undertone. "I saw a vision in my last *Yuwipi*, it was like my Sun Dance vision back when Charging Shield's *wotai* hit the tree."

"Oh huh," Fools Crow uttered his acknowledgement.

"I saw Charging Shield's airplane again, this time he was over the Badlands. He had come back to the reservation with his ally."

"What color was the tail?" asked Fools Crow.

"It was a red plane but the tail turned yellow."

"*Wah ste aloh*," the Oglala's expression was serene. "That mission... he's almost through. His *wotai* could leave him soon. When the tail of his airplane turns yellow, his mission will be fulfilled," Fools Crow reflected Eagle Feather's somber look. The yellow quarter, the warm Southland. It was also the place the spirit first journeyed before it went west to the spirit world. The elder holy man nodded knowingly, "*Ohuze Wichasta*. The Mystic Warriors. Few ever get out of their mission alive." He signaled a finalizing, cutting motion with his hand toward the aft section. "His ally, she'll lead him back."

The statement prompted the aging seers to sit reflecting upon the last Sun Dance. All signs had been good and the young had risen up strong in numbers. It looked like the power of the missionaries over the traditionals would finally be broken. Black Elk had brought his father's pipe and Charging Shield had carried it. The lone sun dancer making the annual gathering last four days gave the people strong hope for the return of the Way. And the young priest, he had become a secret ally.

The Sun Dance absorbed their thoughts. Both men well knew that the ceremony's undiluted return portended a compelling statement far beyond the general welfare of their respective tribes. Fools Crow's blunt remark echoed Eagle Feather's thoughts. "Charging Shield is brave. Courage is a high badge of honor. One of the highest. But the Blue Man escaped. The warrior could not kill the Blue Man." Both men contemplated with nods backward toward the position of the stewardess.

The holy men knew the earth was in danger. In other lands people were being crowded together, animals were disappearing, even in the oceans the finned ones were being over consumed. Worse, the land was becoming scarce for forest growth and agriculture. Great cities were spreading outward. All of the religions were ignoring this, the most dangerous tragedy for the Earth Mother. They had seen much in their visions, spiritual portrayals intricately linked to the elements - to the make up of Mother Earth. Great swaths of forests that made the breathing air were being destroyed with each crossing of the sun. They needed no newscasts to tell them the earth was being over populated, the waters were being poisoned and a grave situation awaited the newly born. Not only visions, but also the spirit ceremonies had told them. The Earth was heating up! The strange weather was telling them already.

It was the Blue Man who was behind all the perils, for it was he who controlled the lives of the nations. The holy men bore looks of chagrin. They had finally realized the folly of believing in the forcefulness of warriors. Warriors would no longer succeed in bringing about the destruction of the Blue Man. The holy men had one last hope. Only a woman could kill it.

The Boeing made a steep descent as Karen adjusted her seat belt. She felt as if she had journeyed back through time. She closed her eyes. The cabin with the stream below swept through her, portraying itself against the trio of badland buttes. She shook her head, fighting the holy man's mesmerization. "Kyle," she whispered, "We're from two different worlds." The flicker in Fools Crow's eyes gave her an answer. "You're from the same world," it said. The answer came and went in a split second.

At the Twin Cities terminal the 737 taxied to the gateway. When she reached in the forward compartment for Eagle Feather's garment bag, several passengers separated her from the holy men leaving the exit. When the two men entered the terminal, Charging Shield broke away from a cluster of waiting well wishers.

Fools Crow shook Kyle's hand for a brief moment. "Wait here," he commanded. Eagle Feather gripped his shoulder, supporting the old man's order with a nod. Charging Shield looked dumbfounded as he watched the pair walk away.

"Kyle," he heard the soft voice.

He was too surprised to do anything but stare when he turned. A wilting feeling seeped through him as he repeated her name slowly. The couple stared at each other for a long moment. He reached out to take the garment bag extending his free hand into hers. At the touch of her, his words came. "I never thought... I can't believe I'd ever see you again."

"Are you still in school?"

He acknowledged but his attempt to reply was feeble.

At that moment Eagle Feather relieved him of the garment bag. "We'll see you later," the Rosebud gave him a friendly pat. He looked at the girl, then back to Charging Shield with a confident smile before turning to join his traveling companion departing down the concourse.

"Are you sure your friends won't be disappointed?" she asked with a worried motion toward Eagle Feather's retreating figure.

He shook his head from side to side before blurting, "How long will you be here?"

"We stay over and go back tomorrow."

He looked at a clock suspended from the ceiling. It was nearly noon. He let go of her hand and placed his arm around her to kiss her gently. She responded by holding him tightly. "God, it's good to see you. Let's get away for awhile," he said.

He carried her travel bag after she returned to the plane for a few minutes. "I thought I was dreaming when I saw you," he said as they walked arm in arm. "It must be Fools Crow's power." He gave her an affectionate tug as they rode the escalator to the lower level parking lot. "I don't think I'll ever let you get away anymore."

"And I suppose you'll turn me into a toad, won't you, Captain Charging Shield?" She doubled her fist pretending to strike him.

"If you try to get away, Fools Crow will," he said exaggerating an impish grin. She squeezed his hand.

He stopped for a second after they stepped from the escalator to admire her legs. "They haven't changed any, have they?"

She feigned annoyance but his words lit a warm smile.

They walked across the parking lot toward his car and soon were chattering endlessly while they drove down the freeway. He related how he had discovered his sister had received and lost her letter. He turned south through outlying suburbs away from the city. He felt suffocated within the heavy freeway traffic. He would be graduating soon. He would listen to Ernie Hale he had decided. He had scored well on his law school application test and realized someday he would have to be a part of the white man's suburbia, either that or live in West River working for Ernie. The lanes of inbound and outbound traffic momentarily pushed aside the exhilaration of Karen's return and forced him to contemplate his future. A future destitute of past adventures, he worried. A broad river carved through hilly farmland. The open space allowed him to dismiss his cares. He looked with an appreciative eye at the girl sitting next to him. He turned to a road that paralleled the wandering stream for miles, passing through sleepy towns.

"Oh look," she exclaimed at a sign advertising a canoe rental. They stopped at a park beside the river, to walk hand in hand down a path, watching a pair of canoes gliding downstream. "Let's rent one," she suggested.

He glanced at the warm fall sun, then nodded to her suggestion.

"There's a pickup point downstream," he said as he returned from the rental office with a pair of paddles. He admired her figure when she stepped from the rest room wearing a pair of shorts from her travel bag. After a few minutes, they pushed their canoe into the Cannon River. The stream narrowed, speeding them underneath a railroad bridge, then the river widened to drift them along at a leisurely pace.

The river divided itself around several islands as it lazily carried the couple. A flock of crows cawed from the river's edge before rising to the high branches of a towering elm. He placed the canoe paddle under his shoulder and aimed it. The crows cawed angrily as they flew away from the river.

"I only hope the eagle is as wise," he said.

"Maybe he's wiser. He's getting as far away as he possibly can," she answered.

"There's an old legend about the eagle, Karen. When man tries to kill the last eagle, the Great Spirit will intervene. Great Spirit will become so angry that it will have to punish man for trying to destroy one of its favorite creations." The advancing spread of the spreading metropolis came to mind. "There's fewer of them all the time. Maybe the legend will come true."

"I've heard they're coming back. There's a ban on DDT. It harms their eggs," she stated.

"I hope you're right," he retorted.

A branch from a cottonwood draped down to the water. He maneuvered the canoe, receiving a gentle brushing from the overhanging branches and fall colored leaves. "The eagle," he thought. 'It still has its freedom.' The lingering rush of suburbia and freeway traffic faded away when he pictured the majestic bird gliding over grazing buffalo and hunters riding among thundering herds. '*Hau!*' He almost exclaimed. 'The eagle was even more free than his native ancestors... or his life before, if ever there was one.'

"Kyle, do you remember when we were on the beach and you said you would like to be an eagle?"

He offered a light-hearted laugh. "I said you should be a meadow lark. I'll be an eagle and watch over you while you sing in a meadow."

She trailed her finger in the water. "And if you were an eagle," she surmised, "you'd outsmart any hunter, wouldn't you?"

"I'd have to, Beautiful, if you were around," he mused. "But you needn't worry, we'd be spirit birds." His thoughts turned suddenly, unquestionably serious. 'His Sun Dance wish.' He asked himself, 'Did she come back because of what he wished at his first Sun Dance?' He felt a heady exhilaration. 'Could he now wish for the impossible? Could he wish for the freedom of an eagle, and, of course, her also?' A stump barely projecting above the surface a few yards from the bow caught his eye. A quick rudder movement with the paddle and the canoe grazed by. The incident brought him from his reverie. 'Foolish thoughts,' he chided himself but deep within, his desire remained, demanding fulfillment. 'If he had a Sun Dance wish', he relented, 'he would wish for the freedom of the eagle.' He felt satisfied with the request, concluding he had managed to avoid being overly specific, for he had sensed too strongly the anxiety that had accompanied his wish. 'Yes, he would wish for the freedom of an eagle, and for her also.' That part, he was definite about.

Close to shore a muskrat pushed a twig upstream. As the canoe drew closer, the long-tailed animal splashed suddenly to disappear beneath the water. The couple passed a bend in the river, catching a pair of mud turtles sunning on a log, enjoying the waning rays of autumn before a long, winter's hibernation.

Charging Shield turned toward the point of an island. "Let's build a fire and let the river flow around us," he said, as he surveyed the shoreline. A log embedded in the sand offered a twisted branch to moor the canoe. They stepped ashore close to a scattered pile of fresh water clamshells, noting hand shaped raccoon prints beside the empty shells.

They strolled to a secluded spot protected by cedar trees. A red-winged blackbird perched on a willow branch, to study the couple gathering a pile of dry twigs. After the fire came to life, he threw several pieces of dry drift wood on the blaze, then savored her outstretched legs while they sat listening to the blackbird call for a mate. He placed his hand on her knee as the blackbird bobbed curiously from its swaying perch. "It's wonderful to be with you, Karen. I missed you a lot."

"I missed you too," she replied.

He leaned forward and kissed her. She took her hands from the sand to put her arms around him. He moved his lips to the softness of her neck and placed both arms around her.

"Nothing feels as good as this," she responded. "I wish today would never end. I wish we could stay here, listening to the sounds of the river, and just holding each other close."

"Close to Mother Earth," he replied before he kissed her, then pulled her closer and soon they were together on the sand.

THE LOST SIX

CHAPTER TWENTY FOUR

Several weeks before Christmas vacation a Cherokee Six rose from the Denver Airport to return five members of the debate team to the University. A professor was at the controls and had recently added an instrument rating to his pilot's license, but he was ill prepared to fly through the severe winter weather that was before them.

The pilot's last reporting was an hour out of Denver heading northeast. It was feared that the dangerous flying conditions caused the plane to crash somewhere within the rugged and sparsely populated Nebraska Sand Hills. Christmas vacation went by, and rescue units hampered by heavy snowfall gave up on the costly search, electing to wait for the spring thaw.

Kyle discussed the tragedy with Mary Bad Hand over a cup of coffee in the Student Union. "He must have gotten vertigo and crashed, Mary. I bet that airplane isn't far from its planned course if the pilot was any good at holding his heading."

"What's vertigo, Kyle?"

"It's a feeling you can get when fog, snow or rain covers up your windows. You don't know if you're upside down or not. Pilots get disoriented and don't know which way is up. Vertigo has killed a lot of civilian pilots and some military ones as well. Military planes have more sophisticated equipment, and the pilots usually have more experience. In the Phantom, if you don't like the weather, you can go over it. Light civilian planes like that Cherokee Six can't get over the big storms. Instrument flying can get pretty dangerous in small planes."

"Those kids are frozen solid out there, Kyle. I've never seen so much snow as I have this year. Makes you wonder how the holy men like Fools Crow get through the winter?"

Charging Shield's eyes lit. "Mary, you know what this school should do? They should have a *Yuwipi* ceremony down here to find those lost students. I bet Fools Crow or Bill could find them."

"Find them through the *Yuwipi*?"

"It's a fact. That ceremony has found people who drowned or were lost. A man killed his wife and buried her by Lay Creek reservoir. Fools Crow found her body and said that the man's pickup would be south, and further to the south the man would be living with a different tribe of Indians. They found his pickup in the Sand Hills south of the reservoir, and law authorities caught up with him in Oklahoma."

Mary Bad Hand shook her head. "It's a good idea, Kyle, but this school wouldn't have sense enough to use a holy man."

Charging Shield disagreed. "The attitude has changed for the better around here. Ever since that Snowman incident, Schmidt and his cronies have lost a lot of ground. Doc Howard is finally getting his say."

"He always did stick up for us 'skins'," Mary added.

*   *   *   *

A week went by. Heavy snows continued to blanket the west. Dr. Howard was sitting in the university president's office speaking into the phone. "Kyle, I want you to contact Fools Crow or Eagle Feather. Ask them if they could come and conduct the *Yuwipi* ceremony you and Mary suggested. We'll pay expenses. We want to find that airplane."

Charging Shield flipped a coin and called Fools Crow's reservation first. The police station told him the Oglala holy man and his wife, Kate had been sent airplane tickets to California by a movie star wanting a ceremony. Kyle chuckled at the information and then called the police station on the Rosebud Reservation. Real holy men seldom had telephones. Within an hour, a squad car delivered Bill to a phone.

"Nephew, I think I know why you're calling." Charging Shield was no longer amazed at the holy man's psychic abilities, and was not surprised with what the Sichangu holy man continued to say. "You want me to come down and do a *Yuwipi* for that airplane that crashed, don't you?"

"That's right, Bill. How did you know?"

"We had a sweat lodge. Grey Weasel came in. He said you'd be calling."

"Did he say anything else?"

"Yes. He said he'd like to steal this new girlfriend of yours."

"Tell him I'll tack his furry hide to a board."

Bill laughed. "I'll be down. We already got our bags packed. Bring that new girl-friend to the ceremony; that one that flies in the airplanes. She's got some power we're going to need," Bill said seriously, then chuckled. "Or are you afraid Grey Weasel will steal her from you?"

"You tell your spirit helper my girlfriend doesn't date weasels. Only eagles."

Bill laughed loudly. "So be it, my friend. We'll be heading out tomorrow morning. I'm going to bring Looking Glass. He's a good singer and his car is reliable."

Charging Shield was pleased that the holy man had asked for Karen. He had told her there was a good chance for a *Yuwipi* ceremony, and she had made some trip trades with other flight attendants to be sure she wouldn't miss the opportunity.

The next evening, Eagle Feather and his traveling companion, Looking Glass, were comfortably settled in the motel room provided by the university. Charging Shield parked his car outside of their room. Karen was with him. "We're a little early. I wonder if this place rents by the hour," he said with a devilish grin, inching his hand above her knee.

She slapped his hand lightly and giggled. "Will you stop. I'm about to meet a holy man, for crying out loud." With that she opened the car door.

Charging Shield held several aviators' maps as he knocked on the motel door. Bill had directed him to bring flight maps covering the territory from Denver to the university.

Eagle Feather took a long look at Karen when he opened the door. He shook the woman's hand warmly when Charging Shield made formal introductions.

"It's nice to see you again," Karen said to Eagle Feather. "We met on the plane a few months ago. You were traveling with Fools Crow."

"Yes, I remember it well," he answered gentlemanly. "My nephew has done well. But I hope you are strong with him. I love him like my son, but I know he can get out of hand sometimes."

Karen laughed as she glanced at Charging Shield. "Yes, I am discovering that."

The big holy man looked at Charging Shield. "I hear that Fools Crow went to Hollywood," he said with a laugh. "Casey Tibbs and Joel McCrea sent him some tickets." He paused and laughed again. "Next thing, we'll be watching Fools Crow in the movies."

Looking Glass and Karen sat on a pair of chairs, while Eagle Feather and Charging Shield spread the maps out on the bed. Charging Shield traced a line connecting Denver to the university. The holy man asked several questions about the speed of the airplane and the pilot's last report to the radar center out of Denver. He ran his fingers slowly over the traced flight line and thoughtfully studied the terrain feature symbols along each side of the line. After a careful study, he sent Charging Shield to the motel office for some tape.

EAGLE VISION

Eagle Feather sensed that Karen wanted to ask a question but was too shy to ask. "You are welcome to come to the *Yuwipi* tomorrow." His invitation answered what she was too afraid to request.

"I feel very honored to be able to attend," her eyes sparkled as she answered. "I believe there is much that your people can teach the rest of the world. Perhaps someday there won't be so much separateness among the races. I only wish there was something I could do to really make a contribution toward that."

"You shall, you shall. You are a woman, and woman is the more peaceful. When woman becomes more powerful, things will change." He held a long somber look as if mulling over seriously what he was about to say. He nodded his head in the direction of the motel office. "Charging Shield. He had a mission to do and in my opinion... he has done it. He stood up to one who was attempting to stop the return of our way." He swept his hand outward and above the girl. "Maybe you will have a mission. A very important mission... someday... maybe not right now... but in a time to come."

His words stirred her deeply. She nodded and turned to see Kyle coming through the door with the scotch tape. Eagle Feather and Charging Shield discussed dinner plans as they taped the maps together and folded them neatly on the bed.

The four of them packed into Charging Shield's car and headed toward a steak house near the motel. Charging Shield regaled them with stories about the university bureaucracy and campus life. Eagle Feather snorted, "How do they ever find time to give you an education, Nephew?"

The conversation was light and sprinkled with warm laughter as they waited for the waitress to take their orders. They laughed about the size of the steaks they would order, since Dr. Howard had informed them the university would be paying for the meal. When the waitress arrived, she directed her attention first toward Karen, who ordered a dinner salad and a baked potato. After the men's orders for T-bones and New York steaks had been placed, Eagle Feather turned toward Karen and winked. "Woman cannot get powerful if she is always dieting."

Charging Shield interjected, "Karen's a vegetarian. She doesn't eat any meat."

Karen spoke up for herself, "The white man doesn't treat his animals with respect. There is too much pain and too much waste associated with our agricultural practices. I guess this is my small way of making a contribution."

Eagle Feather nodded and thought for a moment. "Yes, perhaps you are right. If we don't respect our four-legged brothers and sisters that feed us and the growing things out of the earth, we are not acknowledging and respecting the Creator. You have given me something new to think about."

"I understand from Kyle, you do not drink alcohol. Is that true of most holy men?"

"Yes, I would say that is so," Eagle Feather answered in a mellow tone.

"And peyote, Kyle told me, real Sioux holy men do not use peyote?" her eyes directed her question at Eagle Feather.

"I said real, traditional based Sioux holy men," Charging Shield corrected.

Eagle Feather looked at Looking Glass, who sat shyly across from Karen. The singer of the *yuwipi* songs stammered for a moment under the holy man's stare. "Go ahead and tell them about peyote," the holy man encouraged.

"I... I was into peyote... it was awhile back," Melvin Looking Glass began. "I found out it was too hard on my mind. It was hard on our ministers too. That's what we called the leaders."

"Peyote is an import, like some other religions," Charging Shield added harshly. And they use the word 'ministers'. You can figure that one out for yourself."

"The peyote cactus, it doesn't grow in these parts," Looking Glass explained. "They get it from way down south, mostly in Mexico. They call themselves Native American Church but I'm glad I got away from it. The heavy users, their minds are not keen like Fools Crow and Eagle Feather here."

"Trouble is, when you say Traditional Native American Religion, white folks think we're getting hopped up on peyote," Charging Shield growled.

"We get our spirit power through 'our own juices,'" Eagle Feather added. He then held up his hand with an air of caution. "We cannot condemn the use of peyote if it is sincerely used for ceremony. If it is a people's way and they are sincerely beseeching to the Spirit World..." he shrugged his shoulders and continued. "It is not for me... but we have to be harmonic and respect each other's vision." He ended with an instructive look toward Charging Shield.

Eagle Feather looked at Karen. "You mentioned alcohol. You see, we deal with the spirits that have no use for alcohol... and, of course, they have seen the bad it has done. You must realize, the spirits of this land never had such a thing when they were two-legged. Naturally, an alcohol drinker or a peyote user would have a hard time getting them to come into ceremony. If Fools Crow or myself... if we were drinkers, our *Yuwipi* ceremony wouldn't work for us. Grey Weasel or Big Road, they would not come in and make their predictions."

"Our traditional holy men like Bill here, and Fools Crow, they keep their power through fasting and praying on the vision quest, offering their pain in the Sun Dance and cleansing their spirit in the sweat lodge," Looking Glass commented proudly. "Those are the kind of religion leaders that I want to be part of."

Karen cast a reproving eye at Kyle. "You see, Kyle, you'll have to give up drinking, if you want to become a holy man."

"I don't want to be a holy man," Charging Shield flatly stated.

"Maybe you should think about it," Eagle Feather suggested.

Charging Shield shook his head, "I want to be an eagle."

"And eagles don't drink alcohol, only clear water," Karen kicked him playfully under the table.

Charging Shield smiled, "I can't disagree with that."

Eagle Feather held his hand up to hold their attention. "Nephew, let us say, just to give an example. Let us say, you become an eagle in that next world."

"I couldn't think of anything better," Charging Shield interrupted.

The Rosebud holy man offered a confirming nod. "Then do not develop an appetite, a craving from this world... only what an eagle would have!"

Karen glowed with a knowing look.

Charging Shield was taken aback. "That's good advice, Bill. Real good advice. The more I think about it, the more I believe my beer drinking days can be numbered."

Eagle Feather added, "Some are holy men... some are holy women," he paused to look for a moment at Karen, "... and maybe, some are meant to be eagles... if they earn it. All of us. We must be careful and not let anything of this world... own us. That way we can be free when we enter the spirit world."

The following evening, Charging Shield and Karen drove Eagle Feather and Looking Glass to meet Dr. Howard at the museum. Dr. Howard had thoughtfully placed a thick rug in the middle of a room large enough to accommodate the sizable number of professors and students that were expected. Their early arrival allowed time for a tour of most of the museum. The holy man sensed something from the room adjacent to the one where the ceremony would be held. Dr. Howard opened the door of the room and turned on the light. The room was filled with long wooden boxes that contained human bones. Bill inspected a box and picked out a skull. Geographical co-ordinates and 'Arikara male' were written on the forehead. He picked up another skull marked, 'Mandan female'. He looked at the skull for a long period. Finally, he put it down. "This is not good, Nephew," he remarked when they left the room. "We'll have to make these spirit people welcome when we do the ceremony. No doubt, some of our Sioux people are in some of those boxes too."

"They should be removed from this building and given a proper burial," Karen strongly interjected. Eagle Feather nodded approvingly.

When it came time to begin the ceremony, Eagle Feather set up his altar. He emptied a coffee can of pocket-gopher dirt and mounded it to a peak with his hands, making a flat spot with the bottom of the coffee can. He drew four wavy lines on the flattened area, a face with only eyes and an open mouth for features, and a long straight line with six dots. During this time, Mary Bad Hand arrived with a string of 405 tobacco offerings in red cloths, each cloth slightly larger than a postage stamp and holding a pinch of tobacco. The full-blood woman asked Karen to help her unwind the string and outline a square boundary that would enclose Eagle Feather for the spirit calling.

After everyone invited arrived, Dr. Howard promptly locked the museum doors and took a position close to the light switch. The audience, consisting mostly of faculty members and Indian students, filled the musty room. Charging Shield tied

Eagle Feather's hands behind his back and placed the *Yuwipi* blanket over him, adjusting the quilted covering so that the eagle feather sewn onto it centered over the top of the holy man's head. Charging Shield then wrapped the braided rope seven times around Eagle Feather, starting with a noose around his neck and lowering each succeeding wrap down to the man's ankles.

With the help of Dr. Howard, Charging Shield lowered the huge holy man face first to the rug. Mary Bad Hand, holding Eagle Feather's green jade pipe, sat in the place of honor beyond the dirt altar and just outside the boundary of the tobacco offerings. Dr. Howard turned out the light. Charging Shield stumbled in the dark and groped around to find Karen. He sat down beside her, and the ceremony began.

Looking Glass boomed out the calling song, and after a few minutes the Spirit People entered in the form of blue-green lights. The dotted lights entered from the wall of the adjacent room, the room with the bones of the Indians. Rattles whirled before the audience, bringing gasps and startled expressions from some of the onlookers, most of whom were experiencing their first *Yuwipi* ceremony.

Looking Glass finished the calling song to the spirits. The electrical-appearing lights exited through the wall. Eagle Feather called for the song of Chief Gall, of the Hunkpapas. Looking Glass sang out and at the conclusion Grey Weasel, Eagle Feather's spirit helper, came forth.

"Ho, Grey Weasel is here. It is Grey Weasel. *Wahste aloh*. Welcome, cousin. Let us all pray, brothers and sisters. My friend, Grey Weasel, wants to come in to our pitiful ceremony but will test us first. Let us pray hard and show him that we wish to find those who are lost so that their families will be spared waiting any longer."

"*Hau, Hau*," everyone exclaimed. There was a period of silence while the participants prayed.

A purring sound filled the room. The patter of small feet was accompanied by the excited chattering of a weasel. Eagle Feather began to talk in Sioux to the animal, and the visitor chattered and purred as the holy man spoke. They continued to converse for a long period until finally the animal no longer chattered but purred slowly.

"Ho," Bill called out. "Let us hear once more the beginning of the Song of Gall in honor of our friend, Grey Weasel, who has delivered a message for all here to listen to."

As the song began, the audience heard a woman singing at the top of the adjacent wall. A glowing ice-colored image appeared, superimposed on the wall, roughly the size of a human head. The woman sang briefly before the image disappeared. When her song was finished, a loud crack came from the center of the floor and something slid toward the keeper of the pipe. Charging Shield felt it stop at his feet, and he jumped quickly, nearly landing in Karen's lap.

"What's wrong, Kyle?" she whispered to him.

"There was something by my feet. I think it's still there. Move over."

The song ended and Bill spoke out, "Ho, Grey Weasel has made six predictions. He says that the airplane crashed in a storm not far from a town that has two creeks with almost the same name. We should send an airplane out to look for it. A man and woman will be aboard that airplane. The deer will point to where we should go. If we fly in a line toward where the deer point and head toward the town with two creeks, we will fly over the plane, but it is pretty well covered with snow. Our plane will have to land but everyone will walk away from it. Do not be worried about sending out a plane. In the next day or two some people who are not looking for the plane will be led to it by an animal. A coyote will lead them right across the tail. One of the six bodies will be missing from the wreckage. Her seat belt came unhooked in a big spin. She was thrown out away from the others, but she will not be too far away. Her face will be upon an ice colored rock.

"Those are the six predictions. Now also, a white rock that looks like ice has entered the room. It will have these signs I spoke of and one more prediction upon it. Ho, Nephew, Charging Shield. Reach out in front of you and pick up the rock. Hold it until the final song. You are of the rock clan, and you should welcome your rock brother, not be afraid of it."

Charging Shield reached out for the rock.

"The two who will go out to look for the plane tomorrow are sitting beside this rock. It is the ice rock that holds the seven predictions."

"*Ho Hetch Etu Aloh.*" Looking Glass sang the closing song. After the lights came back on, Eagle Feather was sitting up in the center of the room. His tying ropes wrapped neatly in a ball beside the dirt altar. His blanket was folded in front of Mary Bad Hand.

Karen put her hand on Charging Shield's and leaned close. "This was incredible. Thank you so much for inviting me."

Charging Shield put his arm around her and gave her a quick squeeze. "Thanks for coming. You were meant to be here." He lifted the rock with his other hand for her to see.

She looked with awe at the stone. "This is interesting, Kyle. Here it's almost opaque, like it's cloudy - not clear like ice."

By now the rest of the audience was gathering around Karen and Kyle to get a close look at the mysterious stone. Charging Shield turned the rock over while Eagle Feather knelt beside him and pointed out the predictions. The images showed two lines like creeks coming together, a grouping of deer all pointing in the same direction, a dog-like animal looking back, the tail of an airplane, a straight line ending in six dots, and the face of a young woman with a pageboy haircut and pronounced large eye glasses. The seventh image was not discernible, not even by Eagle Feather. He remarked that it would become evident sooner or later.

The following day, Charging Shield and Karen flew the Cessna 180 from the airport beside the Missouri River to the intersection of South Loop and Middle Loop

creeks. Karen held the stone, mindlessly caressing it with her thumb as she looked out the window for signs.

"There are our deer," Charging Shield said as he directed her attention to the left of the windshield. Deer were bunched up in herds along the draws of both creeks. They all pointed toward a small cattle town. Thick fog was rolling in from southwest of the town, but Charging Shield headed on, following the direction of the deer. Karen pointed out another herd of deer along with a herd of cattle in a meadow.

"The fog is getting lower," Charging Shield remarked. "This doesn't look good." By this time, low-scattered patches dropped light rain on the windshield. Charging Shield pressed on but the lowering ceiling almost forced him to the ground.

Karen tightly gripped the stone, unaware of how nervous she had become. She gazed at the stone in her hand for a few seconds and was suddenly overcome with a sense of calm. She tilted her head back with a sigh. "This is it, Kyle."

"Huh? This is what?"

"The seventh sign. Remember when I said the rock looked cloudy? Well this fog... it's in the stone. I have a strong feeling we are right over the crash site. Fog means warmer weather. Maybe that will melt enough snow to show the airplane."

He glanced at her and smiled with agreement. Then he turned the airplane in a shallow bank to return to the university. "This fog isn't doing us any good, but it might help to melt some of that snow down there," he agreed. Weather conditions worsened. By the time they reached the Missouri River, the ceiling was almost touching the tops of the river bluffs. Charging Shield flew low, close to the water, until finally landing at the airport close by the river.

The next day, close to where Charging Shield had reversed the plane's course, two coyote hunters followed the tracks of a coyote. The animal led them to the wreckage of the Cherokee Six. The tail of the doomed plane was exposed due to the rising temperature from the fog. They reported the position and soon rescue vehicles converged on the scene.

All of Eagle Feather's predictions proved true. Before the holy man and Looking Glass returned to the reservation, Dr. Howard agreed that the bones of the Native Americans would receive a proper burial at a site to be selected, overlooking the Missouri River. Arrangements were also added for Eagle Feather to conduct the ceremony when the spring grasses grew.

BLACK ELK'S WAKE

CHAPTER TWENTY FIVE

I am a fox,
I am supposed to die.
If there is anything difficult
If there is anything dangerous,
That is for me to do!
— Song of the Tokala
The Kit Fox Warrior Society

A March thaw melted the snow on the campus below. A flock of crows banked sharply to avoid the Cessna trainer floating toward the airstrip. "Not bad," he said as they bounced down the runway. He added power to lift the small craft back into the sky and coached her while she held tightly to the controls. Around and around the plane flew to make touch and go landings on the narrow runway.

After the flying lesson, he drove to his apartment. They laughed and held hands as they ran up the stairs in a playful mood.

Her low-cut blouse brought a flash of approval when she removed her jacket. He reached for a bottle of flavored mineral water in the refrigerator, calling for a toast to her first landing while she took two glasses out of the cupboard.

She exaggerated a jaunty expression when they clicked their glasses.

A serene look crossed his face after he sipped the mineral water. He tugged to pull her closer. "They say a sun dancer always gets his wish. I don't want you to get away anymore... Not in this life or any other."

Her smile faded. The longing in his eyes matched hers as they placed their glasses on the table. When they kissed she could feel his strong legs pressing against hers.

The telephone's ring sent a frown across his face. Its annoying ring sounded several more times before he reached for it. After a few minutes' conversation, he placed the receiver down to stare blankly through the kitchen window.

"Who was that?" she asked.

"Mary Bad Hand," he answered slowly. "A friend of mine passed away. His name was Black Elk. Ben Black Elk. They're going to have his wake tomorrow." His eyes wandered across the living room, settling on a sage wreath. Beneath the wreath, on a table, his peace pipe was enclosed within a red cloth sack inside a deerskin medicine pouch along with his *wotai* stone. "He was in the Sun Dance this summer. I carried his father's pipe. It had a lot of power." Charging Shield hesitated. His mind reached back to Ben Black Elk's cabin. 'Black Elk's pipe, Ben's encouragement,' he thought. "It seems so long ago," he said after a lengthy pause.

She waited for a moment to allow him further reflection. "I'm sorry," she offered. "Will you go home to the funeral?"

"I should, but it's clear across the state," his voice sounded troubled.

"Maybe you should go back," she suggested.

He nodded his agreement then shook his head. "Tests are coming soon," he offered for an excuse. "Besides, what would I do with you?"

"I'd go with you," she answered calmly, bringing her index finger to her chin. "If... it wouldn't bother you," she quickly added in a qualifying tone.

"No, not anymore." He looked at her squarely. "You're not the reason I don't care to go to Black Elk's wake." Her eyes held him as he spoke, making him realize that Black Elk was as much a part of the circle as anyone. The circle, this lifetime, had ended for the knowledgeable man, no more - no less, and all things pertaining to life had their endings... yet the circle never completely ended. The *Yuwipi*... did he not hear Big Road, Good Road, Chips and even Ben Black Elk's father... did they not return in spirit? Black Elk's circle would not end, not unless *Wakan Tanka* would end all things. He was glad he was an Indian, for he could believe death was only temporary... and if it was temporary, there was less remorse. The foreboding look that stole for an instant across her features gave him a perplexed expression.

"All right... Whatever." she answered delicately, but he had caught that look, a knowing look, one that hinted strongly it could read his thoughts.

He reached for his glass and drained most of its contents with one swallow. The mineral water seemed to calm his unsettled mood. He had stopped drinking alcohol ever since the supper with Eagle Feather. The holy man had left him with some powerful words. 'Let us say, you become an eagle... develop an appetite... only what an eagle would have'. Mary Bad Hand had heartily approved his newfound conviction. Mary had credited a goodly portion of his mellowing change to his girlfriend, re-entering his life. The two women had become close friends.

The telephone rang again. This time it was his sister, Mildred, informing him of the same news. After a short conversation he left the phone off the hook and strolled toward the couch. Karen joined him. Both placed their glasses on a coffee table. Her skirt pulled above her knees when they sat. He reached across to touch her warm thigh. It was invitingly soft. She put her arms around him to kiss each other. Their breathing came deeper as they caressed. He kissed her at the base of her neck, moving his lips toward her breasts, after he untied the drawstring of her blouse. He cupped his hand around her breast and continued to caress her. After he reached to unhook her bra, he pushed her blouse from her shoulders to savor her firm breasts. 'They're beautiful' he thought, as he pushed the loose blouse down to expose them fully. He cupped her breast in the palm of his hand, then leaned forward to kiss the nipple. He kissed it, rolling his tongue hungrily when he put his mouth over it. Her soft sigh brought his hand above her knee, moving slowly upward and inward, finally stopping where she was warm and wet.

She moaned as he touched her. He bent forward to kiss her thighs, then rose from the couch to carry her to the bedroom.

She was curled beside him when he woke the next morning. He stole an admiring look at her breasts while she slept, arousing his desire.

She stirred in her slumber, her arms reaching out to pull him closer. Her eyes slowly focused, as she put her head to his shoulder with a smile. "I dreamed we were still apart. I'm glad it was just a dream."

He didn't answer but kissed her lips.

She responded, burrowing closer to him.

He caressed her warm buttocks and pressed her against his thigh. He rose up on an elbow and drew light circles that gradually diminished downward, halting beneath her when he kissed the nipple of her breast. He sucked the luxuriant nipple, then parted her moist softness with his fingertip. Her tongue touched his when he left her breast. Their kisses grew passionately until both responded to each other, almost simultaneously. His fulfillment came first although he had wanted to prolong it. He clenched his teeth hard to continue until she cried out loudly when she reached the height of her passion.

They lay side by side staring at each other. She projected a contented glow, her state of excruciating bliss softly ebbing like the quiet magnitude of a receding tide.

They reached out to hold each other in a long embrace. Her breasts and soft thighs nestling against him rekindled his yearning. His knee rose between hers, spreading the wet parting of her enticing legs. After awhile, they made love again as passionately as before. Again, she climaxed, this time longer and before him. When he culminated his desire, he fell into the pillow with an exhausted gasp, savoring their moments as he drifted away.

He was breathing heavily when she jostled him. She was speaking when he woke. "Kyle, I have something to ask."

A tired frown formed.

"I want to go to Black Elk's wake." She was resting on her elbow, half-sitting in bed looking down. Her words were firm; her mouth set. "Would you go? For me?" her eyes drilled through him.

He erased his frown, kissing her gently. He threw the covers back to look at her tantalizing figure knowing it would help dissipate the restful sanctuary he was about to leave. He didn't want to go, but this time he wouldn't disappoint her.

The morning sun offered a calm radiance through the winter haze as they drove away from the campus. Noontime found them in a town overlooking the wide Missouri. After lunch they refueled the car to continue westward. A coiled rattlesnake looked out at them from a billboard advertising a tourist attraction as they ascended the rolling slopes, taking them away from the river. He slowed the car for an approaching curve.

"I've heard the Black Hills were considered sacred. Why is that?" she asked.

"My people say there's all kinds of signs. There's a mountain called Thunder Being Mountain. That's where the thunderstorms are formed. The warm springs and all the different caves are signs that the mountains are a special place. Some caves have crystals and one even has wind that comes out of it. A lot of the rocks have many symbols."

He searched his mind trying to recall the buckskin pouch containing the stone. Eagle Feather's words echoed, 'After awhile it might leave you. Then you can go on... where you want to go.' He absentmindedly toyed with his shirt button as he tried to remember when he had last seen the *wotai*. He remembered taking the stone from his peace pipe bag and placing it in his shirt pocket.

When they reached the top of the river bluffs, she scanned the open range before inquiring about the Sun Dance grounds. She agreed when he explained there wasn't much to see until the circle came to life with people. "Maybe when I see it for the first time, it should be for real," she stated.

After awhile, the Black Hills appeared in the distance. The horizon seemed to grow and expand as they drew closer to the mountain range. A Chinook bid them welcome. Before they reached West River, he turned onto the airport road. He explained that his sister had mentioned that his friend, Ernie Hale, had wanted to see him. "We'll stop by the airport. Ernie owns a flying service," he added.

"Goddamn, Kid, I've been trying to get a hold of you," Ernie yelled as they walked up the sidewalk. "Your sis said you might be out this way. I was hopin' you'd stop in; we got a big political pow wow tonight. Your brother's doin' a good job bein' Alderman and you an' your war background didn't hurt him any." The businessman moaned when Charging Shield turned down his invitation.

"Geesus Chrrisst, where in the hell did you find her?" the heavy man whispered after Karen excused herself to go to the rest room. "Man, she's a looker. What she do, go to school down there?"

Ernie settled in his chair, shaking his head at Charging Shield's answer. "You ain't got it too bad, Kid. Damn them sassy ass flight attendants, they never gave me the time of day."

Charging Shield bent closely to whisper softly in Ernie's ear, "That's because you're from West River, Ernie and you're the only Jew in the whole goddamn wide world that sounds like a good ol' boy!" he leaped back holding his sides, laughing helplessly.

The figure in the chair towered up like a wounded bear, snarling. "Good ol' boy? Where in the hell did you come up with that?" Ernie moaned. "Goddamnit, I never was around my own kind, you know that!" For a moment the big man was genuinely angry but his friend laughing hysterically on the floor made him turn to hide a smile.

He held a frown when he reached inside a cigar box on his desk and sat back down. "You should know better than to joke like that. Ol' Ernie's the best goddamn friend you'll ever find in this state." He took his cigar and waved it threateningly at the still grinning figure rising from the floor. "The last thing I want to be is one of them goddamned, racist, good ol' boys. Them bastards made my life miserable when I was a limping little Jew boy."

Charging Shield was startled back to reality. "I didn't say you was one, I just said you sounded like one," he threw his hands up in mock surrender but he began to worry he may have seriously offended his friend's feelings. He stood up and put his arm around Ernie.

The big man melted like warmed butter. He placed his cigar in an ashtray. "I want to keep your name on my payroll. You going to work for me next summer, ain't yah?" Ernie continued without allowing an answer. "These minority programs... bein' Indian might help me get some government charter flights." He leaned forward to look down the hall, then turned to offer a mischievous wink. "We'd be takin' a few trips out to them Twin Cities, too. Old Ernie would show you a few spots." The telephone on his desk interrupted his conversation for several minutes. When he placed the receiver down, he turned to admire the girl in the hallway. "C'mon you two," he said in a festive spirit. "I got something to show off."

The couple followed the overweight man to a side door of an adjacent hangar. Charging Shield recognized the red Grumman Ag Cat sitting back on its tail wheel, pointing its nose toward the sliding doors.

"There it is, kid," Ernie waved at the biplane. "She's all mine now." Ernie's shoulders raised as he marched toward the aircraft. "Cost me a bundle to fix her the way I wanted," he boasted. "Had to fly her down to Texas to get that engine in her. They just flew her in last week."

Charging Shield studied the bulky radial engine projecting a three bladed propeller. It was the same military engine on the T-28 trainer he had flown in flight school. He stared at the rounded canopy enclosing the polished cockpit. He admired the red fuselage from its three bladed propeller back to the black and white checkered tail. "Looks familiar Ernie," he said as he pointed to the engine.

Ernie laughed. "I knew you'd be familiar with it. Lots a power there for you kid!" What'd you do, make a two-seater out of it?"

"Side by side, kid. I had my boys jazz her up. If we take out the back hopper room, we'll put a bar in there too. If I'd known your girl was so pretty, we'd put a jump seat in back... She could serve us drinks and coffee."

Charging Shield's hands caressed the cowls on the oversized radial engine while the man was speaking. He looked fondly at the heavy acrobatic struts between the wings like most Marines would admire a pinup in a magazine. 'Red, white and black,' he noted. "We'll have to get some yellow paint on her, Ernie. Red, white, black and yellow." he called out. 'Black Elk's colors, Bill's and Fools Crow's,' he thought before realizing Ernie Hale had no idea what they meant or stood for.

Ernie Hale was too excited to care what Kyle wanted to add to the painting of the machine. "What ever you want, Kid." he responded. The big man tapped his fist against the fuselage with an exuberant yell. "She'll get out and roar!" He walked toward the wall to press a switch box that opened the hangar doors. "Why don't you take her up, do some acrabatics', give you a taste of what you can be doin' next summer." Ernie looked upward. "Hell, we'll even do an air show or two - come this summer!"

Charging Shield felt his pulse quicken as he watched the rolling hangar doors bathe the red wings in bright sunlight. He looked at his watch with a pained grimace. "I'm tempted but I have to get down to the reservation, one of our holy men died. They're having his wake."

"They ain't holdin' a war dance in the middle of that reservation runway. Hell, take this bird down."

"You serious, Ernie?"

"You'll be flying this thing sooner or later," Ernie motioned toward the plane. "G'wan, get in that bird. You ain't afraid of it, are yah?" he taunted.

Charging Shield's eyes darted from the plane out to the open sky with frustrated anticipation. "Some other time," he said politely. "I'd take too much of your time checking out."

Ernie threw his head back and laughed. "I ain't flown it yet. We just got her out of the shop. God damn Kyle, I never thought I'd see the day a fighter pilot I taught to fly would be afraid of a Grumman pussycat."

Charging Shield reflected for a moment on his first solo in a fighter-bomber, a supersonic jet fighter with only one set of controls. He nodded his head to Ernie's challenge. "I'll give her some slow flight and some touch and goes, then I'll pick up Karen."

"Oh no, you don't," Karen bristled. "I'm going with you." She gave him a defiant scowl. "We do everything together from now on; isn't that right?"

Charging Shield closed his eyes for a second to manage a weak nod.

Hale regarded the couple with an amused expression. "You've made my day, kid!" he yelled out with childish delight. "You're my first choice for soloing this baby. After that wake, you get back and we'll get you started in politics."

Charging Shield couldn't break his friend's exuberant mood. "Okay Ernie. I'll be back this evening and go to your political rally. My brother is a horse's ass for making fun of my traditional beliefs but for you and this red, beautiful baby that can belch and roar, I'll do anything." He laughed confidently and held out a thumbs up signal.

When the pilot began preflighting the aircraft, Ernie approached the girl. "Honey, with a little cut and polish, I could make this boy into Somebody. All he needs is a little push from the right people." He searched her figure with a bold grin before he winked. "You ain't gonna hurt him any."

"He won't fit into that world, Mr. Hale." Her disconcerting answer was coldly lucid. At that moment, Charging Shield started a loud garden tractor to pull the plane from the hangar. He called for her to bring his flight jacket from the car.

She spun on her heels, leaving Ernie Hale gaping open-mouthed. When she returned with the jacket, the heavy man still carried his chagrined expression. He quietly helped her onto the lower wing and into the cockpit. When the seat belts were snapped, Ernie yelled, "Give me a ring when you kids get back." He cupped his hands to shout, "I'll head you down that white man's road, Kyle. Gonna make you some money too, kid. That's where it's all at."

Charging Shield interrupted his serious study of the instrument panel from the left seat to look over the edge of the cockpit. Before reaching for the canopy handle, he grasped his friend with a warm handshake. "Yeah, Ernie, we'll see you this evening," he answered quietly. "Don't worry about me. I'll put on a big smile and say nice things about my brother. It'll make you and Mom happy, even Hobart."

Ernie Hale stepped down from the aircraft with an accomplished grin after the canopy closed, "Honey, take that wahoo' out of him," he said while tapping on the window. "I got places for him to go. You help me get him outta' this damn fool Indian thing. Them buffalo they're all gone and he's got other... "

"Prop clear!" Charging Shield called out. The starter turned the propeller several times before the engine belched a ring of black smoke through the exhaust port. Within a few moments, the biplane cocked its tail wheel for the gravel taxiway.

"West River Tower, Grumman 3491 X-ray for taxi, over," he called on the radio.

"Grumman 91 X-ray. Cleared to taxi, runway 32," the tower replied.

The biplane made a short roll down the runway before leaping steeply into the Chinook air. The powerful radial engine made the altimeter rise quickly for several minutes before he leveled the aircraft and set the power for cruise. He held his northerly heading to point out Spirit Mountain in the distance, then tested the plane's slow flying maneuverability by pulling back on the power.

Down below, a sudden wind shift broke loose a pile of cottonwood leaves stacked in a corner of a fence line. The breeze rolled its charge across the flight line to deposit some of the leaves at the feet of Ernie Hale, unnerving him. A sudden updraft whirled the gold leaves around the big man. Gold leaves had often brought change to the lonely man. A coyote's lone howl gave Ernie a cold chill.

Charging Shield reset the power for cruise after he was satisfied with the plane's slow flying maneuverability. He banked the biplane sharply for the Sheyela River and the reservation. "Keep flying!" she commanded, pointing back toward the mountain. The tone of her voice was dominant and not to be argued with. He answered with a burst of throttle and a steep left climbing turn, aiming them directly at the lone rise of mountain, distinctly separate from the wall of peaks to the west.

The Chinook rolling down the mountain slopes played out to their ascending altitude. He had to turn on the heater as they approached patches of scud clouds dotting the sky.

When they were but a few miles from the mountain, she exclaimed, "I feel a strange destiny down there." She pointed. Her finger was an eagle's claw but the pilot was looking down at the mountain and was too lost into the depths of his past to notice. He could only stare at the crest, too immersed in memories of his night on the mountain. His subconscious managed to fly the airplane, responding to her commands to circle lower. She could have been a wild eagle sitting beside him and he would not have been aware.

"Kyle, Kyle," he heard her calling. For a moment he was sharing a nest with her high on a badland butte. "I've seen enough. Let's go now." Forcefully the words were spoken. "Come my mate. Let us go now." It was exactly the words that he had heard spoken to him by the female eagle in his vision. The words snapped him from his spell. He banked the biplane sharply for the Sheyela River and the reservation.

Less than an hour had elapsed when he orbited the Oglala community. He flew low over the mission boarding school, then followed a shallow tree-lined creek toward the dirt airstrip at the edge of the town. When he turned down-wind, he noted distant rain showers approaching from the northeast. The biplane settled into the wind for a short rollout on the gumbo soil, then turned at an intersection formed by a car path cutting across the runway to taxi toward a pair of tie-down rings.

A coyote's doleful daylight cry went unnoticed when he waved at a battered pickup passing down the highway beside the airport. The truck stopped and in a short while took them past a white-framed church and the church rectory depositing them in front of the tribal community hall, a long brick building surrounded by cars. He patted a bulge in his jacket pocket. "I brought something from the Sun Dance. It isn't much, but it might have a meaning for Ben."

They walked toward the building to peer through the door. A priest in vestments stood before a portable altar, finishing his Mass service when they entered the hall. "That's Buchwald," he whispered, as they walked past a serving kitchen occupied by several women quietly arranging trays of food. The couple took a seat at the rear of the rafted hall, in time to watch the priest conclude the Mass by waving an over-sized peace pipe at the audience. Two altar boys followed close behind as the procession paraded toward an open casket.

"I would like to offer this pipe in honor of Ben Black Elk." The priest threw a startled stare when he noticed the couple. He waved the pipe awkwardly, momentarily losing his composure. "Ben Black Elk was a man of the Lord," the priest blurted nervously. "Ben believed in our Lord, the Redeemer, sent to fulfill all religious searching." The Jesuit waved the peace pipe at the audience again while he darted his eyes toward the back of the hall. "He is the way. He is the truth. He is the light for all mankind. Without our Lord, the Savior, you are lost and can never receive eternal salvation," he spoke in a rapid staccato. "You must accept him to be saved from eternal damnation. Ben knew that the church's way was the only way." Buchwald's words were rote, as though he had said the same pattern of words hundreds of times; the deceased one's name inserted mechanically into the perfunctory monotone. "Yes, he was a man of the true way. He believed in our Lord and Savior. He loved our Lord and received eternal salvation. Ben followed the path of the Lord and set an example for all to follow. Without the Lord, you are doomed to everlasting fire. Your soul forever lost."

The missionary droned on. Despite the doomsday speculation of the priest, the audience sat through the uninspiring monologue with a look of detached melancholy as if they had heard the statements too often and too long. Finally, in conclusion, two women accompanied by an organ sang as the priest raised the peace pipe above the casket. "Mary, dear, oh pray for me."

The Jesuit waved the pipe like a conductor until the song was finished, then walked toward a table, aided by the pair of altar boys as he removed his Mass vestments.

A woman from the mourners in the front row rose to approach the couple. As she drew closer, Charging Shield recognized her as the attractive older woman who accepted the peace pipe in his first Sun Dance. "*How Kola* (Hello, friend)," she spoke in Sioux. "I am an adopted relative of Ben's. After the Sun Dance this summer, I heard him talk about you." The woman motioned with her head toward the casket, then looked scornfully at the priest retiring to the kitchen. "Some of us don't like it when a white man thinks he knows more about someone we are close to. Come up and say something if you wish."

Charging Shield replied with a nod. He reached into his flight jacket to retrieve the sage wreath that he had worn in the Sun Dance. The woman indicated her approval by offering a package of cigarettes. He stripped several cigarettes and placed them in the palm of his hand.

The woman marched away to stand stiffly with her back to the open casket facing the audience. She paused to allow a bouquet to be placed among the many wreaths and flowers before she spoke in a formal tone. "I have asked someone to say a few words. He has seen war and has gone through our Sun Dance." She turned to motion him forward. "It is good that an Oglala warrior should say some words on behalf of my cousin lying here."

Charging Shield carried the wreath toward the front of the audience. Before he spoke, he offered the wreath to the four directions, ending his offering by sprinkling the tobacco over Black Elk's casket. "I came to say goodbye to an old friend," he began. "I am an Oglala and want to be truthful, therefore I will not invent what Ben's thoughts were since I cannot read people's minds, but I can truthfully say what Ben did and what he told me." Charging Shield related the events set in motion by Eagle Feather leading toward Black Elk's presence in the Sun Dance lodge.

Charging Shield glanced back at the casket. "Uncle Ben was in the lodge on the morning of the fourth day at last year's Sun Dance. He said, 'Nephew, I want you to carry my father's pipe.'

"You could hear the wind howling outside the tent as we talked. It looked like we were going to be in for some bad weather for the first time at the Sun Dance. Ben told me to take his father's pipe and not be afraid. He told us that his father predicted that we would gather around a tree and our spirit would come back. He said to go on with the Sun Dance and we did. When I stepped into the circle with his father's pipe, the wind died down and I had courage to carry through with the ceremony." Charging Shield stiffened and spoke with increased volume, "Have courage, Nephew. My Father's spirit will be with us today. These are the words of encouragement that I heard directly from Uncle Ben."

He turned sideways and spoke with added resolve. "My Uncle Ben lying here showed his stand at the Sun Dance. I hope that all will think of him as a warrior for the Indian way." He held the sage high. "I brought something from that Sun Dance. I ask that his relatives place this in his casket, if that is agreeable to them."

An elderly couple came forward to accept the wreath. They walked slowly toward the casket to place it on Black Elk's chest. An old man approached at that moment. "*Wahste aloh. Wahste, wahste aloh.*" (Very good, very good.) Another man reached out to offer his hand. A tremolo broke out from the audience. A murmur of approval swept the room.

A few minutes before, Father Weitz had entered the hall through the rear door of the kitchen and now stood inside the serving counter watching the well wishers surrounding the speaker. He had heard Charging Shield's brief eulogy and both had exchanged a polite nod to each other, the mutual greeting not missed by Buchwald, who was glowering at everyone as he stood beside the old portable altar, stacking his mass vestments.

Father Weitz was too overcome by a keen sense of exhilaration to be concerned about anyone except for the presence of Kyle Charging Shield, a man he hardly knew. The warrior's presence seemed to catalyze a mysterious force. 'Here it was again. The flash of future! This time it was stronger... far stronger than the time when he had first paid a visit to Fools Crow. Ahhh, he could so easily predict the oncoming moments; Buchwald would scurry to the organ. The loud playing organist and another woman would sing a hymn to still the mounting conversations. He could even predict the hymn! And, of course, Buchwald would come up to him with an order to meet at the rectory across the parking lot.' After the senior Jesuit left, Weitz took his time leaving, even stopping to shake the speaker's hand and exchange a greeting.

When Charging Shield finally returned to his chair, Karen reached across the table to touch his arm. "I'm so proud. I loved every word you said."

Before another hymn could begin, the Indians politely asserted themselves, introducing another speaker that offered accounts of the deceased flavored with traditionalism. The evening sunlight slanting through the high windows of the community hall caught Charging Shield's attention. "We'd better leave," he said with a tired smile. "Don't want to disappoint Ernie."

He stopped by the kitchen to inquire about his sister. After a brief conversation with one of the cooks, he took Karen's hand and left the hall. "My sister couldn't make it today. She'll go to the funeral with us tomorrow." He showed a slight scowl. "I still think she lost your letter purposely. She's got a hang up about me not marrying an Indian girl. Course my brother-in-law Ralph is a white man." He glanced at the sunset before they started down the road for the dirt airstrip.

"I sent you two letters, Kyle." Karen responded. "What's her excuse?"

"Two letters! Wait until I get a hold of her." He held a pained grimace. "She says one of the two of us should marry our own race and she's already married."

"Sounds real democratic." Karen quipped with mock humor. "Tell her I'm an Indian," she said as she turned up her nose.

"Then she'll complain we're not from the same tribe," Charging Shield retorted.

"Sounds like she wants you single, Kyle."

He stopped and kissed her long and hard. "We'll be mates forever, Beautiful." He said with passion, "I like my sister but this warrior was family weaned a long time ago." With that statement he took her hand and turned toward the airstrip. "When I'm around you Karen," he shrugged. "It might sound silly, but you make me feel like an eagle."

She laughed. "That's what we are then, my love. We really are." She tossed her hair, which was starting to change. It was beginning to take on the hue of the golden eagle and was even beginning to pick up the patterned whitish spots, but he failed to notice.

Her voice sent him back to his vision quest. As they walked down the side of the road toward the airplane he gripped her hand tightly. "Eagles," he replied with a vacant look. "Yes, how mysteriously wonderful that would be. A pair of eagles forever free." He concluded without noticing the serious grin and knowing stare that captured her face. The same pickup truck that had carried them earlier honked as it approached and they hopped on board.

Across the parking lot in the rectory, Reverend Paul Buchwald threw the peace pipe beside a wine bottle in a dresser drawer. His eyes focused through the window on the two altar boys skipping across the parking lot. Next to the dresser behind a rolltop desk, his assistant spoke in a consoling tone, "Come now, Paul. We've always held our wakes this way. You said so yourself, it's a blending of both traditions."

"That devil, he couldn't wait to run up there and call me a liar," Buchwald directed a reprimanding scowl. "Father Weitz, I wouldn't waste time making excuses for a militant. He didn't come out here to pay respect to Black Elk. He came to show off. Flaunting some sex arousing woman around; worse, he insulted our Lord who was speaking through me."

"Paul, that community hall isn't exactly a church." Weitz had difficulty appearing concerned despite Buchwald's anger. His mind wanted to race back and dwell upon that euphoric experience - the ability to predict!

"The Blessed Sacrament was there, therefore it was a church," Buchwald answered smugly.

"But the people, Ben's relatives, they asked him to say a few words."

"That woman who asked him, she's a pagan," the senior Jesuit retorted; "Claims she's a traditionalist." He locked his chalice in a drawer and hung his keys on a peg above the desk. "If she'd known anything about tradition, one of the elders would have been up there speaking - not some upstart."

The missionary placed his cassock in a closet, before looking through the window with an impatient scowl. "I told those people to load up my altar. Used to be... that altar stamped out witchcraft; now they're probably using it for a supper table." He left the rectory for the community hall. After awhile, he stalked back, followed by several men carrying the portable altar toward a pickup in the driveway. The priest dropped the truck's tailgate, then bounded up the steps. "I found out that militant flew an airplane down here. He's got the people stirred up. That damned Charging Shield, he's possessed."

"Now Paul, you've always been hasty with ... " The assistant's words were greeted by a postman's knock on the screen door.

A special delivery letter was handed to Buchwald. "Only reason he's flying an airplane is to show off. Why doesn't he drive down here like ordinary people? I'm telling you, he's possessed." Buchwald spoke from the side of his mouth while he signed for the letter. He drew his breath to deliver another tirade but the return address, bearing Gothic print made him exhale and then gasp. The return address read, "Chancellors Office, Western Diocese." Midway through the first page, the priest's hands trembled. Over the senior priest's shoulder Weitz hurriedly picked out the wordage before Buchwald turned to the second page.

Following the initial plaudits from the Bishop, Diocese of Western Dakota, commending the senior pastor's service, the letter took a differing tone.

'... social and political pressures in these changing times... potential constitutional challenge... a year's sabbatical has been arranged in accord with the provincial abbot for reassignment transition... '

The ending was explicit.

'Hereafter, no interference with indigenous ceremonies or related forms of religious expression will be instigated by pastoral members, Diocesan members or Order members, within the Western Diocese.'

The air weighed heavily. Father Buchwald's face contorted with a bitter grimace. The letter fell to the floor before he grabbed the keys off the peg above the roll-top. He turned slowly then sprinted out the door and down the sidewalk, waving out of the pickup's box, a man who was buckling a pair of weather-beaten leather straps securing the altar to the cab. After the motor started, the truck screeched backwards.

Father Weitz ran from the rectory and reached for the door handle as the truck came to a stop. He jerked the door open to yell across the seat, "Paul, where are you going?"

Buchwald glowered, shifting the truck out of reverse. "I've dedicated my life on this desert and never been appreciated." His grip tightened on the steering wheel as he turned to glare in the direction of the airport. "I'm going to let that red devil know where the law stands. I can't interfere, they say. By God, he can't interfere either. He can't get away with interfering... interfering in the Lord's work."

Weitz felt the piercing stares of the silent men that had carried the altar. He closed the door and leaned close to plead in a low tone through the open window, "Paul, I know your feelings are hurt. Why don't you come back and we'll have a drink?"

The words offered in consolation brought a cold rebuke. Buchwald's choked voice was barely audible, "Maybe you're behind this. You've never said much against witchcraft."

Weitz felt his spine stiffen. "You've brought it on yourself, Paul. I'll admit I'm not worried about how these people see their Creator through their own way." His manner relaxed. "You know how I feel about that."

"Blasphemy! Left wing, communist, Satanist blasphemy!" Buchwald yelled hotly before he pressed the accelerator to race away, roaring past and barely missing a sedan driven by the Mission Superior, turning from the street. Weitz shook his head in dismay at the truck with its altar standing high, speeding rapidly away from town.

Father Superior parked the sedan in the vacant space left by the pickup. His knowing look as he stepped from the car answered Weitz's probing stare. "The Bishop sent me a copy of the letter. I thought I'd better get down here," he said as he leaned his heavy frame against the black sedan. "I don't relish this, but it had to be done. There's too much at stake. The times, you can blame it on the times," he said, throwing his hands up helplessly.

Weitz gave a cursory glance. "The Indian Movement, they'll eat Paul alive this summer - if he's still here." He spoke his words to the distant buttes. He paused to acknowledge the older priest's worried frown. "My sources tell me the Movement can't wait for Paul to interfere with this year's Sun Dance, even if it's behind the scenes like last year's politics. It's pretty dramatic material for the media."

Father Superior cringed and bobbed his balding head. "That would be bad, very bad. I don't want any trouble with the Indian Movement."

"The publicity wouldn't do us any good," Weitz clarified.

"Where's Paul going?" Father Superior asked.

"To the airport. He's blaming it all on Kyle Charging Shield. At least, he'd like to."

"The ex-marine who was in the Sun Dance?" Father Superior looked puzzled and then relieved.

Weitz nodded.

"I need a drink," the Superior declared, shaking his head lamely as he followed Weitz up the steps. He didn't want his priests tangling with the militants. There again, Paul was disobeying his orders. The old priest took a chair beside the rolltop, rejecting a glass of altar wine for a stronger drink of whiskey, which he drained in one gulp. He held out the empty shot glass, which was promptly refilled. Seldom did he drink whiskey but the situation had even made him forego an early supper. He appreciated the burning sensation the liquor left on his empty stomach. He downed half of the second glass before he sat back. The tenseness began to fade. The crumpled pages on the floor relaxed him further. He bent to pick up the two pieces of paper with tender care, rereading the letter thoroughly. Afterwards he looked longingly through the screen door at the sunset; his thoughts many miles away from the reservation. Weitz allowed the old superior his long period of contemplation. 'This will help the retirement fund. It had to be done,' was the issue of his thoughts. Finally, the senior Jesuit turned to speak, slowly and emphatically, "I want him out of here soon. Real soon. In less than a year I retire."

"But what can I do? You're the boss," said Weitz.

Father Superior pointed at the letter. "The Bishop, he should have been more explicit. You go to the Bishop. Get a sabbatical date set for Europe, Ireland, somewhere. I don't want that damned zealot coming back here trying to take on the militants." He hushed his words, "The Father General wants it that way."

Weitz nodded. "I know what you mean."

The old priest reached for the shot glass to drain its remainder. "It is better that you set this up," he spoke quietly. "Within the Order, only the Father General, and you and I know about this. In a short time, I will be with my peers in the retirement community. Most of them will never comprehend the changes that are taking place. Some of them were as bad as Paul, worse, if you can believe that, and... I will have to live with them." He lifted the glass and swallowed the whiskey.

"I can believe it," Weitz answered strongly.

"They were good men, mind you. They meant well." The priest's pause for a comment from Weitz was met with silence. "They meant well." He repeated within a tired expiration. "Thank the Bishop for helping us out of this dilemma." Father Superior looked up to add hurriedly, "The Father General understands. I performed my stewardship well. He appreciates that. He has been most understanding over this whole matter. Yes, all the way to Rome it has traveled. " Father Superior turned to look at Weitz squarely. "You drove a hard bargain for your cooperation, Jim. At first

I was skeptical, I'll admit, but I have to give you credit. Your predictions were right. The school board; the boarding school will have an elected board. We'll have it underway by next fall. Some of the white ranchers and the government employees will want to be on it, of course."

"I want an Indian majority and by second semester we fill the school board. Otherwise I won't be seeing the Bishop."

"All right, you'll get it."

"And the school buses and day school project?"

"That can't possibly be until next fall. The funding hasn't been allotted," the old priest argued.

"School buses and day school pilot project by second semester, at least for this part of the reservation," Weitz's voice was adamant. "Father Superior, get the project going by this school year. The Indian Movement isn't going to fool around! They've targeted the boarding schools as top priority and the media loves it." His composure carried an aura of impatience.

"But there's no funds, not that soon," Father Superior argued.

Father Weitz held him with a hard stare. "The land, Father, mortgage or sell some of the goddamn land that was taken from the Indians."

Father Superior gasped, "That land was freely given. It was last rites gifts. They donated to the Church. We worked it all out with the BIA. "

"All those acres, what's a section or two?" Weitz persisted. "It's against the law. The BIA broke the rules. Only Indians can own reservation land."

Father Superior looked beaten. "All right, all right," he moaned with exasperation. He banged the empty shot glass on the rolltop desk so hard it left a dent. He extended three fingers indicating a refill. He looked up at Weitz as the whiskey was poured, "And you'll see the Bishop?"

"I'll see the Bishop," Weitz complied.

The arrangement satisfied, Weitz decided to join the older priest by boldly pouring himself three fingers. When he held up his glass in a commemorative toast, the force descended again... as powerful as before. Reflected in the whiskey glass he could see Buchwald standing out on the prairie, surrounded by a whirlwind of splinters. 'A whirlwind of splinters?' he almost asked aloud. And then his mind raced on, just beyond, causing his hand to shake. There was something he didn't want to predict. He grimaced painfully. 'Was he traversing too far into this culture, was he responsible for what he saw in the glass?' He scowled at the glass, then gulped down its contents. 'There, maybe that could be a sacrilege, maybe that could destroy a prediction,' he wished as the liquid burned his throat... but the force remained, as strong as ever. He knew he had to get to the airport. Something was happening to Charging Shield or was it Buchwald?

Charging Shield reached for the starter switch. When the engine came to life, rain droplets from the cowling sprayed the cockpit. He savored the fresh smell of the brief rain shower while he taxied on the damp gumbo. The tailwheel left an arc across the car path intersecting the glistening runway as he taxied to midfield. Noting the windshift from the bend of the sagebrush and tumbleweeds he taxied north. At the north edge of the narrow strip, he turned south into the wind to check his magnetos and controls. The restricted forward view of the bulbous nosed plane caused him to lean out of the cockpit to align the aircraft with the runway. He closed the canopy; the tinted glass and fading sunset made him twist the rheostat, brightening the instrument panel. He dropped his right hand from the controls to his passenger's knee for a moment and winked at her before opening the throttle.

She gripped his forearm for a moment and said strangely, "Soon, we will be flying, my Love. Yes, soon," but the blast of engine and prop wash drowned her words.

In a culvert at midfield, beneath the gumbo road leading into the airport runway, an exceptionally large coyote waited. It looked more like a prairie wolf but such an animal had been extinct in the area for fifty years. The canine twitched its bushy tail as it leered expectantly at the approaching pick up truck. Crouching lower and retreating slightly back into its hiding place, the four-legged emerged after Father Buchwald turned and crossed over its hiding place. Just before the truck approached the runway, the animal bounded out in front of the vehicle to capture the priest's attention.

The biplane lumbered, swaying as it gathered speed for its takeoff roll. The pilot scanned the airspeed indicator and manifold pressure when the woman's startled yell jerked his head from the cockpit in time to see the pickup careening sideways as it approached the damp, slippery runway. He clenched his teeth as his eyes shot to the airspeed indicator, then back to the pickup to watch it slide to a stop at the edge of the narrow runway. His gaze froze on the altar protruding above the pickup cab as he fought his urge to pull back on the control stick. He took an agonized glance at the slowly rising airspeed indicator before pushing the stick forward to clear the tail wheel from the damp alkali. The aircraft danced on the main landing gear, gaining added lift when the fuselage came parallel with the ground. Only a few plane lengths remained between the closing machines before he jerked back on the controls; the rudder and control stick were pushed hard port to clear the wings. The stall horn blared as the biplane leaped skyward. The lower right wing slammed into the altar. The old relic, brought to the mission by wagon train three quarters of a century before, exploded out of the pickup box, scattering itself into a thousand pieces across the sage and buffalo grass. The pilot felt the jolt and cringed as he looked down at the sage plants flashing past his lower left wing tip. He pushed the nose forward to silence the stall warning horn and leveled his wings. As the aircraft gained speed, he began a shallow left climbing turn. He took a deep breath before he looked at his passenger. "That was close," he gasped. He checked the left wing.

"I think we might have brushed the sage with our wing tip. It felt like we hit something."

"My God, that was scary," she answered shakily. "Whoever was in that pickup, he was diving for the floor. A bushy tailed dog was out in front of him."

He held the upwind turn; the powerful engine produced a high rate of climb as he turned a half circle to look down at the intersection of the airport. The steep climbing attitude caused the figure below to diminish swiftly. Before the nose blocked the runway from view, she looked out of the window. "That pickup driver's waving at us!" she exclaimed.

The throttles eased back from the maximum power setting before the plane was leveled. He dipped the left wings to catch a glimpse of the lone, unrecognizable figure growing smaller on the runway. He waved his wings before turning northwest. "Probably some rancher, Karen. I bet he never saw us until it was too late. They shouldn't allow a road through the middle of a runway."

Down below, Reverend Buchwald waved his fist frantically at the belly of the Grumman. "Don't you wave your wings at me you pagan dog. I pray to God you get what you deserve. I hope you crash in your show-off machine. Yes! Crash you pagan dog! The Devil to you- Kyle Charging Shield and the old Badlands witch who stole your soul!" The Jesuit turned in rage to survey the altar pieces scattered on the gumbo soil. A broken leather strap hanging from a sage plant caught his eye. He grabbed the strap and threw it in desperation at the disappearing plane.

Weitz watched a whirling dust devil picking up bits of grass as it crossed the airport boundary. He parked behind the pickup, feeling no compassion for the older priest blubbering incoherently over a piece of the scattered altar that had been reduced to countless pieces on its tumbling, crashing journey out across the sage clumps. Buchwald flailed his arms wildly at the wreckage when Weitz stepped from the car. "That Devil," the older priest choked, "Damn him," he poked a jagged piece of wood in the direction the airplane had flown. "Call the sheriff. He tried to kill me. Damn his infidel soul to hell."

Weitz glared at the priest with mounting anger. "Yes, you would condemn a man's spirit, a man's eternal soul, over an inanimate piece of wood," he muttered with contempt. "I pray to that Great Mystery of theirs that we mere two-legged never be granted that power to condemn a man's destiny to the spirit world." At that moment, the growing whirlwind twisting its way from the south, began picking up the strewn altar pieces before crossing over both men. The pieces twirled upward then rained down like hail around Buchwald. None descended near Father Weitz. Startled fear covered Buchwald's face as he fled to his pickup.

Weitz watched with a look of stern chagrin. But his sober expression suddenly changed to breathless awe. The revelation he had seen in the glass returned so strong that it blotted out Buchwald's truck swerving away in a roaring, gumbo clod-spinning exodus. Charging Shield flashed strongly in the young priest's mind, a foretelling mind absolutely detached and oblivious to Buchwald's near collision with a fence post at the entryway to the airport. And then he understood! Charging Shield was a throwback to a past... a past where there was no white man... no Jesuits... before all of the white men's interpretations. A past where God-created Nature revealed, unblemished, undistorted, a Nature that could never be deceptive. That was why those old time traditionals were not deceptive!' The wide sky above him seemed to add to the immensity of his thoughts. 'Yes, and somehow, Kyle Charging Shield could have the power to return back into that Nature. Really there was no such thing as time. It was only a present reality. What could be was really... yes... it really was... and maybe the entities were all a part of the great whole. Such was the clear depth of his perception as he stood in the midst of the heavily sage scented prairie.

The whirlwind died away before it reached the end of the airfield. And for Father James Weitz, S. J., it was like Kyle Charging Shield; no longer a force for him. The revelation came and went, swiftly. It was gone like the blown wind, like the sweep of the tide, a beat of goose wings, a pod of orcas, the swirl of a trout and the mournful howl of a coyote at that moment. Yes, he knew, Fools Crow and Eagle Feather would conduct a ceremony within a matter of days... not a sweat lodge or a *Yuwipi*... some kind of honoring ceremony for Charging Shield. What kind it didn't matter... because afterwards he would sit before Fools Crow. In time, Fools Crow would prepare him with a sweat lodge. He was bewildered by a sense of mystery, yet calm and certain that the mystique of the land that was subduing him, because of its powerful uniqueness; this force would not require him to give up his way. Yes, all two-legged were diverse. Diverse because of the different experiences from day one and yet there was the commonality of the whole. That commonality was always there because there was but the one origin and it was truly universal. Yes, it even reached way out there in space, or rather it had reached from there into mere two-legged space. His mind whirled with heavy thought. Fools Crow would prepare him for a vision, a vision bound to a new destiny... a fearsome destiny out there in time. He would have to sit under this great universe and become connected with all in this mysterious Way.

The coyotes set up a chorus of howls, trailing a connection to the deep recesses of the badlands. The chorus followed the direction of the plane flying serenely into the golden sunset.

Charging Shield switched on the navigation lights as he watched the top of the sun slowly settle. He tugged her thigh to pull her closer. "Before it gets dark, I want to show you my grandmother's cabin."

She looked at the fading rays bathing a towering thunderhead above the western horizon. "I'd love to see it." She spoke with calm expectation.

He pushed the mixture to rich and added power. He made a slight adjustment on the propeller setting before he put his arm behind her. When she kissed him, he laughed, "That makes a close call worth it!"

They flew in silence for several minutes before he cocked the plane to scan the rugged terrain. After they passed over a ridgeline, he stared through the windshield, intently studying a twisting stream. A smile broke across his face before he lowered the nose to point toward a trio of badland buttes. "We're getting close," he exclaimed over the rush of wind and mounting whine of the radial engine. "Pretty soon you'll see my grandmother's place." He crossed a gravel road before he spotted the dim outline of an abandoned cabin. He held his glide for a few moments then adding power he pulled the nose up. He tugged the control stick back, then pushed it to the left. The aircraft rose to stand on its left wings for a brief instant.

The wing over-pressed him against the side window.

She leaned against him to look down at the tall cottonwood sheltering the cabin. "Oh, it's so beautiful."

The biplane dipped to gather speed. "You can see it better from your side," he spoke over the pull of the G forces. He leveled the wings to follow the road away from the cabin, then turned sharply to face the trio of badland buttes. He passed over the road, pulling the nose into a steep climb followed by a gentle roll to the right. At the top of the maneuver, he pointed the right wings toward the abandoned dwelling.

"I see the cabin, I see the cabin!" she yelled as she leaned against her window.

She strained against the G forces to look at him, managing a smile. "It's got a stream in back." When she pointed... her hand was an eagle claw. He looked with wide-eyed awe at the curvaceous claws. She looked at him with yellow eagle eyes, "You have your wish, my love. We're going back. Back where you really want to be!"

He felt the aircraft shudder before it rolled on its back. He kicked the opposite rudder pedal and pushed the stick sideways, but the biplane snapped its nose into a spin. Just before the spin began, he saw a jagged crease race across the lower right wing. The wing tore free at the mid-way point before the Grumman impacted into a dry wash ravine. An exploding gold flame enveloped the two still forms, the red fuselage and the white checkered tail. Black smoke rose from the twisted mass. Red, white, black and flame gold yellow were the last colors of the once powerful machine.

After the consuming flames, the setting sun painted the unburned tail yellow before disappearing behind the quiet loneliness of badland walls. An object the size of a *wotai* glimmered above the wreckage for a few moments then danced gaily like a firefly over the darkening buttes. A pair of eagles lifted to rise above a gold etched meadow.

The victorious cry of a prairie wolf howled tauntingly as it approached the buttes. The female eagle broke away to attack the creature, tearing out a piece of fur as it streaked for safety into a badger's cave bored into a badland gully. The wolf howled mockingly at the circling eagle while it waited for nightfall. The eagle knew that it was no ordinary four-legged for this species had been extinct ever since the white man had entered the territory. When darkness came, the wolf journeyed north to its domain within a bush covered ravine below Spirit Mountain.

SUN DANCE FOUR

CHAPTER TWENTY SIX

"It may be that some little root of the sacred tree
still lives. Nourish it then, that it may leaf and
bloom and fill with singing birds."
— Black Elk

The following summer, the morning sun heralded the fourth day of the Sun Dance. "Oh-huh," Eagle Feather exclaimed to Catches in the ceremonial lodge while the pair studied an agate that Catches held. "There is a buffalo in it."

"Yes, that is what I saw," the soft-spoken Catches replied. "I was getting water from the creek when it flashed at me. Last night I had a strange dream. I dreamt that a woman with a purple shawl would be here today. She will work for our Way in some later years, just before I go into the spirit world. She will help spread these ways because they're going to be needed." He placed the stone in a pouch tied to his waist, then knelt on one knee to gather dirt from the tent floor to make a mound about the height of the empty coffee can that he used to flatten the crest. The Oglala looked over his shoulder for a few moments to the north, facing Spirit Mountain. Both men knew that Fools Crow would be preparing Father Weitz with a sweat lodge at the base of the mountain. Purposely, the timing of the young priest's Vision Quest was planned to coincide with the Sun Dance. Catches placed four miniature flags in a square on the mound's crest then reached into a pocket of his shirt to pull out a piece of paper. He dropped it within the boundaries of the four flags. He turned to his startled companion with an awkward look. "The priest... he asked that I should do this," his tone apologetic.

Eagle Feather tempered his scowl with an air of approval. "If that's part of his medicine, then it should be so." He deferred a nod down to the mound and then over to the tent wall closest to the arena. "That and the Sun Dance, he will need all the help he can get."

Catches reached down to retrieve the slip of paper. He handed it to Eagle Feather. "The priest... he asked that I should read this aloud."

"Then read it," Eagle Feather commanded with irritation, pushing the paper back to Catches.

Catches looked perplexed. "My eyes... I... I don't read very well without glasses," his words barely audible.

EAGLE VISION

SUN DANCE FOUR

Eagle Feather grabbed the typewritten note. He held it far away, demanding focus from his aging eye muscles. Fortunately, the words were typed in bold capital letters. He read aloud. "Nation will not lift sword against nation, neither will they learn war anymore." He paused to study the name, Isaiah, typed below the message. "Is-sy-ah," he mispronounced. "*Hau!*" he exclaimed with satisfaction. "Those are good words."

"Yes, those sound good. My medicine tells me they are the words of a holy man," Catches added.

"*Hau,*" Bill agreed. Eagle Feather, who had been facing east, now turned to face the south. He reached down to his medicine pouch for his peace pipe. He lifted his pipe and pointed it toward the south, then read the message of Isaiah to the south quarter of the universe. "Nation will not lift sword against nation, neither will they learn war anymore." He repeated the message to the west quarter, and then to the north quarter. "Nation will not lift sword against nation, neither will they learn war anymore." The words had a pealing ring for both men. While he read the words to the north quarter, Catches joined in, having by now, almost memorized the prophecy word for word.

Eagle Feather's voice lowered to a growl. "They talk endlessly of their interpretation of the Great Spirit... they claim their Christ and Moses knew *hahn bla chee yah* (vision quest)... yet this young priest today is probably the only one of them in that whole big outfit that will be up there praying and fasting on a mountain like what their old-timers were claimed to do." Eagle Feather made one last fine adjustment to the position of his buffalo horned headdress. "I always told Charging Shield that they could have killed us all but there was something inside of them that kept them from doing it."

"Did he believe you?" Catches queried.

Eagle Feather shrugged with an emotionless smile. "You know how hard headed some of them warriors are. He's an eagle now. He probably knows now. He's with his mate and better off." He rose to accept the stone from Catches. After studying it briefly, he spoke. "This is not the stone of my vision. No doubt this *wotai* will go to some one important today, maybe that woman who will wear a purple shawl." He paused to ponder for a brief moment. "The woman in my vision had a *wotai* like mine. Strange... it was exactly like mine and we all know that the Great Mystery makes every stone different." Not one to over analyze mystery, Eagle Feather dismissed the puzzle to the time span where it belonged with an upward sweep of his hand. "That mate of Charging Shield's. She has got something powerful to do. They'll be back. She will come into her own power." He exhaled a whooing gasp almost sounding like the warning call of the prairie owl. "Me and Fools Crow. We tried to destroy the Blue Man through the ways of the warrior and we found out that it wasn't meant to be."

Catches grunted. His tone sounded like the grunt of a bull buffalo. "The Blue Man is very much in power. He is everywhere. My thoughts are that only a woman can do it."

Eagle Feather held his horned head low, agreeing with a nod and a chagrined look. "My vision tells me she will return." He paused, "She will come back and fight that Blue Man but that will all be in another time coming." He groaned a muttered, "Ooh huunhh," almost sounding like the buffalo Catches impersonated. "Ooh huunhh." he bellowed dolefully once more. "The woman power. I even told Charging Shield's mate about that and yet I did not do more about it while she was here."

"It is not quite yet the time but it is coming close." Catches advised.

"Huuuunnhhh." Bill Eagle Feather bellowed harshly. "Then I vow, brother. I will help whoever it is that will have a stone like mine. No doubt, this woman who will have a stone like mine, I will help her too," he added, "if I am around."

"You can be both," Catches sounded strangely prophetic.

"Oh huh." Eagle Feather answered in affirmation.

"And the young priest on the mountain?"

"No, he is only getting started. He has got plenty to do with his own kind. He will not be confronted by the Blue Man. He would think it is some sort of devil that those over him have invented for a long time."

"That has kept them from seeing many things within the Earth Mother, especially who the Blue Man really is," Catches stated.

At that moment, far to the north, Father Weitz crawled from a steaming sweat lodge. The Blue Man watched from a thicket of buffalo berry, concealed by a stand of tall clover weed. Fools Crow stood with a peace pipe and four colored flags to send Weitz to the top of Spirit Mountain.

The wizened holy man sensed the presence of the Blue Man and whirled with the pipe, pointing it like a rifle at the hiding place. 'Truth! Truth! You can be defeated if only these *washichus* can learn truth." he snarled in Lakota. The Blue Man cringed to the ground, trembling as if the peace pipe was spitting out a cannonade of destruction to his realm. The Oglala looked up to the top of the mountain where four puffs of white clouds billowed, arranging themselves in four directions. The young priest quit toweling himself dry and stood in naked awe at Nature's acknowledgement to the holy man's words. Weitz did not understand Lakota but he could understand clearly a powerful sign issued by the controlling power of all. His training made him sink to his knees and bow his head.

"Stand up! Stand up!" Fools Crow ordered in English. "We look at our God, especially when it is speaking to us." The priest leaped to his feet to watch the billowing puffs revolve slowly and then disappear.

Fools Crow turned his attention back to the buffalo berry bush and spoke in Lakota. He told the Blue Man to leave the young priest alone but more important, to get ready for the battle of his life. "A woman shall come to destroy you. Eagle Feather and I, we have learned that warrior force will no longer work in this land. This woman shall be like the mountain. She will know truth." With that, the Blue Man shivered and crept back to his lair, pondering the ominous warning issued by the stern holy man who did not know how to lie.

After Weitz had dressed, Fools Crow offered him the peace pipe and the colored flags each tied to four sticks. He pointed to the top of the mountain as he spoke. "The Blue Man controls the *washichus* across the cities and towns of this land. All over, the white man is in control, he has lost the meaning of truth. If this Blue Man is not destroyed within all of us, we will lose the planet. You are a young man. It is your mission to teach those in control to know that they are missing a great truth by ignoring what the Great Spirit can teach from its creations. We did not spend our time on making up new weapons for war and creating great armies of warriors. Your people have used up most of this land's resources because of wars after wars... and most of them caused by your relatives in Europe. Our people spent their time contemplating truth and didn't have to come up with new weapons. Now we have to contemplate a Blue Man. A Blue Man of untruth, greed and earth destruction. When our people roamed these Great Plains, the Blue Man had no power. He did not even exist before us! Truth is truth!"

Eagle Feather rose to face the Sun Dance lodge opening. "We'd better get out there and get the dancers ready."

The holy men lined up the procession of sun dancers. The drummers began their rhythmic throb when the line of dancers entered the arena.

The sun was high above when the piercing song was finally called out. Eagle Feather watched with the rest of the dancers when a Vietnam veteran, named Hare, stood to be pierced below his shoulder blade. The woman with a purple shawl stood next to Hare. It was Mary Bad Hand. The sun dancers admired the courage that the Yankton Sioux displayed. Disregarding the pain, the only expression the dancer showed was humility as he danced slowly before the silent crowd, dragging a buffalo skull. When he completed one circle, Eagle Feather walked over to Mary Bad Hand and handed her the *wotai* stone that had first appeared to Catches.

Catches walked toward another young sun dancer named Horn Chips to hand him his braided rope. "You'll pierce next, Nephew. Come and lay down on the sage." All told there were more than twenty young pledgers that came forth to be pierced. An equal amount of young women also experienced the August heat before the Tree of Life.

The dancers gathered at the base of the tree for the fourth and final time, then they were free to break their bonds.

High above the Sun Dance grounds, no one, except Eagle Feather and Mary Bad Hand, saw the pair of circling birds. The Sichangu holy man issued a confident smile. It was exactly like his prediction. The pair would wait for the rainbow in the east and the tree would come to bloom, the tree of many nations and many hoops, many circles. A tinge of disappointment clouded his thoughts for the moment. He was well aware that the Blue Man still lived upon the mountain. He watched the larger of the two eagles. Charging Shield had performed one of the missions. Buchwald had been defeated and no longer would the missionaries be a threat to the return of the Way. He thought about the young priest. Now, these younger Jesuits, some were even coming over to respect the Way. Such a change! His eyes trailed to the female eagle. The sunlight cast a special reflection from her tail feathers back to him as if she was signaling her reception to his thoughts. She flapped her mighty wings and took the lead. The male went into trail position behind her. 'I hope we will meet again.' He sent the message to the she eagle. In afterthought, he added, 'I

know we will meet again,' for he knew her destiny would be fulfilled upon the mountain. "The woman power. The woman power," he muttered in Lakota, "it will have to be the power to kill the Blue Man." He spoke as a man with renewed hope.

Mary Bad Hand's thoughts were also mesmerized by the pair of departing birds heading towards the badlands. The stone in her hand turned hot, acknowledging that her destiny would be with the pair of eagles within her own life span.

The great birds flew toward a trickling stream and the abandoned cabin shaded by the towering cottonwood. The pair set a glide for the topmost branches. When they landed, they rested together for a while. The female pushed close to the male for a moment, then flapped her wings to drop down to the meadow. She changed to a small yellow bird. The huge eagle stood watching while the meadowlark sang.

ABOUT THE ARTIST

Daryl No Heart is a Lakota full blood; born on the Standing Rock Reservation in the Dakota Territory. He is a Hunkpapa descendant from the homelands of Sitting Bull. His ancestors include medicine people from the Lakota Nation and victims at the Wounded Knee Massacre.

No Heart received a diversity of education at Flandreau Indian Vocational High School, the United States Military, and University of California at Los Angeles. The different concepts of education at these American institutions has not equated nor displaced the original teachings and native philosophy, which he has received from his parents, grandparents and all his relations.

No Heart is a native man, who has received the artistic gift from his generous creator and developed his unique style and personal methods through constant practice and life experience. The strongest influence in his artistic creations are his Indigenous heritage, culture, and spirituality, handed down through the spirit of his ancestors. It is through his personal spirituality that he would like to educate the non-native and preserve the wealth of human value, which his ancestors have nobly and humbly lived.

For custom made limited edition prints of Eagle Vision art work, contact:

ANCESTORS, INC.
Daryl & Sharon No Heart
P.O. Box 40025, St. Paul, MN 55104-0025
Phone (612) 225-1437; Fax (612) 225-9399
d.noheart@worldnet.att.net

BOOKS, VIDEO & AUDIO TAPES
by Ed McGaa, Eagle Man

☐ **Eagle Vision**, $18 plus $1 postage

Enclosed is $15 plus $1 postage for:

☐ **Native Wisdom**

☐ **Mother Earth Spirituality**

☐ **Rainbow Tribe**

☐ **Finding Wakan Tanka**
    (Audio Tape) Eagle Man narration and song.

☐ **Black Elk's Prayer & Vision**
    (Audio Tape) Eagle Man narration and song.

☐ **Native Wisdom**, $25 plus $1 postage
    (Video Tape) Outdoor setting

☐ **Eagle Vision Poster (Cover)**, $25 plus $1 postage
    Full color, 14" x 30"

Upon Request; Books will be Autographed by Author

Add $1 postage for each additional book or tape.

Check or Money Order only.

Please remit in U.S. funds.

33% off for any book or audio tape delivered
to a state or federal prison.

Four Directions Publishing
Box 24671
Minneapolis, MN 55424
Phone (612) 922-9322
Fax (612) 922-7163
E-mail: eagleman4@aol.com
Website: http://members.aol.com:/eagleman4

ABOUT THE AUTHOR

The Author was born on the Oglala Sioux reservation and is a registered tribal member, OST 15287. Following the earning of an undergraduate degree, he joined the Marine Corps to become a fighter pilot. Captain McGaa returned from 110 combat missions and danced in six annual Sioux Sun Dances. The Sun Dance led him to the tutelage of Chief Eagle Feather and Chief Fools Crow, two Sioux holy men. Eagle Man holds a law degree from the University of South Dakota and is the author of *Red Cloud*, (Dillon Press, 1972), *Mother Earth Spirituality*, (Harper & Row, 1990), *Rainbow Tribe*, (Harper/Collins, 1992), and *Native Wisdom*, (Four Directions Publishing, 1995).

* * * *

American Indian books generate many letters. It would be appreciated if you will enclose a self-addressed stamped envelope (SASE) and a <u>return address & date</u> upon your correspondence. Your letters are most appreciated but it has become difficult to answer all correspondence, especially while I still continue to journey upon the world to seek more adventures and knowledge. Advice: E-Mail seems to be becoming the most efficient and most productive communication. Eagleman4@aol.com